PELICAN BOOKS

A SHORT HISTORY OF FRENCH LITERATURE

Geoffrey Brereton has specialized in French literature as a literary critic and historian since 1947, when he resigned from the BBC to become an independent writer. He had already taken a first degree in Modern Languages at Oxford and a University Doctorate at the Sorbonne and had worked in education and journalism. In the Second World War he was attached to General Eisenhower's North African Command to conduct psychological warfare through the press and radio together with his French and American colleagues. He has since contributed many articles and programmes to periodicals and the BBC and has translated or edited a number of modern plays, from Claudel to Sartre and Adamov. He has done occasional university teaching and recently acted as French Adviser to *Cassell's Enyclopaedia of World Literature*.

His principal books are *Jean Racine* and *An Introduction to the French Poets*, both republished recently in revised editions, also *Principles of Tragedy* and *French Tragic Drama in the Sixteenth and Seventeenth Centuries* (1973). Among his most popular works has been the present book, now reissued in an extensively revised edition. His other Penguin publications are Froissart's *Chronicles* in the Penguin Classics and the 16th–18th Century section in *The Penguin Book of French Verse*. He is a Fellow of the Royal Society of Literature.

A SHORT HISTORY
OF FRENCH LITERATURE

Geoffrey Brereton

SECOND EDITION

PENGUIN BOOKS

Penguin Books Ltd, Harmondsworth, Middlesex, England
Penguin Books Inc., 7110 Ambassador Road, Baltimore, Maryland 21207, U.S.A.
Penguin Books Australia Ltd, Ringwood, Victoria, Australia
Penguin Books Canada Ltd, 41 Steelcase Road West, Markham, Ontario, Canada

—

First published 1954
Reprinted 1956, 1961, 1965, 1966, 1968
Second Edition 1976

—

Copyright © Geoffrey Brereton, 1954, 1976

—

Made and printed in Great Britain
by Richard Clay (The Chaucer Press) Ltd,
Bungay, Suffolk
Set in Monotype Fournier

Contents

To Anne

Introduction

SOME eight hundred and fifty years of continuous production, with few of the stagnant pockets which occur in all literatures, have given France a literature of unequalled richness and variety. They have also given the Western mind an image of itself. Europeans in any age have had few thoughts, desires, or fantasies which a French writer some-where has not shared and expressed. In this sense, French literature, though it may not always contain the original source, has served as a pool in which several cultures meet. If its significance had to be summed up in terms of one quality, 'universality' would inevitably be the choice.

But although it has become part of a common heritage to an even greater extent than the ancient literatures of Greece and Rome, that is not its main interest. Certainly it often presents the familiar in new forms, or the unfamiliar in more accessible ways, but if that were all French would be merely a kind of Basic European designed for those who found the more local idioms too difficult. It is so obviously more than this that it is hardly necessary to point to the many writers from Villon and Rabelais to Valéry and Proust who are so characteristic of France that one cannot begin to imagine them existing elsewhere. Even the most 'universal', such as Montaigne, Molière, Rousseau, Gide, belong primarily to their native – or adoptive – country and only secondly to the world. In every case it is the native and personal qualities which give most pleasure and reward whatever effort may be entailed in penetrating to them.

This book aims at suggesting the individual flavour of at least the greater writers, if necessary even by impressionistic means. It is often neither possible nor desirable to do more in a brief survey of so vast a field. At the same time, the field has to be surveyed, the kinship between different authors pointed out, and their work related to the thought and social history of their times.

The plan adopted here preserves the three main chronological divisions into which French literature falls most naturally. The first, the Middle Ages, is treated in broad outline since it is very largely the domain of the specialized student. The second runs from the sixteenth to the eighteenth centuries, a period in which literature was coloured, if not dominated, by the Greek, Latin, and Italian influences introduced at the Renaissance; it includes the great age of native French classicism under Louis XIV, as well as the period of liberal and rationalistic thought which followed, to culminate in the Revolution. The third opens with the Romantic Movement and runs through the successive or overlapping phases of realism, symbolism, surrealism, and existentialism.

Within these chronological divisions, the main genres are followed through in chapters which group together poets, novelists, dramatists, or other kinds of writers. In this way, the history of poetry is traced consecutively from Marot to Chénier and later from Lamartine to today, the history of the drama from the Pléiade to Beaumarchais, then from Hugo and Ionesco and beyond, and so on. In each period the genre treated first is that which possessed the greatest contemporary importance and occupied the majority of outstanding or representative writers. So, in the Middle Ages, the long poem, whether narrative, allegorical, or satirical, has pride of place. The great prose-writers – many of them moralists – are the best guides over the next period taken as a whole. In the nineteenth and twentieth centuries the novelists, previously of secondary importance, take precedence as the chief interpreters of the spirit of the time.

For the scale on which this book is written, such a framework has seemed the best of several alternatives. But it has been conceived as a framework and not as a strait-jacket. No general classification can be entirely adequate, since literature consists of individual writers and their works, interesting precisely for what they do *not* have in common. It is hoped that this principle will emerge even from this short history, whose chief purpose is to help the reader to see his way before he enjoys some of the original works described; or better still, while he is enjoying them.

Note on the Second Edition

The original edition has been re-scrutinized throughout and corrections made in the light of recent scholarship and critical opinion. The most drastic revision bears on the twentieth century. Some writers who appeared important when this book was first published in the nineteen-fifties seem less so now, while others have won increasing recognition. Besides this, substantial sections have been added on entirely new writers and tendencies – particularly in the novel and the drama, but not only there – so bringing the record as nearly as possible up-to-date. The bibliography has been completely overhauled and considerably expanded. But the original conception of the book as a reliable general guide and an unpedantic companion for the reader of French literature has not, I hope, been impaired.

G.B.   1974

I

THE MIDDLE AGES

CHAPTER I

Narrative and Allegorical Poetry

FRENCH literature – more precocious than Italian or Spanish – may be said to begin early in the twelfth century with the *chansons de geste*. It was a vigorous beginning, in keeping with an age alive with social and artistic energy. The spirit of the first Crusades, a growing sense of national unity, and a revolution in architecture were some of the signs of its fertility. In literature, the century also produced the great network of the verse romances, of which the Arthurian legend and the story of Tristan and Iseut are part, the sly and earthy satire of the *Roman de Renart* and of the first *fabliaux*, and the earliest known Mystery play. In southern France, it was the golden age of troubadour poetry. So, a hundred years before Dante and two hundred before Chaucer, poets writing in a French tongue had set out most of the modes and themes which underlay the medieval literature of Western Europe. They were enabled to do this by the comparatively advanced state of their language.

The Old French of the twelfth century was a clumsy but fully-formed language. To anyone at home in modern French it looks oddly half-familiar and it can be read after considerably less study than, say, modern Italian. It was quite adequate for straightforward story-telling and for the description of outward appearances, though not yet flexible enough to express inner feelings of any great complexity. This is where the early writers seem, to a modern mind, to be weakest. But their psychology was by no means as elementary as their style at first suggests.

They were using a language which had gradually developed from very humble origins. The colloquial Latin spoken by Roman soldiers and settlers had been taken up by the original Celtic inhabitants, then still further garbled by the Germanic peoples who invaded Gaul after the fall of Rome. For several centuries it hardly was a language, but a number of dialects, each with its local peculiarities, known collectively as Romance. In France these dialects divided into two main groups – the *langue d'oc* of the south, where

oc was the word for *yes*, and the *langue d'oïl* (*oui*) of the centre and
north. Chiefly because of the political ascendancy of the north its
language has become standard French, as Tuscan has become
standard Italian and Castilian standard Spanish. With the important
exception of Provençal lyric poetry, which will be described in the
next chapter, the 'French' literature of the twelfth century was
written in the *langue d'oïl* – and of this the variety which eventually
predominated was that spoken in the Île de France, the region
round Paris. Many of the texts which have come down to us are the
work of regional authors, or were copied by regional scribes –
Picards, Burgundians, Poitevins, Normans, and Anglo-Normans.
But the local differences are comparatively slight. Less than a
hundred years after the Norman conquest of England, a single kind
of French was being written and understood from Westminster and
Winchester to Angoulême and Lyons.

Before that, the written language had been predominantly Latin.
Of the few early Romance writings which survive, the first which
has any literary significance is a thirty-line fragment of the *Cantilène
de Sainte Eulalie*, composed at the end of the ninth century. Other
lives of saints and martyrs followed. They were the popular counterpart of the numerous Lives of Saints which industrious monks
had been writing in Latin for centuries. Their interest is that they
were in verse, for verse and not prose was the medium unquestion-
ingly used in writing for the non-learned public. The flat, monotonous lines of the *Vie de Saint Léger* and the *Vie de Saint Alexis*, with
their assonanced endings, foreshadow the metres of the *chansons de
geste*, and no doubt were intoned to mass-audiences in the same way.

The *chansons de geste* were recited to the music of the *vielle* (a
stringed instrument originally played with a bow, violin-wise) by
the professional story-tellers or *jongleurs* who performed in castles,
abbeys, and in market-places on public holidays. They are long
chronicle-songs – some as long as 20,000 lines – and they must have
been chanted in several instalments. But they are not deliberately
episodic and there is a unity of action about them which distinguishes them from the chain-story. Because of their length and
unity and the fact that they deal with national or regional heroes,
they constitute the most important body of medieval European epic
poetry.

The finest, which may also be the oldest, survives in an almost complete copy made by a Norman scribe in about 1170, and now in the Bodleian Library at Oxford. This represents an original composed near the beginning of the century, and the story is based very freely on historical events which occurred over three hundred years before that. It tells how Roland, the impetuous nephew of Charlemagne, was left in command of the Frankish rearguard while the main army passed back northward over the Pyrenees; how, through the treachery of his step-father Ganelon, Roland was overtaken by the Saracen hordes – in history, they were the Christian Basques; how through over-confidence he refused to blow his marvellous horn, the olifant, which would have brought back Charlemagne to his help, until it was too late; and how he fought to the last beside Oliver and Turpin and died only when the enemy were in full retreat. The story does not end with Roland's death. Charlemagne, the King-figure, avenges him in another battle which is described in full. The traitor Ganelon is torn in pieces by four horses. A captured Moorish queen is baptized and at the close of the poem Charlemagne hears in a dream the voice of Gabriel summoning him to a new holy war. The wandering, yet concrete, narrative is full of descriptions of councils, warriors, armies, arms, horses, and fighting. Not all is realistic. The poet's fancy plays with numbers – the huge numbers of the pagan hosts, the numbers slain single-handed by each of the twelve peers, the number of gifts which the treacherous Saracens propose to send to Charles:

> You will give him bears and lions and hounds,
> Seven hundred camels and a thousand mewed hawks,
> With gold and silver four hundred mules laden,
> Then fifty carts to drive it away in.

But these are the fantasies of simple, direct minds, more accustomed to action than to introspection and firm in the belief that a pagan cleft from chaps to chine will open the road to heaven.

Whether this was the first *Chanson de Roland* and what was the *cantilena Rollandi* which William of Malmesbury declared was sung before Duke William at Hastings are unsolved questions. So is the identity of the poem's author – or perhaps two authors. The old theory that popular ballad songs dating from the time of Charle-magne himself were gradually built up into the complete epic was discarded early in this century in favour of the explanation put for-ward by the great French scholar, Joseph Bédier. According to him, the origin of the *chansons de geste* was learned and ecclesiastical and they were conceived as epic poems from the outset. Many origin-ated, like the verse Lives of Saints, in monasteries and abbeys which had a particular interest in popularizing the hero who had founded them or whose relics they housed. The halts along the pilgrim routes to Spain and Italy were especially suitable places for combin-ing history and legend and narrating them as an incentive to religious faith. Thus Roland's olifant was preserved in the church of St Seurin at Bordeaux. The pilgrims, like any modern tourist, would be glad to have its history explained to them. More generally, the recent expeditions against the Spanish Moslems and the Palestinian Crusades, which began in 1096, had an undoubted bearing on the militant Christianity of the *chansons de geste* and supplied a motive for reviving these half-mythical champions of Christendom at that particular date. Just as the Elizabethans looked back over the cen-turies for reflections of their own times and dramatists like Shake-speare supplied a mirror in historical plays, Frenchmen of the twelfth century looked back to the days of Charlemagne and Louis the Pious.

Today it is realized that some of the French epics may have an older pedigree than Bédier supposed, also that laymen (the *jongleurs*) probably played a larger part in composing them than he allowed. But his theory as a whole has not been superseded. It can be applied convincingly to most of the *chansons de geste*, of which about eighty survive.

In their purest form they belong to the twelfth century, though their popularity (with an inevitable debasement) continued for a hundred years after that. Traditionally, they were divided into three main cycles, or *gestes*, which still serve to classify the majority of them. *La Geste de Roi* deals with the struggle of Charlemagne and his family against the heathen and makes the King a dominating figure. Besides the *Chanson de Roland*, it includes the burlesque *Pèlerinage de Charlemagne*, whose unknown author was the first to use the twelve-syllable line – the alexandrine – instead of the usual line of eight or ten syllables. The *Geste de Guillaume d'Orange* is concerned with the deeds of a great southern family in warfare against the Spanish Moslems; the King's authority is respected and the vassal's duty to serve him is made clear, but the real hero is Guillaume. So the defence of Christendom and the family saga are intertwined. The third main group, labelled – though inadequately – the *Geste de Doon de Mayence*, is more openly feudal. Here the enemy is no longer the pagans but some rival baron – and often the family or supporters of Charlemagne himself against whom the hero is forced to revolt by some act of injustice. To this group of 'rebel epics' belong *Gormont et Isembart* (a poem perhaps as old as *La Chanson de Roland*, though only a fragment remains), *Girart de Roussillon*, *Raoul de Cambrai*, and *Renaud de Montauban*, known also as *Les Quatre Fils Aymon*.

There is usually room in the same period for a literature of action and of dream. While the *chansons de geste* were still developing, there began to grow up another conception of literature which expressed itself in the Romances. These also were long narrative poems, but technically they were less simple than the *chansons*. The most important difference was that they were rhymed, not assonanced, and were intended to be read by the lettered society of the courts rather than to be chanted to the crowd by *jongleurs*. This relatively cultivated public was interested in leisurely descriptions of jousting, hunting, armour, decoration, and costume, fascinated by problems of courtly etiquette and the right conduct of amorous relationships, and imaginative enough to welcome stories of magic very different from the restrained Christian supernatural. Such themes could not be fitted to the heroes of the *chansons de geste* at a time when these were still in their prime. Later, romance invaded the battlefield, crusaders were changed by sorcerers into swans, and the figure of Charlemagne himself was enmeshed in the enchantments of Oberon – as in the thirteenth-century *Huon de Bordeaux*. Roland and his peers had no true literary descendants. They survived only by being assimilated to the heroes of romance, and it is with a shock that we meet them again in the sixteenth-century poems of Ariosto or Tasso – Italianized beyond recognition – or find them among the knights-errant whose deeds bemused Don Quixote.

But in the twelfth century no such confusion was possible. The new heroes were taken from non-national and non-Christian sources, and, first from Greek and Latin literature, read often at second hand. Through Latin abridgements of Greek romancers and pseudo-historians, or through Virgil, the 'matter of Rome the Great' reached writers who re-told it in the idiom of their age. The most popular theme was the adventures of Alexander the Great, which inspired a *Roman d'Alexandre* almost contemporary with the *Chanson de Roland* and reappeared in several other versions through the century. A mythical Alexander, chivalrous and open-handed, campaigns in fabulous eastern lands where vines grow jewels and plants speak. The medieval French writers had fastened eagerly on the hints thrown out by an imaginative Greek of the second century. Fantasy of the same sort runs through some of the *romans d'antiquité*, of which the most famous were the *Roman de Thèbes*, the *Roman d'Enéas*, and Benoît de Sainte-Maure's *Roman de Troie*, all written towards 1150. In these, however, the love element is equally important. It reflects the influence of Ovid, the master of the sentimental casuists of the twelfth and thirteenth centuries, and prized by them even above Virgil as the greatest Latin poet. In the *Roman de Troie* the story of Troilus and Cressida appears in European literature for the first time. It was probably Benoît de Sainte-Maure's own invention.

It is interesting to see that almost at the beginning of their literature some French writers turned out of the main-stream of their national culture, which stemmed from the Christian tradition, because they felt a temperamental affinity with Greece and Rome. The two currents were to run through French literature until the present century, when Péguy and Claudel took one road, Valéry and Giraudoux the other. They are not invariably opposed, but can coexist as the two main sources for the writer, apart from contemporary themes. A third source which might have been added practically disappeared in France after the thirteenth century, though it proved more persistent in England and Germany.

The 'matter of Britain' embraced the whole legend of King Arthur and his knights and, eventually, of the Grail. The story of Tristan and Iseut, which originally had nothing to do with Arthur, became annexed to it. From where did these legends come?

The ordinary reader may think of them as essentially Celtic and may look for justification to such relics of ancient Welsh poetry as the medieval tales of the *Mabinogion*. But some of the Arthurian themes in the *Mabinogion* were clearly borrowed from the French, while others have no connection with the main Arthurian canon as it grew up in the twelfth and thirteenth centuries. An alternative line of descent, exclusively literary, is at least clearer.

In 1137 Geoffrey of Monmouth, Bishop of St Asaph, produced his *Historia Regum Britanniae*, a Latin chronicle purporting to describe the reigns of British kings from pre-Roman times on. Most of his account was completely unhistorical and he was the first to tell how a great warrior-king, Arthur, fell in battle in the sixth century and was taken to the enchanted island of Avalon for his wounds to be tended. In 1155 the Norman poet Robert Wace made an adaptation of Geoffrey's chronicle in French verse. His *Roman de Brut* expanded the story of Arthur, adding such new features as the Round Table. How far these writers drew on their own powers of invention and how far they were echoing popular tales which might, for example, have been brought to their Norman ears by Welsh and Breton minstrels is, of course, a crucial point – but one on which it is difficult to pronounce either way. The only certainty is that Arthur and his knights were first launched in literature by Geoffrey and Wace and that very soon afterwards French poets took them up, remoulded and developed them almost beyond recognition, and in so doing gave them a much wider circulation. The first great poet to work on the material – which he so transformed that he made it his own – was Chrétien de Troyes.

His surviving work was written between 1165 and 1190, most of it at the Court of the Countess Marie de Champagne at Troyes. This was a small closed society devoted to the arts and to a dilettante study of human relationships. Later, he had another cultured patron, Philip of Alsace, for whom he began his last poem, *Perceval*. Apart from *Perceval*, three of his verse romances – *Erec et Enide*, *Lancelot*, and *Yvain* – concern Arthur and his knights. A fourth, *Cligès*, takes place mainly in Greece and Constantinople, though its characters visit Arthur's Court.

In all these, Chrétien treats the Knights of the Round Table as idealizations of the nobles of his own day. His zest for narrative conducts them through endless adventures and feats of arms, love affairs, enchantments, imprisonments. The lonely tower, the dark forest, the damsel on the palfrey, the evil dwarf, all appear in curiously-detailed descriptions and were hardly intended as symbolic. The animated surface-flow of the story does not cover great psychological depths, and it is always a question of conduct rather than of passion. Yet he has some skill in analysing the effects of love on his characters. His observations are shrewd and sometimes witty, rarely profound. He is preoccupied with two themes: the knight's duty towards his calling – his honour and his prestige as a fighter – and his duty towards his lady. The hero of *Erec et Enide* deliberately humiliates his young wife in a successful attempt to vindicate his 'honour' as a knight. The burden of *Lancelot* is the opposite: the knight gladly submits to every test that his lady requires, even to the unspeakable humiliation of riding in a peasant's cart. While Chrétien placed women on a high level, he was incapable of that extreme idealization which raises them above humanity. He makes them beautiful, sensual, and – within certain limits – interesting. He is far from subscribing to the medieval cult of virginity, but farther still from the gross popular conception of woman as a naturally vicious being.

In *Perceval*, or *Le Conte del Graal*, his attitude appears to change. This poem introduces into the Arthurian canon the myth of the Grail, but without clearly showing what it was intended to symbolize. Since Chrétien died before completing the poem, it is impossible to know how far he himself would have developed it in a Christian and mystic direction, but his beginning certainly lends itself to such a development.

The young knight Perceval comes in his wanderings to a mysterious castle whose master is a wounded king. During supper a page enters bearing a white lance with a bleeding point, followed by a maiden with a gold chalice set with precious stones – this is the Grail – then by a second maiden carrying a silver dish. The little procession passes through the hall and disappears. Over-courteous, Perceval asks no questions. In the morning the castle seems to be deserted. Unseen hands lower the drawbridge and he rides away, never to find the place again. Later, he learns that he should have questioned his host about what he had seen. The spell would then have been lifted from the castle and the wounded king would have been healed, but the opportunity has been missed.

A slightly later writer, Robert de Borron, re-telling the tale in his *Joseph d'Arimathie*, explains the Grail as the vessel used at the Last Supper, then given to Joseph of Arimathea, who preserved in it the blood of Christ. It has been handed down among Joseph's descendants and brought to Britain to be kept in the castle of Corbenic. This version was adopted by the unknown author of a vast prose romance written between 1220 and 1230 which shows Arthur's knights undertaking the quest to find the way back to Corbenic, and with it the Grail. Only a knight without fault can hope to succeed, and this proves to be Galahad, who dies as his quest is fulfilled. The world of the Round Table comes to an end in a twilight battle in which all the knights are destroyed. The two outstanding motifs are now the triumph of purity, in Galahad, and the interpretation of the earthly quest of the knights as a heavenly quest.

The prose romance which set this forth is the main repository of the Arthurian legends. It incorporates in one great cycle the love of Lancelot and Guinevere and all the courtly adventures which went with it, the exploits and death of Arthur, and the Grail theme fully developed as a Christian myth.

A few years later another long prose romance recounted the story of Tristan and Iseut, which from then on became part of the Arthurian cycle.

The legend of Tristan and of Iseut the wife of Marc, bound together by a love stronger than themselves, knowing that it must lead them to suffering and disaster yet unable to resist it, needs forcing before it will enter into the code of chivalry. And it cannot be given a Christian significance, however it is treated. The original Tristan may have been the Drostán of Pictish legend who became the Drystan of the Welsh. But his story was probably first told in a complete and dramatic way by a French poet writing in the middle of the twelfth century, whose work has been lost. On this were based the earliest surviving versions – the poems of the *trouvères* Thomas and Béroul. Although their poems are not complete, enough of them survives to show what they were like, and they can be eked out from slightly later imitations and translations. Thomas

(an Anglo-Norman) was a little too addicted to the mannerisms of
the courtly code as Chrétien de Troyes understood it. Since Chrétien
says that he too wrote a poem on Marc and Iseut, which has disappeared like so much else, it is not impossible that Thomas read it
and was influenced by it. Béroul's simple and direct style is better
suited to the subject. It suggests a savagery and melancholy of
passion which, whatever theories are put forward, will always remain associated with the ancient Celtic lands, from Ireland to
Brittany. The Forest of Morois, the heathland, and the sea seem an
integral part of the legend. There could be no other setting for one
of the world's greatest stories of tragic love. For the general reader
an excellent re-telling of the story is Bédier's *Roman de Tristan et
Iseut* in modern French.

So in the twelfth and thirteenth centuries the great legends which
have become a European heritage were built up in literature by
French writers. Their international ramifications are too numerous
for it to be possible to mention more than a few of the most interesting.

In German, Eilhart von Oberg worked parallel with Béroul,
inspired, it would seem, by the same lost French poem which
Béroul had used. The greater Gottfried von Strassburg based his
Tristan (c. 1210) on the version of Thomas, and from Gottfried the
line runs to the Wagnerian *Tristan und Isolde*. Gottfried's contemporary, Wolfram von Eschenbach, worked from the *Perceval* begun
by Chrétien de Troyes to produce his own highly idealistic and
allegorical version of the Grail legend, and his *Parzival* was also
used by Wagner. In English literature – beginning with Layamon,
who stems from Wace – the whole Arthurian tradition derives
from French-language writings. The greatest embodiment of the
stories in our language, Sir Thomas Malory's *Morte d'Arthur*, was
compiled in the late fifteenth century, from the long French prose
romances of the thirteenth century, and in its turn became the
source of such poets as Spenser, Tennyson, and Swinburne. Arthur
gave Rabelais his starting-point. For years Milton meditated on the
Round Table, before finally discarding it in favour of the biblical
theme of *Paradise Lost*. No wonder that the vast edifice of Arthurian romance, built, extended, decorated, and looted by so many
poets and prose-writers, fought through by generations of scholars

and ransacked by mythologists and fairy-hunters, should have become almost synonymous with romance *tout court*.

Another small window into that enchanted world was opened by Marie de France, whose work contains some of the 'Celtic' atmosphere. Her subjects are not Arthurian, but she wrote one poem on Tristan. Her *Lais* are short episodic poems re-telling with a somewhat stiff grace stories which she may have heard from Breton *trouvères*. She is concerned with the adventures and intrigues of young lovers, perfect in body and innocently wanton in mind. She likes pathos. She admits magic – the talking deer, the werewolf, the lover who comes in the form of a goshawk – as the most natural thing in the world. Who she was is quite uncertain. Possibly she was the same Mary who became Abbess of Shaftesbury towards 1180. It is at least likely that she lived in England and frequented the Court of Henry II at much the same time as Chrétien was writing at the sister-court at Troyes. She knew his works and believed in the same chivalrous code, with slightly more emphasis on the rôle of the woman. She is the first poetess to emerge in Northern French literature, though strictly she is a story-teller rather than a poet. In a later age she would have used prose for her fanciful, unsubstantial plots. The *lai narratif*, which she probably invented as a literary form, has technically nothing in common with the full-length romances; but the spirit behind them is much the same. She also wrote an *Isopet*, or collection of verse fables in the tradition of Aesop.

One more type of romance proper enjoyed great popularity in the thirteenth century and includes some of the freshest works in medieval literature. The *romans d'aventure* belong to no definite cycle and are best thought of as the light reading of a sentimental élite. Unlike the *romans bretons*, they rarely have magic elements, nor do they carry the same wealth of psychological overtones. Unlike the *romans d'antiquité*, their settings are not in the past, but contemporary. This is their main characteristic and, when due allowance is made for the romancer's licence, many of them may be read as delicately realistic reflections of the actual life of the time. Among them are *Floire et Blancheflor*, *Guillaume de Dôle*, *L'Escoufle*, *Le Roman de la Violette*, *Le Châtelain de Coucy*, *La Châtelaine de Vergy*. None are inordinately long. Some are long-short stories in verse. With them may be grouped the sparkling, buoyant *Aucassin et Nicolette*. This is a 'chantefable' consisting of alternate passages of prose and verse, to be now recited, now sung. A tale of two lovers who refuse to be separated by their parents, it depicts the resilience of youth and its ultimate triumph, after surprising adventures, over the crabbed and calculating. Only the sceptic would class it among dream literature.

These light-weight stories have been overshadowed by *Le Roman de la Rose*, the most popular single work of the thirteenth century and perhaps of the whole medieval period. Begun towards 1230 by Guillaume de Lorris, it was completed nearly fifty years later by Jean de Meung, who added some eighteen thousand lines to his predecessor's four thousand.

There were three reasons for the poem's contemporary success. It was, in its first part, the clearest and most complete statement of the courtly conception of love that had been made, and so formulated the ideals which had been implied in a hundred romances of chivalry. Its second part was didactic and satirical in a vein which became increasingly popular through the thirteenth century. Most important of all, it was the first big allegorical poem in an age ready to adopt allegory as its favourite means of expression. The story is a dream which, says Guillaume de Lorris, he had in his twentieth year. He found himself in a garden peopled by personages such as Idleness, Pleasure, Soft Looks, Evil Tongue, Danger, and Reason. Helped by some and opposed by others, the Lover – the poet himself – seeks to pluck the Rose which grows there, jealously guarded. The Rose is the Beloved, passive, perfect, and scarcely attainable. She can only be reached by circumventing innumerable pitfalls and difficulties. The beauty of this invention is that it can be interpreted at two different levels. It can be an Art of Courtship according to the most refined social standards – an early *Carte de Tendre* – or it can be given an almost mystical sense, in which the search for the Rose resembles the quest for the Grail.

Allegory today may appear tedious and 'unreal', though it must be remembered that only a small proportion of literature has ever been realistic and the writer's problem at any period is the same. He has to find the most effective convention for representing the human personality as he sees it. It is always a convention; he never draws in the round. The thirteenth-century technique of isolating one quality and personifying it was merely an extreme example of abstraction, or analysis. It developed naturally from the romance-writers whose characters had been sketchily drawn and moved like puppets through the ingeniously-imagined circumstances. In their work, the psychological machinery was explained by the narrator or occasionally shown as a debate in the character's mind between such half-personifications as *Prouesse* and *Amour*. From here it was a short step to jettisoning the 'human' character altogether and writing solely in terms of abstractions. Psychology expressed through allegory or symbol need be no more hackneyed than its expression through character. Success depends not on the system, but on the insight and skill of the individual writer. Guillaume de Lorris's insight was considerable.

Jean de Meung's long continuation is in an entirely different spirit. Using the same personages and continuing the same story, he ends it at last with the plucking of the Rose and the triumph of the Lover. But his outlook is so different that it is a mystery why he was attracted by this particular poem. He looks on love as a force of nature (as did the poets of the Tristan story) to be endured because it cannot be avoided. Far from idealizing women, he considers them as dangerous and cunning jades both in and outside marriage. He attacks the social ills of the time – the arrogance of kings and nobles, the parasitism of the mendicant monks. He was a rationalist and something of a pedant, while Guillaume de Lorris was a courtier and a poet. He fills out his story with displays of learning which have nothing to do with it. But his contemporaries drew no clear distinction between entertainment and instruction, and this did not mar the poem for them. It served rather to complete it and bring it up to date. The composite *Roman de la Rose* may lack artistic unity, but it contains nearly all the features which interested the medieval mind. Only earthiness (though not sexuality) was missing, and for this one must look to the early drama, the *fabliaux*, and the vast, rustic-humoured *Roman de Renart*.

This grew up principally in the north-east, where Picard meets Fleming in hard-headed fellowship. The world gets what it deserves – plenty of sly comment and an occasional belly-laugh: no pretty fancies. When there is fantasy it takes the form of humour, closely linked to the physical. The literary ancestry of the *Roman de Renart* can be traced back to Aesop's fables, with their derivatives in Latin and early French, such as Marie de France's *Isopet*. But whereas in the fables the interest is dispersed over a number of different animals, other works showed a preference for one central hero. In a long poem of the tenth century by a renegade monk, the *Ecbasis captivi*, this character is the wolf – though he is finally vanquished by the fox. Another Latin poem, the *Ysengrimus*, written by one Nivard of Ghent towards 1150, took up the same story and was the immediate literary source of the French *Roman*. But popular tales must also have been used to enrich it.

The original *Roman de Renart* as we know it was a composite work by a number of different authors, such as Pierre de Saint-Cloud, writing during the last quarter of the twelfth century and the first few years of the thirteenth. Its sole unity consists in the metre – the eight-syllable couplet of many of the courtly romances – and in the fact that the same characters appear in the different stories and remain true to type. In a score of episodic poems, Renart the fox, crafty and resourceful, wages an intermittent war against the more stupid wolf, Ysengrin, and his wife Dame Hersent. In his turn he is often outwitted by weaker animals – Tibert the cat, Chantecler the cock, or Tiercelin the crow. If Brer Rabbit had been of this particular company, no doubt he would have played his part too. These characters have become part of a general heritage and their names are familiar to many who know nothing of their origin. Renart has given his name to every French fox, displacing the old word *goupil*. Many an English and Belgian cat is Tibby, Brun the bear was the first Bruin, and one can only regret that Tardif the slug and Couart the hare have not had wider currency. Is it necessary to see in *Le Roman de Renart* more than a reflection of that almost universal interest in the personality of animals which begins in childhood and invents half-human qualities and adventures for them? The original *Roman de Renart* told the stories chiefly for their own sake, though it is possible to read a certain social significance into the triumphs of Renart and the smaller animals over more powerful opponents. Like the 'little' peasant and the small citizen, they must get by cunning what is denied them by force. But the only open satire is against the Church. Renart 'tonsures' Ysengrin with boiling water, since his delicious fried eels are for monks only; miracles occur at the tomb of Dame Coupée, the hen, and the other creatures swoon with ecstasy; Renart undertakes a pilgrimage to Rome, since only the Pope could absolve such a sinner. But such episodes are comparatively rare, and at least King Noble the Lion is always respected.

In the thirteenth century the huge, rambling story was taken over by moralists, satirists, and even parodists. *Le Couronnement de Renart*, composed in Flanders soon after 1250, is a medieval *Animal Farm*. It tells how Renart obtains Noble's throne by a trick, throws over his own most faithful supporters, rewards the rich and oppresses the poor, and is welcomed with acclaim in every country he visits, particularly in Rome. The ironical moral is that money is the prince of this world, and possibly of the next. In *Renart le nouvel*, written towards 1300 by Jacquemart Gelée of Lille, the animals have become practically human. They hold a tournament at the court of Noble, as in the romances of chivalry. There is a love-intrigue. And beside the animal characters allegorical characters are placed, giving the same hybrid effect as the presence of actors in the later Disney films. With a fourteenth-century *Renart le contrefait*, the career of Renart as a distinctive character is finished. Here he is at once an arch-criminal and a moralizer over his own misdeeds. The original fox is lost in the anonymous author's eagerness to impart his own encyclopaedic knowledge and to stress the moral so strongly that only the underlinings can be seen.

The reign of Renart was also the age of the *fabliaux*, which have the same popular and satirical flavour. They are short narrative poems, usually with a humorous point. Not all of them are entirely distinct from the other short stories in verse such as Gautier de Coinci's *Miracles de la Sainte Vierge* (*c.* 1220) which contain such well-known stories as *Le Jongleur de Notre Dame* and were written in a pious spirit. Some, on the other hand, belong to the courtly tradition and resemble the *lais*. But the typical *fabliau* is realistic, shrewd, and based on a quizzical observation of life. Wives deceive their husbands and, far from being found out, talk them into leaving home on lengthy pilgrimages. Another husband, less gullible, holds an auction to sell the cupboard in which his wife's lover – a priest – is hiding. A thief, hiding in a sheep-pen, answers 'Here I am!' when the shepherd calls his dog (conveniently named Estula) and the priest is sent for to exorcize the evil spirit. When there is a moral, it is starkly practical, as: 'Parents, treat your children well, or when you are old they will turn you out to starve.' The *fabliaux* are a storehouse of anecdotes which continue to crop up in different forms even today. They are not all very subtle and the broadest must have appealed to a very rustic sense of humour. But such a story as *Auberée*, with its sketch of the ingenious procuress, already brings us near to the world of Boccaccio and Chaucer.

The authors of many of the *fabliaux* are known. Among them was Rutebeuf (*fl.* 1250–85), the author of the short violently satirical *Renart le Bestourné* and of more personal-seeming poems also. But in a sense the *fabliaux* are all impersonal. They belong to a class of popular literature in which the author's identity is of small importance. It is only in lyric poetry that the personal note is heard, or at least simulated.

CHAPTER 2

Lyric Poetry: Troubadours to Rhétoriqueurs

LYRIC poetry originates in song, and for most of Western Europe the song was invented by the troubadours of the *langue d'oc*. They in their turn may have learnt their art from the Spanish Arab poets, or they may simply have adapted to their needs the Latin models with which they were familiar, particularly the hymns and chants of the Church. The question is still debated and goes well beyond the limits of any one literature.

It is at least certain that an advanced culture existed in southern France as early as the eleventh century. The aristocracy participated in it more fully and with less dependence on the learning of the monasteries than their northern counterparts. Though traditionally called Provençal, this Mediterranean culture was not confined to the geographic Provence, but extended to the whole region in which the *langue d'oc* (embracing the four main dialects – Provençal, Languedocien, Auvergnat, and Limousin) was spoken. This language in its standard literary form was used by troubadours not only in France, but also in Spain and Italy as the language of poetry *par excellence*. The same verse-forms, though not the language, were taken up in the thirteenth century by the Sicilian school of poets and so stand at the origin of Italian poetry. Dante and Petrarch admired the mastery of such troubadours as Arnaut Daniel and Guiraut de Borneil.

The earliest known troubadour was Guillaume Count of Poitou and Duke of Aquitaine (1071–1126), who ruled vast domains in the south-west and is a striking example of the nobleman-poet. Kings did not disdain the art, while of over four hundred troubadours whose names are known many belonged to the feudal nobility. Even when composed by professionals, the Provençal song-poem is an aristocratic art-form, stamped with the curious refinement of the little courts which fostered it.

Unlike the *jongleur*, who usually did not compose his material and who intoned the *chansons de geste* to a probably monotonous twanging, the troubadour composed words and music himself. His short songs were of great technical subtlety. They divided into stanzas, with complete rhymes and usually some sort of refrain. Strict stylistic rules were evolved which, together with the requirements of music, led to great ingenuity in the handling of the verse. Though the personal note so often appears to be present, it is subordinated to the conventions of the genre. One theme is predominant and runs through the most representative of the troubadour forms – the *canso d'amor*, or love-song. This is devoted to the praise of the poet's mistress, whom he only hopes to win by a submissive and faithful love. To make himself worthy of her is his guiding principle in life. He is ready, he declares, to worship her from afar in the sole hope that she will accept his homage and acknowledge his existence. If the troubadour's art really stemmed from the Latin hymn, it is easy to understand this assimilation of human love to a religion. In any case, the courtly verse-forms came themselves to be used, by such poets as the thirteenth-century Guiraut Riquier, to hymn the Virgin. For the more spiritual of the troubadours, the line between earthly and divine love may have been indistinct.

The greatest significance of the *canso d'amor* was that it reflected a sexual attitude which was to remain in European lyric poetry for centuries. Dante's love for Beatrice, Petrarch's for Laura, and the vast body of medieval and Renaissance poetry which stems from Petrarch; later, the Romantic idealization with, in England, its Pre-Raphaelite offshoot: all this, with or without mystical associations, can be traced back to the troubadour's conception of courtly love, which was, of course, similar to the knightly code of many of the romances, but was expressed with greater formal elaboration and presented as a more specialized sentiment shorn of narrative and descriptive elements.

The *canso d'amor* has also been explained as the product of a society in which the husband was often engaged in a crusade or a local war, while in his absence the wife was unwilling to risk the consequences of a complete love-affair. But apart from the fact that adultery is not often implied in this poetry, such social generalizations cannot fairly be drawn from literature. What would be thought of a future historian who concluded from the vogue of the detective-novel that after 1920 the majority of the British middle classes became actively interested in ingenious methods of committing murder?

After a brilliant development in the twelfth century, Provençal culture began a decline from which it never recovered. The principal reasons for this eclipse were political and attach to such events as the stamping-out of the Albigensian heresy by the northern armies. But meanwhile the northern *trouvères* had begun to practise the Provençal verse-forms and in the last quarter of the twelfth century the troubadour tradition passed into the *langue d'oïl*. The first generation of *trouvères* includes Conon de Béthune, the Châtelain de Coucy, Gace Brulé, and Blondel de Nesle. In the thirteenth century, some of the best known are Jean Bodel, Guillaume de Ferrières, Richard de Semilli, Roger d'Andeli, Thibaut de Champagne, Richard de Fournival, Baude Fastoul, Adam de la Halle, and Colin Muset. As with the southern poets, there is a mingling of great nobles, such as Conon de Béthune and Thibaut de Champagne, King of Navarre, with commoners. But the latter write with the same refinement. It is true that an important *confrérie* of poets existed at Arras through which a new bourgeois influence might be expected to have made itself felt. But though Jean Bodel and Adam de la Halle among the Arras poets write, as dramatists, in a more popular vein, they are far from being so free in their courtly songs. Only a few poets, such as Colin Muset, introduce occasional mockery or parody into the courtly verse-forms. But for the most part these medieval poets respected the genres as religiously as the most rigid purist of the seventeenth century. You did not jest in the *canso d'amor*. Why should you, when you had the *fabliau*?

The *trouvères* took over the forms used by the troubadours and developed new ones of their own. There were dialogue-songs known as *chansons à personnages*, such as (to give them their northern names) the *jeu-parti* (a debate on love between two *trouvères*), the *pastourelle* (encounter between shepherd and shepherdess), the *aube* (lovers separating at dawn), the *reverdie* (May song). Various kinds of dance-song – the *ballette*, the *estampie*, the *rondet* – also suggest the light pastoral vein. Another notable type, native to the north and possibly of great antiquity, was the *chanson d'histoire* or *chanson de toile* (sewing-song). This was a

simple ballad often concerned with the unhappy love of a girl or
young wife. Fair Yolanz is love-sick for Count Mahi, in spite of her
husband's black looks and her mother's scolding. Fair Doette waits
in vain for the return of her lover Doon, killed in a tournament.

Some of these must originally have developed from the folk-
song, but in the forms in which they have come down to us they
have clearly been worked over by skilled poets and it is impossible
to separate the popular from the literary elements in them.

In the later Middle Ages the history of lyric poetry is still a history of forms, developed with great artistry from the verse-patterns
of the troubadours. The fourteenth and fifteenth centuries are
dominated by the *rondeau* and the *ballade*. The second has nothing
in common with the English or German ballad and was not intended
for narrative. At its simplest it is a poem consisting of three stanzas
followed by a final half-stanza or *envoi*, through the whole of which
the same three rhymes recur. Each stanza ends with the same line,
which serves as a refrain. The *rondeau* is a shorter and equally
stylized poem on two rhymes only. Though different poets introduced certain variations into these two master-forms, their basic
design did not allow for much freedom. The composer of the
shortest *ballade* has to find fourteen similar rhymes of one sort, six
of another, and five of another – besides working in an identical
line four times. The sonneteer needs a maximum of only four
rhymes of the same sort and he does not have to repeat any of his
lines. It was on such forms as the sonnet that Italian poets were
working at the very time when the French were manoeuvring
within their cramped and elaborate patterns. They achieved at their
best an almost Chinese delicacy, or perhaps after all an Arabic
virtuosity of design, but it is a closed design. For the lover of intricate repetitions, of perfection constantly mirroring itself, the *rondeau* and the *ballade* have a steady fascination, but it must be said
that the psychological content is very much simpler than the artistic
form. The majority of the French medieval poets seem to have exhausted their ingenuity in fashioning their verses. In feeling they
are neither complex nor decadent. Paradoxically, their love-songs
leave an impression of fresh simplicity sometimes tinged with sadness.

Of the fourteenth-century poets, Guillaume de Machaut (*c.*

1300–77) was chiefly responsible for popularizing the newly-elaborated *ballade* and *rondeau* and for establishing the *virelay* and the moralizing *dit*. His chief successors were Eustache Deschamps (*c.* 1346–*c.* 1406); Jean Froissart (*c.* 1337–*c.* 1405), better known for his Chronicles; and Christine de Pisan (*c.* 1365–*c.* 1430), an early humanist scholar. The biographical fact of Christine's early widow-hood lends more poignancy to her songs of lost love than we should perhaps find in them if we knew nothing of her life. A personal note can be detected in Froissart's verse, though no echo of the great events which it was his life's work to record. Only Deschamps uses the *ballade* for political and satirical themes, but he is not entirely successful in this literary heresy; too often his verse is flat. The fifteenth century saw a revival of still older modes in the work of Alain Chartier (*c.* 1385–*c.* 1430), whom it considered as its master-poet. His *La Belle Dame sans merci* renewed the courtly theme of the lover who tries in vain to win his lady and finally dies of despair. However, his long *Livre des quatre dames* was topical enough in theme; it is partly a lament, partly a debate between four women who have lost their lovers in the disaster of Agincourt. Though it may wear the appearance of the rhetorical exercise so frequent in medieval poetry, this particular debate bears the marks of a nationally-felt bitterness. Yet Chartier's main commentary on the unhappy state of the country, *Le Quadrilogue Invectif*, was written in prose. It is on the whole true that the poets who lived through the grim and turbulent period of the Hundred Years War remained, as poets, in their formal garden, insulated by art against public anxieties and private passions alike.

This applies with particular force to Charles d'Orléans (1394–1465), the most accomplished writer in the medieval lyric tradition and one of the last great aristocratic poets. The nephew of Charles VI of France and himself one of the most important figures in the kingdom, he was taken prisoner at Agincourt at the age of twenty and spent the next twenty-five years in captivity in England. Released at last, he retired to his château at Blois and surrounded himself with poets. His own exquisitely delicate work, which rivals that of the troubadours in its handling of the serious short poem, reflects nothing of his considerable political activity. While his personal experiences give it a general tone of quiet melancholy, few poems can be attached to any specific phase of his life. Imprisonment forces tears from such varied poets as Villon, Verlaine, Wilde, Apollinaire, but a quarter of a century of it draws from Charles d'Orléans a few *ballades* of restrained regret for the pleasant land of France.

Into this literature of discreet self-effacement the figure of François Villon (1431–63?) makes a startling entry. Half victim-crook, half moralist-clown, he writes with a directness largely due to the absence of any shadow of a lost musical accompaniment in his verse. It could not be sung, nor does it look back to the conventions of song. In reading it, we meet the author squarely in the medium in which he composed. Nevertheless, Villon continues to use the *ballade*, which acquires a new vitality in his hands. He rhymes *ballades* in thieves' slang, *ballades* to beg a small loan from a noble patron, to lament the passing of youth in women, to ask compassion for the hanged swinging on the gallows, to hymn the Virgin, to describe a singularly unplatonic love, to commend the soul of his friend Jehan Cotart, the Homeric drinker. No one else had asked the prim, stylized *ballade* to do all this and, quite naturally, no one else had won such a generous response from it. Villon's other metre, an eight-line stanza built on three rhymes, is closely related to the *ballade*-form in which, no doubt, his thought was cast and of which he is the chief master. Unlike Charles d'Orléans, he based his work freely on his life. Obscure in many details, its general features are clear enough.

Born in Paris, he was brought up by a parish priest, Guillaume de Villon, from whom he took his name. While studying at the university, he acquired an early taste for the tavern and the bawdy-house and from student disorders slipped readily into actual crime. For his part in various killings and robberies he was imprisoned several times – the last under sentence of death. An eleventh-hour pardon saved his life, but on condition that he should leave Paris for ten years. This was in January 1463, when he was a little over thirty. After that, no authentic trace of him has been found.

His work divides into *Les Lais* ('The Legacies'), sometimes called *Le Petit Testament*, a light burlesque poem of three hundred lines (1456); a longer, graver poem, *Le Testament* (1461 or 1462), which is his masterpiece; and a score of independent short poems written at various dates and which include the famous *Epitaphe Villon* (*Ballade des Pendus*) and the half-dozen *ballades* in thieves' jargon. *Le Testament* in particular is the work of a man who has known poverty, hunger, humiliation, frustration in love, fear, sickness, and perhaps torture, but who has preserved an intense interest in the small, inconsequent happenings in life. Much of it is malicious gossip about his friends and enemies, but Villon can suddenly swing from trivial mockery into high (though conventional) moralizations on the destiny of man. The idea of death haunted him and he faced it as a physical horror unmitigated by allegory or sentiment. While his grossly realistic vein is paralleled in other medieval poets, the emotional sweep of some of his verse and the bitter pathos of certain passages are unapproached elsewhere.

In Villon, lyric poetry had moved a long way from song, whether 'folk' or sophisticated. It had digested realism and satire without ceasing to be personal. But if a way was pointed here, no one was capable of taking it. The main poetic movement continued to be concerned with formal subtleties.

Late fifteenth-century poetry was dominated by the *Rhétoriqueurs*, a school of writers centred on the Court of Burgundy,* whose dukes proved enlightened patrons of culture at a date when the kings of France were absorbed in politics and war. Georges Chastellain (*c.* 1404–75) led a group which included Olivier de la Marche (*c.* 1422–1502) and Jean Molinet (1435–1507). All considered Chartier as their master and favoured, like him, a certain rolling eloquence in prose and verse based on the ample style of Ciceronian Latin – hence their name. They brought the long didactic and allegorical poem, practised before them by Chartier, Deschamps, and Christine de Pisan (a legacy of the *Roman de la Rose*), to a new pitch of ornamented abstraction. Their short poems reflect an excessive delight in verbal ingenuity which often ends in making verse dependent on the pun, the riddle, or the acrostic for its effects. For all their preoccupation with style, they had little to say. They might

---

*A paper by P. Jodogne in *Humanism in France* (Manchester U. P., 1970) virtually proves that the title *Rhétoriqueurs* was never adopted by contemporaries and was first coined by a nineteenth-century critic. But the term is convenient and is used in nearly every modern history and dictionary of French literature. The origin of the term *Pléiade* is much the same.

be said to mark the exhaustion of the medieval inspiration but for some of the later *Rhétoriqueurs* (no longer confined to Burgundians) who establish a faint link with the poetry of the Renaissance. Such was Jean Lemaire de Belges (1473–*c.* 1524), who travelled in Italy and introduced echoes of Dante and Petrarch into his verse. He attempts new metres: the *terza rima* and even the alexandrine. He shows a Latin learning in his *Épître de l'Amant vert* and a classical sensuality in his *Temple de Vénus* which distantly foreshadow Ronsard.

CHAPTER 3

Prose Chronicles and Fiction

PROSE lagged behind verse as a medium of expression until well into the fourteenth century. Not only was the chief fiction of the time – the *chansons de geste* and the romances – written in verse, but so were works which purported to record real events. The rhymed chronicle by the professional writer became an institution side by side with the monkish chronicle in Latin, on which it was often based. Usually it was commissioned by some noble patron who required either a record of his own achievements or a flattering genealogy. The Normans, who felt themselves to be *parvenus*, were especially addicted to this form of ancestor-worship. To their encouragement most of the early verse chronicles owe their existence, from Geoffrey Gaimar's *Estoire des Englès* to Benoît de Sainte-Maure's *Chronique des Ducs de Normandie*. Wace, who besides the Arthurian *Roman de Brut* wrote the *Roman de Rou*, extolling Duke Rollo, the founder of the Norman line, summed up the position ingenuously enough:

> Je parol a la riche gent
> Ki unt les rentes et l'argent,
> Kar pur eus sunt li livre fait.

(I write for the rich people who have the rents and the money, for it is for them that books are made.)

Nevertheless, it was the chronicle in prose which occupied four of the most interesting medieval writers: Villehardouin, Joinville, Froissart, and Commynes. Between them they span three centuries and represent changing approaches to the writing of history.

Geoffroy de Villehardouin (*c.* 1152–1211) wrote his *Conquête de Constantinople* in the last few years of his life to justify himself and his comrades-in-arms of the Fourth Crusade of 1202–4. This Crusade, after assembling at Venice, had conquered and sacked the Christian city of Byzantium instead of making for the Holy Land as originally intended. From the castle which he had acquired in

Macedonia – and from which he never returned to France – Ville-hardouin looks back to the councils and campaigns in which he has been a leader. He explains the reasons for the diversion as he sees them and insists on the good faith of the majority of the French knights. But he recounts rather than argues. If things happened so, it was God's will; those who did wrong have been punished by death in battle. He has a fatalistic respect for Providence which he shares with the authors of the *chansons de geste*, though he lacks their positive faith. Years of hard and weary fighting have left him simply with a stock of memories which he reviews in the somewhat flat and realistic manner of a soldier.

The personality of Jean de Joinville (1225–1317) is more interesting, and there is far more life in the detail of his book, the *Histoire de Saint Louis*. He wrote it at the age of eighty as a biography of Louis IX, who by then had died and had been canonized. But it is also an autobiography, since it describes in the first person the relationship between Joinville and the king, whom he accompanied on the disastrous Crusade of 1248. The narrative of this Crusade forms the main and most coherent part of an otherwise disjointed work and is written with such vivid directness that it is supposed that the octogenarian Joinville was using a personal memoir he had written much earlier. The honest rendering of personal experience, the anecdotic treatment, and the open, simple character of the author make this an outstanding work among the numerous Crusader chronicles.

Villehardouin and Joinville were noblemen – both from Champagne – who wrote of events in which they themselves had played a part. The next great chronicler, Jean Froissart (c. 1337–1410), was a professional writer who worked for several patrons, including Philippa of Hainault, Edward III's queen, who brought him from his native Flanders to England. The later part of his life was spent in Flanders and France, where he travelled extensively. While he also wrote of the events of his own time, it was as an historian-reporter rather than as a participant. The early part of his *Chroniques* is drawn from a chronicle by his compatriot, Jean Le Bel. For other passages, such as his famous account of the Battle of Poitiers, he talked with eyewitnesses before putting pen to paper. He was no mere compiler. By obviously whole-hearted research and inquiry he re-creates his period, picturing with great skill not only the Hundred Years War, whose chief historian he is, but the Scottish wars of Edward III, the rebellions of Étienne Marcel and of Wat Tyler, the feasts and tournaments which furnish the colour, if not the sinews, of history. Too close to his subject to analyse it, he excels as a descriptive artist. He is better than invariably accurate; he depicts the fourteenth century as it saw itself. A hundred years after his death his *Chroniques* became famous in England through Lord Berners's translation. His other work:, apart from his short poems, include a long verse romance, *Méliador*, which at that date was a pastiche.

Froissart's *Chroniques* were continued in the fifteenth century by two writers at the Court of Burgundy, whose Dukes, as we have seen, protected Chastellain and other *Rhétoriqueurs*. Several of these same poets also wrote prose chronicles. Among them might have been Philippe Commynes (*c.* 1445–1511) if, as a politically ambitious young man, he had not abandoned the service of the Burgundians to attach himself to Louis XI of France. He was rewarded by high office as a diplomat and political adviser. Towards 1490, after Louis's death, he began to write his *Mémoires*, which deal with the character and diplomacy of this most astute of French kings. Unlike Froissart, Commynes is not a great verbal artist, but he has other qualities. He is the first French writer to show the true historian's interest in cause and effect. Confronted with the anarchy of the times and the obvious bankruptcy of the old feudal-chivalrous ideas, he attempts, behind the pattern of events, to descry new principles of government. For him the ruler, like Louis XI, must use moderation and intelligence rather than force. Commynes did not evolve a complete political system, but he grappled, some twenty years before Machiavelli, with the same problems which the Florentine analysed in his more abstract and conclusive work.

For the familiar details of everyday life, French medieval literature has nothing quite equivalent to the English *Paston Letters*. But much may be learnt from two instructional books. *Le Livre du Chevalier de La Tour Landry pour l'enseignement de ses filles* (the title defines the work) paints incidentally the life of provincial aristocratic society in the fourteenth century. *Le Ménagier de Paris* (1392) was ostensibly written by an elderly husband to educate his fifteen-year-old wife in household management and sound moral principles. Whether it was intended for a real wife or for the general public, it is an admirable introduction to the world of the rich Parisian *bourgeoisie*. A diary, *Le Journal d'un Bourgeois de Paris*, covers the years 1405–49, but it is less concerned with personal doings than with the political reactions of its unknown author during a stormy period which included the Burgundian and English occupations of Paris.

Imaginative literature in prose hardly became important before the Renaissance. The evolution of fiction required, first the reduction of the verse romances into prose, then the development of new forms and themes – leading eventually to works which could fairly be called novels. The French word *roman* covers both 'romance' and 'novel', usefully underlining the continuity of a narrative genre from the twelfth to the twentieth centuries. But while such continuity exists in a very general sense, it is hard to find anything comparable to the modern novel much before the seventeenth century. The Middle Ages saw the thirteenth-century prose versions of the great Arthurian romances, (see pp. 16–19 above), then little worth noting until the middle of the fifteenth century. The work which was then produced illustrates the problems of transitional writers caught between contemporary reality and a powerful but wheezy tradition.

The tradition of chivalry inherent in the romances was so strong that only a Cervantes could have shaken it off or a Scott could have renewed it, and these writers were not of that calibre. Saddled with moral values which had become anachronistic, the contemporaries of Villon and Commynes had three possible choices. The first was to continue to write of knights-errant and their fabulous adventures in a purely entertaining way, as the modern Western treats of cowboys and Indians who have ceased to exist, together with their peculiar code of honour. Authors who did this were assured of a wide audience which was to grow vastly in the next century. By then the printing-press had come into general use and was clamouring, like radio today, for more material than original writers could provide. The answer was translation and adaptation – the adventures of Fierabras, Huon de Bordeaux, Ogier le Danois, Perceval le Gallois, Palmerin de Bretagne, Lancelot du

Lac, Amadis de Gaul – all legendary characters in conventionally imaginary settings.

A second course, taken in a few works only, was to assume that the code of chivalry was still alive and to apply it to contemporary characters.* This was done in the anonymous *Livre des Faicts de Jacques de Lalaing* (*c.* 1468), which romanced the exploits of a real knight who had died a few years before and could only have taken part in the practical cut-throat fighting of the Hundred Years War. In a sense this was as legitimate as the liberties taken in the earlier verse-chronicles, but there at least a decent time had usually been allowed to elapse. A more imaginative variation of the same approach is found in *Le Chevalier délibéré* (1493) by Olivier de La Marche. Here the author's patron, Charles the Bold of Burgundy, is presented as a knight-errant moving among allegorical characters and exploits. This was a propaganda treatment not dissimilar to Spenser's allegory of Elizabeth in *The Faerie Queene*. It has often been attempted, never with complete success.

But the most interesting development occurs in the work of Antoine de La Sale (*c.* 1386–*c.* 1460), the best-known fiction-writer of his age, though more books have been attributed to him than he probably wrote. His chief book, *Le Petit Jehan de Saintré*, deals with the whim of a great lady who takes up an impoverished page and begins to educate him as a perfect knight. All goes well until she tires of her protégé and allows her new lover, a robust and insolent monk, to beat him up in her presence. In the end the hero is avenged on the pair of them, but not before the courtly idea of the relations of the knight and the lady has suffered an irreparable blow. This story is not yet a parody, but by admitting realism into the most sacrosanct part of the courtly convention, it points unmistakably to the decadence of romance. A genre begins to die when it is corrupted from within – i.e. when it no longer takes its own ethic seriously.

Fully realistic fiction had a different ancestry. On one side it stemmed from the native *fabliaux*, and it is in this tradition that the ironically-entitled *Les Quinze Joyes de Mariage* (*c.* 1440) was written. Its theme is the tribulations of a young husband whose simplicity is exploited by all the women of his household. It echoes

*There is a modern parallel in the novels of Dornford Yates.

the anti-feminism of Jean de Meung and points once more to Woman as the unassimilated element in the medieval writer's scheme of things. If he could not believe with the troubadour that she was semi-divine, he had to agree with the monk that she was allied to the devil; in neither case was she quite of this world. A second source was the *Decameron*, which now joined the *fabliaux* as an inspiration for short-story writers. The first French work to be outwardly modelled on it was *Les Cent Nouvelles nouvelles* (c. 1460), which, like *Les Quinze Joyes de Mariage*, has been unreasonably attributed to Antoine de La Sale. These hundred racy after-dinner anecdotes by an unknown writer at the court of Burgundy are told by a circle of noblemen – the same device as in Boccaccio. But their subjects and popular style owe nothing to him.

CHAPTER 4

The Medieval Drama

THE Middle Ages had no 'theatre' in the modern sense of buildings specially constructed for the performance of plays, with which goes a professional corps of actors and other specialists. Our very notion of drama as a series of surprising situations presented in a general atmosphere of suspense which hinges on a conflict between different characters, or between characters and their circumstances, would have been foreign to medieval people. But if they had no 'theatre', they had two of the apparently universal urges on which any sort of drama depends. One is the appetite for spectacle and the other the desire, especially strong in primitive temperaments, to 'represent' a story in physical action rather than simply to tell it or to hear it told. Add to this their strongly developed community life and the fact that in the churches they had both a social centre and a public building which could be used for performances, and it is plain that their resources were not so limited.

The main types of medieval drama, the Mystery plays and the Miracle plays, had their origin in the ceremonies of the Church and so were common to all Western Christendom. In the course of centuries different countries introduced their own variations, but the original root has been traced back to a development of the Easter ritual already widespread by the tenth century. In this, a chorister standing by the altar exchanged chanted questions and responses with three others who moved down the church towards him, so 'acting' – though the word is at first too ambitious – the visit of the three Marys to the empty tomb. Similar small ceremonies, with the same kind of embryonic dialogue, were used to represent the Christmas visit of the shepherds to Bethlehem and the Epiphany visit of the Three Kings.

A second line of development was from a stock sermon 'against Jews, Pagans, and Arians' preached in many churches at Christmas. Here the preacher quoted the words of various biblical prophets who had foretold the coming of the Messiah. It was easy for a histrionic priest to turn the sermon into a 'dramatic reading', then other voices were interpolated, and finally the prophets emerged as separate characters, with parts to act as well as to recite. Others were added who were not strictly prophets, such as Adam (with Eve, Cain, and Abel), Abraham (sacrificing Isaac), Balaam (and his ass). In such ways as this the rich material of the Old Testament was added to the Passion-story of the New Testament, to which it could be made to serve as a natural prelude.

For a long time this rudimentary drama was performed inside the churches as a supplement to the services. The performers were ecclesiastics and the language used was the Latin of the ritual. Probably because the spectacles became too boisterous and required more space, they were eventually moved outside the church and performed against its western wall, which provided an excellent background with its great porch forming a focal point and a means of entrance and exit. Here there was usually a square giving ample room for spectators. 'Scenery' could be set up, consisting of scaffolding and other wooden erections. They ranged from Heaven on the spectator's left to Hell, figured by a dragon's open mouth through which fire belched from cauldrons of pitch, on his right. Between were whatever settings or *mansions* the action called for – as Nazareth, Jerusalem, Herod's palace, Calvary. All this was solidly built by carpenters before the performances began and formed a *décor simultané* or multiple setting which provided almost the only means of indicating changes of scene until the introduction of movable sets in the specially-constructed theatres of the seventeenth century. The medieval actors simply moved from one *mansion* to another according to the demands of the story and the bidding of the *lector* – a producer-conductor who directed the complicated performance with his book open before him. He was often the author too.

Such was the method of staging preferred in France. (The English adopted the processional method.) It was evidently followed in performing the *Jeu d'Adam*, the earliest known Mystery in any language other than Latin, though Latin is still used in it for the directions to the actors and for the chant of the choir. The play has come down in an incomplete manuscript copied by a Provençal scribe, but the original appears to have been written in

Anglo-Norman towards the middle of the twelfth century. It is an expansion of the 'testimony' sermon. With a stiff but not unmoving simplicity it shows the tempting of Eve and the expulsion from paradise, then the killing of Abel by Cain. Other Old Testament figures then come forward, speak their lines, and are carried off by the waiting devils. The whole bears witness to the vigour of the early Mysteries. The only other text at all comparable in date is a fragment of a Resurrection play belonging to the early thirteenth century.

The *Jeu d'Adam* was transitional in that it was still attached to the liturgy. Gradually the Mystery plays drifted further away from the Church, while acquiring enormous popularity which caused the activities of an entire town to be focused on them at festival times. By the fifteenth century, when they reached their heyday, the actors were laymen, the language always French, and the site usually the main square of the town. Hundreds of actors might be concerned if we include the angelic choir, the numerous semi-comic devils, the Roman soldiers at the Crucifixion, and other crowd-parts. The responsibility for organizing this had passed to the municipalities and thence to the *confréries*, or local associations which grew up. The earliest known was formed at Nantes (1371), followed closely by Rouen (1374), then Paris, whose famous *Confrérie de la Passion* was granted royal letters patent in 1402. From that time until about 1550 date the great Mystery plays, of which about sixty survive. Some are immensely lengthy compositions, containing from thirty to sixty thousand lines of eight-syllable verse – the stock medieval metre. Thus they are up to fifteen times as long as *Hamlet*, though the acting-time would be proportionately longer still because of the great amount of physical action involved. Their production lasted over days or perhaps over several Sundays. They mingle, with little art or integration, a simple and sometimes moving piety with crude humour, or combine scholastic theology with scenes of homely realism. In spite of their length they lack the broad sweep of the epic and also the tension of great drama. While this was perhaps inevitable in the circumstances in which they were produced, one is left wondering why there has never been an outstanding dramatic treatment of what might appear to be the tragic subject *par excellence*. If any period could have achieved it, it should have been medieval

France, which possessed faith, naiveté, strength of communal emotion, and a sufficiently developed artistic tradition. But the spirit which expressed itself in the Gothic cathedrals never in the drama achieved the same sense of form.

Composed, often collectively or anonymously, for particular towns, most of the Mysteries borrowed from each other. It is sufficient to name the best known. Among the earliest – dating from the fourteenth century – are the Palatinus Passion (so named from the manuscript in the Vatican Library), and the Autun Passion. The Arras Passion, which opens with an allegorical debate before the heavenly throne, was probably written by Eustache Marcadé, who died in 1440. The most famous of the Passions, by Arnoul Greban, was composed and acted at Le Mans towards 1450; a development of it by Jean Michel was performed at Angers in 1486. Arnoul Greban perhaps collaborated with his brother Simon in the *Mystère des Actes des Apôtres*, the longest of all.

By 1500 all the great cycles had been built up and during the next century the Mysteries slowly died out. The humanistic spirit of the Renaissance and the Protestant Reformation were both opposed to the spirit which had conceived them. After 1560, the bitter religious wars were still more unfavourable to such collective displays of piety and merriment. The edict of 1548 by which the Parlement de Paris banned the performance of Mystery plays in the capital was a symptom of the decline, though not, of course, its cause. Occasional provincial performances continued for another fifty years, but their significance was not greater than the contemporary performances found in England until the end of Shakespeare's life. Attempts to write non-religious Mysteries also came to nothing. A *Mystère du siège d'Orléans* was produced in 1439, only ten years after the relief of the town by Joan of Arc. Some eighty years later Pierre Gringore composed a Mystery on Saint Louis, and between the two we find a *Mystère de la destruction de Troie*. But neither national history nor the old *romans d'antiquité* could replace the inspiration of Bible and Church and the possible development of the French Mystery into the national chronicle-play does not occur.

The Miracles were a second type of religious play. Sometimes they merged into the Mysteries, but their distinguishing marks were that they were comparatively short and that their subjects were not biblical. They were connected with the cult of saints or of the Virgin Mary. The earliest examples in French – there had been others in Latin – are the *Jeu de Saint Nicolas* (c. 1200) by Jean Bodel of Arras and the *Miracle de Théophile* (c. 1284) by Rutebeuf. Both authors were professionals who were probably fulfilling commissions from some college or fraternity. The first takes the then topical theme of a crusader who is captured by the Saracens but saved by the miraculous appearance of his patron saint. The second tells of a clerk who has sold his soul to the devil; in this case it is the Virgin who saves him when he repents before her statue. This story anticipates the most important group of Miracle plays, the *Miracles de Notre Dame*. Forty in number, they belong to the middle decades of the fourteenth century and were performed by the Paris Guild of Goldsmiths at their annual gatherings. The plots of most of them are drawn from secular sources such as the *chansons de geste*, the romances, and even the *fabliaux*. Into these stories of human activity, sometimes with realistic contemporary settings, the medieval writers felt it not at all incongruous to introduce the Virgin to bring about the dénouement by her miraculous aid.

Independently of the religious drama there existed an irregular comic theatre whose origins have been traced back by some authorities to the *jongleurs*. It is surmised that these gave monologues with mime, performing in the market-places or the great baronial halls. Sometimes several may have banded together to give what was more than a collective recitation but not yet quite a play. There is no certain evidence of this, only a strong presumption that such was the ancestry of the non-ecclesiastical drama. Other suggested sources are the early medieval Feast of Fools, in which the Church allowed its own ritual to be parodied, and the Mystery plays themselves, from which comic scenes might have split off to form separate entities. If, however, some lay tradition of acting was not already established in the thirteenth century, it would be difficult to account for the plays of Adam de la Halle (c. 1250–87). This *trouvère* from Arras, also known for his song-poems, composed a kind of revue in which he himself, his wife, and various citizens of the town appear in a series of gaily satirical scenes. The occasion is supposed to be the departure of Adam for student life in Paris; the title is *Le Jeu de la Feuillée*. His second play, *Le Jeu de Robin et de Marion*, is a pleasant expansion of the troubadour *pastourelle* theme. Its main characters are a shepherd, his shepherdess, and a debonair knight whose honied words cloak the worst intentions. Fortunately Marion is equal to the situation and after much rural merriment the *jeu* ends in her marriage to Robin. Since the story is told in a combination of dialogue and song, this has been boldly described as the first comic opera. It is worth recalling that the English Robin Hood and Maid Marian are perhaps descended from the French Robin and Marion, though not necessarily from Adam de la Halle's pair. These were stock names for greenwood lovers.

Adam de la Halle had no known successors. The records of comedy in the fourteenth century are virtually blank and it is only towards its end that we hear of the formation of societies who went under the general name of *Sots* (Fools) and were contemporary with the *Confréries de la Passion*. The *Sots* were found all over France. They wore a distinctive green-and-yellow costume and a fur bonnet garnished with ass's ears. Each company had its Prince of Fools and its Mother Fool. Probably they were recruited from the ranks of irreverent youth. Two famous Parisian companies were the *Enfants sans souci* and the *Basochiens*. The latter were made up of lawyers' clerks and other junior members of the legal fraternity (*Basoche*). Anyone who, sitting peacefully in a modern Parisian café towards the end of the examination season, has had his drink snatched suddenly from before him by a marauding student dressed chiefly in feathers and drained to the accompaniment of warwhoops will have witnessed a reminiscence of the medieval *Sots*. The spirit of the student rag entered powerfully into the plays which these performed and which divide into three main kinds, though a clear distinction was not always made in practice. The *sotie* was a short satirical piece directed either against the general follies of mankind or, more riskily, against contemporary personalities, as in Gringore's *Sotie du Prince des Sots* (1512), which satirized the Pope. The characters were usually allegorical. The *moralité* (a speciality of the *Basochiens*) also had allegorical characters, so following the literary fashion of the time. The moral lesson which it generally pointed might be religious, but more often it warned against such ordinary secular vices as avarice, gluttony, or filial disobedience. It inclined to broad clowning more freely than the English Morality and was sometimes indistinguishable from the *farce*.

Unlike the *sotie*, the *farce* was not satirical. It was concerned with simple contemporary characters in knock-about situations. In its social approach and its plots it belongs to the popular tradition of the *fabliaux*, though it lacks their bitter undertones. It flourished especially between 1450 and 1550 (as did the *moralité*) and, unlike the other medieval genres, it had a future which the Renaissance did not block. Although the recipe of the farce as Molière was to write it was renewed from Italy, he often strikes the same note as the anonymous medieval writers. Racine's *Les Plaideurs* sometimes seems to echo the far less sophisticated tones of *La Farce de Maître Pathelin*, which is easily the most successful example of its kind. Written by an unknown author probably in 1464, *Pathelin* sketches in a few short scenes a convincing caricature of legal cunning and commercial stupidity, both of which are routed by the deceptive simplemindedness of the shepherd Thibaut l'Agnelet. From the rapid and economical dialogue, the Judge's exclamation, *Revenons à ces moutons*, has been picked out, altered, and given proverbial force.

Such small touches are all that remains alive of the medieval drama, much of which was evidently not thought at the time to be worth writing down. What does emerge powerfully, taking the most ambitious Mysteries together with the slightest farces, is the image of a society and its mentality of intense interest to the social historian, since this is the fullest transcription of the people's voice. The historian of the drama is also enthralled by the many still obscure points of origin and presentation which the subject raises. What he has before him is often spectacle rather than drama in its narrower modern sense. As poetry, the medieval plays are flat and diffuse; they compare badly with the other genres. On the whole, the example of the Middle Ages discourages the idea that a people's theatre – as this certainly was – can rise to the same heights as a professional theatre which attracts and holds a body of specialists. If the community is an ass when it watches passively, it is still something of a goose when it puts on its own entertainments. It should do so in the pursuit of happiness rather than of art. This began to be realized in the sixteenth century, when new models were adopted which put the medieval conception permanently out of date.

II

FROM THE RENAISSANCE TO
THE REVOLUTION

CHAPTER 5

General Prose: The Outline of Man

In the sixteenth century a new wave of creative energy, originating in Italy, passed through the thought and art of Western Europe. While it is true that the significance of the Renaissance has sometimes been over-stressed and the qualities of the medieval mind at its best correspondingly undervalued, there is no doubt that literature at least needed this new injection of vigour. The old lines of thought were running into an impasse. The forms which expressed them were becoming fossilized. It was necessary for French culture to break out of the elaborate cage which it had begun to construct for itself in the fourteenth century.

In France, as elsewhere, the renewal had two main aspects: the intellectual and philosophical, which developed in the reign of François I (1515–47), and the aesthetic, which became fully apparent towards 1550. This second development, though naturally linked to the first, affected the shape of literature quite as much as its content and left its strongest marks on poetry and drama. It can best be considered in the chapters dealing with those genres. Meanwhile the philosophical aspect, understood in its widest sense as an exploration of the nature of man and of his response to his environment and his own conscience, begins to occupy the great prose-writers in which French literature is particularly rich. For the most part these writers are not specialists in philosophy, theology, or history (as were their nearest counterparts in other countries). Some, as Montaigne, Pascal, La Rochefoucauld, even Rousseau, can be classed as moralists. Others, though equally engaged on painting that portrait of man which, as has been well said, was the main work of the French genius up to and through the age of Louis XIV, attempt no systematic commentary. Such are Brantôme, Mme de Sévigné, Saint-Simon. Others again, particularly in the eighteenth century, advocate a social or political theory, but in so doing they rarely lose sight of the individual example. All rank as high in literature as in the history of ideas; when the ideas they put forward are no longer of interest they can still be read for their vitality as writers. Except that they wrote in prose, they are not identified with any one literary form, though on occasion (as with Voltaire and Diderot) they used the short story when it served their purpose. Through them may be traced the evolution of the French mind over nearly three centuries. The picture, of course, will be incomplete until we have reviewed the drama and the novel. But the main lines at least can be discerned in the great general writers from Rabelais to Rousseau.

The two main factors in the early Renaissance were the revival of classical studies and the religious reformation. The classical revival began with the Italian scholars of the fourteenth century – Petrarch among them – who first studied Latin literature for its own sake and in its own historical context. This movement was reinforced in the fifteenth century by the arrival in Italy of Greek scholars driven from Constantinople after its conquest by the Turks. The Greek learning and manuscripts which before 1453 had been centred on Byzantium now became available to the West. A generation later the movement began to spread northward and was incarnated in such men as the great Dutch scholar Erasmus. Of international reputation, he worked for a time in France and was the contemporary of France's first great Hellenist, Guillaume Budé (1468–1540). Budé persuaded François I to found the free Collège de France in opposition to the traditional teaching of the University of Paris. Other great names in French Renaissance scholarship are the evangelical humanist Lefèvre d'Étaples (*c.* 1450–1536), the Italian-born Julius Caesar Scaliger (1484–1558), whose interpretation of Aristotle had great influence on French literature and whose son was the classical scholar Joseph Justus Scaliger (1540–1609), Étienne Dolet (1519–46), the philologist and printer, Théodore de Bèze (1519–1605), who was the chief disciple of Calvin, and the Estiennes, a great family of printers and linguists whose work spanned the century. Three men are chiefly remembered for their influence as teachers: the Scot George Buchanan (1506–82), who numbered Montaigne and some of the young Pléiade poets among his pupils; the Frenchman Muret (1526–85); and Dorat (1508–88), who figures in the Pléiade as Ronsard's master.

The new learning was important, not for pedantic reasons, but because it threw fresh and apparently more authoritative light on vital problems. The chief of these, as always, was the relationship of contemporary man to his environment. The explanation given by the medieval thinkers, who were almost exclusively theologians, had been perfectly suited to its own time and place. It supposed a hierarchy of powers, spiritual and temporal, among which authority was derived downwards through the pope and his bishops and the king and his vassals. When the papal authority was shaken by schism within the Church itself and the feudal conception of government ceased to correspond to political realities, the time seemed ripe for a new philosophical interpretation. Thanks to the classical scholars, whose researches led them into a world of thought independent of the medieval cosmos, humanism was born. Humanism took man as its yardstick and worked outwards and upwards from that scale instead of starting with a fixed system of dominations, spirits, and angels among which man occupied a very humble place. While humanism was not necessarily anti-Catholic, it naturally tended either to revive pagan values, or else to link up with the Protestant Reformation through its rejection of the idea of universal hierarchy. Original research bred original judgements and with them the awakening of the individual conscience. For it is inevitable that if the spirit of free inquiry is taken far enough and applied to big enough issues, it must end in a clash with established dogma. You begin by trying to make better sense of an obscure sentence in one of the Fathers of the Church and you end after ten years' work with a new interpretation of his whole teaching. Humanism and Protestantism were especially liable to overlap when biblical texts were subjected to the same methods of criticism as were applied to classical authors. The men of the Renaissance, with their universal curiosity, saw no good reason to separate the two. The revival of classical studies and the religious reformation were therefore complementary parts of the same movement, at least in France.

There, the official attitude was at first not unfavourable to reform. François I, the contemporary of Henry VIII of England, was well disposed towards it and would have been a sufficiently vigorous monarch to carry it through. He would have been supported by his sister, Marguerite d'Angoulême, and by several of the highest figures of the realm, ecclesiastics as well as laymen. There was a reformist movement within the French church itself, in spite of the implacable opposition of the Sorbonne (the Faculty of Theology of the University of Paris, in effect the highest ecclesiastical court of France). It was not until 1534, when an over-bold protest by the reformers (the *affaire des placards*) was interpreted as a direct challenge to the King's authority, that the royal policy hardened against the 'evangelicals'. Two years later the leader of the French Reformation, Jean Calvin, published his articles of faith in *L'Institution de la religion chrétienne* (in Latin, 1536; in French, 1541) and fled to Geneva, where he was to rule as a virtual dictator. In the next decade numerous Frenchmen were burnt at the stake, including Étienne Dolet. The persecution of heretics was intensified until the outbreak of civil war between Catholics and Huguenots in 1560. This open struggle continued intermittently until the reconciliation of the two factions in 1598 by Henri IV.

For the writer and controversialist, the century was divided into three roughly equal periods. In the first – the age of Erasmus – the debate was open and the scholar with heretical views might well believe that he was pleading a case with a reasonable chance of peaceful acceptance. In the second – the age of Rabelais – the issues were more clearly defined and attacks on orthodox doctrine were fraught with greater danger, though the offender with influential patrons might still escape. In the third period – the age of Ronsard, d'Aubigné, and Montaigne – the intellectual must either definitely take sides or become circumspect enough to avoid controversial subjects altogether.

While the scholars and theologians provided literature with an indispensable background of ideas, as well as with most of its sources, their own writings do not bulk large as literature. They wrote for their fellow-specialists, employing a pure Ciceronian Latin which they contrasted somewhat contemptuously with the debased yet more 'native' Latin used by the French medieval scholars. When – as with the Protestant pamphleteers of the second half of the century – they aimed to reach a popular audience, their prose was clumsy and undistinguished. The great age of humanism produced only one outstanding prose-writer.

François Rabelais was born towards 1490 near Chinon in Touraine. He became a monk, got into trouble for his interest in humanistic studies, then, leaving his order, qualified as physician. He was appointed town doctor at Lyons, where he probably met his principal patron, Cardinal Jean Du Bellay (the uncle of the poet), whom he accompanied as secretary and personal physician on several missions to Italy. Thanks to Du Bellay and other protectors, he escaped the consequences of his cutting attacks on the Sorbonne and in the last few years of his life even enjoyed the income from two parish livings. He resigned them both before his death in 1553.

If Voltaire, who has already said everything of an epigrammatic order, had not described Rabelais as a 'drunken philosopher', it would be tempting to call him a drunken scholar. He was intoxicated with the general potentialities of learning – not merely with his own learning, considerable though this was. His contemporaries esteemed him for his knowledge of Greek and Hebrew, his scientific publications (on medicine), and his professional competence. He is believed to have been one of the first doctors to practise dissection, no doubt in the desire to correct by experiment the fantastic theories of the medieval anatomists. The appeal to the concrete reality would at least be typical of him. It would, however, be misleading to insist too exclusively on Rabelais's medical knowledge. For his generation all branches of knowledge were related and his idea of learning was encyclopaedic rather than specialized. Without such an outlook he would never have crammed his monstrous book with such a diversity of material.

Gargantua and *Pantagruel* were published in four parts over a period of twenty years (1532–52), while the posthumous Fifth Book (1564) was probably completed by another hand from Rabelais's unfinished manuscript. In outward appearance the whole forms a grotesque adventure-romance probably suggested to Rabelais by a popular chap-book entitled *Les grandes et inestimables chroniques du grand et énorme géant Gargantua*, which appeared at Lyons in August 1532. Here the parents of the giant Gargantua are magically created by the enchanter Merlin in order to assist King Arthur against his enemies. Gargantua's vast size enables him to perform prodigies in battle and, after serving Arthur for 'two hundred years, three months, and four days', he is transported to fairyland by Morgane and Melusine. Just possibly to divert his patients ('Most illustrious drinkers and you, my poxy darlings') and more certainly

himself and his patrons, Rabelais continued this popularization of
the old romance material, writing *Pantagruel* (late 1532), then, two
years later, *Gargantua*. Since Gargantua is Pantagruel's father, these
two books were subsequently switched. In the new order Gargantua
virtually disappears as a character after Book I; the narrative from
Books II to V is concerned with Pantagruel and his chief companion, the mercurial and many-sided Panurge. Though Rabelais
drops all mention of King Arthur, the extraordinary feats, wars, and
journeys of his giants still conserve the romance tradition, though
at the same time they burlesque it by sheer exaggeration. Into this
are mixed, like plums in a pudding, a hundred and one more or less
scabrous anecdotes of the kind found in the *fabliaux* or the *Cent
Nouvelles nouvelles*. The whole is told in a style which never uses
one adjective where forty will serve, which welcomes equally words
of learned, provincial, foreign, technical, and popular origin,
imitates accents and sounds, and in short behaves like a paint-gun
in the hands of a child of genius.

Rabelais's work can be read purely as an example of fantastic
fiction enlivened with the scatological humour which one might
expect from a ribald medical student or a half-emancipated monk.
He occupies a high place as a comic story-teller in a line continued
after him by such writers as his near-contemporary Noël du Fail,
La Fontaine (*Contes en vers*), or Balzac (*Contes drolatiques*). But the
other aspects of *Gargantua* and *Pantagruel* make any such classification too restrictive. Rabelais writes also as a philosopher and a
satirist passionately interested in the theories and institutions of his
age. He attacks the lazy and stupid pedants, the garblers of Latin-
ized French, the over-subtle scholastic intellectuals, the corrupt and
rapacious lawyers. He joins in the chief controversies of the time.
How is the new all-round man to be educated since the medieval
methods are rejected? His answer is in the programme drawn up for
Gargantua by the enlightened teacher Ponocrates. It embraces
equally the physical and mental development of the young giant.
He learns less from books than by 'doing' and by direct observation of the world around him. Nothing depends on theory or constraint, everything on experiment and the joy of discovery. In a
rather wider context, Rabelais imagines the Abbey of Thélème,
built by Brother Jean des Entommeures, as his reward for helping

Gargantua in his war against Picrochole. First, it is to be the exact opposite of the ordinary cloister – it shall be a pleasant and luxurious place, admit women, have no walls, no clocks, and no rules except *Do what you will*. Its positive character is its insistence on freedom, which Rabelais sees as an essential requisite to right living. He does not, however, reach the point of preaching the innate goodness of all human nature once it is liberated. The inhabitants of Thélème are of gentle birth, carefully chosen and nurtured. They resemble rather one of those idealized medieval communities ruled by a code of honour than the ordinary run of Rabelais's own century. Their abbey is in fact a Utopia, illustrating what might be accomplished in the most favourable circumstances by purely human means.

Another question debated by Rabelais is the status of women, which provides the chief thread of the *Tiers Livre* (1546). Panurge is wondering whether he should get married and his consultations with various advisers recall the old dispute begun in the *Roman de la Rose*. It had, however, been freshly raised in Rabelais's time by Platonists and anti-Platonists and Rabelais could not resist parading his anti-feminism. His attitude, less crudely expressed, recurs in Molière a hundred years later: the place of a woman is in the home. Receiving no satisfactory answer to his questions, Panurge sets sail with Pantagruel to consult the Oracle of the Holy Bottle (whose final word will be *Trink*) and their voyage is the subject of the last two books.

Rabelais had been interested by recent voyages of discovery, particularly those of Jacques Cartier to Canada, and his heroes reach India by the North-West Passage after calling ungeographically at a number of fabulous islands. Among these are the Isle of the Papefigues (Protestants), of the Papimanes (Catholics), and of Messire Gaster or Stomach (Epicureans), whom he prefers to both. Ferocious satire is mingled with chaotic fantasy while the Rabelaisian obscenity begins to grow mechanical.

Though Rabelais's work abounds in allusions to contemporary events and personalities, it is not all symbolical. It is also a reflection of personal experiences and the expression of an imagination content simply with imagining. If many of the episodes and characters can be 'explained' historically, others cannot. The five books are therefore an epitome both of an age and of a man whose personal character remains somewhat enigmatic. The most definite philosophy which emerges is an immense zest for living allied to a thirst for discovery whether through literature, science, or direct experience. All are tools to reveal the actual world. With this goes an almost boundless confidence in the ability of man to know and shape his environment, under a beneficent Creator. In religion Rabelais was a deist, rebelling against the institutions of the Catholic Church but also repelled by the rigidity of Calvinist doctrine. Better than any-one else he symbolizes the uncouth vitality of the early Renaissance whose shaggy scholars, ravaging through the formal pastures of the medieval rhetoricians, left havoc behind them but also fertility. The problem after them was how to reduce this chaos to a new order.

Michel de Montaigne (1533–92) already belonged to a more sober generation. Equally a product of humanism, he used his reading and his experience with method and humility. He did not ride life easily, but saw it as a dangerous beast which the prudent man should study to control. Outwardly, he is the perfect example of the lettered country gentleman who plays an able part in local and even national affairs. He travels for health and social reasons, but his true centre is the little castle of Montaigne in Dordogne which his great-grand-father, the Bordeaux wine-merchant Ramon Eyquem, had acquired some fifty years before he was born. By this act the family had bought their way into the landed aristocracy. A father with 'pro-gressive' ideas made him mingle on equal terms with the villagers and at the same time employed a tutor to teach him Latin by the 'direct' method and to develop his mind – as though he were Gar-gantua – 'in all pleasantness and freedom'. After a severer schooling at the Collège de Guyenne at Bordeaux, Montaigne studied law and became a counsellor at the Bordeaux bar. The post was little to his taste, but it accustomed him to the weighing of evidence and brought him the friendship of Étienne de la Boétie, a talented young judge who strengthened his taste for philosophy and whose early death affected him deeply. At thirty-five he inherited his father's estate and could realize a long-cherished project of selling his legal post and retiring to his château to study and meditate. Ten years of this life resulted in the first two books of the *Essais* (1580). He now felt free to travel and visited Germany, Switzerland, and Italy – partly in search of treatment for the painful disease of the stone. On his return he was forced into active public life by his election as mayor of Bordeaux. In a time of pestilence and renewed civil war he carried out his duties with political skill (he was re-elected for a second term) though without gratuitous heroism. He is accused of having deserted his post during an outbreak of plague. In fact he was away at Montaigne, his second term was just expiring, and he decided not to return to Bordeaux for the formal handing-over of his office. One misses the grand gesture, but Montaigne never pretended to have more than the minimum courage necessary to face unavoidable evils. When the plague reached his own district, he fled before it with his household, dependent on the grudging hospitality of neighbouring squires who turned him out 'if one of the company so much as complained of a sore finger'. They returned home after six months to find the estate pillaged by soldiers, but the château still habitable. These experiences enriched the third book of *Essais*, published in 1588. Montaigne spent his last few years quietly, refusing Henri IV's offer of a court appointment, and died, as he had hoped, in his bed.

His life and character are the stuff of his book, but they only became so by a gradual process. He began, flatly enough, by simply annotating his reading. Then, desiring to organize his impressions and no doubt to focus his hopeless memory (he could hardly remember the names of his servants or of the plants in his garden), he took to compiling groups of quotations and anecdotes on a common theme, such as *By divers means one reaches the same end*, *On Warhorses*, *On Smells*. Threading these compilations on the briefest of commentaries, he called them *essais* ('testings-out' or experiments), so inventing the name and the thing. Fortunately he did not stop there. His authors and their subjects became as real to him as living persons. 'That villain Caligula', he writes, with real heat; and, still more revealingly, of Seneca and Plutarch: 'My familiar acquaintance with these personages and the assistance they have been to me in my old age, compels me to defend their honour.' What more natural than that Montaigne should join in the discussions begun by his authors, citing, for example, his own sensations after a riding accident which nearly killed him? At first he is merely one more witness, but there grows in him the desire to paint his own portrait in detail – not, like Rousseau, because he is a unique case, but because, in his phrase which sums up the whole classic approach to literature, 'each man bears the complete stamp of the human condition'. What is true of Montaigne should therefore be true of humanity in general.

Was this only an excuse for the pleasure of exploring his own ego? To an age which can see no one psychological norm, but at most a variety of predominant types, it must appear so. But the subterfuge was unconscious. Montaigne does not cheat by displaying himself in an advantageous light, nor does he abase himself in order to appear more interesting. Painting in breadth rather than in depth, he gives us an honest self-portrait according to his ability. It is one of the most engaging in literature – and the chief cause of his success. He is lastingly readable – apart from a few rather stiff essays at the beginning – for his familiar approach matched by a familiar style. He writes as he would have spoken. The secret of his prose – far less encumbered than Rabelais's – is still in a preference for the concrete and the particular. 'Oh, what a soft and easy pillow is ignorance!' he exclaims. Of the wrong approach to a problem: 'It is like trying to harness a donkey at the tail-end.' He did not – as French prose did not yet – handle abstractions easily.

Yet beneath this naïf charm of language there lies a considerable philosopher. At first, following his master Seneca, Montaigne is predominantly a Stoic. To his most constant question – How should a gentleman live and, above all, face death? – he finds the answer in Epictetus: With the dignity and resolution acquired by the exercise of both reason and will. With these two weapons one can conquer the weaknesses of the natural man and school oneself to face the inevitable 'philosophically'. In middle age, however, Montaigne began to question the power of reason. He had reached the point of reading his authorities critically and noting the contradictions between them; he was also struck by travellers' accounts of the New World which suggested that what was held right and logical in one country was not so in another. What particularly impressed him was the relativity of knowledge and hence the impossibility of reaching any certain truth through the human mind. His new attitude is developed at length in the long *Apologie de Raimond de Sebond* in the second book of the *Essais*. Finally, in the third book, written after his most shattering experiences, he tends to be an Epicurean. He abandons the heroic constraint of the Stoics and considers it best to let nature have her way. These three attitudes of Montaigne were each developed by later writers, but it is important to remember that he himself evolved no philosophic system. He was simply concerned with seeking a practical philosophy, concordant with experience. If he is to be pinned down to anything, it is to his middle phase of empirical doubt. This led him not to indifference but to greater freedom of speculation. Throughout he contrived to remain – as many of his followers did not – a devout Catholic. He held that political and religious institutions were outside the scope of his inquiry.

Montaigne's great man was Plutarch, whom he read in the translation of Jacques Amyot (1513–93), a university lecturer who became a tutor to princes and finally Grand Almoner of France. His racy and vigorous translations of Plutarch's *Lives* (*Vies des Hommes Illustres*, 1559) and *Moralia* (*Œuvres morales*, 1572) had a bracing influence on French prose, both through Montaigne and independently. North, translating Amyot's French with the same colloquial freedom with which Amyot had treated Plutarch's Greek, made the *Lives* a favourite Elizabethan book and the source of Shakespeare's Roman tragedies. Plutarch's enormous success in the sixteenth and seventeenth centuries rested on the never-failing attraction of the biographical approach to history and (thanks to his translators) on his easily understandable picture of the Ancient World. He also gave examples of noble conduct which to some extent provided a new secular morality to take the place of the old code of chivalry. The conception of 'Roman' virtue found in Corneille and his contemporaries (though Corneille himself used Plutarch very little) owed much to this source. Later, Racine read his beloved Amyot aloud to Louis XIV. One of Molière's most philistine characters uses the heavy volume for pressing his neck-linen – a proof at least of the author's safeness. Amyot's translations of Greek romancers (Heliodorus and Longus) also provided lighter material for French novelists and dramatists.

Other notable books of Montaigne's time were written by political theorists or historians. Jean Bodin (1530–96), writing his *Six livres de la République* (1576) partly to refute Machiavelli, set forth the theory of national sovereignty vested in the crown which was to be practised by Richelieu and Louis XIV. As a political philosopher, achieving the broad view at which Commynes had only hinted, he belongs to the same line as Montesquieu and Rousseau. Étienne Pasquier (1529–1615) was a barrister and poet who explored the national past in his *Recherches de la France* and can claim to be the earliest historian of French literature. With him may be mentioned Claude Fauchet (1530–1602), who explored French literature back to the thirteenth century in his *Recueil de l'origine de la langue et poésie française* (1581). But the most living history is contained in the memoirs of Blaise de Monluc (1502–77) and Brantôme (1540–1614).

At the age of seventy Monluc looked back on fifty years of professional soldiering in Italy and in the French wars of religion. The eldest son of an impoverished Gascon nobleman, he had risen to be Marshal of France and Governor of Guyenne. He wrote his *Commentaires* not for 'learned young gentlemen' but for 'the captains, my companions'. He gives a vivid picture of sieges and battles, remembered with a wealth of detail and sometimes interlaced with moral reflections. But he is more than a military historian. From his rugged, clumsy prose there also emerges the self-portrait of a relatively honest soldier, courageous, capable, and ruthless by way of duty, when the interests of the King his master seem to demand it. Pierre de Bourdeille, seigneur de Brantôme, was another Gascon. He also served as a soldier and travelled adventurously. But his element was the Court and the atmosphere of private and political intrigue which he found there. His reputation as a licentiously-minded gossip-monger is based particularly on his *Vies des dames illustres*, but this, like his *Vies des grands capitaines*, is only part of the long *Mémoires* or *Œuvres* which he left to be published after his death. Through personal knowledge, hearsay, and sometimes cool borrowings from literature, he creates through his anecdotes an impressionistic image of sixteenth-century society. One goes to him not for truth but for colour, as no doubt did such writers as Mme de La Fayette, when she wished to describe the Court of Henri II in *La Princesse de Clèves*; or later Mérimée in *La Chronique du règne de Charles IX*. Given more energy and stronger hates, Brantôme might have been the Saint-Simon of his age.

The tumultuous sixteenth century ended with internal peace

under a strong king. The predominant desire of Frenchmen was now for harmony and order, which would presently lead to a new conception of hierarchy under Louis XIV. However, there could be no going back, politically or ideologically, to the medieval system. The philosophic discoveries of humanism had become as much part of the world of the educated man as had the geographical discoveries of the great navigators. The task of incorporating them in a new system of thought was undertaken by men whose intention was to be not revolutionaries, but conciliators. Thus, Guillaume du Vair (1556–1621) was concerned to show that the morality of the Stoics – the virtuous life based on a strict control of the passions – was entirely compatible with Christian teaching. Pierre Charron (1541–1603) systematized the ideas of Montaigne, whose friend and disciple he was. In his chief work, *La Sagesse* (1601), he did not recoil from using Montaigne's scepticism to prove the insecurity both of human knowledge and of traditional moralities, founded on custom. Yet this book full of subversive possibilities, one of whose declared aims was to demonstrate 'the excellence and perfection of man as man', was not meant as a weapon against the Church. It was meant to persuade 'reasonable' men who were not theologians that Christianity could be reconciled with both reason and nature.

Without some appreciation of this attitude it would be difficult to understand the point of view of René Descartes (1596–1650), one of the most influential thinkers of the seventeenth century and a forerunner of eighteenth-century rationalism. Descartes himself was not a rationalist in the sense that he opposed reason to faith or science to revelation – though the ultimate effect of his work was to encourage just those tendencies. But this only became possible when the context altered. Descartes's context was an ordered universe functioning according to laws established by a Creator whose existence he took for granted. This Creator had endowed man with reason, together with his other natural faculties, in order that he should use it in the pursuit of truth. If reason, submitted to the most rigorous discipline and used with all humanly conceivable precautions and cross-checks, should still lead us astray, that would be equivalent to saying that God has cheated us, which is unthinkable.

Descartes's argument satisfied most orthodox minds of his age, though it rested on the ultimately humanistic assumption that man is a microcosm of the universe (i.e. all qualities are to be found in him, and among them the capacity for ascertaining truth). By postulating a Creator and then holding him responsible for the perfection of his work, Descartes could safely display an unwitting intellectual arrogance that would have staggered even Rabelais's generation.

His method of reasoning was set out after long meditation and practical experience of life as a soldier and traveller in *Le Discours de la méthode* (1637). He lays down what seems an obvious procedure similar to the proving of a proposition in geometry. Its simplicity was in fact novel, as can be seen if it is compared to the complicated rules for conducting a demonstration in medieval logic. It has two striking features. It omits all reference to higher authority or doctrine and requires the thinker to use only those factors which he himself can conceive with absolute certainty and clarity. Secondly, it is a purely intellectual process with no appeal to experience. The Cartesian method, typical of one side of the French genius, is to start from the simplest possible postulates (as that a triangle has three sides) and to build up, by impeccable reasoning, to the most complex philosophical or metaphysical conclusions. Where the Slav or the German will seize the Absolute by the hair, this Frenchman patiently catches it in a trap. The results are not the same, since the means condition the end. But we are not concerned here with Descartes's contribution to philosophy proper, or to science, except to note that perhaps his main achievement was to have created analytical geometry. His theory of the physical universe, involving astronomy and optics, was displaced within fifty years by the work of Newton and his contemporaries, founded on better scientific observation. Descartes's importance, in the general history of thought, and hence of literature, was that he set an example of clarity and 'natural' logic in succession to the somewhat chaotic speculations of the humanists. He also gave his century the notion of an orderly environment which could be understood by an effort of the intellect. In writing *Le Discours de la méthode* in French, rather than in the Latin which was still generally used by philosophers, he set up a landmark in French prose remarkable for the unpedantic ease with which it handled its necessarily abstract material. However, his other main works, the *Méditations méta-*

physiques (1641) and the *Principes de la philosophie* (1644), and much of his correspondence, were originally written in Latin. Most of his work was done in Holland, where he settled in 1628. Going to Sweden on the invitation of Queen Christina, he died of pleurisy in his first winter in Stockholm.

Had Descartes wished to dissent he might have become in his own lifetime the philosopher of the minority tendency known as *libertinage*, a position which was filled rather unsatisfactorily by Pierre Gassendi (1592–1655). Gassendi's spoken theories were evidently bolder than his written work (published posthumously in Latin as the *Syntagma philosophiae Epicuri*, 1658). This can be read as yet another attempt at reconciliation, this time between the Epicurean philosophy of reasonable enjoyment and Christian doctrine. But however evasive their spokesmen, the *libertins* were important as the only true rebels against the Church and State in the predominantly conformist society of the seventeenth century. They might be rakes in practice, ruthless nobles whose type-portrait Molière drew in *Don Juan*, or they might be cultured and punctilious gentlemen like Charles de Saint-Evremond (1616–1703), who spent the last forty years of his life in political exile in London and is buried in Westminster Abbey. He expressed his Epicureanism in essays and letters not intended for publication, followed Parisian literary taste closely, and was an acute critic of the drama. He judged the contemporary scene lucidly if not profoundly, foreshadowed Voltaire as a dryly urbane stylist and Montesquieu as a philosopher of history, and in fact formed a bridge between the rationalism of two centuries.

Other *libertins* were simply free-thinking scholars like La Mothe le Vayer (1588–1672), who prolonged the humanism of the Renaissance in a sceptical and 'pagan' direction. Others again – particularly in the first half of the century – were naturally turbulent spirits like the poet Théophile de Viau, or like Cyrano de Bergerac (1619–55), whose character Rostand romanticized for the stage some 250 years after his death. Cyrano's main works are *Les États et Empires de la Lune* and *Les États et Empires du Soleil*, pleasantly lunatic accounts of journeys to the sun and moon. Cyrano would be merely another writer of 'burlesque' if he had not laced his fantasy with satire directed against orthodox religious belief.

Thus the *libertinage* of the seventeenth century was an undercurrent of free thought, used sometimes as a justification for free conduct, connected usually with atheism and linked with one or more of the three great pagan systems: Scepticism (nothing is certain beyond the senses), Epicureanism (follow nature and enjoy the moment of life), and – more rarely – Stoicism (dominate the moment of life). Any of these could be found in the original pre-Christian philosophers, or they could be developed from Montaigne, whose works were finally put on the Index in 1676. But *libertinage* does not come to the surface in any writer of quite the first rank. The cynical La Rochefoucauld and the sensual La Fontaine both fail to declare for it. Molière was perhaps a Gassendist, but only if the opinions of some of his characters are taken as his own. It remained as a potential threat to orthodoxy of which the preachers and theologians seemed constantly aware. It was often allied to social merit and could enter (as with Saint-Evremond) into the composition of the *honnête homme*. For though the century often succeeded in merging its conceptions of the gentleman and of the Christian, the identification of the two ideals was never total.

On the Catholic side there had at first been a desire to win over all people of good will by presenting Christianity in not too forbidding a light. The wars of religion having ended, the French solution was to clinch the counter-reformation by sweet reasonableness rather than by an over-exclusive austerity. This tendency shows in the persuasive writings of St François de Sales (1562–1622), whose *Introduction à la vie dévote* and *Traité de l'amour de Dieu*, with its interesting psychological treatment of love, traced out a 'primrose path to heaven'. The Jesuits, influential as educators and confessors, were equally concerned to attract rather than to repel.

But there remained the stumbling-block of original sin, which meant that man was imperfect in his essence and could never reach unaided the heights of virtue (let alone of knowledge or power) claimed by the humanist philosophers. The theological answer was in the doctrine of grace, according to which the ability to act rightly and to escape damnation is divinely granted to some or all Christians. The immense complications of this doctrine cannot be set out here, but it is at once obvious that it involves the questions of divine justice and predestination. Have we or have we not any control over our destiny? To what extent do we possess free will? For the seventeenth century this was the key question, not confined to theologians, since, once it has entered into a writer's consciousness, it is likely to affect any literary analysis of character and motive. Catholic opinion on it shaded from the broad viewpoint of the Molinist wing of the Jesuits, who taught that grace is a universal gift, always effective provided we are willing to make use of it, to the narrow viewpoint of the Jansenists who held that grace is reserved for a limited number of the elect. The salvation of these, like the damnation of the non-elect, depends on what seems an arbitrary act by the Deity.

The Jansenists took their name from Cornelius Jansen, Bishop of Ypres (d. 1638), in whose book, the *Augustinus*, the doctrine of predestination was expounded in its full severity. They were a strict-living sect who, for their morality as well as their doctrine, have been compared to Calvinists within the Catholic Church. They set up at the Abbey of Port-Royal a remarkable community which included a nunnery, a school, and a group of theologians and scholars. Led by such teachers as Antoine Arnauld and Nicole, they waged a long theological war with the Jesuits which finally ended in the dispersal of Port-Royal. But before this they had influenced both the cultured bourgeoisie and the more serious-minded aristocracy, had educated Racine, and helped to form Pascal.

Blaise Pascal (1623–62) was the highly-strung son of a magistrate from the Auvergne, who moved to Paris after his wife's death to bring up his children in more cultivated surroundings. Pascal's genius first showed itself in mathematics and physics – interests which never left him. He displayed also a strong practical sense in inventing and marketing an early calculating machine and in launching (in 1662) the first Paris omnibuses – the 'five-sou coaches' – which died out after a few months for lack of public support. Ambitious and intellectually arrogant, he frequented aristocratic society for a short time after his father's death, then turned to Port-Royal, which he already knew through his family and where his sister Jacqueline had become a nun. A series of spiritual crises, precipitated no doubt by growing ill-health (he died at thirty-nine of intestinal tuberculosis combined with a blood-clot on the brain which had caused him years of headaches), led him to humble himself religiously, though he never lost his terrible lucidity or his sovereign contempt for those with whom he disagreed. He remained a layman and in fact spent his last days in his house in Paris, away from Port-Royal.

Pascal's first main work, the *Lettres provinciales* (1656–7), was a series of eighteen pamphlets written in defence of the Jansenist doctrine of grace at a time when Antoine Arnauld was being accused of heresy in the Sorbonne. Adapting his tone to the general public, Pascal shows the apparent contradictions of Jesuit theology, then swings into a scathing attack on their over-indulgent moral standards. From the technical material provided him by the experts of Port-Royal, he weaves a still readable indictment of his opponents in an easy, familiar style often lightened by wit. The *Provinciales* establish Pascal as a controversialist of the first order. One can only regret from this point of view that he did not live a century later to measure himself against Voltaire, and Voltaire seems to have had the same regret. The logic and irony of Pascal, together with his gift for finding the concrete illustration to point his argument, make him a master of urbanely malicious prose.

His second and greater work, *Les Pensées*, consists of the disjointed notes which he made in the last few years of his life in view of writing a book in defence of religion. Had the book been finished, it is safe to say that it would have had less interest than those observations, some of one staccato line, others of several pages, which put us in direct (if sometimes baffling) contact with the author's mind. Different editors have worked on them, grouping them according to their interpretations of Pascal's general plan, but there can, of course, never be a definitive edition. The order in which Pascal would have combined his notes, what he would have used and what discarded, cannot be reconstructed with certainty. His guiding intention, however, was to convince the *libertin*, the worldly unbeliever, of the truth of religion and so of its vital necessity in his own life. He therefore dissects human nature in terms to which the non-religious can assent, and in so doing shows himself to be equal to the greatest of the secular moralists. But his sense of the divine leads him beyond neat conclusions, whether cynical or reassuring, to consider the terror and mystery with which human life is surrounded. Nothing could be more opposed to the seeming complacency of some of the French classic writers, as they settle down to map out the psyche, than Pascal's disturbing glimpses of the infinite. Indeed they suggest that the clarity and confidence which appear to characterize the *Grand Siècle* were perhaps a desperate bid at self-preservation by minds only too conscious of the chaotic gulf around them. Because this was so near they felt obliged to establish at least a small area of floodlit sanity. Pascal admitted the gulf because not to have done so would have meant denying his own nature; as Baudelaire said, it moved with him; also because he found a protection in his religious faith. He was, perhaps, a mystic (it must not be forgotten that what he accepted as a minor miracle led to the healing of his own niece at Port-Royal in 1656), but he never disdained the use of reason to support his religion so far as it was capable. Beyond that, 'The heart has its reasons of which Reason knows nothing.' While criticizing Montaigne for intellectual timidity and Descartes for having wished to erect a philosophical system without God (but, needing a First Cause, 'He could not help letting Him give a flick to start the world moving'), Pascal is familiar with their works and uses them freely, as he uses St Augustine, Charron, Du Vair, and the Bible. Because of this breadth of interest, disciplined by a rigorous intellect and filtered through a hypersensitive personality, he is one of the most universal and profound of writers. The fragmentary *Pensées* have a sharpness of impact and a power of suggestion which would both decrease if they were fully worked out. What might have been a great but dated apologia for Christianity has lived on for many readers as a source-book of human psychology.

None of the theologians proper has the interest of Pascal, but the preachers demand a brief consideration. The parallel between the pulpit orator of the sixteenth and seventeenth centuries and the newspaper leader-writer has often been drawn; it might be extended to the radio commentator, particularly in the United States. The preacher's function was to lead opinion, to arouse a passionate interest in his case, sometimes to provide a solemn emotional entertainment. He often borrowed the technique of literature. Pascal's general remarks on 'eloquence' (meaning: the art of persuasion) can be applied equally to the written and spoken word. But the orator addressing a mass-audience must seek larger effects than the writer. His poster-like style is often too crude for the library. Nevertheless oratory has often forced its way into literature and it is impossible to draw a clear dividing-line. The great seventeenth-century preachers achieved some of the poetical qualities which the verse of the time lacked in the rhythm, pomp, and colour of their sermons. (The Hebrew poetry of the Bible was often in the background.) Easily the greatest was Bossuet (1627–1704), best remembered for his funeral orations on members of the Royal Family. But he has a wide range of tone, extending far beyond the sonorous lament. His very exaggerations (as they appear on the written page) light up the more typical qualities of French classical writing: dignity, balance, the slow and cumulative development of a theme, the organization (but not faking) of emotion by reason, the foreseen yet decisive image thrown in to clinch the rhetorical victory. Apart from his sermons, Bossuet engaged in numerous controversies. His *Discours sur l'histoire universelle* (1681) interpreted human history from the Creation to Charlemagne as a manifestation of divine providence. Other preachers were Bourdaloue (1632–1704), less emphatic and more Cartesian than Bossuet and preferred to him by Louis XIV; Fléchier (1632–1710), whose style bears traces of *préciosité*; Mascaron (1634–1703); and Massillon (1663–1742), whom Voltaire praised for his 'civilized moderation'. Fénelon, who was roughly of the same generation, is considered in Chapter 7.

CHAPTER 6

General Prose: The Window on Society

WHEREAS most of the writers just considered had used prose
functionally to clear or diffuse their ideas, others had begun to
develop a more self-conscious attitude towards the style in which
they wrote. The main literary 'reforms' of the seventeenth century no doubt concerned poetry; the main incidence of the 'rules'
was upon the drama. Prose, not being considered by contemporary
critics to fall into any recognized genres, escaped legislation by
escaping classification. But it nevertheless reflected current preoccupations with correct ways of speaking and writing. Malherbe's
insistence on purity of language did not apply only to verse. The
most famous of the early salons, that of Mme de Rambouillet, was
also in its playful way a school of urbane French. The affectations
of the *précieuses* of other salons were part of a search for a fashionable
style in language to match the fashionable style in manners and
clothes. The importance conceded to critics and grammarians such
as Vaugelas (*Remarques sur la langue française*, 1647) reflected a
general desire to purge the language of both plebeian and extravagant terms and establish standards of French which should be
common currency among people of culture. As a stylistic model,
the elegant and easy prose of Jean-Louis Guez de Balzac (1597–
1654) had considerable influence, exercised principally through his
carefully composed letters to fellow-members of Mme de Rambouillet's circle and of the French Academy, to which he belonged
from its foundation. He was also the author of moral and political
essays and of a series of *Dissertations critiques*. The correspondence
of the poet Voiture, another member of the Rambouillet group,
was equally admired, but his wit appears forced in a way that
Balzac's does not.

In no genre did preoccupations with style go so far as to amount
to a true aesthetic movement. The greatest writers, as always,
wrote as they could and made a virtue of their own peculiarities.
But they wrote at least with a greater awareness of style than their

sixteenth-century predecessors and were more ready to linger over
the elaboration of a passage. Hence a tendency, particularly among
the leisured amateurs who formed an important proportion of
the seventeenth-century prose-writers, to seek to impress or
amuse as much by their handling of words as by their actual
material.

This prose is built on three technical resources, more or less
consciously employed: the anecdote, the maxim, and the portrait.
The first was not new: it had abounded in Rabelais, Montaigne,
Brantôme, and Amyot's Plutarch – to go back no further – and it
would continue to be the memoir-writer's mainstay. The maxim
was akin to the 'sentence' – the short philosophical reflection whose
secret the sixteenth century had learnt from Seneca – which Montaigne relished and of which Bacon's more mannered essays are
largely constructed. 'Revenge is a kind of wild justice' can serve to
introduce or to wind up a moral discourse; or it can replace it altogether, in which case it becomes a maxim. 'Hypocrisy is the
homage which vice pays to virtue' (La Rochefoucauld) is a maxim
which is almost an epigram. 'The world may be divided into people
that read, people that write, people that think, and fox-hunters'
(Shenstone) is an epigram that is almost a wisecrack. It would be
pedantic to insist on exact gradations, but it is broadly true that the
seventeenth century wittingly shortened and polished the earlier
'sentence' while still seeking to convey a valid psychological
truth. Its maxims often carry a sting, but they rarely sacrifice
everything, as so often in a writer like Wilde, to mere verbal smartness.

The third resource, the portrait, was cultivated as a social
pastime in the salons of Madeleine de Scudéry and of Mlle de Montpensier ('La Grande Mademoiselle'). Portraits composed by various
habitués of the latter were collected and published by her secretary,
Segrais, in 1659. The vogue continued for another forty years,
attracting the most candid (or the least skilful) pens, such as that of
the second Duchess of Orleans, who wrote of herself:

'My figure is monstrously fat. I am as square as a cube. My skin
is red mottled with yellow. My hair is going entirely grey. My nose
is pitted with smallpox, like my cheeks. I have a big mouth, with
bad teeth. Such is the portrait of my pretty face.'

More or less flattering or satirical, physical or psychological, the portrait is written for its own sake or incorporated in novels, memoirs, or letters. Its close companion is the set description of a place or a natural scene, but this appears more rarely in a predominantly urban literature.

On these three elements the chief 'classical' prose-writers built their work which, however many volumes it may fill, is never long-winded. It has the opposite defect. However Cartesian the clarity of the detail, the long development, the sweep of sustained argument or narrative, is missing. These people sketch, relate, or comment without insistence (that would be fastidious) and pass on. In short their prose, being based on techniques which demand a very brief space to reach perfection, is impressionistic. The only 'monumental' writers of the age of Louis XIV are theologians and the authors of unsuccessful epic poems.

The memoir-writers, letter-writers, and worldly moralists of the time are still intensely interested in man – that is in their fellow-members of a limited but stimulating society who may happen to fill them with envy, hatred, or malice, but never with indifference. Without the tolerance of a Montaigne or the long views of a Pascal, they are nevertheless sufficiently skilled in deducing the general from the particular to make up a formidable school of psychological observers. On this score the habit of the maxim, embodying a generalized conclusion, balances the anecdote, which is restricted to a single instance and occasion.

The greatest of the maxim-writers, Duke François de La Rochefoucauld (1613–80), led a stormy personal and political life, was imprisoned by Richelieu, cold-shouldered by Mazarin, fought on the wrong side in the civil war of the Fronde, was dangerously wounded, exiled, then pardoned and received back at court. At the age of fifty he set up house (platonically, it seems) with the twenty-five-year-old Mme de La Fayette. Earlier, he had belonged to the circle of the marquise de Sablé, who provided a meeting-ground for the high aristocracy with the most prominent Jansenists (including Pascal) before she herself retired to Port-Royal. At her salon the maxim was cultivated as was the portrait elsewhere. Having thus been shown the way, La Rochefoucauld could use the last twenty tranquil but somewhat disillusioned years of his life to meditate on his considerable experience. His *Mémoires*, published in 1662, are a fairminded and unexciting account of his active career. His reputation rests on his *Réflexions ou Sentences et Maximes morales*, first published in 1665, then modified and augmented through several editions of which the last (1678) contained over five hundred maxims.

La Rochefoucauld's basic assumption is the simple one that *amour-propre* (self-regard) is the mainspring of all human activity. There are no disinterested acts or impulses. Friendship, generosity, pity, courage are all motivated by egoism, often unrecognized, for 'Nous sommes si accoutumés à nous déguiser aux autres qu'enfin nous nous déguisons à nous-mêmes.' He therefore unveils our various pretensions one by one, sometimes by a mere quip such as: 'We are all strong enough to bear other people's misfortunes', or 'Old men love to give good advice to console themselves for no longer being able to give bad examples.' Sometimes he has a wider resonance, as in: 'We are never as happy or as unhappy as we imagine,' or 'A fool has not enough stuffing to be good.' He is more than a facile and amusing cynic, but not so much more as to be the founder of a true philosophy of pessimism. The Jansenists, who admired his work, held that he had exposed 'the misery of man without divine grace', i.e. the emptiness of secular morality. If he had, it was with no conscious religious intention. He deflates the pomp of human virtues as the élite of his own social circle conceived them, but no spiritual balloon goes up in their place. The view of him as the ironically wise commentator who could be deceived by nothing on his own level but was unaware of other levels sums him up not unfairly.

Among his circle of friends was Marie de Rabutin-Chantal, marquise de Sévigné (1626–96), who had been left a widow at the age of twenty-five by her husband's death in a duel. She devoted the rest of her life to her two children, to the care of her country estates, and to a vivacious and cultured social life from which she carefully excluded fresh emotional attachments. She regarded as frank misanthropy La Rochefoucauld's dissection of friendship, while no doubt sharing her great friend Mme de La Fayette's opinion of the destructive effects of passion. Her letters, of which about fifteen hundred survive, were written for the most part between

1664 and 1696 to friends and relations such as Cardinal de Retz, the Jansenist statesman Pomponne, her uncle and guardian Christophe de Coulanges, her cousin Bussy-Rabutin, her son Charles, and – by far the greatest number – to her daughter Françoise-Marguerite, who by her marriage in 1669 became the comtesse de Grignan and went to live in Provence. Mme de Sévigné's topics are the day-to-day happenings in Paris and at Versailles – a trial, an execution, the news of a victory, a death, a picnic, a sermon by Bossuet, the première of a play by Racine: all this interlaced with tittle-tattle about persons famous or now unknown. We learn from her that Turenne has been killed, also that some innovator has just had the idea of serving coffee *with milk*. Besides this intimate running commentary on public events, there is Mme de Sévigné herself, her emotions, her reading, her reflections, her journeys, her quiet life at Les Rochers, her estate in Brittany, where she entertains provincial neighbours and revels in the moonlight and the butter. For whom was she writing?

First, no doubt, for her correspondents; but through them for a circle of mutual friends round which her letters would be passed as would a newspaper in later periods. She reports to Grignan what has happened in Paris, though naturally with no attempt at objectivity. Very occasionally this entails a note of self-consciousness, as in the too famous *Lettre de la Prairie*, where one sees her sitting down to compose a set piece. But usually she appears completely spontaneous, writing for publication only among a small, appreciative group. And she also writes for herself. She is in this a true writer and not a dilettante. However expressive her conversation may have been, she still needs to put pen to paper to form and realize her true impressions. 'How do I know what I feel until I have seen what I have written?' might have been said by her. When Mme de Grignan is travelling for the first time from Paris to Provence, she sends letter after letter after her. 'My heart is torn. At last I feel what separation means.' And then: 'Be careful of yourself. The coach might upset. You are coming to the Rhône. That dangerous Rhône. It terrifies me.' 'Stop worrying, mother,' her daughter replies. 'It's only water.' How could the cool and serious Mme de Grignan understand that this solicitude, real though it is in a way, is as much an effect of creative art as are the tears which a novelist may shed over a situation which he had not invented an hour before?

Of all the correspondences of a century which prized and culti-vated the letter, Mme de Sévigné's almost alone can entertain for long stretches a reader unfamiliar with the events and personalities involved. Garrulous but with art, a wonderful observer of externals but reflective when necessary, she stamps history with her own impressionistic outlook. This was also the outlook of the most sympathetic section of a class.

What happened when the world of power and fashion was observed by an outsider (other than Molière) is instanced by the work of Jean de le Bruyère (1645–96). He was a soured little man of middle-class origin living in the garrets of the Prince de Condé, to whose grandson he had been appointed tutor on Bossuet's recom-mendation. The tutorship over, he stayed on as a retainer, unable to tear himself away from the fascinating spectacle of the Court though too often for his dignity confused with the lackeys and lapdogs. He published the first edition of *Les Caractères ou les Mœurs de ce siècle* in 1688 as an appendix to his somewhat free translation of the *Characters* of the Greek philosopher Theophrastus (fourth century B.C.). In the seven subsequent editions published in his lifetime, La Bruyère tripled his own contribution, completely dwarfing Theo-phrastus. His success brought him election to the French Academy but no fortune, since, expecting little of the book, he had signed away the profits as a present to his publisher's daughter. They are said to have amounted to over 200,000 francs.

Materially *Les Caractères* is a collection of portraits, short maxims, and reflections sometimes developed to the length of several paragraphs. The book in its final form is divided into chap-ters which allow La Bruyère to group his literary, social, political, or psychological observations in some sort of order, but there is no logical development and the book is best regarded as a filing-cabinet for his ideas. His intended target was not only the court, but the whole of society, as his sub-title *Les Mœurs de ce siècle* suggests. But he is most at home at Versailles, among the Parisian bourgeoi-sie, and in the slippery world of letters. Outside that, he is a tourist. His sympathy with the people, expressed in a famous passage liken-ing the toiling peasants to animals ('Yet, when they rise to their

feet, they show a human face'), his constrasting of personal worth
with titles and honours, of riches with poverty, make him appear
something of a social reformer. He seems to be preaching equality.
But such passages, exceptional though they are for the date, are
scattered among a mass of different opinions, some supporting the
class-system of his day. There is certainly no revolutionary intention, but at the most the personal dissatisfaction of a talent-conscious
man with the unequal distribution of rewards and, behind that, the
discontentment of the bourgeoisie in a time of financial stringency.
For La Bruyère wrote when the decline of the *Grand Siècle* was
setting in and the country was beginning to feel the pinch of wars
and of a top-heavy economy. He grumbles but has no thought of a
new order. It was in a spirit of acceptance that he wrote: 'A man
born Christian and French finds that he is restricted in satire; the
great subjects are forbidden him.'

For this reason his satire has not the scope of Voltaire's or
Swift's. On balance, he is more humorous than bitter. Rather than
a satirist, it would be more exact to call him a caricaturist. The
ordinary run of salon 'portraits' strike us as chocolate-box or
pavement art beside the little masterpieces of Cubist painting in
which La Bruyère perfected the genre. They are of types or of
people who have grown into types, labelled with the pseudo-Greek
names dear to seventeenth-century comedy – Ménippe, Ménalque,
Cliton, Arténice. The inevitable belief that all had 'keys' (that this
was representational art) earned the book its scandalous success in
spite of La Bruyère's denials. There is at least no need to read them
in that light today. One can make the application where one will,
or leave it on a general level. As for the maxim, it is less condensed
and polished than in La Rochefoucauld, but in La Bruyère's hands
it acquires greater psychological depth and gains in effect by being
distributed among the portraits or embedded in longer passages.
'The man who cannot be an Erasmus should think of becoming a
bishop' is a passable epigram, but is improved by being part of a
longer paragraph on talent *versus* dignities. A whole psychology, or
physiology, of love is behind such remarks as: 'A man can deceive
a woman by a feigned attachment, provided he has not a real attachment elsewhere.'

As a prose-writer La Bruyère is among the greatest of his

century, and indeed in French literature. He can range from the Bossuet-grandiose to the clipped dialogue of stage comedy. He has a store of expressive, savoury, or technical words which he does not hesitate to use, while he himself has written the classic paragraph on the *mot juste*. He is a master of the picturesque or concrete image. He writes of a little town that is 'painted on the slope of a hill', of a 'pressing and irresistible urge to flee to the east when the bore is to the west'. Some of his comparisons are so bold that they skirt surrealism, as when he compares a blue-stocking to a gun – a beautifully ornamented and technically perfect show-piece which 'serves neither for war nor for hunting'. His eccentrics flower beyond humanity. There is Diphile, the bird-fancier, who 'passes his days – those days that slip by and never return – in pouring out seed and cleaning up droppings'. When he goes to bed, 'He meets his birds again in his sleep; he himself is a bird, he is crested, he twitters, he perches; he dreams at night that he is moulting or broody.' To hear such notes of fantasy again in French literature, we have to wait a long time. It is perhaps unexpected – though by no means so unusual as is sometimes supposed – to find them in one of the great classical writers.

After the professional excellence of La Bruyère, the amateur memoirs of the time have a smaller literary appeal. One reads chiefly for their historical or biographical interest the *Mémoires pour servir à l'histoire d'Anne d'Autriche* of Mme de Motteville (1621–89) or the lively *Historiettes* of Tallemant des Réaux (1619–92), who retails sometimes scabrous gossip on cultivated society in the period 1630–61. For the second half of the century, Mme de La Fayette's *Mémoires de la cour de France pour les années 1688 et 1689* and her *Histoire d'Henriette d'Angleterre* are written with sympathy and charm, as are the *Souvenirs* of Mme de Maintenon's niece, Mme de Caylus (1673–1729), who describes life at court as she knew it as a girl. The *Histoire amoureuse des Gaules* (1665) of Mme de Sévigné's irrepressible cousin Bussy-Rabutin (1618–93) deals indiscreetly with the early love-affairs of Louis XIV and others and was described by Pepys as 'a pretty libel against the amours of the Court of France'. The *Mémoires ou Histoire amoureuse de la cour d'Angleterre* of Anthony Hamilton, chevalier de Gramont (*c.* 1646–1720), performs a like service for the Court of Charles II.

The *Journal* of the marquis de Dangeau (1638–1720) dryly records day-to-day happenings at court between 1684 and 1720 and is valuable as a 'document'. Among early journalists, Théophraste Renaudot founded *La Gazette* in 1631, a weekly giving official and Court news, and the first regular newspaper. The first notable review, devoting considerable space to literature and the theatre, was Donneau de Visé's *Mercure Galant*, of which six numbers appeared in 1672–4 and which from 1677 became a regular monthly. It continued as the *Mercure de France* from 1714 to 1825.

However, two authors of personal memoirs tower well above the rest and claim places among the major French writers.

Paul de Gondi, Cardinal de Retz (1614–79), was a political conspirator on the grand scale who perhaps saw himself as a second Richelieu. He followed his early *Conjuration de Fiesque* (written in 1639) with the *Mémoires*, whose chief subject is the civil troubles of the Fronde (1648–53), in which he himself played a prominent part. The complications of that violent period spring to life in his episodic pages. There is no overall view, but a breathless unfolding of situations as they appeared at the time to those taking part. What is it like to be a political freebooter faced with immediate decisions on often inadequate knowledge? De Retz gives the answer. He also sketches a number of 'portraits', for the most part hostile and so well pointed. He demolishes his contemporary La Rochefoucauld, whom he knew and disliked ('He has never been a great fighter, though he was very much the soldier'). His style has vigour and animation, but he tires when read at length.

Some fifty years later an unsuccessful intriguer of another type appeared, with a more formidable pen. Louis de Rouvroy, duc de Saint-Simon (1675–1755), was equipped for literature with frustration, snobbery, malice, and a hawk-like eye. The heir to a great name, he served at first in the army, but finding that promotion came too slowly, resigned at twenty-eight. Promotion always came too slowly for his impatient ambitions. Disliked now by Louis XIV, who prized service above temperament, he remained at court and joined the cabal round the young duc de Bourgogne, heir presumptive to the throne. The aim was to prepare a more liberal monarchy and, though Saint-Simon's reformist leanings were bound up with his personal ambitions and dislikes, he might, in England, have been one of the great Whig nobles. His ideal was a government by enlightened peers, like himself. Bourgogne died before reigning. Saint-Simon might still have obtained an important post through his friendship with the regent, Philippe d'Orléans, but the regent's death in 1723, together with his own fundamental incapacity and pride, robbed him of any chance of power under Louis XV. In retirement he worked over the notes he had begun to keep towards 1694, read Dangeau's *Journal*, which he found 'repulsively flat', and between 1740 and 1750 wrote his splendidly-coloured *Mémoires*, covering the last part of Louis XIV's reign and the Regency (1691–1723).

Often historically inaccurate, Saint-Simon uses the anecdote with a rare zest, not disdaining the tales brought him by grooms and valets. He is often on the stage himself, whispering in a corner or exulting over the discomfiture of an enemy. He can paint the large canvas – the set scene of an ambassadorial reception or a royal deathbed. But his portraits are his great successes. Where La Bruyère's are anonymous and general, these are in the highest degree particular. The names are pinned on, the physical peculiarities are detailed mercilessly. 'Her arms were thicker than a normal thigh, with a slim wrist and a tiny little hand at the end, as pretty as you could wish for. She had exactly the face of a large parrot with two big bulging myopic eyes. She walked too like a parrot.' For the French Court at the end of the Great Century, one goes to Saint-Simon as one goes to water, without caring if the images are refracted. His long, involved sentences – particularly when he is excited – carry on the reader in their ducal sweep, jolted here and there by the occasional pungent word or grammatical solecism. Because of his winding style, together with his interest in etiquette and in the exact degrees of relationship among royalty and *noblesse* – which transcends snobbery and becomes a passion like mathematics – he has been compared to Marcel Proust, who certainly learnt something from him. Both, it might be added, wrote of a society that was dying or about to die and which is more living in their pages than it ever was in reality.

In Saint-Simon (who belongs in spirit to the seventeenth century), in La Bruyère, and in Mme de Sévigné, we have three writers who collectively have perhaps never been surpassed for the colour and life of their prose and for their psychological insight into the human material immediately before them. They are magnificent painters, bold and free within the generous limits of the contemporary manner. The only reservation that might be made from the viewpoint of another age is that their subject was man in captivity.

CHAPTER 7

General Prose: The Social Conscience

THE period of virtually unchallenged absolutism lasted for rather less than forty years. Old nobles who had taken part in the Fronde, like de Retz and La Rochefoucauld, lived nearly long enough to see the régime again in difficulties (this time entirely of its own making) and to hear the whispers of honest doubt echoed by such writers as La Bruyère as France entered the sombre sixteen-nineties. A reform of the monarchy in a less absolute direction was felt to be necessary and the hopes of the reformers centred upon the little duc de Bourgogne, Louis XIV's grandson and probable successor. We have already seen Saint-Simon trying, a few years after, to climb on this particular band-wagon. A more disinterested nobleman, Beauvilliers, who happened to be linked with Mme de Maintenon and with Racine, was entrusted with the general education of the young prince. He appointed as his chief tutor François de Salignac de la Mothe-Fénelon (1651–1715), a brilliant young ecclesiastic who had already fulfilled missions in the La Rochelle district, where he had dealt in a conciliatory spirit with the Huguenots forcibly converted after the revocation of the Edict of Nantes. He had also expressed liberal pedagogic ideas in his *Traité de l'éducation des filles* (1687), which, though it could hardly advocate Rabelais's full-bodied acceptance of nature, did maintain that nature should be coaxed and encouraged, never repressed. Applying his principles to his royal pupil, Fénelon composed for his reading a new episode to the *Odyssey*. Telemachus, son of Ulysses, goes in search of his father, accompanied by his guide Mentor. The literary convention followed was that of the adventure novels of the earlier part of the century, and this in itself was a bold notion for a man in Fénelon's position. The novel was didactic in that it painted the Utopian purity of primitive times – so different from the corrupt artificialities of Versailles. More dangerously, it told the young prince that kings are not above the law, that national states are not above humanity, and that war is a crime. It preached a certain measure of social equality. These ideas, as much as the somewhat insipid charm of the narrative, stood out when *Les Aventures de Télémaque* was published without Fénelon's authority in 1699. By then he had lost his tutorship and had been exiled to his diocese of Cambrai for expounding the Quietist approach to religion in his *Explication des maximes des saints sur la vie intérieure* (1697). Quietism, introduced to the court by the pious Mme Guyon, was a passively mystic method of entering into direct communion with God through unspoken, and indeed unconscious, prayer. It attracted a man of Fénelon's anti-rationalist temperament, but brought him into conflict not only with the Jansenists, whose religion demanded constant vigilance and effort, but with the watchdog of orthodox Catholicism, Bossuet. Fénelon was condemned by Rome, submitted, but was never again a power at court. From Cambrai he wrote various political memoranda, developing the ideas already contained in *Télémaque*, and set out his literary principles in his *Lettre à l'Académie* (1714). He remains as a liberal-minded Catholic inevitably reminiscent of that earlier conciliator, St François de Sales, and foreshadowing Rousseau in his feeling for simplicity and primitive innocence – though that feeling owes something to the fact that he was writing for a child of ten. He was a master of a graceful, rhythmic prose style, elegant and unemphatic like his character.

In the year of Fénelon's death, the marquis de Vauvenargues was born (1715–47). His short life, marred by physical suffering resulting from smallpox and war injuries (he served as an officer in the War of the Austrian Succession), was just long enough for him to raise an emotional plea in the peak period of eighteenth-century rationalism. On this count he forms a bridge between Fénelon and Rousseau. His *Introduction à la connaissance de l'esprit humain, suivie de réflexions et maximes* (1747) places him among the great secular moralists and in no doubt deliberate opposition to La Rochefoucauld. For Vauvenargues, human nature is potentially both good and evil. Instead of despising it, the philosopher should sympathize with it and applaud it when it produces good results, irrespective of the hidden psychological motive. Hardly a Christian, Vauvenargues is a relatively optimistic humanist concerned with seeking the best in different systems and natures and with placing it at the service of the community. Though non-political, he makes the connection between individual and social virtues. That was his novelty. Such a maxim as 'The mercenary sacrifice of the public welfare to private interest is an infallible mark of vice' could hardly have been written in the seventeenth century. If his maxims in general lack the steely snap of La Rochefoucauld's, that is because disgust is a firmer literary foundation than tolerance.

So far we have traced the dawning of new mental attitudes more significant in the light of what followed than conclusive in themselves. We now come upon a more systematic attempt to map out a new road.

Charles-Louis de Secondat, baron de Montesquieu (1689–1755), was born in the château of La Brède near Bordeaux, in Montaigne's country. The background of the two writers was somewhat similar. Like Montaigne, Montesquieu belonged to the legal and country aristocracy. He inherited a magistrate's post in the Bordeaux *parlement* which he gave up after a few years in order to mix with Parisian salon society and to travel abroad. His first considerable work, *Les Lettres persanes* (1721), brought him literary fame of a kind not at once suggestive of the serious social and political philosopher. In part the book is a novel told in letters recounting a harem intrigue of a lightly licentious nature. But two of the 'Persian' characters visit France, so giving Montesquieu the opportunity to describe and satirize Parisian society through their eyes. The device of the foreign or other-planetary visitor, worn threadbare today, was almost Montesquieu's invention and it enabled him to take up La Bruyère's example from a new angle, though his 'portraits' of contemporary French types are less incisive. But his treatment of political and religious questions is much bolder. His Parsee travellers compare the Christian religion with other religions and prove to be anti-clerical rationalists. The Utopian race of Troglodytes whom he describes date all their misfortunes from the day when they elected a king. So this light-seeming book does reflect the serious interests which occupied Montesquieu's thought for most of his life.

Having written a few political essays and two dull erotic novels without political undertones, *Le Temple de Gnide* and *Le Voyage à Paphos* (his authorship of the second has been disputed), Montes-

quieu travelled Europe from Italy to Holland and ended by spend-
ing two decisive years in England (1729–31). Here he found what
he considered the ideal political system: a monarchy in which the
sovereign's powers were curbed by Parliament. He went home to
spread the somewhat theoretical admiration for English institutions
which was to play so large a part in French political thought until
the American Revolution of 1776, and to write his first long serious
work, *Les Considérations sur les causes de la grandeur des Romains
et de leur décadence* (1734). The key-word here is *décadence* and the
whole is an attempt to show that rational causes led to the conversion of the early Roman republic, founded on liberty and austerity,
first into a monarchy, then into a vast, unarticulated empire. It is
less a history of Rome than a theory of history, inspired by the
principle that 'it is not chance that dominates the world, but general
causes, either moral or physical, which are at work in each monarchy
to raise, maintain, or destroy it'. Divine providence, which had
explained history for Bossuet, does not enter into Montesquieu's
analysis.

The ideas, as well as some of the historical material of *Les Considérations sur les Romains*, occur again in his greatest work,
L'Esprit des lois, which he had first conceived as a young law
student and which he published in 1748 after twenty years of in-
tensive work on it. While it is not a well-planned book and it alternates in style between plainly-reasoned argument and a smartness
designed to catch the fashionable public, certain important points
stand out in it. It is a study of political theory written by a jurist,
who begins by examining the constitutions of various states, both
ancient and modern, from the angle of their legislation. When he
finds a wide variation in laws, as, for example, between Imperial
Rome and the England of his own century, he explains the difference in terms of climate, geography, and the occupations and political development of the population. This principle of the relativity
of legality, popularized though not discovered by Montesquieu, is
of course the counterpart to Montaigne's earlier discovery of the
relativity of morality. But while Montaigne was chiefly interested
in the consequences for the individual, Montesquieu's interest is
in the national consequences. From such and such a body of laws,
he claims, can be deduced a nation's character and its history. He

divides governments into three classes: the despotic, which he detests, founded on fear and servility; the monarchic, founded on honour (that is, class and caste obligations); the republican, founded on virtue (the civic-moral qualities of the individual citizens, as noticed by Vauvenargues). Montesquieu's preference goes to monarchy, and to prevent it from slipping into despotism he proposes his theory of the separation of powers. In other words, the laws should not be made by the sovereign (the executive power) but by an independent legislative body; their application should be decided by another independent body, the judiciary. Only this system (which he had observed in England and had studied in the writings of Locke) could give sufficient guarantees of personal liberty.

The principle was to be adopted by the Constitution-makers of the Revolution, but by then the political situation had so deteriorated that it was not applicable in the form Montesquieu had desired. Still Utopian in 1748, by 1791 his theories were not radical enough. For this reason the real political influence of his writings is highly debatable. It is at least certain that the situation he envisaged was not revolution, but a modified reform of the monarchy in which traditional institutions such as the Estates should be preserved or revived. While politically he was not a democrat, he was, however, acceptable to the most liberal democrats for his warmly human insistence on tolerance, his concern for individual rights, and his condemnation of slavery, judicial torture, and capital punishment.

In one important respect Montesquieu went fully with his generation and with its successors. In a poetic 'Invocation to the Muses' intended for *L'Esprit des lois* he writes of reason as 'the most noble, the most perfect, the most exquisite of our senses'. This curious phrase, which neither Pascal nor Fénelon nor Vauvenargues could possibly have used, reflects the revival of reason as Descartes and the seventeenth-century *libertins* had conceived it – as an unrivalled instrument of perception – preparatory to its idealization by later rationalists as the one true source of light. Down this channel there flowed into French thought a spirit of free inquiry not totally different from the humanism of a Montaigne, but equipped, thanks to Descartes and Locke, with deadlier methods, more narrowly and effectively directed against more clearly-defined social abuses and strengthened by an embryonic scientific materialism. On the upper reaches of this stream can be placed two men: Pierre Bayle (1647–1706), a Protestant rationalist who had attacked from Rotterdam the supernatural basis of religion in his *Pensées sur la Comète* (1682) and his *Dictionnaire historique et critique* (1697); and Fontenelle (1657–1757), a nephew of Pierre Corneille, who achieved success as a scientific popularizer, became permanent secretary of the *Académie des Sciences*, and insinuated his religious scepticism in such works as the *Entretiens sur la pluralité des mondes* and the *Histoire des oracles*, both written as early as the sixteen-eighties. From such critical and materialistic writers one line leads to the 'philosophic' movement and to the Encyclopaedists who dominate French thought after 1750. The other, a more abstract rationalism less dependent on the material 'fact', is typified by Voltaire.

Voltaire was the name taken by François-Marie Arouet (1694–1778), who made his first appearance in Parisian society during the dissolute period of the Regency and was in contact as a young man with the Epicureanism of the new *libertins*. The son of a notary, he had a flair for business which was to keep him wealthy and independent throughout his life. He shone socially by his malicious wit; at first he seemed destined to be known as a poet and writer of highly successful plays. The plays, on which the least durable part of his reputation rests, have small social significance, in spite of their 'philosophic' pretensions, and belong to the history of the drama (see Chapter 9). His verse, though it includes philosophical poems, has no ideological features that do not also appear in his prose. The best of this prolific and varied writer is in his prose works.

A turning-point in his life came when, at the age of thirty, he dared to quarrel with a member of one of the great noble families, the chevalier de Rohan. As a result Voltaire, whose social successes had led him to imagine that the aristocracy accepted him on an equal footing, was beaten up by the chevalier's lackeys, rudely refused the honour of a duel, and imprisoned in the Bastille without trial. He was released on condition that he left France for a time. His two years' stay in England (1726–8) gave him, in contrast, an even rosier view than he might have taken of English political and religious tolerance, and he came back with as great an enthusiasm for liberal institutions as Montesquieu was to conceive a year or two later. The most direct result of his visit was his *Lettres philosophiques*, or *Lettres sur les Anglais* (1734), but more generally also his thought became concentrated on the attack on privilege, whence it widened into an attack on injustice of any kind, behind which (since he was temperamentally incapable of accusing the whole aristocratic order) he saw increasingly the obscurantist hand of the Church.

The *Lettres sur les Anglais* attacked French despotism chiefly by inference, but having unwisely included in them a violently anti-religious section, the *Remarques sur Pascal*, Voltaire saw his work condemned by the *parlement* and was advised to leave Paris. He went to live at Cirey in Lorraine as the guest and lover of the marquise du Châtelet. Encouraged by this highly gifted woman, he set himself to study science and wrote a good popularization of Newton's theories, but his final verdict was: 'I liked science so long as it did not threaten to overshadow literature. But now that it is dominating all the arts, I can only regard it as an ill-bred tyrant.' He continued to produce plays and wrote most of his *Siècle de Louis XIV* (finished and published in 1751) which together with his earlier *Histoire de Charles XII* (1731), was to make his reputation as an historian. Both works dealt with almost contemporary periods – the earlier with the struggle between the great Swedish monarch who died in 1718 and Peter the Great of Russia, the later with the impressive reign of which Voltaire's generation were the products or the heirs. Voltaire documented himself by wide reading and personal conversations. 'Ten lines of a chapter sometimes cost me a fortnight's reseach', he says somewhere. All things considered, he is remarkably objective. He conceives history as not only political and military and includes surveys of commerce, civil institutions, and the arts. He is, however, a better narrator than analyst, has no comprehensive theories, and pins events to individual men and often fortuitous causes. Towards 1740 he began writing an *Abrégé de l'histoire universelle*, which was ostensibly to continue Bossuet's *Discours sur l'histoire universelle*, prolonging the record from Charlemagne to Louis XIII. This became *L'Essai sur les mœurs* (1759, augmented 1769) and is a polemical and not very scientific survey of 'world' history showing the slow progress of the peoples through superstition towards rational enlightenment. But the plan, which takes in the Asian and American nations as well as Europe, is remarkably advanced for the date.

After ten fruitful years at Cirey Voltaire, by now perfumed with success, returned to Paris to be accepted by the court and protected by Mme de Pompadour. Tiring in time of this life and much shaken by the death of Mme du Châtelet, he accepted in 1750 a long-standing invitation from Frederick the Great of Prussia to go to Berlin. Received at first as a fellow-philosopher and an ambassador of French culture, Voltaire – whose own quarrelsome nature was also at fault – soon came to feel that Frederick was treating him as his tame poet. He left Prussia in 1753 and from that time settled on the Swiss-French border, where he could dodge persecution by both the French and Genevan authorities. Of several properties which he rented or owned, the chief was Ferney. Here he lived as a local magnate, running profitable local industries in a philanthropic spirit, championing the victims of religious fanaticism like the Calas and Sirven families, and multiplying his polemical writings with increasing brio. Besides the thousands of letters and scores of pamphlets which he poured out – the latter signed with fantastic pseudonyms – longer works such as the *Traité sur la tolérance* (1763) and the *Dictionnaire philosophique* (1764) expounded his ideas in more developed form. Above all, his philosophic tales earned an immediate popularity which they have never lost. In 1747, he had written the first of them, *Zadig*, a pseudo-oriental story which may owe something to Montesquieu's *Lettres persanes*. Others carry suggestions of *Gulliver's Travels*, but Voltaire's satire has not the savagery of Swift's. He is the reasonable man, smiling dryly enough at follies in which he is not too closely involved. *Micromégas*, written in Berlin (1752), shows a giant visitor from Saturn examining the puny wars and philosophies of the earth. *Candide* (1759), a product of the Ferney period, satirizes an exaggeration of Leibniz's philosophy of optimism by spinning an uproarious tale of disasters, known wherever French is read. *L'Ingénu* (1767) shows what happens when a Noble Savage is actually introduced into polite society. These and three or four other stories represent at its best that light, dry prose of Voltaire's which is 'classical' in a different way from the prose of Bossuet or La Bruyère. Reason is no longer a controlling but an initiatory factor. Clear, simple concepts expressed in clear short sentences suggest what seems to be the stylistic model for the academic rationalist. But it is a dangerously misleading model. This style, wonderfully strained of colour and of all but the subtlest flavour, becomes intolerably flat without the point of malice which only a Voltaire, or possibly an Anatole France, can mix into it. It is not the international precision-language for untechnical philosophic discussion that it appears to be. It is the language of the controversialist, sliding aces on to the table with no change of expression, or occasionally distracting attention with a dry joke or an urbanely blue anecdote. Without the polemical intention, Voltaire's style would be arid and a poor vehicle for communicating ideas.

As a 'philosopher', he made social thinking popular and indeed fashionable – a necessary condition to its application to the social system. His ideas may appear fragmentary and destructive, but the most urgent task as he saw it was to break down a complacent acceptance of abuses which had become petrified in the structure of institutions like the Church. There could be no millennium until that had been done. He misjudged both the forces against him and the strength of his own weapons. Assuming that prejudice was a vested interest from which the majority of mankind did not profit, and that most men need only to be shown the light of reason in order to follow it, he gravely miscalculated human nature. This was a field in which the eighteenth century in general was inferior to the seventeenth but independently of the age the character of Voltaire must also be taken into account. His personal psychology has not been adequately studied and perhaps there is not the material to do so, but he clearly suffered from an emotional frigidity which prevented him, like Bernard Shaw, from ever entering into intimate contact with another human being. Mme du Châtelet may have been the exception, but this relationship, which in any case ended unhappily, was predominantly an intellectual one. Denied both personal knowledge and emotional satisfaction, Voltaire turned to humanity at large. To his concern for it and certain unhappy specimens taken from it (but always specimens) can be attached his positive qualities: his passion for justice, his charity, his spasmodic courage in facing influential enemies. This humanitarian rationalist was not a pure materialist. He hated the mystery of religion, which he thought must lead to fanaticism, but he believed, like Rabelais, in a Creator, or at least in a principle of goodness above all religions and all worlds. In this sense he was not an atheist, but a deist.

At the age of eighty-three, a physical skeleton powered with a still vigorous brain, he left Ferney to see the Parisian production of his latest tragedy, *Irène*. The delirious ovation which he received was a homage both to the man and to his ideas. But the strain was too great. A few weeks later he died, fittingly, in the capital.

The open triumph of Voltaire, eleven years before the outbreak of the Revolution, was a triumph also for the whole philosophic movement. For the eighteenth century a *philosophe* was almost any progressive-minded intellectual and the movement embraced men with interests in science, mathematics, sociology, and economics. Anything which could throw new light on man as a social being or point to a theoretical solution of the problems of the age could be comprehended in it. It brought together – as sixteenth-century humanism had not quite succeeded in doing – cultured society with the man of letters and the specialist. It forced the writer to take notice of social and scientific questions and to shape his knowledge and his output accordingly. It encouraged the specialist to use language intelligible to the cultivated but often frivolous layman (the descendant of the *libertin*), to eschew jargon and dullness. In fact, the writer and the specialist often merge and take on the appearance of a superior kind of journalist. This is evident in the most important grouping of 'philosophic' thought, the *Encyclopédie*.

In 1747 the publisher Le Breton commissioned Diderot to bring out a French adaptation of Ephraim Chambers' *Cyclopaedia or Universal Dictionary of the Arts and Sciences*, published in London nineteen years before. He produced in the event an entirely different work, whose conception owed something to Bayle's *Dictionnaire historique*, wrote many articles himself, and persuaded most of the distinguished men of the age to contribute. Some articles contained deliberate propaganda, but the vast majority were factual. But then, as in most ages, merely to state the latest position in science or speculative philosophy in non-technical terms could be a subversive act. After the appearance of the first two volumes (1751), the *Encyclopédie* was temporarily banned, though never effectively suppressed. Against great difficulties and working more or less clandestinely, Diderot had succeeded by 1765 in producing the seventeen volumes which compose the main body of the work. Supplementary volumes followed, mostly of plates, whose publication continued through the seventeen-seventies.

The name of Encyclopaedists is extended as much to sympathizers as to substantial contributors. Jean d'Alembert (1717–83), Diderot's assistant editor until 1759, was a mathematician and rationalist thinker in the *libertin* tradition. He wrote the *discours préliminaire* of the *Encyclopédie*, expounding its aims and methods, but has left nothing substantial. The Abbé de Condillac (1714–80) had considerable influence as the author of the psychological theory of sensualism (which he developed from Locke), according to which the human personality is formed by physical sensations after birth, not by innate qualities. This theory was applied to sociology by Helvétius (1715–71), who saw the pleasure and profit of the individual as the basis of society. The condemnation of his *De l'esprit* (1758) involved the *Encyclopédie* in new censorship difficulties. The German-born Baron d'Holbach (1723–89) presented a similar philosophy in books in which Diderot collaborated (*Le Système de la nature*, 1770). These writers represent a quasi-scientific movement of thought in which the pendulum has swung so far away from the spiritual as to give almost a parody of materialism. But the reaction was inevitable and not unproductive in the realm of psychology. With them may be linked a younger man, Condorcet (1743–94), who as an economist belonged to the physiocrat school of Quesnay ('all wealth derives from the land') and who was also one of the first *Idéologues*, a group of mechanistic psychologists active under the Revolution and Napoleon. There remains the man without whom there would not have been an *Encyclopédie*.

Denis Diderot (1713–84) was an eclectic writer whose character and career remind the English reader in some measure of his contemporary, Samuel Johnson, though his interests were wider. Of provincial middle-class stock, he left home against his father's wishes to live wretchedly in Paris as a hack-writer. His marriage to a linen-draper's assistant, Antoinette Champion, further annoyed his family and improved his prospects in no other way. The crushing labour of editing the *Encyclopédie* – which did not interrupt his flow of other writings – brought small financial reward but gave him connections with all literary Paris and an entrée to influential salons. His contributions to the *Correspondance littéraire*, a cultural news-letter for foreign sovereigns edited by Baron Grimm, carried his name to the courts of Europe. At fifty, his worst difficulties were over. Catherine of Russia, by way of tactful subsidy, bought up his library for 15,000 francs but left him the use of it for life, adding 50,000 more francs as fifty years advance of salary for 'her' librarian. In 1773, the grateful Diderot travelled to Russia and spent six months at St Petersburg. He enjoyed himself better than Voltaire in Berlin. The story of the uninhibited philosopher slapping Great Catherine on the thigh in the excitement of their discussions is typical as well as authentic. Her solution was to have a table placed between them, behind which 'I was under cover from his gesticulations.'

This perennially excited eccentric was something more than a great journalist, but perhaps less than the profoundly advanced thinker he is sometimes claimed to be. If he hit before the letter on dialectical materialism and the theories of transformism and of evolution, he did not develop them systematically but merely sparked them out in his ceaseless and unprejudiced exploration of ideas. He was interested, less amateurishly than Voltaire, in the science of his time, but was more ready to leap to bold conclusions than a specialized scientist would be. His philosophical writings, which are extended essays, or else dialogues, show first the rationalistic influence of Shaftesbury and Locke (*Pensées philosophiques*, 1746), then that of Francis Bacon, from whom Diderot largely took his conception of experimental philosophy as opposed to philosophy based on reasoning. An eighteenth-century Rabelais might have written, as he did: 'Only a man who has practised medicine for a long time is entitled to write on metaphysics.' His enthusiasm for Condillac's theory of sensualism inspired the *Lettre sur les aveugles* (1749), which earned him a term of imprisonment, and the *Lettre sur les sourds et muets* (1751), in both of which he argues that thought is a function of matter and morality is dependent on our physical circumstances. His most original speculations are to be found in *Le Rêve de d'Alembert* and *Le Supplément au voyage de Bougainville*, both written in 1769 but published posthumously. The second contains a picture of the 'natural' happiness and morality of the Tahitian islanders – Diderot's version of the Noble Savage.

Diderot also expressed his ideas in tales. *La Religieuse* (written 1760), condemns the enforced celibacy of the convent. *Jacques le fataliste* (written 1773) pursues the theory of sensualism: man is predestined by his physical environment. The best known, *Le Neveu de Rameau* (written 1762–73), is a dialogue containing personal and social satire between *Myself* and the old Bohemian music-teacher of the title. These have been explained as the two voices of Diderot, the moralist and the cynic. For Karl Marx they represented the *honest consciousness*, thinking in terms of static values, and the disintegrated consciousness, aware of flux and confusion and so capable of connecting widely separate ideas. In their apparent formlessness these philosophic tales are quite different from Voltaire's chiselled products, but their power of suggestion is correspondingly greater.

It is as a theorist of the drama that Diderot is best remembered. His theory of the *drame bourgeois*, advocating a new type of serious play in prose with contemporary characters to replace the now languishing classical tragedy in verse, became the accepted formula of domestic drama in the nineteenth century. It is considered more fully in Chapter 9 (pp. 140–41). One of Diderot's recommendations was for static tableaux and scenes of mute pathos, which seems to stem directly from his admiration for painters like Greuze, whose work he describes in his *Salons* written for Grimm's *Correspondance littéraire*. Before a picture pointing a moving moral, Diderot's heart leaps up, the tears flow, and the eighteenth-century paradox is complete.

This materialist, offering scientific explanations of right and wrong, nevertheless responds emotionally to what he calls 'the morality of the heart'. He feels and obeys a natural predisposition to 'virtue' – the same civic-cum-personal morality in which Vauvenargues believed. Virtue leads to *bienfaisance*, a word only translatable in this context as *active* (one might almost say *utilitarian*) *goodness*. In thus combining the amoral conclusions of experimental science with an emotional humanitarianism, Diderot resembled many of his contemporaries. As he felt, he wrote – rapidly, under the stress of emotion, without bothering to have some of his works published once they were finished. Fanatically industrious, then indifferent to the results, he has defined his own influence in his description of Rameau's nephew: 'If one such person appears in a gathering, he acts like a grain of yeast that starts a fermentation and restores to everyone part of his natural individuality.'

Diderot, according to one version, suggested to Jean-Jacques Rousseau his first serious work, the *Discours sur les sciences et les arts*, which was awarded a prize by the Académie de Dijon and started him on his career as a social and political philosopher. (Rousseau maintained later that the idea was his own.) Until then Rousseau (1712–78) had been known only as a hanger-on of cultured society and as a composer of music. A Genevan, whose mother died at his birth, he had been brought up by an emotionally romantic father who was expelled from the city when his son was ten, leaving the remainder of his education to others. At sixteen he demanded shelter from the Catholic priest of a village outside Geneva, who turned him over to Mme de Warens, a pious woman of imprecise morality interested in potential converts from Calvinism. In the region where St François de Sales had once worked on a very different scale at the same task, she radiated a lax religion of the heart in which to feel good was to be good and which was just the development of Fénelon's well-meant Quietism that Bossuet had feared. For twelve years, amid many wanderings and short-lived jobs, the rootless youth was intermittently dependent on his *maman*, returning once on foot from Paris without a penny in his pocket. During two unforgettable summers she gave him the use of the little country house of Les Charmettes, near Chambéry, where he worked avidly to educate himself in philosophy and literature. Then, his ambition awakening, and seeing his future as a dramatist or composer, he moved to Paris. He became secretary to various personalities, began his lifelong association with Thérèse Levasseur, an inn-servant who bore him five children, and walked out one July day to Vincennes to visit Diderot in prison.

The *Discours sur les sciences et les arts* (a reply in the negative to the competition question: 'Has progress in the sciences and arts contributed to an improvement of morals?') posed his theory of natural goodness (1750). The more important *Discours sur l'inégalité* (1754) developed it, invoking the virtue and liberty of primitive times before the formation of societies. In 1758, the *Lettre à d'Alembert sur les spectacles* condemned on moral grounds another creation of advanced societies, the theatre. Until about this time Rousseau had been considered as one of the Encyclopaedist group, and had used the same methods of rational demonstration, though more fervently. But he now broke violently with Diderot, Grimm, and d'Holbach, the quarrel being complicated by the emotional undertones of his stay at the *Ermitage*, a country house in the Forest of Montmorency, near Paris, lent to him by a new patron, Mme d'Épinay. Here he fell hopelessly in love with his hostess's friend, Mme d'Houdetot. The situation is transposed and romanticized in *La Nouvelle Héloïse* (1761), a novel so successful that it went through seventy editions in the next forty years. He completed it while living in another house in the neighbourhood, offered him by the Maréchal de Luxembourg after his break with Mme d'Épinay. This period (1758–62) was the most productive in his life. Besides the *Lettre à d'Alembert* and the *Nouvelle Héloïse*, he wrote or finished *Le Contrat Social* (1761), his treatise on political theory which became one of the scriptures of democracy,* and *Émile* (1762), his irresistibly attractive book on 'progressive' education. Here nature is the great educator and the problem is at last faced of how to preserve or foster in a modern individual the qualities generally lost when mankind emerged from its primitive simplicity. To say that it is solved would be an exaggeration. *Émile* contained *La Profession de foi du vicaire savoyard*, a lyrical section exalting natural religion, which Rousseau – a mystic in this – made a matter of

---

* Rousseau postulates the *social contract* as an unformulated agreement by which individuals have pooled their individual liberties in order to form an association (the State) giving them protection against enemies outside and criminals within. The sovereign is the people, which makes laws and decides policy – as far as possible by a general vote. The executive (the 'government' or the 'prince') can never initiate policy or legislation; it can only carry out the general will. If the contract is broken – by a foreign conqueror or through seizure of power by a tyrant – the 'natural' basis of the State collapses and each citizen is entitled to recover his individual freedom of action.

'inner certainty'. One of his intentions was to refute the atheists of d'Holbach's clan, but he went on to deny the necessity of revealed religion and of Christian dogma. Where their work escaped, his was condemned and his arrest was ordered by the Parlement de Paris. From that date, his miseries began.

In flight from Paris, he was soon repulsed by Geneva and after four years' wanderings accepted the invitation of the philosopher David Hume to take refuge in England (1766-7). But he fancied Hume was in league with his enemies and returned to France, a half-crazed victim of persecution-mania. In 1770, the protection of the Prince de Conti allowed the pariah (as he felt himself to be) to settle in quiet lodgings in Paris. In May 1778, another patron offered him a country cottage at Ermenonville, near Senlis. He died there two months later, no doubt of a stroke.

His last years saw the composition of his openly autobiographical works, inspired by the wish to justify himself against his enemies. All were published posthumously. *Les Confessions*, the most important, was composed between 1764 and 1770. *Les Dialogues* or *Rousseau juge de Jean-Jacques* (written 1775-6) was a frenzied appeal to public opinion, to make which he divided himself into two personalities, Rousseau the man and Jean-Jacques the writer. *Les Rêveries d'un promeneur solitaire* forms a calmer epilogue, left unfinished at his death.

Besides his significance as a writer, Rousseau has become a kind of prophet. It is not difficult to see why. Of all the eighteenth-century thinkers who expressed similar ideas in various forms and places, none proclaimed with such intimately felt conviction the superiority of the natural over the civilized man. In his origins man was free, happy, and virtuous: society has robbed him of his birth-right. Such is the basic theme, worked out in different contexts, of the *Discours sur l'inégalité*, *Émile*, and the *Confessions*. Rousseau's working-out is often faulty. We know that if primitive men ever did live alone, and not in packs ruled by violence and superstition, their lives must have been nasty and brutish. Some of the subter-fuges to which Émile's tutor resorts to educate him 'naturally' are as artificial as they are transparent. Nevertheless, Rousseau did put his finger on a supremely important point – the only point, in a general sense, that is ever at issue in any debate on human nature and destiny. If Rousseau was right, nearly all French thinking since the Stoical Montaigne had been misdirected. More than that, any philosophy which demands discipline and effort because it assumes that the personality has to be moulded for virtue – or even moulded for existence – becomes pernicious. It can only damage the perfect being we once were.

This leads to the question: When were we perfect? For the Christian, in Eden; for the classical-minded, in Arcady; for Freud, in the uterus; for poets from Traherne to at least Rimbaud, in childhood. As mankind is driven by improved knowledge from one illusory paradise after another, and not only from Rousseau's pastoral Elysium, the nostalgia for some such refuge still persists. Even Pascal recognized 'the desire for happiness, which no man can fail to have'. Since there can hardly be a desire without an object – and, though less certainly, a memory – of satisfaction, this has been generally taken as proof that it exists somewhere. Rousseau's immense achievement was to have defined that object in terms which his age could accept. In face of such a violent release of hitherto repressed nostalgia it hardly matters that his placing of paradise was historically wrong, his definition of nature questionable, or that psychologically the whole conception can be related to certain happy phases in his own life and to his social ineptness.

His second achievement, smaller but still vast, was to have capped all the tentative and diffuse rusticity of his century with a genuine feeling for the country and country life. After Rousseau, 'pastoral' is dead in literature for some time and the untamed landscapes of the Romantics are in sight. Thirdly, the *moi* of Rousseau, detectable by the biographer in *La Nouvelle Héloïse* and by the psychologist in *Émile* (the child brought up as he himself would have wished to be), emerges openly in *Les Confessions*. His declared intention of recounting his own life without concealment or attenuation (because 'if I am not better, at least I am *different*') breaks down in some passages of doubtful sincerity, but on the whole what a devastatingly intimate portrait it is. Either through conventional modesty or because they were incapable of reaching down consciously to the same levels of self, no one had done this before. Too many writers were to attempt it later. Another feature of *Les Confessions* is the curious lack of class-consciousness. The tramp, the lackey, is no longer the character from a slightly different world found in comedy and the picaresque novel: it is Rousseau. Not that he was unaware of snobbery in real life, but in his book he puts on unashamedly any uniform that circumstances give him, confident that the *moi*, the real self, sanctifies the costume.

Rousseau's often lyrical and sometimes rhetorical style – a development beyond Fénelon, an anticipation of Chateaubriand, an inspiration for several Romantic poets – makes unfamiliar reading today, particularly in his long descriptions of nature. But its historical influence is undeniable. In *Émile* and *Les Confessions* at least the interest of the subject carries the reader on and makes these two of the lasting books in French literature.

CHAPTER 8

The Novel and Short Story

ONE looks to the novel less for its significance in the history of ideas than for its connections with social history, of which it is often a transposition or a more or less deliberate commentary. It may show us the physical manner in which people lived at a particular date, but it is also likely to deal with the personal relationships of people living together in a social group and regulated in their conduct by the prevailing conventions. These conventions may derive from religion or philosophy as the mass-produced fashion derives from the exclusive model of the *grand couturier*, but to say that is not to belittle them. They are what has become of the ideal after it has been popularized, in which process it takes on what often appears to be new life of its own. The impact of an ideal conceived by an individual mind, then transposed and diffused by society, back on to the lives of individuals dependent on society, gives the novelist his most fascinating subjects – and in fact is the material of most novels.

In this sense, the French novel in the seventeenth century was a *défilé* of idealized conduct, punctuated by one or two instances of more searching analysis – as in Mme de La Fayette – and accompanied by a ground rumble of realists or parodists who were powerless against the tide of fashion. In the eighteenth century the realists came more nearly into their own, but then again they are swamped by a new wave of middle-class moralizing from which only the libertine writers escape by affecting to swim with it. The sixteenth century hardly developed a novel of its own, but it gave standing and popularity to the *nouvelle* (the short and long-short story), a genre in which French writers have since excelled. (One thinks particularly of Voltaire's stories and of Mérimée and Maupassant in the nineteenth century.)

The historical source was the Italian *novella* as written by Boccaccio and his successors. His work, as we have seen, had already inspired the *Cent Nouvelles nouvelles* in the fifteenth century. In

1532 his longer story, *Fiammetta*, was translated, and thirteen years later a new translation of the *Decameron* was made by one of the secretaries of Marguerite d'Angoulême (1492–1549). The sister of François I of France and herself Queen of Navarre, Marguerite was one of the great cultured princesses of the Renaissance. She was a patron of letters, favourable to heretics and reformers (Rabelais's *Third Book* is dedicated to her ghost), who wrote metaphysical poetry strongly influenced by the new Platonism of the time (*Le Miroir de l'âme pécheresse*, 1531, and *Les Marguerites de la Marguerite des Princesses*, 1547). She also wrote plays, but her most lasting work is the *Heptaméron* (1559), an unfinished collection of seventy-two stories told on seven days, as the *Decameron* is a hundred stories told on ten days. Marguerite's narrators are an aristocratic group of men and women temporarily cut off by floods in an abbey in the Pyrenees, a district which she knew and described as Boccaccio knew and described the country near Florence. Her stories are original and for the most part are amorous tales based on the real experiences of her contemporaries in the French courts. She is not a prude, but her serious intention is evident in the discussions which take place between the stories.

Such sentimental and moral analyses, separated though they are from the narrative, are not found in the other story-tellers of the century. To their work the native soil of France clings more closely. While often borrowing anecdotes from the Italians, they suggest the *gaulois* spirit of the old *fabliaux* and the new influence of Rabelais in its most immediately popular aspect.

Bonaventure des Périers (*c.*1510–44) was a protégé of Marguerite d'Angoulême, thanks to whom he probably escaped the stake for his satire the *Cymbalum Mundi*, a set of dialogues violently attacking religion. His short stories, the *Nouvelles récréations et joyeux devis* (published posthumously in 1558), are the work of a broad humorist who was a good observer of the social types of his age. His contemporary, Nicolas de Troyes, collected equally coarse anecdotes, some of which he may have heard in his saddler's shop at Tours, in *Le Grand Parangon des Nouvelles nouvelles*. Written towards 1535, this book remained in manuscript until the nineteenth century. There is a more definite personality behind the work of Noël du Fail (1520–91), a Breton squire who went to war and travelled round the universities in search of learning, but wrote of the local life near his manor. In *Les Propos rustiques et facétieux* (1547), *Les Baliverneries* (1548), and *Les Contes et discours d'Eutrapel* (1585) he paints the peasants and their conversation with humour and realism. The priest, the notary, the doctor are there too. Certainly he moralizes, but as a philosophic farmer; the case is hardly comparable to the platonizing Queen of Navarre.

After the *Sérées* of Guillaume Bouchet (c. 1514–94) – presented by the author as after-dinner anecdotes for the amusement of the merchants of Poitiers – the genre reaches into the next century with *Le Moyen de parvenir* of Béroalde de Verville (1556–1629). These stories, also ostensibly told at a banquet, are related with much narrative skill and are, in the popular meaning, Rabelaisian. They were published anonymously towards 1610, by which time a new movement of refinement had begun in society and literature. The versatile Béroalde himself played some part in its coming. His prose romance *Les Aventures de Floride* and his translation of Montemayor's *Diana* from Spanish into French (1592) were together representative of the two strands from which the long French novel was being woven. It sprang from romance modified and renewed by pastoral.

In the earlier part of the sixteenth century, the invention of printing had called into being a large number of hack-written tales based somewhat distantly on the old French verse romances. But long before this, in the thirteenth and fourteenth centuries, the verse romances had found their way abroad and had developed new growths of their own in – particularly – Italian and Spanish literature. These offshoots now returned to France invested with the novelty of the exotic to re-combine with the native stem. The most successful importation was the Spanish *Amadis de Gaula*, which Herberay des Essarts translated for François I in 1540–8. The Italian contribution possessed the added glamour of a new kind of poetry, more accomplished than anything yet written in French. Ariosto's *Orlando Furioso* had as its hero the Roland once killed at Roncevaux, but the poet's fantasy and his treatment of love had completely obscured the rugged *chanson de geste*. Tasso's *Gerusalemme liberata* looked back in theme to the thirteenth-century Crusader epics, but in sentiment it was romantic and passionate.

From such examples alone a new type of softened romance could develop.

But pastoral introduced a further refinement. Here again the principal impulse came from Italy. The first *Arcadia* had been published by Sannazzaro in 1501–4, in mingled verse and prose. Before the end of the century, pastoral had invaded the drama, as in Tasso's *Aminta* and Guarini's *Pastor Fido*, to quote two famous examples. The vein, though not the form, already existed in French poetry. Its invasion of romance has an historical connection with the improvement in firearms, which spelt the disappearance of the man in armour. Bayard, the last of the *preux chevaliers*, was killed by an arquebus shot in 1524. Some sixty years later, Sir Philip Sidney, a lingering survival of knightly chivalry, and incidentally the author of an English *Arcadia*, was also killed by gunfire at Zutphen. Sailing on board the Armada, Lope de Vega used as musket-wads the verses he had written for a discarded mistress. Henceforward war would be one thing and love-making another. In garden, orchard, or by the riverbank the perfect courtier could express his feelings unencumbered with horse and lance and, more than that, rid of the constant reminder of danger and duty which they constituted. It is perfectly true that, as far back as the troubadours, love had been treated in a carefree country setting in such forms as the *pastorela*, while the long *Roman de la Rose* is placed in the garden. But in the first case these were song-poems representing a temporary 'escape' or relaxation; in the second the garden was a formal, almost Cartesian, affair, and Guillaume de Lorris was a gentle clerk rather than simply a gentleman. Pastoral took its characters into real country, natural though not wild, and dressed them as shepherds and shepherdesses. By extending from lyric and didactic poetry into the early novel, it acquired greater social meaning and became a reflection and, to some extent, an arbiter of aristocratic manners. At the beginning of the seventeenth century, when France had just emerged from the barbaric wars of religion and was seeking a more peaceful and civilized way of life, it was particularly acceptable to society.

To such circumstances can be ascribed the immense vogue of *L'Astrée*, which might reasonably be called the first French novel. Its author, Honoré d'Urfé (1567–1625), was a nobleman related to the Duke of Savoy, in whose service he spent part of his life. Inspired by models of the kind already mentioned, particularly the Spanish *Diana* – to which may be added the Greek romances translated by Amyot – he wrote as a leisured amateur, publishing the first part of his book in 1607. The fifth and last part, completed by his secretary Baro, appeared only in 1627, after his death. The geographical scene is Le Forez, a district west of Lyons watered by the little river Lignon, which because of this book has become a French Forest of Arden and which d'Urfé knew intimately as his native province. The faithful love of the shepherd Céladon for the shepherdess Astrée may have had a biographical source in his own love for Diane de Chateaumorand, who became his brother's wife, was divorced from him, then married Honoré, from whom she also separated. If so, *L'Astrée* is in part an idealization of the author's youthful feelings. The 'historical' setting, however, is the fifth century A.D., in which it is supposed that these sophisticated country-people wooed and intrigued under the moral guidance of the Druids – who had the advantage of not involving the author in possibly dangerous problems of Christian theology. The most immediately noticeable feature of the *Astrée* is its great length. D'Urfé's method allows of the introduction of innumerable complications and adventures which, together with the stories of the lesser characters which are also told at length, can prolong the book indefinitely. Ultimately, one knows, it will end in the final reconciliation of the two principal lovers, but there is no inevitable point at which, aesthetically or dramatically, this must occur. As has been seen, d'Urfé died before he reached it. The episodes are interwoven with discussions on the etiquette of love in the same way as the stories in the *Heptaméron*, and it was these discussions which in a still half-polished age gave the book its popularity as a guide to feeling and its polite expression. D'Urfé's unemphatic and rhythmic style, diametrically different from that of the great sixteenth-century writers, is civilized in its smoothness. Although it marks one of the starting-points of *préciosité*, its affectations are not exaggerated.

D'Urfé's full title was *L'Astrée, où par plusieurs histoires et sous personnes de bergers et d'autres sont déduits les divers effets de l'honnête amitié*. Love according to rules accepted by both the sexes – *l'honnête amitié* or virtuous love – predominated in most of the novels written in the next fifty years. The gradations of passion were neatly ticketed by a literary bishop, Jean-Pierre Camus (1584–1652), now chiefly remembered for his biography of St François de Sales, whose friend and admirer he was. Wishing, however, to use the worldly novel for religious edification, he wrote some fifty examples of it. A fair sample would be *La Pieuse Julie, histoire parisienne* (1625). For Camus, 'One begins by virtuous love; then frivolous love slips in; from there it is but a short step to sensual love, and thence to the precipice of carnal love.'

The immense virtuosity of French writers in their presentation of the different facets of love rests largely on a literary tradition as old as Chrétien de Troyes, but renewed by the contemporaries of d'Urfé and constantly enriched up to Stendhal, Proust, Mauriac, and beyond. If it sometimes appears to be an over-limited approach to human nature, d'Urfé himself provides a fair answer: '*Aimer ... qu'est-ce autre chose qu'abréger le mot d'*Animer, *c'est-à-dire faire la propre action de l'Âme?*' The play on words contains a psychological observation. More than religion, war, or grief, love is an excellent *animator*, under whose influence the human reactions are enlarged as under a microscope and the perceptions sharpened to a needle-fineness. None of the other passions can furnish such profound or such comprehensive readings in psychology, and the central tradition that the novelist should write about love carries him very far beyond a narrowly erotic field.

The *honnête* or virtuous love of d'Urfé and Camus is much in evidence in their successors, who trace its course through multi-volume novels enlivened by journeys and adventures. The setting is no longer pastoral but pseudo-historical and the characters bear names taken from antiquity or more recent centuries. Warfare is not ruled out, but it is a more conventional thing than in early romance and is usually undertaken only to win some relentless fair. There is never a conflict between martial duty and the claims of love, since the second are paramount. If one could ignore the sentimental element in these books and read them only for their adventures, one could describe them as early historical novels, but that would mean ignoring their main social significance for their contemporaries.

Among the chief names which remain is that of Marin Le Roy

de Gomberville (1600–74), the author of *Polexandre* (1637). His heroic courtly characters belong nominally to the fifteenth and sixteenth centuries. They travel, not only to Palestine, but to Mexico, Morocco, Turkey, in the description of which there is some conventional attempt at local colour. The novels of La Calprenède (1614–63) have a similar general tone, though politics are accorded greater importance. His ten-volume *Cassandre* (1642–5) has Alexander the Great as its hero. *Cléopâtre* (1646–57) is also set in a vaguely historical antiquity. In 1661 he began but did not finish *Faramond, ou l'Histoire de France*. The relationship of such works to the verse epic has been noticed. It remained for Fénelon, at the end of the century, to make the connection quite open by linking his adventure-novel *Télémaque* with the Odyssey. These novelists were eclipsed by Madeleine de Scudéry (1607–1701) who, with some collaboration from her brother Georges (1601–67), produced works as popular in their time as *L'Astrée* had been in its. Her chief novels were *Ibrahim ou l'Illustre Bassa* (1641), *Artamène ou le Grand Cyrus* (1649–53), and *Clélie, histoire romaine* (1654–60). Ibrahim in the first is a Genoese gentleman who becomes grand vizier to the Sultan of Turkey, so creating the opportunity for oriental scenes of passion and jealousy, though virtue finally triumphs. Cyrus the Great was the Persian conqueror of the fourth century B.C. who in this story woos Mandane, Princess of the Medes, under the assumed name of Artamène. Disguised identities were a favourite device of all this fiction, beginning with *L'Astrée*. In *Clélie* the scene is ancient Rome in the time of the Kings, based somewhat freely on Livy.

Mlle de Scudéry was a famous salon hostess who put on, towards 1650, the mantle discarded by the marquise de Rambouillet, whose *chambre bleue* had reflected the earlier influence of d'Urfé. Much of her contemporary success sprang from the hardly-veiled portraits which her novels contained of habitués of her salon or other prominent social figures. The Great Cyrus was the Great Condé, while Mandane was the Duchess of Longueville. She conducted an idealized society of the age of the Fronde through the intricate mazes of mannered love and illustrated by examples the true *précieuse* doctrine of the fundamentally respectful yet witty approach of the man to the enthroned woman. She undoubtedly helped to set the tone for polite intercourse and her influence spread beyond France. Mrs Pepys, who is first noticed reading *Le Grand Cyrus* in December 1660, was still enthusiastic about it more than five years later.*

The limitations of Mlle de Scudéry were illustrated – literally – by a plate in the first volume of *Clélie* showing the *Carte de Tendre* which had been worked out in the author's salon. The way through this pastoral country of the affections begins at *Nouvelle Amitié* and leads (ignoring dead ends such as the Lake of Indifference) by three alternative routes to either *Tendre-sur-Reconnaissance*, *Tendre-sur-Inclination*, or *Tendre-sur-Estime*. Beyond that lies *La Mer Dangereuse*, rocky but otherwise uncharted, and beyond that again are *Terres Inconnues*. This was country into which novelists had so far refused to venture, fearing no doubt the precipices mentioned by Camus. Passion accelerating beyond control was not a pretty subject – nor, with its split-second complications, was it an easy one to handle. They had preferred not to look.

However, another woman writer was prepared to face it, while still keeping a light, almost Jane-Austenish hand on the wheel. Mme de La Fayette (1634–93) was an educated and sensitive woman, enjoying high connections at court but somewhat unhappy in her private life. She was a girlhood friend of Mme de Sévigné and numbered among her circle the writer Jean Regnault de Segrais (1624–1702). Segrais published a collection of 'portraits' (1659). He also wrote *Les Nouvelles françaises ou divertissements de la princesse Aurélie* (1657), short stories with exotic settings such as Spain and Turkey. Mme de La Fayette's first considerable book, *Zaïde*, was signed by Segrais when it appeared in 1670 and probably he had collaborated in it. It was a short novel of sentiment and adventure set in ninth-century Spain, with Spanish and Arab characters. Except for its shortness, there was little exceptional about it. In 1678, Mme de La Fayette published (anonymously) *La Princesse de Clèves*, in which has been suspected the influence,

---

* 'I find my wife troubled at my checking her last night in the coach at her long stories out of *Grand Cyrus*, which she would tell, though nothing to the purpose, nor in any good manner. This she took unkindly, and I think I was to blame indeed.' *Diary of Samuel Pepys*, 12 May 1666.

though not the hand, of La Rochefoucauld, with whom she lived. This book is the first great short novel in French and is the nearest counterpart in prose fiction to the plays of Racine, though the expression of emotion is far less intense and its effects are more mildly depicted. The characters belong, like those of de Gomberville, to a sixteenth-century court, that of Henri II. The lovely and virtuous Mlle de Chartres, newly married to the Prince de Clèves, a husband for whom she can only feel 'esteem', falls deeply in love with the brilliant duc de Nemours. Nemours, though about to be married to the King's daughter, tries to seduce the Princesse de Clèves and meets with her distressed resistance. In desperation, she makes a confession to her husband, begging him to take her away to the country. He realizes her innocence, but in face of his own hopeless passion for her he is tortured by jealousy and ultimately dies. Nemours approaches the Princess again, but although she is now free she refuses him and retires to end her life in a convent.

This is the *fatal amour* of the Tristan legend subjected to a moral discipline so rigid that, though principle is victorious, the only possible end for the individuals concerned is disaster. The main psychological interest is in the self-searchings and vain twistings of the heroine unable to escape her heart, set against the apparently artificial background of a sophisticated court. Dry, stiff, colourless are the adjectives which look applicable to the manner of telling, but on closer acquaintance they are discarded for decorous and economical, so conveying better than any explicit description the social moment to which the book belongs. This, to confront Mme de La Fayette again with Racine, is passion in an accepted cage, by which it is conditioned but not broken. All the basic elements can be found in earlier novelists – chiefly, that is, the 'historical' convention and the method of self-analysis – so that it is possible to consider Mme de La Fayette as a Madeleine de Scudéry grown up and trimmed of verbiage; her greater impact depends largely on her greater concentration. But when all such general features have been noted, the fact remains that one particular author wrote an outstanding book where others failed. So let us not break down Mme de La Fayette into a bundle of tendencies and influences. That she may have had some deep personal interest in her theme is suggested by the fact that she experimented with similar triangular situations in two short *nouvelles*, *La Princesse de Montpensier* (1662) and *La Comtesse de Tende*, published posthumously.

Mme de La Fayette's generation temporarily deserted the long novel in favour of shorter fiction. Many stories were presented as memoirs or personal confessions, so lending a fictitious attraction to their sentimental plots. They were the work of minor writers, such as Mme de Villedieu (1632–92), who wrote some thirty novels, Edme Boursault (1638–1701), who was also a playwright, and Mme d'Aulnoy (1650–1705). The last was more successful in her fairy-tales (*Les Illustres Fées*, 1698), a genre which enjoyed great popularity in the eighteenth century. But here she is overshadowed by Charles Perrault (1628–1703), whose *Contes du temps passé* (1697), published under the name of his son Pierre, told for the first time in literature the stories of Red Riding-hood, Bluebeard, Cinderella, and other immortals. To these stories, seemingly gathered from genuine popular sources, Perrault added cautionary morals, in the manner of the fable-writers.

We must now return to the beginning of the century to trace the course of the realist opposition. 'Realist' is a relative term which serves here to characterize writers who dealt in humour, parody, and the more material aspects of low and middle-class life. It has little in common with nineteenth-century realism and it contains nothing more 'real' than the reactions of the Princesse de Clèves to the dilemma inherent in her social situation. It begins with the anti-sentimental and the anti-heroic and may be said to prolong the broad *gaulois* note of the sixteenth-century story-writers. But this thing had been better done by the Spaniards and their influence was more important than the native one on this branch of the French novel.

Cervantes, after trying his hand at a pastoral novel (*La Galatea*), which d'Urfé probably read, published the two parts of *Don Quixote* in 1605 and 1615, at much the same time as *L'Astrée*. *Don Quixote* originated in the desire to deflate romance, with several side-glances at pastoral. From another angle, it is a picaresque novel of adventures which, in spite of the hero's delusions, take place very much in the actual physical world. While it was not, of course, the only source, it contains all the features which the French 'realists' used. In 1627, when the last volume of *L'Astrée* appeared, a deliberate parody of it, entitled *Le Berger extravagant*, was published by Charles Sorel (1600–74). Sorel's hero is a young Parisian merchant crazed by novel-reading. He buys a shepherd's outfit and goes down into the country to lead the pastoral life depicted in the books. The rather mechanical humour hinges on the contrast between the shepherd's imaginary world and the intrusions of material reality. It is a symptomatic book rather than a great one. Seven years earlier Sorel had published *La Vraie Histoire comique de Francion*, a satirical picaresque novel based on his own experience in which several different levels of Parisian life are realistically described. Both here and in his short stories, Sorel proves a pleasantly loquacious writer with a familiar style and a keen power of observation. His vein was continued by Paul Scarron (1610–60), who is perhaps more important as a poet and dramatist and whose name is associated with 'burlesque' or parody of the epic poem. He responded temperamentally to the exaggerations of Spanish humour, to whose influence most of his work bears witness. In his *Roman comique* (1651–7) he writes of the adventures of a troupe of travelling players in and around the town of Le Mans, where he had lived for some years. He uses openly his local knowledge of places and persons, and if none of his characters from life seems very lifelike it is because they are so often engaged in violent physical action that they have no opportunity to develop a personality. The work of a third 'realist', Antoine Furetière (1619–88), shows the same lack of individual characterization. His *Roman bourgeois* (1666) paints Parisian middle-class types – particularly from the legal and literary worlds – in their urban milieu. It points distantly to the kind of Parisian novel that Restif de La Bretonne, Balzac, Anatole France, Jules Romains will write later. But it remains a series of sketches – a notebook more than a work. Furetière was a versatile though secondary author. He also deserves mention for his *Fables* (1671) in imitation of La Fontaine, but more so for his *Dictionnaire Universel* (1690), which earned him expulsion from the French Academy for infringing its monopoly of dictionary-making. His revenge was his *Factums*, in which he used the technique of the portrait to satirize individual academicians.

The novel as presented by such writers is a loose, episodic work consisting chiefly of a number of developed anecdotes and

descriptions. In an overall sense, it does not have a plot but a
narrative frame. Psychology is not explored. The characters do
not develop, nor do they reveal themselves in action, as did
Rabelais's characters. On the other hand, it represents the beginning of the novel of manners, in so far as there can be a novel of
manners distinct from the novel of individual psychology. All the
term means is that greater stress is visibly laid on social and
professional habits. It is a question of emphasis, of foreground and
background, rather than of kind.

To the novel of manners, then, should be attached Alain-
René Lesage (1668-1747), the first considerable French novelist
of the eighteenth century. He resembles his predecessors in taking
with both hands from the Spanish, and even in affecting Spanishness in inventions of his own. He follows the picaresque method,
pegging on one unheroic hero different adventures of which some
are really self-contained *nouvelles*. Over Scarron he has the advantage of having lived after Molière and La Bruyère had written,
so that his social observation and his conception of character-types
are more pointed. In effect, he is beginning to use the 'portrait' and
the 'character' in a non-stationary way. They blend into and flow
with the narrative – not yet perfectly, but sufficiently for Lesage to
be counted among the creators of the modern novel. In England, his
contemporary Defoe was doing the same thing in such novels as
Moll Flanders. A little later Smollett would acknowledge Lesage's
influence on his typically picaresque *Roderick Random*. Lesage
stands by two books. *Le Diable boiteux* (1707) is a free adaptation
of a forgotten story by Vélez de Guevara. In it, the little lame devil
Asmodée flies up with the narrator above Madrid and, by taking
the roofs off the houses, shows him 'what goes on inside'. Anecdotes, studies of characters and customs follow automatically. His
greater work, *Gil Blas de Santillane* (1715-35), has all the appearance of a genuine Spanish picaresque novel, yet source-hunters
have retired baffled before it and have left it with Lesage. The
young Gil Blas goes to study at Salamanca. On the way he is
captured by brigands, escapes, and wanders about Spain serving
different masters. He rises to high political power, loses everything,
then again makes good and retires to live in peace and luxury. In
both books the 'Spanish' personalities and ways of life have an

oblique reference to France, but the satire is tolerant and unparticularized. Human nature in general is the target.

Lesage's other novels, nearly all nominally Spanish, are *Guzman d'Alfarache* (1732), *Les Aventures de M. Robert Chevalier* (1732), *Estebanille Gonzalès* (1734), *Le Bachelier de Salamanque* (1736). He also succeeded as a playwright, composing or adapting some hundred short farces for the popular theatres of the Paris fairs, and one full-length comedy, *Turcaret* (1709). This is a Molièresque study of the powerful financier, a character (illustrating the rise of the bourgeoisie) which Molière had not attacked. It stands midway between Jonson's *Volpone* and Marcel Pagnol's *Topaze*, but if anything nearer to the latter.

Lesage led a quiet, laborious life in Paris. He belongs to a new generation of men of letters and was one of the first writers to earn a living solely by selling his work. Before that, even the professional writer had depended on individual patrons or on pensions, posts, or livings connected only indirectly with his pen. This was another sign of the rise of the bourgeoisie, translated into a wider tendency to read and buy books and so enlarge the writer's public.

Lesage's near-contemporary Marivaux (1688–1763) did his best work for the theatre and is considered more fully in another chapter. As a novelist, he introduced into the novel of manners some study of individual psychology and showed the characters not only falling in love but reasoning about it from the delicate, adolescent point of view more fully explored in his plays. His chief novels, *La Vie de Marianne* (1731–41) and *Le Paysan parvenu* (1735–6), are both 'success' stories of innocent and charming young people who on their way to position and happiness encounter many conditions of men. The description of these gives a gallery of Chardin-like genre-pictures of town and country life at different levels of society. Otherwise, these are trailing stories still in the picaresque tradition and both were left unfinished.

Marivaux's incipient tendency to moralize, or at least – through his characters – to reason, becomes an inescapable feature in the abbé Antoine-François Prévost (1697–1763) who, together with the Englishman Richardson, illustrates the chief characteristic, or vice, of eighteenth-century fiction. Educated by the Jesuits, he became an officer, then a priest, and wrote novels in secret. Difficulties with the Church caused him to emigrate for six years to Holland and England. On his return he was able to publish openly, and he continued his vast production of novels, memoirs, history, and travel books to a total of fifty volumes. Volume VII of his *Mémoires d'un homme de qualité* (1728–31), which like most of his work is semi-autobiographical, contains the only story by which he is now remembered: *L'Histoire du chevalier Des Grieux et de Manon*. This short 50,000-word novel, of about the same length as *La Princesse de Clèves*, is the love story of a weak-willed and passionate young man and a girl who becomes *déclassée* because they elope when she is intended to enter a convent. Manon Lescaut is charming, morally not overscrupulous, but fundamentally faithful to Des Grieux, whom she 'adores'. After many vicissitudes, she is included in a convoy of prostitutes and deported to New Orleans. Des Grieux goes with her, and the final scene is their escape into the wilds of Louisiana, where Manon dies of exhaustion.

This touching and indeed gripping tale seems marred today by the sentimentality which once made it popular and typical of its time. The stylistic mixture of the real and the hyperbolic is hard to swallow. There is something unintentionally macabre in: 'I dug a wide grave; I put in it the *idol of my heart*, having carefully wrapped it [her] in all my clothes to prevent the sand from touching it.' And to what plane of reality, at a moment when Manon is literally dying from exposure and Des Grieux is in not much better plight, belongs: 'I warmed her hands with my burning kisses and the ardour of my sighs'?

The purpose of *Manon Lescaut*, claims its author, was to show the 'disastrous effects of the passions', and the hero, who survives unwillingly, makes a religious repentance. Whether this was the kind of moral lesson which Bishop Camus would have accepted had he lived a hundred years later is open to question. But there is no doubt that Prévost, in his more worldly and emotional way, was intending to put the edifying novel into practice. All he achieves, however, is a study of untidily passionate love with a footnote that if directed unsuitably – against the trend of society – it will lead to ultimate unhappiness.

Prévost was an anglophile. Sympathetically-drawn English

characters appear in his long *Philosophe anglais ou L'Histoire de M. Cleveland* (1731) and *Le Doyen de Killerine* (1735–40). But more important were his translations of Richardson, beginning with *Pamela, or Virtue Rewarded* in 1742. It was the secular middle-class moralizing of Richardson, rather than Prévost's half-ecclesiastical kind, which was to strike most deeply into French literature.

This influence is reflected in Rousseau's *Nouvelle Héloïse* (1761), a novel told in letters, like all Richardson's. The biographical starting-point was Rousseau's stay in the pleasant country neighbourhood of Montmorency – transposed in the novel to a more 'romantic' site on the Lake of Geneva. He fell passionately in love with his hostess's friend, Mme d'Houdetot, as the tutor Saint-Preux falls in love with the Julie of the book. But Mme d'Houdetot remained faithful to her lover, the poet Saint-Lambert. More *bourgeoisement*, the fictional Julie d'Étanges makes a marriage of duty with the elderly M. de Wolmar. No longer entitled to woo, Rousseau–Saint-Preux can at least write letters exhorting Julie to virtue. Fiction now separates entirely from biography. Julie tries to find consolation in her duties as a wife and mother, but confesses her feelings to M. de Wolmar, who generously invites Saint-Preux to live with them as a proof of his confidence in them both. This confidence is justified, but Julie finally dies when nursing a sick child.

What La Rochefoucauld, or even Mme de La Fayette, would have thought of this can be imagined. The seventeenth-century triangle, when not frivolous, was indeed a dreadful thing. You did everything to avoid it, or escaped from it into a convent. Failing that you invoked the strictest social discipline to endeavour to control it. But here control of the passions is handed over to individuals – and emotional individuals at that, with no defence except their innate feeling for 'virtue'. It is the psychologist's business to determine which system sets up the worse inhibitions, but some are revealed unconsciously in the work of Rousseau himself. Historically, however, this restoration to eighteenth-century readers of the individual human heart and the parallel withdrawal of conventional disciplines earned the novel its immense success. It seemed an epitome of all previous novels, except the novels of manners and of adventures. It was concerned with the psychology of individuals; it was passionately, then nostalgically, sentimental; it philosophized indefatigably; it had a country setting drawn directly from nature. This might have been the outstanding novel which the eighteenth century never quite succeeded in producing. But with all its theoretical qualities, today it is readable with difficulty.

The rustic and philosophical novel, which owes so much to Rousseau, has worn badly. Jean-Pierre Claris de Florian (1755–94) is still faintly remembered for the verse *Fables* (1792) in which he followed in La Fontaine's footsteps, but hardly at all for his simple novels idealizing country life in his native Cévennes (*Galatée*, 1783; *Estelle et Némorin*, 1788). Of Bernardin de Saint-Pierre (1737–1814) all that survives of a mass of well-observed nature-descriptions and a back-to-nature philosophy consciously derived from Rousseau is the one charming tale *Paul et Virginie* (1787). It is the fresh and innocent love-story of a young French couple which ends with the death of Virginie in a shipwreck, while Paul dies of grief soon after. Set in Mauritius, the exotic landscapes are an integral part of the book and point to the background effects which Chateaubriand will presently draw from American landscape. This in a sense is pastoral, but renewed by a rediscovery of wild nature and finally severed from its connections with courts and the courtier.

A farm-labourer's son was potentially the most comprehensive novelist of the century's end, though except in *La Vie de mon père* (1778) he wrote of urban subjects. Rétif de la Bretonne (1734–1806) found work in Paris as a printer and set up some of his books directly in type. He was a prolific and careless writer, producing some two hundred and fifty volumes filled with the inexhaustible moral comments which the impact of Paris released in him. His typical *Le Paysan perverti* (1776) and *La Paysanne pervertie* (1784) illustrate the demoralizing effects of the city on the virtuous countryman. Fortunately he possessed a talent for observation and a collector's love of cataloguing it, so that in the forty-two volumes of *Les Contemporaines* (1780–5) we have, for example, descriptions of the two hundred and fifty trades in which the Parisian woman engaged, from herb-selling to *grande couture*. This zeal to collect and classify, but without the classic selectiveness of a La Bruyère, inevitably reminds us of another descendant of peasants, Balzac. There is in Rétif de la Bretonne's work the material for an early *Comédie humaine*, but it is only material and in no sense a finished product.

Besides the emotional and sometimes rustic novel, the eighteenth century had a more sophisticated type of fiction, often thought of as typical of the age. It usually took the form of the short story or, at most, of the single-volume novel. Its brittle and artificial colouring borrowed from the fairy-tale and from an orientalism akin to the Chinese lacquers which began to appear in gentlemen's houses, or from such sources as the *Arabian Nights*, translated by Galland in 1704–17. Such influences, dating from the beginning of the century, appear in Montesquieu's *Lettres persanes*, Voltaire's *Contes*, or Diderot's *Les Bijoux indiscrets*. These had satirical or philosophic intentions. Others laid claim in their prefaces to a moral purpose, and it is sometimes difficult to decide whether what we are reading was conceived wholly as a light tale of *libertin* society or whether indeed the *moralité* was seriously intended. If the latter, their whole case rests on the proposition that to know vice is to love virtue. There is at least no difficulty with Marmontel (1723–99), whose *Contes moraux* (1761) are anodyne enough and belong in their faded charm to the tradition of stage comedy. He further proved his sincerity in his novels *Bélisaire* (1766) and *Les Incas* (1777) – preaching respectively tolerance and anti-slavery – and in his readable *Mémoires d'un père*. The verdict must go the other way against the earlier writers Charles Pinot Duclos (1704–72), the author of *Les Confessions du comte de ...* (1742), and Claude-Prosper Jolyot Crébillon (1707–77), the son of the dramatist. The chief works of Crébillon *fils* are *L'Écumoire* (1733), a Japanese tale, *Le Sopha* (1745), and *Le Hasard du coin du feu* (1763).

These and more minor licentious *conteurs* wrote, often wittily, to entertain an unpuritanical section of society, whose manners they may be taken to reflect. The marquis Donatien-Alphonse-François de Sade (1740–1814) is a different case. His pathological writings indicate a personal obsession with sex, and he may be seen as a pioneer of modern sexual psychology. At thirty-two he was sentenced to death on inadequate grounds for immoral practices and attempted poisoning, fled, but spent most of his later life in prison and in the lunatic asylum of Charenton, where he ended his days. In his way de Sade was also a 'philosophical' writer, who set out in long novels such as *Justine, ou les malheurs de la vertu* (1791), or *Aline et Valcour* (1795), to expose the iniquities of contemporary society.

The libertine tradition produced one great novel in *Les Liaisons dangereuses* (1782) of Choderlos de Laclos, but its libertinism is psychological rather than physical and is the more impressive for that reason. Laclos (1741–1803) wrote only one novel. He moved in good social circles and rose to be a general in Napoleon's armies. He pleads the usual justification of the moral lesson, gives one of his characters a name (Volanges) used in Marmontel's *Contes moraux*, quotes from Rousseau, and was an admirer of Richardson. Like *La Nouvelle Héloïse* and *Clarissa*, his is an epistolary novel. Its letters show two experienced libertines, the vicomte de Valmont and the marquise de Merteuil, planning in concert to seduce two innocent characters, Cécile de Volanges and her lover the chevalier de Danceny, whose lives they thus destroy. A helplessly sentimental married woman, Mme de Tourvel, is also seduced by de Valmont, then abandoned in obedience to the marquise de Merteuil's commands. In the end, it is true, the pair receive exemplary punishment, but what emerges from the book is the triumph of the male and female libertine over their victims, whom they exploit not so much for sensual pleasure as for vanity. La Rochefoucauld would have understood this conduct, though it is unlikely that his generation would have approved of it.

The hard, dry psychology of *Les Liaisons dangereuses* is rendered by a style which echoes in places the economical directness of the traditional Don Juan and which had been pre-described by Saint-Simon in another context: 'Nul verbiage, nul compliment, nulles louanges, nulles chevilles, aucune préface, aucun conte, pas la plus légère plaisanterie, tout serré, substantiel, au fait, au but.'

This book might be considered as a parting kick from the eighteenth century to the romantic nineteenth, were it not that there is no complete break and that a Stendhal will carry reminiscences of the narrower Choderlos de Laclos. In the same way, de Sade and the tamer 'licentious' writers leave a heritage to the *diabolique* minority of romanticism and post-romanticism – Gautier in *Mademoiselle de Maupin*, Baudelaire (externally), Barbey d'Aurevilly, Villiers de l'Isle-Adam, and Huysmans. On the other hand, the more important legacy (at least immediately) was that of the emotionalists, who taught the expression of feeling without fear, favour, or reserve, and in some cases hymned the marriage of human nature with wild nature in language as ecstatic and cadenced as the prose of Chateaubriand or the verse of Lamartine.

CHAPTER 9

Tragedy and its Satellites

THE fact that this chapter begins and ends with minor names may serve to suggest the parabola described by French tragedy in the course of two hundred and fifty years. The top of the curve is the period of fifty years from about 1630 to 1680. The rest appears in retrospect as an experimental leading-up to the age of Corneille and Racine, then a decline, shading out into various attempts at renewal or innovation, none of which was conclusive in itself.

A similar curve for English drama would reach its peak more quickly, in the Elizabethan age, and would be seen to rise directly out of the Renaissance. In this lies the main difference – one might almost say, the main misunderstanding – between the English and French conceptions of tragedy. If the Mystery plays, which had lost all vitality by 1550, had been rapidly replaced by vigorous new forms of drama, the outcome might have been much the same as in England and Spain. But in France the transition was slower. Several hardly related factors – the wars of religion, the material conditions of the theatre, the preoccupation with classical models and their inhibiting effect on playwrights – delayed the flowering of a national drama until well into the seventeenth century. And the delay profoundly affected its nature. Between Montchrestien and Hardy, who were Shakespeare's contemporaries, and Molière and Racine, who were Dryden's, the social climate changed even more radically than in England. Reflecting back on the drama, it encouraged the growth of qualities which the sixteenth century had disregarded – measure, sophistication, and that special distillation of realism called *vraisemblance*. These qualities belonged to the French drama in its prime and for long remained woven into its fabric. They did not, as elsewhere, grow up after a great period of poetic melodrama from which different standards could be invoked to challenge their supremacy. Instead, they marked a culminating point, historically and aesthetically, to reach which various interesting experiments had been tried out and relegated to a secondary place. The queen-genre which flourished when the fertilizing drones had been discarded was tragedy in its Louis-Quatorzien form – a polished and lethally concentrated type of play, whereas the Elizabethan (and the Spanish) type was exuberant and dispersed. The second gives more margin to the dramatist who is not absolutely of the first class: the minor Elizabethans and Jacobeans were able to achieve more than the lesser contemporaries of Corneille and Racine. But at the point of highest genius, there is nothing to choose. Each tradition or convention can lead in its own way to the same intensity of tragic emotion which, for that matter, Sophocles and Euripides also attain in their way.

In discussing the drama of the sixteenth to the eighteenth centuries, French critics have invariably treated it as the history of two main genres, tragedy and comedy. This traditional approach, though a simplification which is sometimes misleading, was inevitable. The intermediate kinds had considerable vitality, but their failure to attract writers of the calibre of Corneille, Racine, and Molière has kept them on a lower eminence, whether as literature or as theatre. When, in the eighteenth century, the strict distinction between the two genres begins to grow irksome, the prestige of the classic dramatists still prevents any really radical attempt to break it down. At any time after 1750, there would have been an opening in the French theatre for a Dumas *père* and a Dumas *fils*, if not for a Victor Hugo and an Ibsen. But what dramatic theory stipulates, history fails to provide.

The path which led to fully-developed tragedy began as a movement among scholars and learned poets. It was the same movement, rooted in classical humanism, which produced the poetry of the Pléiade. The first tragedies were translations from the Greek, such as Lazare de Baïf's *Electre* (1537) and G. Bochetel's *Hécube* (1544), or Mellin de Saint-Gelais's *Sophonisbe* (1559) from the Italian of Trissino, an author who himself based his work on the Greek dramatists. Other plays were written in Latin by teachers for performance by their pupils. Montaigne recalls with pride that at the age of eleven (so in 1544): 'I played the chief parts in the Latin tragedies of Buchanan, Guérente, and Muret, which were acted with some dignity at our College of Guyenne.' Such experiments led to the first original tragedy in French, the *Cléopâtre captive* of

Étienne Jodelle (1532–73), a poet of Ronsard's group. It was performed by the author and his friends before the Court of Henri II –
it is thought in the winter of 1552–3 – and a little later at the Parisian College of Boncourt.

Everything in that production, including the 'Bacchic triumph'
with which the actors celebrated their success – a stray goat was
garlanded with flowers and a 'Paean' was sung in honour of the
Muses – bore the marks of a student affair. Yet *Cléopâtre* is an interesting ancestor of a great genre. It is divided into five acts, with
choruses. The verse-forms are mixed: alexandrines are used in
two acts only. The story is taken, like Shakespeare's *Antony and
Cleopatra*, from Plutarch's *Lives*, but it opens when Antony is
already dead. Only his ghost appears in the first scene. The play
contains a debate on the fate of the queen between the victorious
Caesar and his officers and Cleopatra herself. At first she pleads for
mercy, but her fundamental resolve to kill herself remains unshaken,
as the audience soon realize. Her death occurs off-stage between the
fourth and fifth acts. In the last act a witness relates the scene in the
death-chamber.

Most of the features of later French tragedy were present here
in germ – the lack of action on-stage, the debating-hall ring of much
of the dialogue, and the faintest of hints of psychological conflict
in the minds of the chief characters. Jodelle and his contemporaries
were still uncertain of the form a play should take. Having deliberately broken with the medieval tradition, they had no living
stage conventions of any sort to guide them. They wrote for what
must have been almost static 'readings' given in the courtyards of
colleges and, occasionally, of the great châteaux. For literary models
they looked back to the Greeks and – increasingly as time went on –
to the Latin tragedies of Seneca. From Seneca they concluded that
tragedy should deal with episodes of death and horror expressed
in long declamatory speeches interspersed with moral comments or
'sentences'. The subject, according to one of the earliest theorists,
J. C. Scaliger, whose commentary on Aristotle's *Poetics* was published in 1561, should be 'the fate of an illustrious person, with an
unhappy ending, told in solemn style and in verse'. In agreement
with this prescription, Jodelle's contemporary La Péruse wrote
Médée (*c.* 1553), Jacques de La Taille (1542–62) wrote *La Mort de*

Daire and *La Mort d'Alexandre*, Jacques Grévin (1538–70) wrote *César*, and Jodelle himself a second tragedy, *Didon se sacrifiant*, a dramatization of Book IV of Vergil's *Aeneid*. These works are less drama than solemn lamentations before and after the death of the hero, which the audience soon sees to be inevitable.

There was a little more movement in the tragedies composed on biblical subjects, no doubt because of the contagion of the native *mystère*. In fact the first original so-called tragedy in French, the *Abraham sacrifiant* of the Protestant Théodore de Bèze, was too near to the *mystères* to displace Jodelle from his position as a pioneer of new forms. Another Protestant, Louis Des Masures, published in 1563 a trilogy of plays on King David. But the best of the early sacred tragedies, constructed this time on the Senecan model, was *Saül le furieux* of Jean de La Taille (*c.* 1535–*c.* 1607), the elder brother of Jacques. The play depicts the madness of Saul, his increase of misery at the news of Jonathan's death, and his final resolution to perish in battle. Written in 1562, *Saül* was published ten years later with a preface (*L'art de la tragédie*) which specifically prescribed for the first time the unities of time and place – although Scaliger had foreshadowed them in his earlier treatise. Of the five tragedies which Pierre Matthieu (1563–1621) wrote for performance by students, three had biblical subjects (*Esther*, 1585; *Vasthi* and *Aman*, 1589). In short, the principle of drawing tragedy from religious as well as secular sources was established from the beginning by Protestant writers and presently adopted by Catholics. It was not abandoned until the close of the seventeenth century after it had given such masterpieces as *Polyeucte* and *Athalie*.

Nearly all the plays so far mentioned were the work of young men in their early twenties or of their teachers, and it is noticeable that none of the finest poets of the age attempted tragedy. Sixteenth-century France produced only one dramatic poet of much inherent merit. Robert Garnier (*c.* 1545–90) was a barrister and judge whose literary technique can be assimilated, as later Corneille's, to the argumentative and declamatory traditions of the law courts. Nevertheless, it is in the pathetic qualities of some of his more lyrical scenes that his talent shows to best advantage. This is especially true of his one biblical tragedy, *Sédécie, ou Les Juives* (1583), whose subject is the massacre of the royal family of Judah by their conqueror, Nebuchadnezzar. Onstage is the spiritual drama, the supplications and lamentations; the scenes of physical horror, such as the blinding of a captive which Shakespeare shows to the audience in *Lear*, occur offstage in Garnier. His other six tragedies were *Porcie* (1568), *Hippolyte* (1573), *Cornélie* (1574), *Marc-Antoine* (1578), *La Troade* (1579), and *Antigone* (1580). Drawn from Roman history or Greek legend, these were more closely modelled on Seneca than *Les Juives*. All, with their choruses, owe something to Greek tragedy through Seneca. Garnier's Roman plays were not without effect on the more learned type of Elizabethan tragedy. *Cornélie* was translated by Kyd as *Pompey the Great* (1594), while two years earlier Sir Philip Sidney's sister, the Countess of Pembroke, had translated *Marc-Antoine*. In another play, *Bradamante* (1582), Garnier broke new ground. He takes his subject from Ariosto's epic, *Orlando furioso*, and the story, with its happy ending, develops in the spirit of the romances of chivalry. *Bradamante* was among the first of the tragi-comedies, a type of play with a considerable future before it.

Little is known of the conditions in which Garnier's plays were acted, since the history of the French sixteenth-century theatre outside the universities is still obscure. The secular theatre had at first no theatre buildings, and without some such meeting-ground connection was difficult between the academic writers and the popular entertainers. But it is now evident that the severance was not as complete as was once supposed. From research in municipal archives it appears that wandering troupes of professional or semi-professional players were growing up to replace the old local *confréries* of amateurs, and that such troupes were numerous. Some perhaps hardly deserve the name of actors, but were groups of tumblers, musicians, and mountebanks. One of the earliest documents is a contract signed by a woman at Bourges in 1545. She engages with a *joueur d'istoires* to play 'Roman antiquities, consisting of sundry moral histories, farces and capers'. The word *tragédie* in such documents first appears in a licence to perform issued at Amiens in 1556 and becomes steadily more frequent at the expense of the old *histoires* – which seem to have been chronicle plays which did not evolve – and *moralités*. Since the details of the players' repertoires are rarely given, it is possible that the more up-to-date name of *tragédie* was at first given to plays which were really *histoires* or even modified *mystères*, but it is certain that by the fifteen-nineties authentic tragedies such as Jodelle's and Garnier's were being performed professionally. Three at least of Garnier's, including *Les Juives*, were in the repertoire of the company of one Adrien Talmy, which toured the north and south-west, as well as Paris. At about the same date the indispensable condition of a permanent theatre in the capital began to be fulfilled.

In 1548 the Parisian *Confrères de la Passion* in association with the *Sots* had purchased a building called the Hôtel de Bourgogne for the performance of their plays. But in the same year the Parlement de Paris issued its decree forbidding them to perform Mysteries. Though other medieval genres remained, the activity of the *confrères* steadily declined and they became ready to rent their hall to any professional troupe that would take it. Among the first recorded lessees were an English company in 1598, of whom little is known. A Spanish company was there as late as 1625, the Italians often. But the most regular lessee was the Frenchman Valleran-Leconte, who first took the Hôtel in 1599, and several times later in the early years of the seventeenth century. From the end of 1629 the troupe which he had founded, led by his successor Bellerose, was given sole tenancy of the Hôtel, where it was to remain for fifty years as the *Comédiens du Roi*. A few years later (1634) a rival troupe led by Mondory acquired the tennis-hall of the Marais, so providing the Parisian public with its second regular theatre.

Among the first tragedies acted in Paris was *L'Écossaise* (1601) of Antoine de Montchrestien (*c.* 1575–1621). It was a play in Garnier's vein on the pathetic fate of Mary Queen of Scots, a figure in whom French poets took a special interest because, before going to Scotland, she had been the queen of the short-lived François II. Montchrestien's other five tragedies are also literary and elegiac rather than dramatic. They include two biblical plays, *David* and *Aman*, both printed in 1601. The second has the same subject as Racine's *Esther*. The author, a Norman like Garnier, led an adventurous life. A duel in which he killed his opponent led to his flight to England. On his return he founded a successful cutlery business and wrote a *Traité de l'économie politique* (1615) advocating protectionism. He was killed in a Huguenot rising.

The chief author of the early seventeenth century was, however, a professional. Alexandre Hardy (c. 1570–1632) served Valleran-Leconte and Bellerose as their 'paid poet' (*poète à gages*) and may also have been an actor. Little is known of the man, but his boast four years before his death that up to that date he had written six-hundred plays gives some idea of his fertility – though 'written' often means 'put together'. Thirty-four of his plays survive – enough to show him as an exponent of robust melodrama, with a taste for violence. He reduces the rôle of the chorus, ignores the unities, and presents on the stage rapes, fights, and executions. A contemporary stage-manager, Laurent Mahelot, lists as require-ments for Hardy's *Parthénie*: 'Two palaces, an enclosed room and a bed, a stretcher, a dummy head, a basin, a halter, a dagger, a flask filled with wine or water, trumpets, a sheet for the ghost, flames, and fire-crackers.'

Hardy found his subjects in Greek and Roman history and in the contemporary or near-contemporary Spanish and Italian writers of romance and pastoral. He adapted them skilfully enough for the stage, but had few literary qualities. His language is often a pastiche of the weaker verse of Ronsard's group, which in Hardy's lifetime was already archaic. Had he been a more original poet he might have done something to change the course of French drama, for he came at a moment when the sixteenth century's theoretical concep-tion of tragedy had lost support and when a more exuberant and popular type of play might have been implanted and maintained even against the general run of the new century. Between 1600 and 1630 three kinds of play – apart from comedy – were to be seen on the French stage, and all were practised by Hardy. The *pastorale*, a romantic play concerned with the sophisticated loves of 'shep-herds' and 'shepherdesses', was the stage parallel to the pastoral novel and corresponded to the contemporary work of Honoré d'Urfé. Theatrically, it derived from court entertainments of the Masque type, which had usually introduced music and ballet. It continued under its own name until about 1640, but to-gether with the *pièce à machines* (a play first found in the sixteen-fifties and based on elaborate scenic effects), it grew closer to opera, into which it finally merged altogether. This was really an instance of the Italians, with their love of romantic decoration and sometimes of the romantic grandiose, taking back their own. What had begun in the verse of Ariosto culminated at the Court of Louis XIV in the music of Lully, whose chief librettist was Philippe Quinault, a deserter from spoken tragedy.

Tragedy, marked out for the noblest destiny, was scarcely distinguishable from melodrama in the hands of Hardy and his contemporaries. Very near to it was tragi-comedy, for Hardy a slightly freer genre in which the sentimental interest was usually stressed. A few years later, when stricter distinctions began to be drawn, a tragi-comedy could be defined as 'a tragedy with a happy ending'. In general, it belonged to the romance tradition, dealt in complicated surprise-plots and the romantic loves of heroes from legend or history, and had its literary counterpart in the novels of La Calprenède and Madeleine de Scudéry. When the term disappeared in the sixteen-sixties, similar plays were called *comédies héroïques*. When first published in 1637, Corneille's *Cid* was called a tragi-comedy; his *Pulchérie* (1672), was a *comédie héroïque*. One of the first of the French Don Juan plays, Villiers's *Festin de Pierre* (1659), was called a tragi-comedy. Molière's *Don Juan*, a play of deeper significance but in prose, was a 'comedy'. In *Don Garcie de Navarre* (1661) he wrote a *comédie héroïque*. It is pointless to establish finer distinctions than contemporaries themselves attempted. But the name of tragi-comedy may fairly be used to cover the complicated, often sentimental play with 'noble' characters which at first overshadowed 'pure' tragedy, then competed with it, and finally fell before it. Like tragedy, it was, of course, always in verse. The infection, or lure, of tragi-comedy was constantly felt by the writers of tragedy, and all but the greatest and the driest succumbed. The battle which first established 'pure' tragedy was fought by Corneille, however reluctantly, and his contemporaries. The fortunes of battle sometimes hang on a hair, or – which is the same thing – on a critical interpretation of a few lines of dialogue (as in *Le Cid*). Had Corneille not won at least some victories as a precedent and example, it might have remained for Racine in the sixteen-sixties to do the pioneer work – and the greatest admirers of Racine would hardly swear that he would have succeeded.

Mechanically, the development of tragedy was related to the unities and these had a connection with stage practice. The stage for which Hardy wrote used a multiple setting, inherited no doubt from the *Confrères de la Passion* (whose machinery was that of the old *mystères*) but modified in accordance with the ideas of the sixteenth-century Italian architect Serlio. A different décor was set for each play, but remained unchanged during its course. Instead of scene-changes, different parts of the stage represented different places. For example, the centre background might represent a palace, the left-hand side of the stage a village and, nearer the audience, a country house, while the right-hand side would represent a hermit's cave and a prison. It is supposed that the actors indicated which part of the décor they were using by standing near it, but that once their imaginary position was established in the audience's mind, they might move freely about the whole stage. The arrangement remained in being at the Hôtel de Bourgogne throughout the sixteen-thirties, and was also used at the Marais theatre for Corneille's early comedies and for the first production of *Le Cid*. As far as tragedy was concerned it began to disappear in the sixteen-forties, with the acceptance of the unity of place. Conventional décors were then introduced, such as a pillared hall in a palace, but any scenic illusion was marred by the practice of placing seats for spectators on the two sides of the stage. The overall area of the interior of the Hôtel de Bourgogne was probably about the same as in the Elizabethan theatres, but whereas the Elizabethan playhouses were square or circular, the French were rectangular, with boxes running round three sides. The French theatres either were, or were modelled on, the numerous indoor real tennis courts which became available for hire when the game declined from the popularity it had enjoyed in the sixteenth century. It is interesting to note that France saw its first semicircular auditorium in 1689 when the new Comédie-Française was built. By then, the age of the great 'classical' dramatists was over.

The principle of the unities, though it may be regarded partly as a conventional framework, led to the concentration of emotional effect typical of French tragedy. The unity of place, which meant that the whole action occurred on the same spot, could be observed when the *décor simultané* had been discarded. The unity of time was justified by the specious argument that it was unrealistic to suppose that an action represented in two hours had in fact extended over a much longer time. Some theorists allowed twenty-four hours for the time spread of a play, but the stricter interpretation (as in Racine) was 'the period between sunrise and sunset'. This apparently artificial convention forced playwrights to single out the most intense period of emotional crisis and to construct their plays tightly around that. As for the unity of action, it tended in a less mechanical way to the same result. The interest was to be centred on a single plot, usually not too complicated, and this also involved economy in the number of characters.

The supporters of these rules backed them with the authority of Aristotle, who had, however, insisted on only one unity – that of action – in the course of his attempt to define tragedy. In the sixteenth century Scaliger and Jean de La Taille had invoked his name, but their recommendations had since been ignored by Hardy's generation and the argument which broke out in the sixteen-thirties was to all intents and purposes a new one. Jean Mairet (1604–86), at first a writer of tragi-comedies, had the distinction of setting forth the doctrine in the preface to his *Silvanire* (1631) and of putting it approximately into practice in his *Sophonisbe* (1634), which goes into history as the first 'regular' tragedy. At the same time the critics looked at the new rules and saw that they were good for discussion. In particular, Jean Chapelain (1595–1674), who occupies between Malherbe and Boileau an intermediate though lesser position as a literary pundit, was in favour of them. As a member of the Académie Française, founded on Richelieu's order in 1634–5, he had behind him the official authority of that body and of its patron, with all the trend towards classification and uniformity which this entailed. In 1637 the Académie was called upon to examine in the name of the dramatic proprieties Corneille's successful play, *Le Cid*. The judgement, drawn up chiefly by Chapelain and published in 1638, was a cautious condemnation worded to offend Corneille as little as possible. Probably because of this tepid document and the greater violence of his non-academic critics, the sensitive Corneille wrote nothing else for three years. But the incident also made for the definite triumph of the unities in tragedy, both in critical theory and in the practice of dramatists such as Corneille, who now bowed to the inevitable.

Pierre Corneille (1606–84) was born at Rouen of a Norman legal family, qualified for the bar, and became a magistrate in his native town. Rouen remained his principal home throughout his life. In Paris he always appeared a visitor and was awkward and aloof. Of his first eight plays, six were comedies, beginning with *Mélite* (1629) and including *La Galerie du Palais* (1633), *La Place Royale* (1634), and *L'Illusion comique* (1636). In 1635 Corneille attempted his first tragedy, *Médée*, and followed it in the winter of 1636–7 with the epoch-making *Cid*.

Le Cid is a variation on the common theme of two lovers whose love is thwarted by enmity between their families. In this case the lovers themselves are obliged to become the protagonists in the feud. Rodrigue's father having been mortally insulted by Chimène's father, the comte de Gormas, Rodrigue challenges the Count to a duel and kills him. Chimène, while still loving and on the moral level of 'honour' approving Rodrigue, is driven to demand his punishment as her father's murderer. The King puts her off, the more so because Rodrigue meanwhile proves himself to be a great military leader and so invaluable as the Count's successor. The play ends in compromise. The still reluctant Chimène receives the King's command to marry Rodrigue, who meanwhile has sufficiently proved his respect for her feelings. But in order not to violate her scruples he is to wait for a year longer, during which he will accomplish new feats of arms which will make him still more worthy of her and will efface the 'point of honour' which prevents Chimène from openly obeying her heart. The delayed happy ending would be in accordance with the romance tradition of chivalrous love dominant in the novel of the time and in tragi-comedy. Contemporaries interpreted the play in this light, even criticizing Chimène for forgetting her dead father too easily. Some modern critics, however, have detected a psychological barrier, which will prevent Chimène from ever belonging to Rodrigue. For them, the optimism of Rodrigue and the soothing promise of the King with which the play actually ends are hollow. The true ending is in Chimène's last speech: 'Am I to submit to the eternal stigma of having stained my hands in my father's blood?' If this were so, the standing and nature of the play might alter. It would no longer be a long-drawn struggle between 'inclination' and 'duty' finishing in an acceptable compromise, but a true inner tragedy of blood against blood – almost as in *Oedipus* – and the first of its kind in French. Corneille's stature would grow correspondingly. He would become a great pioneer of psychological tragedy and the somewhat similar dilemma treated by Racine over thirty years later in *Bérénice* would look petty in comparison. But there are few signs that either Corneille or his generation understood *Le Cid* in this way. Discussing the play in one of the *Examens* first published in 1660, and which contain his considered views on dramatic theory, the author shows his awareness of the impropriety (both social and theatrical) of allowing Chimène's marriage to be arranged on the same day as Rodrigue has killed her father – an absurdity to which he was nearly driven by the unity of time. He even suggests that in the year's interval allowed some obstacle might occur to prevent the marriage, and that the audience can think this if they like. But in opposing 'virtue', 'honour', and public opinion to love, and then leaving the outcome uncertain, Corneille has done what he believes to be his moral duty as a playwright. Never for a moment does he conceive his tragedy as an essentially instinctive conflict between two feelings of equal depth. His chief concern is to reconcile what was acceptable on the stage of his time with the truth of history – for the 'historical' Chimène married Rodrigue.

The play was an adaptation of the Spanish *The Youth of the Cid* (1621) by Guillén de Castro, who dramatized an episode in the life of the eleventh-century national hero, Rodrigo de Bivar, named *Cid* (Sidi) by the Moors whom he defeated. Corneille toned down the style of the original, at once florid and violent, and gave his play smoother dramatic qualities while losing the epic qualities and diluting the 'Elizabethan' vitality of Castro. But it is difficult to admit that in compensation he so changed the meaning of his model as to create at this one stroke the element which makes the greatness of French tragedy at its best: the notion of a human dilemma so deeply rooted that it involves the whole personality.

The well-known formula of inclination mastered by duty – which is Corneille's version of the Christian stoicism put forward by Du Vair – applies adequately to the four 'Roman' plays which, after three years' silence, Corneille produced between 1640 and 1643: *Horace, Cinna, Polyeucte*, and *La Mort de Pompée*. Love, or simply safety, is opposed to moral obligation and personal reputation (*gloire*), and the triumph of the latter is ruthlessly clear-cut. It was as though Corneille was now determined to keep his characters, men and women, on a superhuman level. These four plays, which are his most typical contribution to literature, illustrate the doctrine of heroic energy often venerated in periods of strong physical activity and intellectual conservatism. Horace (Horatius) butchers his sister because she is unpatriotic enough to reproach him for killing her fiancé from the enemy side. Émilie, though brought up and royally treated by the Emperor Augustus, plots fanatically to kill him in revenge for her father's death. Polyeucte drives away his wife unless she is willing to go to the stake with him as a Christian martyr. Though there is some discussion of motive and much of conduct, any attempt to look on these as dramas of individual psychology is misdirected. The significance of Corneille's characters is quite different. They are not cases for analysis but symbols of human endurance and heroism, sure of their destinies and fundamentally unchanged throughout.

In 1643–4 Corneille wrote his last two comedies, *Le Menteur* and *La Suite du Menteur*, vivacious comedies of intrigue both adapted from Spanish models. Then, with *Rodogune* (1644), he embarked on a line of nearly twenty plays, only a few of which were successes. He gave up the theatre temporarily in 1652–9, then returned to experience the disappointments of the aging author who persists too long and to watch with some bitterness the rise of Racine. After his Roman period, he had gone back in spirit, if not in name, to tragi-comedy, inclining sometimes to melodrama. He wove plots as complicated as those of the comedy of intrigue and while, judged by the standards of Racinian tragedy, this appears a weakness, it would, in another convention, appear as Corneille's greatest strength. Such plays as *Héraclius* (1646), *Pertharite* (1651), *Othon* (1664), and *Attila* (1667) contain surprising and sometimes violent incidents which suggest that Corneille was the dramatist whom France failed to produce in Hardy's time. In another vein is the note of true lyrical tenderness in *Psyché* (1671), a play with music and ballet, written in collaboration with Molière and Quinault.

But Corneille is predominantly the author of the energetic historical play in which the 'political' interest is in the foreground, as in Shakespeare's *Julius Caesar* or Sartre's *Les Mains sales*. To this the moral conflicts of the characters are related. As a dramatic poet, Corneille is firm and sonorous if sometimes stiff, but ready to soar into the kind of rhetoric beloved by men of action, politicians, and even the most cultured in their less guarded moments. It is productive also of those Senecan 'sentences' which can be detached as quotations and remain memorable when the dramatic context is forgotten. In this language the gods converse when they are sure of being overheard.

Corneille's contemporaries lived through the same evolution of the unities and experienced the same double pull of tragedy and tragi-comedy. The greatest of them, Jean Rotrou (1609–50), wrote comedies as well. Like Hardy before him, he was retained on salary by the Hôtel de Bourgogne. His best works, almost worthy of Corneille, are the religious tragedy *Saint Genest* (1645), *Venceslas* (1647), a theme from Polish history in which politics are crossed with love, and *Cosroès* (1648). Pierre Du Ryer (*c.* 1600–58) wrote chiefly tragi-comedies drawn largely from novels and was influenced by pastoral (*Les Vendanges de Suresnes*, 1633). His biblical tragedies *Saül* (1640) and *Esther* (1642) continued a still live tradition. Tristan L'Hermite (1601–55) first became known as a poet (*Les Plaintes d'Acante*, 1633) who expressed a certain personal melancholy in his ingenious verse. He retraced his own impecunious youth in a picaresque novel, *Le Page disgracié* (1643). His principal plays are *Mariane* (1636), one of the first successful regular tragedies, then *La Mort de Sénèque* (1643), and *La Mort de Chrispe* (1644).

Such dramatists, representative of a very abundant theatrical production, are themselves hardly read today except by specialists, and can never be seen on the stage. The same fate has overtaken the most commercially successful author of the whole century, Pierre Corneille's younger brother, Thomas Corneille (1625–1709). He ranged from the Spanish comedy of intrigue to tragedy and, writing usually in the romance or the romanced historical manner, scored outstanding successes with *Timocrate* (1656), *Camma* (1661), *Ariane* (1672), and *Le Comte d'Essex* (1678). After Molière's death

he became the regular author of his company and in 1677 produced
a softened version of Molière's *Don Juan* which proved more
acceptable to the ecclesiastical authorities. His success in spectacular
musical plays led him to write opera libretti for Lully in the sixteen-
eighties, and this was perhaps the logical outcome of his whole
dramatic career. His work shows that less rigorous types of drama,
whether melodramatic or sentimental, persisted strongly throughout Racine's working life, and were important theatrically, however
small their literary value.

In Jean Racine (1639–99) the French conception of 'pure'
tragedy reaches its height. The son of an official in the taxation
office at La Ferté-Milon, he lost both his parents in infancy and
was brought up by pious middle-class relatives with Jansenist
connections who had him educated at Port-Royal. The influence of
Jansenist religion on his plays (the Christian doctrine of predestination colouring the Greek conception of fatality) is highly con-
testable, but the sound knowledge of Greek which he obtained at
Port-Royal is a certain factor. Having discovered his theatrical
vocation, he broke publicly with his puritanical teachers and produced his first tragedy, *La Thébaïde*, in 1664 and the second,
Alexandre, in 1665. These were experiments, of which the second
reflected the influence of the contemporary novel. *Andromaque*
(1667) was his first great play and was followed by his one comedy,
Les Plaideurs (1668), then by a series of six remarkable tragedies
culminating in his masterpiece, *Phèdre* (1677). The success of
Phèdre was at first threatened by a rival clique which supported an
inferior play on the same subject by Pradon. This and no doubt
more fundamental personal considerations led Racine to renounce
the theatre, take up the post of royal historian to Louis XIV, and
seek a reconciliation with Port-Royal. Twelve years later he was
persuaded by Mme de Maintenon to write two biblical plays for
private performance at the girls' school which she had founded at
Saint-Cyr. These were *Esther* (1689), a short but charming piece
in three acts with music, and *Athalie* (1691), a tragedy which retains
some of the monolithic barbarity of the Old Testament. Apart from
plays, Racine wrote a small number of poems on topical, official, or
religious themes (as the *Cantiques spirituels*, 1694), some waspish
epigrams foreshadowing Voltaire, and, in prose, an *Abrégé de*

l'histoire de Port-Royal (not published until 1767), which was his act of restitution to his old teachers. His letters, many of them exchanged with his friend Boileau, are interesting for their familiar details of his life and time.

To consider Racine in the aspect of a dramatist building plays for the theatre is to remark the most immediately striking difference between his work and that of Corneille and the writers of tragi-comedy. *Andromaque* has a relatively complicated plot, worked out with great skill and clarity. It hinges on the 'chain of lovers', in which A loves B who loves C who loves D who, since she is Andromache, has her mind faithfully set on her dead husband, Hector. Hector, together with his still living child, constitute E. If, to save the life of his child, D would turn to C, then B might turn back to A and this reversal of the chain would give a mechanical happy ending, as in comedy. In fact, since these are human characters, the links in the chain rebel and the end is the confusion and disaster proper to tragedy.

In *Britannicus* (1669) Racine seemed consciously to tread on Corneille's ground by taking a subject from Roman history in which political ambition and treachery overshadow the love-element. His now simpler plot deals with the first crime of Nero (the murder of Britannicus) and the fall from power of the old Empress, Agrippina. This was followed by *Bérénice* (1670), also set in Rome, in which two characters, deeply in love with each other, nevertheless bow to circumstances and part. This deliberate experiment in simplification hardly has a 'plot', while the plot-machinery is phantomatic. In contrast *Bajazet* (1672) is a violent play set in a Turkish harem, full of passion, murder, and dramatic devices. It is a freak in his total production and the nearest he ever came to melodrama, though the story is straightforward enough. After *Mithridate* (1673), in which Roman and Asian history cross to yield a more restrained story of love and ambition, Racine turned to the world in which he seems most at home – that of Greek legend in which the fabulous can touch the human with its wing. *Iphigénie* (1647) treats of the sacrifice of the daughter of Agamemnon to secure favourable winds for the Greek fleet sailing to Troy, though this is integrated in an exciting plot having a well-developed love interest. Finally, in *Phèdre* the main interest is concentrated on the incestuous desire of the wife of Theseus for her stepson Hippolytus, and the plot, though not without its contrivances, is entirely subordinate to the march of human passion contained from the outset in the characters and their situation.

No sane popularizer would contemplate writing 'Stories from Racine' or even 'Characters from Racine'. The latter, though they live intensely and are not symbols, are not separable from the passion which fills them during the crisis so exactly focused by the dramatist. For a few brief hours they are incandescent with desire, hatred, or jealousy. Any existence they may have apart from that is irrelevant. Working effortlessly within the unities, Racine is expert in leading up to that unbearable moment of truth called, in dramatic language, the *reconnaissance*, the recognition. In farce and comedy this is the literal recognition of a person: that character dressed in woman's clothes is one's fiancé, Ganymede turns out to be Rosalind. At a higher level, the recognition is of oneself and of one's situation; it is rather a 'realization'. Othello realizes that Desdemona was innocent and that he has killed her, Lear – suddenly quite sane – that Cordelia is dead, Macbeth that the wood is moving. In the greatest example of all, Oedipus realizes what he is and what he has done, and that the two things are the same. To show this dreadful moment with its intimate connection with everything that has gone before and its inseparability from the essential personality is a specialized function of tragedy which few dramatists have managed to fulfil. Cocteau, rewriting *Oedipus Rex* as *La Machine infernale*, emptied the legend of its profound significance by making the whole disaster a contrivance of the gods. Corneille's characters arrive by rational debate at self-knowledge, perhaps, but self-knowledge which leads to a decision – it may be to sacrifice their lives. Racine's characters have no decision to take. Their world and they themselves have disintegrated. There is no place anywhere for them, they can only disappear. So, in Shakespeare, the desolate cry: 'Where should Othello go?' So the exclamation of Phèdre: 'Où me cacher?'

The only considerable Racinian character who remains intact and defiant after the 'recognition' is the biblical queen in *Athalie*. The psychology of this impressive play is extremely curious and incompatible with the theory that Racine (through his Jansenist upbringing) was fundamentally – perhaps unconsciously – imbued with Christian doctrine. Athalie alone, in this 'religious' tragedy, does not admit the god working within her, but only the god working against her:

> Impitoyable Dieu, toi seul as tout conduit.

As a poet, Racine wrote dramatic poetry – that is, verse exactly relevant to the situation, character, or emotion being represented by the actors. It is only necessary to say this because Racine has been invoked by the theorists of 'pure poetry' – under that or different names – who claim for his verse an aesthetic-emotional value independent of the plays. If a Frenchman could be found who had no knowledge of the plays (of the 'situation' behind the verse) and yet was capable of judging the poetry as poetry, this contention might be tested out. Needless to say, it never can be. Racine's verse is as functional as Corneille's plots are in their different way. It renders the inner feelings of the characters with all their complexities and resonance, but there is no overspill. One can go about murmuring 'Absent thee from felicity awhile' without a thought for Hamlet, but the lovely conundrum 'La fille de Minos et de Pasiphaé' instantly calls forth the answer 'Phèdre'. What may mislead the reader of Racine's verse is its incantatory power. Magically simple words used in a way which seems not quite usual (as in Valéry) are used by Racine to establish the remoteness of atmosphere which is essential to the plays as plays. Without it they would be sordid crime-stories and the whole inner drama of the passions would be as wasted on the audience as they would be on a bench of fact-judging magistrates. But this language is not hyperbolic. You can shoot down, if you are a destructively analytic critic, such a lovely winged metaphor as, 'L'ennui cherche son ombre aux royaumes d'Arsace' (Saint-John Perse). But you can do nothing of the kind with the Racinian line from which it derives: 'Dans l'orient désert quel devint mon ennui.' It comes at you on your own level and has you by the throat before you can reflect. Of the seventeenth-century French poets, Racine alone combines in any sustained manner this directness with the slight haze always necessary to poetry and produced in this case less by the music of words than by their intimately and intricately secret connections.

The dramatists of Racine's generation and that immediately following appear minor in comparison, whatever their contemporary success. Philippe Quinault (1635–88), whose talent was for sentimental tragi-comedy, turned from the 'legitimate' stage in 1672 to write libretti for Lully's operas. He wrote over a dozen, ending with the triumph of *Armide* (1686). The abbé Claude Boyer (*c.* 1618–98) crowned a long and undistinguished career with two biblical tragedies, *Jephté* (1692) and *Judith* (1695), following Racine's *Athalie*. The abbé Charles-Claude Genest (1639–1718) was a man-of-letters who wrote tragedies incidentally; the best was *Pénélope* (1684). Antoine d'Aubigny de La Fosse (*c.* 1653–1708) is similarly remembered for one play, *Manlius Capitolinus* (1698), suggested by Otway's *Venice Preserved*, but with ancient Roman in place of modern Venetian characters. Jacques Pradon (1644–98), notorious for his *Phèdre et Hippolyte* (1677) vamped up to compete with Racine's *Phèdre*, wrote some ten other tragedies which, for their romantic-sentimental tone, would have been better cast as tragi-comedies. Jean Galbert de Campistron (1656–1723) began with tragedies, as *Andronic* (1685), and became a librettist for Lully and other composers. Joseph La Grange-Chancel (1677–1758) claimed on slender enough grounds to have been a pupil of Racine, but re-worked what may have been the master's discarded projects in *Oreste et Pylade* (1697), *Amasis* (1701), and *Alceste* (1703), beside writing for the opera.

For most of these writers it is obvious that the mould of regular tragedy was too narrow and that their true affinity was in the pseudo-historical or pseudo-Greek sentimental novel whose natural dramatic development was opera. Nevertheless, the conventions of tragedy, established by the seventeenth century and apparently justified by the unique genius of Racine, continued to rule in the eighteenth century. Critics and authors still venerated them in the letter if not in the spirit, while stage practice, a still more conservative force, for a long time made any serious change impossible. The great tragic dramatists of 1700–50 were still Racine and Corneille – in the sense that their plays served not only as models but themselves provided the chief acting successes of the time.

Variations on these two were provided by Crébillon *père*

(Prosper-Jolyot de Crébillon, 1674–1762), whose penchant was for a tangled plot with sentimental or horrific episodes. He substitutes pathos and horror for the true tragic formula of pathos and cleansing terror and represents indifferently the urge to go back to the violence and confusion of Hardy's theatre or forward to the still unborn melodrama. But his horrors are restrained by stage convention. Dramatizing the Greek legend of Thyestes, a barbaric revenge-story in which a father is served at a feast with the bodies of his own children, Crébillon can merely show an actor holding a goblet of blood on the stage. This play, *Atrée et Thyeste* (1707), was among seven others he wrote between 1705 and 1726, including *Électre* (1709), *Rhadamiste et Zénobie* (1711), and *Sémiramis* (1717). He returned to the stage at the age of seventy-five with two indifferent Roman political tragedies.

In Voltaire, the plight of the eighteenth-century dramatist becomes more evident. In a life marked by a passionate interest in the theatre, he produced some twenty tragedies, from *Œdipe* (1718) to *Irène* (1778). He was considered the greatest tragic dramatist of the age and was sometimes hailed as the successor of Racine. But the psychology of his characters and the means used to reveal it are mechanical in comparison. In *Zaïre* (1732), one of his best tragedies, too much depends on a case of mistaken, or rather concealed, identity. In *Mérope* (1734) there is a literal 'recognition' of a son by a mother and the same tragi-comic device is used elsewhere. Human passion is jerked into being instead of flowing irresistibly from the initial situation, yet Voltaire, the apostle of 'taste' in literature, would not go the whole way and write melodrama. He attempted instead to introduce new, but ultimately incompatible elements into a genre whose nobility he respected. The first was an enlargement of the subjects treated by tragedy, until then predominantly Greek or Roman. *Zaïre* deals with the Crusades, *Alzire* (1736) with the Spaniards in Peru, *Mahomet* (1742) with the rise of the Prophet, *Adelaïde du Guesclin* (1734) and *Tancrède* (1760) with the Middle Ages, *Sémiramis* (1748), following similarly named plays by Longepierre and Crébillon, with ancient Egypt. But the local colour is only a veneer and the situations are the same as those used by the earlier dramatists, whose verse also Voltaire echoes too often for an original poet. His second tendency, typical of the age, is to use his plays for 'philosophical' ends. *Mahomet* was openly directed against religious fanaticism – but saved from censure by being dedicated, with typical Voltairean effrontery, to the Pope. Plays entitled *Brutus* (1730) or *La Mort de César* (1732) carried a condemnation of political tyranny. Thirdly, Voltaire, who was highly interested in play-making and play-producing, did much to advance the contemporary movement for more colourful scenic effects. The famous cannon-shot fired off-stage in *Adelaïde du Guesclin* was a signal for the minor revolt which culminated in 1759 when on Voltaire's initiative spectators were at last cleared from the stage to their rightful place in the auditorium. Crowd-scenes and tableau-scenes became possible and after 1760 the Comédie-Française, which held a monopoly of serious drama, grew accustomed to changing the scenery at least once in the course of a five-act tragedy. This greater liberty was won in the name of Shakespeare, whom Voltaire claimed to have introduced to France, though later he condemned him as 'a drunken savage'. Another current was through the actor Garrick, who visited France towards 1750 and much impressed French actors by his naturalistic technique. Shakespeare's major tragedies were timidly adapted for the French stage between 1769 (*Hamlet*) and 1792 (*Othello*) by Jean-François Ducis and, besides this palely polite rendering, Frenchmen could read the good translation made by P. Le Tourneur in 1776–82, though they could not see it acted. But interest in Shakespeare, as later with the theorists of the Romantic drama, was more important as a stick to beat the narrowing classic tradition than as a sign of real appreciation of Elizabethan drama. It will be remembered that Garrick himself rearranged Shakespeare radically to suit contemporary taste.

Thanks to such influences, the latter part of the century witnessed tragedies with slightly more movement and colour and a preference for non-classical subjects, as in *Guillaume Tell* (1766) and *La Veuve du Malabar* (1770) by Antoine Lemierre (1723–93). The play drawn from national history, with a strong patriotic or republican tinge, was the speciality of Dormont de Belloy (1727–75), who wrote *Le Siège de Calais* (1765) and *Gaston et Bayard* (1771). This tendency culminated under the Revolution in Marie-Joseph Chénier (1764–1811), the brother of the poet (*Jean Calas*,

1791; *Fénelon*, 1793). Such plays marked the decadence of the
five-act tragedy in verse which dramatists persisted in attempting
as though the seventeenth-century formula had had some magic
virtue of its own. But the great magicians being dead, they were
in much the position of the sorcerer's apprentice who knows the
words of the spell but cannot control it. Poetic tragedy had come to
such a pass that the youthful Stendhal could speak of the dramatic
alexandrine as a *cache-sottise* – as though an English critic should
speak of the Shakespearean line as a device to conceal intellectual
nonsense.

Meanwhile, there had begun to grow up a type of play which
could replace regular tragedy – the serious drama in prose whose
characters might be contemporary and were not necessarily noble.
Some of the earliest *drames* were written by Baculard d'Arnaud
(1718–1805), though his were still in verse. His *Comte de Comminges*
(1764) tells a story of Gothic horror enacted among yawning
graves and rattling skeletons in the burial-vault of a monastery. His
Euphémie (1768) makes equally gruesome use of the macabre. This
was a step beyond Crébillon in the development of melodrama
(meaning originally a drama with incidental music – to announce
the villain or underline the pathos) which filled the small popular
theatres from 1770 on and reached its height under Napoleon. The
Comédie-Française also admitted the *drame*, but avoided horror. It
favoured the historical type (the freer counterpart of historical
tragedy) or the sentimental type, both of which were written successfully by Louis-Sébastian Mercier (1740–1814), author of *Le
Déserteur* (1770), *La Destruction de la Ligue* (1782), and other plays.
Many authors, including Beaumarchais, attempted the modern
family drama, but only Michel Sedaine (1719–97) produced, in
Le Philosophe sans le savoir (1765), an example with any lasting
qualities.

This variety of *drame*, with an obvious future before it, had
already been defined and recommended by Diderot in *Les Entretiens
sur Le Fils naturel* (1757) and *Le Discours sur la poésie dramatique*
(1758) – stimulating writings on the theatre of which the second
contains very interesting analyses of Racine, Corneille, and Molière.
Diderot wanted a type of play intermediate between tragedy and
comedy (neither of which it would supplant), which should be

realistic in its themes and characters – both taken from everyday life – naturalistic in technique, social because it would take into account the effect of trades and occupations upon the individual's psychology, moving in its homely pathos, and of course, given Diderot and his age, moral. This well-reasoned formula fails badly when Diderot tries to put it into effect in *Le Fils naturel* and *Le Père de famille*, but that is due to the extreme technical slowness of these plays and his over-reliance on mime and the pregnant silence. He had no dramatic gift and failed to realize the many pitfalls of the slice-of-life formula, but as a theorist he is extremely fertile. As he created at least the conception of the *drame bourgeois*, so Nivelle de La Chaussée (1692–1754)) before him created the play called derisively the *comédie larmoyante* or 'tearful comedy' (*La fausse antipathie*, 1733; *Le Préjugé à la mode*, 1735; *Melanide*, 1741; *L'École des mères*, 1744). La Chaussée's plays have been condemned on all hands, but the main difference between them and the *drame* is that they occasionally add laughter to the other ingredients of realism, pathos, and the moral lesson. This is the exact prescription for modern popular drama. In the nineteen-fifties a film entitled *I believe in you* could be described by a critic as: 'A film I am sure you will enjoy enormously ... will have you laughing one minute and trying not to cry the next.'

A contemporary of La Chaussée observed that he made his audience snivel. To snivel and yet be sure of a happy ending is a luxury in line with deep-sprung seats which the austerer genre of tragedy cannot provide. Yet the reality of tragedy, illuminated by a necessary poetry, is certain, while the glossy realism of the basically prosaic slice of life is an illusion obtainable only by blurring the focus.

CHAPTER 10

Comedy from Jodelle to Beaumarchais

As the humanistic poets of the Renaissance had aimed at building French tragedy from the rediscovered Greeks and Latins, they also sought to develop a new comedy in the same way. With *Cléopâtre* Jodelle wrote *Eugène* (1552), which is technically the first French comedy. Other members of the same movement, while prizing tragedy as the nobler genre, tried their hands at lighter entertainment. In 1561 Jacques Grévin published *La Trésorière* and *Les Ébahis*. In 1573 Jean de La Taille published *Les Corrivaux* and *Le Négromant* – the second a translation from Ariosto. A year after the death of the poet Rémy Belleau (1528–77) his friends printed his comedy *La Reconnue*. These were comedies with stock characters, a love intrigue, and 'recognitions', modelled either directly on Latin originals by Terence and Plautus, as was J.-A. de Baïf's *Le Brave* (1567), or influenced by them indirectly through the literary comedy of the Italian Renaissance. While all of these were occasional or amateur experiments, rather more weight must be given to the lively adaptations of plays by various Italian authors made by Pierre Larivey (*c.* 1540–1619), a writer of Italian parentage who lived in France and became a canon at Troyes. His nine surviving comedies, published in 1579 and 1611, depend for their effect on the humour or surprise of situation and plot. Larivey transposed his originals to French settings and, writing in prose, put popular and stage-worthy dialogue into his characters' mouths. Whether his plays were acted is not known, but they were certainly suited to the needs of the small travelling companies.

A second Italian influence, this time non-literary, reached France through the Italian actors who visited the country several times before becoming a regular feature of French life in Henri III's reign (1574–89). They brought with them the broad clowning technique and improvised dialogue of the *commedia dell'arte* as well as its standard characters – the ridiculous old man (Pantalone), the Doctor or Pedant (Montaigne protested against this popular travesty of the learned man), the picaresque valet or trickster with his several alibis (Arlecchino, Brighella, Scapino, Scaramouche), the fire-eating soldier with his terrifying moustaches (the Capitano or Matamoros), and of course the pair of youthful lovers under various names, with whom goes the pert serving-maid Columbine who eventually pairs with Harlequin.

Such characters would be identified with an actor throughout his career and would often be acted in masks, to preserve the stylization still further. Their influence on the characterization of literary and 'serious' comedy is of course immense, though not often precisely calculable since the dramatist's conception of characters he has himself imagined or observed in real life becomes interwoven with his impressions of conventional stage types. The French had the Italian characters physically before their eyes for longer than in any other non-Italian country. Frequent visits to Paris and the southern provinces led in the middle of the seventeenth century to the establishment of a permanent troupe in the capital, headed by the first Scaramouche. This troupe was to share Molière's theatre with him, then, in 1680, to take over the Hôtel de Bourgogne, which in the previous thirty years had become the home of high tragedy and had produced Racine's greatest plays. The over-broad buffooneries of the Italians and, it was whispered, a lifelike caricature of Mme de Maintenon in their play *La Fausse Prude* led to their expulsion in 1697. But twenty years later they were back again, to remain well into the eighteenth century, merging in time into the Opéra-Comique (1762). French playwrights not only watched them but wrote for them. Racine says that he first conceived *Les Plaideurs* as a scenario for the Italians. Regnard and Marivaux in a later generation composed most of their lighter sketches for their stage.

The *commedia dell'arte* of Renaissance times must have struck Frenchmen as a more exciting variety of their own native farce. The latter continued, with a few vigorous borrowings from the Italians, to delight popular audiences in the first quarter of the seventeenth century. It was in the hands now of professional comedians, such as the famous trio of Turlupin, Gros Guillaume, and Gaultier-Garguille who capered and sang at the Hôtel de Bourgogne. Others performed at fairs or, like Tabarin on the

Pont-Neuf, gagged irrepressibly to attract customers for their sponsors – in Tabarin's case his brother, a quack doctor and drawer of teeth. Naturally, little of their material has been printed and what has been is inferior in wit and characterization to the medieval *Maître Pathelin*. In spite of the experiments of the Pléiade group, in 1630 French literary comedy was still waiting to be created.

Most of its exponents from that time until Molière were men who also wrote tragedy and tragi-comedy. They still consciously looked abroad for models, sometimes adapting the Italian or the old Latin comedy, but also exploring a new field of great richness. Spanish comedy, then at its height, was part of a whole drama predominantly concerned with the moral problems of a particular society, magnified or dignified for the purposes of the stage. Comedy attacked these problems from their lighter side, choosing for preference sentimental and sexual themes, and finding a reassuring if not always a convincing solution. Transposed into French, much of its social meaning evaporated. The peculiar Castilian sense of *appearances*, of family honour and personal dignity with the hand always on the sword-hilt ready to defend it, was not exportable. What the French used was the complicated imbroglio by means of which the problem had been posed and worked out, names, settings, and social customs stripped from their context, and sentiment neither wholly of one nation nor of the other. The main impression left by French comedy between 1630 and 1650 is that it takes place in a Cloud-Cuckoo-land suspended above frontiers in which characters not quite like real people behave according to what seem to be their own rules of conduct. This comedy is in verse which, by giving it a language and style of its own, removes it still farther from the everyday world. Knowing that Molière will soon appear, the historian of literature inclines to search too exclusively in his predecessors for signs of realism and reflections of contemporary French manners. Sometimes he finds them, but at the cost of neglecting the typical flavour of playwrights with a different norm. These playwrights hardly created a 'school' of comedy, but their work is more than a mere preparation for Molière.

Foremost among them is Pierre Corneille, whose comedies, already mentioned in the previous chapter, entirely suited audiences ready to appreciate a new *comédie des honnêtes gens*. In part his is sentimental comedy, concerned, like *L'Astrée*, with love, but the sentiment is brisk and not pathetic as it was to become in the hands of eighteenth-century dramatists. In part it is a comedy of intrigue, in that much of the dramatic effect depends on a skilful tangling of the plot. It is true that in *La Place Royale* and *La Galerie du Palais* (the Palais de Justice, which had shops and a whole merchant population unders its arcades), Corneille sets the scene frankly in Paris and makes use of contemporary realism, but in *L'Illusion comique* he introduces a magician as well as a rip-roaring Capitano from Italian farce and so blends fantasy into the astonishing mixture of this play. In his best-known comedy, *Le Menteur* (an adaptation of Alarcón's *La Verdad Sospechosa*), we are back again in the French–Spanish sentimental imbroglio. The hero, a man so instinctively expert in lying that even when he tells the truth he is not believed, might provide the basis for a comedy of character. There is also a moral lesson in his discomfiture. But as handled by Corneille, neither of these constituents develops any importance. The chief interest is concentrated on the gay dance of the plot.

Corneille's contemporary, Rotrou, composed a dozen comedies for the Hôtel de Bourgogne, including *Filandre* (1633), *Clorinde* (1635), *La Belle Alphrède* (1636), and *La Sœur* (1645). Nearly all were adaptations, several from the Spanish. Here are the same romantic intrigues as in Corneille, conducted by characters who live on the borderland of pastoral. A little later, the poet and novelist Scarron drew heavily on Spanish models for the eight comedies which he wrote between 1643 and 1657, of which the best are *Jodelet, ou Le Maître Valet, Don Japhet d'Arménie*, and *Le Marquis ridicule*. These plays are the work of a poet, full of a rich verbal humour echoed later in the plays of Victor Hugo and Edmond Rostand, of racy and invented words, of lines parodied from Corneille's tragedies, and of the kind of patterned dialogue (which became the speciality of opera) in which one character continues or echoes the lines of the previous speaker. As in the Spanish theatre, most of the broader comic effects are entrusted to the valets and the serving-maids. Two at least of Scarron's plays contained important parts for the nasal-voiced comedian

Jodelet, who lived just long enough to be included under his own name among the dramatis personae of Molière's *Précieuses ridicules*. The comedies of intrigue which Pierre Corneille's younger brother, Thomas, was adapting from the Spanish at the same time as Scarron are, in comparison, featureless. They are rather the work of a slick young poet cleverly exploiting a current fashion.

In default of a great comic dramatist, isolated plays must show the other directions which the French stage was exploring. Literary satire appears in *Les Visionnaires* (1637) of Desmarets de Saint-Sorlin (1595–1676), which is a kind of early *Femmes savantes* with its picture of three literature-crazed sisters; in Saint-Evremond's *Les Académistes* (c. 1637), which parodies the early meetings of the Académie française; and social satire in *La Belle Plaideuse* (1654) of François de Boisrobert. Cyrano de Bergerac's *Le Pédant joué* (1653) derived in contrast from the *farce* and the *commedia dell'arte*.

It was from this tradition, with only minor traces of Spanishness, that Molière sprang. His early, essentially practical, experience of the theatre was acquired in touring the provinces. Establishing himself in Paris at the height of his powers, he built a drama of acute social observation on his cruder early technique. The clown may lack refinement, but he has never been accused of losing touch with humanity.

Molière (1622–73) was the stage name of Jean-Baptiste Poquelin. He was born in Paris of the prosperous merchant class, educated at the Collège de Clermont, and could have followed his father's profession of tapestry-maker and upholsterer which carried with it a lucrative appointment at court. He preferred instead to join with a family of actors, the Béjarts, in their attempt to found a new Parisian theatre, the *Illustre Théâtre*, which rapidly proved a financial failure. In 1645 they set out on their long Odyssey as a travelling company, performing in towns as far apart as Nantes and Grenoble, but nearly always in the south. Molière became the leader of the troupe, probably wrote or adapted his first Italian-style farces and certainly composed his first two full-length comedies, *L'Étourdi* (1653 or 1655) and *Le Dépit amoureux* (1656), before re-establishing his company in the capital in the autumn of 1658. This time their experience was greater and their backing more solid. They acquired as patrons first the Duke of Orleans, then Louis XIV, and in 1661 were given, jointly with the Italian players, the use of the excellent theatre hall which Richelieu had had constructed in the Palais Royal.

As success grew, Molière had two masters to satisfy: the Parisian public, whose entrance-money provided the company with its basic maintenance at the Palais Royal, and the King, who gave a yearly pension and occasional special grants in return for the court entertainments which Molière produced, sometimes at incredibly short notice, at Saint-Germain, Versailles, or Fontainebleau. Usually the two demands could be reconciled. The spectacle and ballet enjoyed at court was also applauded by paying audiences, though there would probably have been less of it if Molière had performed only for a town public. On the other hand, 'bourgeois' plays could be taken by the King with a good dose of balletic interludes, though such a play as *L'Avare* was not made for him and was not much liked.

Highly-placed protectors were important to Molière, whose outspokenness created enemies. The short *Précieuses ridicules* (1659), his first play written in contact with Parisian society, was ostensibly a broad satire on the ignorant imitators of the great salons of the capital, such as Mlle de Scudéry's. But the affected speech and manners of Molière's pseudo-*précieuses* struck the general public as very like the real thing and the laughter which went up ruffled the truly refined. Molière followed *L'École des maris* (1661) – on the theme of two elderly brothers, who plan to marry their young wards – with *L'École des femmes* (1662), which provided the occasion for a general attack on his rising fame. This play deals with a middle-aged bourgeois who tries to fit a young girl to be his dutiful wife by bringing her up in moronic simplicity. Her native wit combined with her innocence defeat him and she escapes to marry the gallant of her choice. This commendable theme, worked out in a lighthearted vein which leaves nothing sinister in the middle-aged Arnolphe, was attacked by literary exquisites who found the language coarse and remembered the *Précieuses ridicules* and by the partisans of the rival company of the Hôtel de Bourgogne. The resulting 'Comic War' gave Molière much publicity and drew from him two witty short plays, *La Critique de L'École des femmes* and

L'Impromptu de Versailles (both 1663). The second has the historical interest of putting Molière's company on the stage under their own names and of expressing his preference for 'natural' acting as against the high-flown artificiality of the Hôtel de Bourgogne. His views are not unlike those which Shakespeare lent to Hamlet in his advice to the players.

This had been a literary and professional quarrel. Molière, moving into his greatest period, now came into collision with the Church. *Tartuffe ou l'Imposteur* was acted once before Louis XIV in 1664, then virtually banned for five years on the initiative of ecclesiastics who felt that this portrait of a wolf in priest's clothing might cast reflections on genuine religion. The same forces ensured the disappearance after a short run of *Don Juan* (1665), a great though uneven play on a subject which other contemporary dramatists had treated without censure. Don Juan, here a representative of the contemporary *libertins*, argues with mathematical logic on the non-existence of the supernatural and goes down unrepentant to the traditional hell-fire beneath the stage. His final sin has been to become hypocritically religious, because 'hypocrisy is a privileged vice which shuts everyone's mouths and peacefully enjoys complete immunity'. Hypocrisy is also under discussion in Molière's most perfect play, *Le Misanthrope* (1666). If one were to follow a narrowly biographical interpretation, one might see the author himself in the outspoken, rigidly honest Alceste who loses everything because he cannot make a few concessions to social convention, or alternatively because he cannot betray his principles. Since nothing can save Alceste from his own nature, *Le Misanthrope* becomes comedy on a tragic plane, with the hero going out at the end into a social wilderness instead of a personal limbo.

No one boycotted *Le Misanthrope*, and from then on Molière's career was one of professional success but of deteriorating health and of private anxiety arising from his marriage, in 1662, to Armande Béjart, a young member of his company. He wrote *Le Médecin malgré lui* (1666), one of his several short farces on the charlatan-physician; *Amphitryon* (1668), a mythological play on the love of Jupiter for a mortal; *George Dandin* (1668), on the wronged husband whose wife always outwits him; *L'Avare* (1668), a development from the *Aulularia* of Plautus; and in 1667 and 1669 two very different comedy-ballets, the delicate *Le Sicilien ou L'Amour-peintre* and the farcical *Monsieur de Pourceaugnac*. In these the comedy is loosely linked with interlude dancing and music which can at a pinch be omitted. The type includes *Le Bourgeois Gentilhomme* (1670), the immortal portrait of a snobbish merchant, and Molière's last play, *Le Malade imaginaire* (1673), whose chief character is a healthy man absorbed in the medical treatment of his imaginary ill-health. Just before this, Molière had given *Les Femmes savantes* (1672), one of his funniest social comedies. In its mockery of pseudo-literature and pseudo-learning it is a full-scale development of *Les Précieuses ridicules*.

Having written some thirty plays of several kinds, Molière died on 17 February 1673, a few hours after acting the part of the imaginary invalid. His company, with his wife now at its head, at once merged with the old Theatre of the Marais which had produced Corneille's first plays. A few years later, in 1680, a royal order compelled the Hôtel de Bourgogne to amalgamate with them in its turn, and the result of this triple merger was the Comédie-Française. The monopoly of the Comédie-Française extended to everything but opera, operette, the Italian players, and the small 'irregular' theatres in the fairs. For more than a hundred years another individual venture like Molière's was out of the question, though on the credit side, he, Racine, and Corneille were – unlike Shakespeare – assured of constant productions by a strong company with fairly continuous traditions.

It is useless to stick labels on Molière. Certainly he practised the comedy of character to such effect that it became an obsession with his successors in Europe. But Tartuffe is more than *the* religious hypocrite, Harpagon than *the* miser, Argan than *the* hypochondriac, or George Dandin than *the* baffled husband. They are more than an accumulation of true strokes adding up to a type – an error of which even La Bruyère was sometimes guilty. They utter sudden realistically lifelike cries, have sudden fantastic whims which seem to prove that their own imaginations are working. To find such things in models is uncanny, and can be developed by a sensitive actor into something so macabre that we want to disbelieve it. The Misanthrope, in particular, can be rendered not as a pig-headed individualist being jollied along by a ring of cheerful puppets, but as a soul undergoing torment in an only formally frivolous drawing-room. Such interpretations may not have been consciously intended by Molière, but the fact that they are possible is disquieting – notwithstanding that the predominant atmosphere is 'healthy' (i.e. un-Freudian) and that one can love and enjoy Molière simply for his sunny mockery of the ridiculous excess. The devil, after all, was an old and harmless favourite in comedy; it is when his victims appear on the stage that one likes to feel quite sure that their writhings are merely simulated. In Molière's comedy, unlike tragedy, the dream which is broken at the end has been seen by the audience to be foolish from the outset and its breaking is a matter for laughter in which the dreamer must appear to join. But a dramatist who even occasionally raises the question: What became of him after that? – to Orgon without Tartuffe, to Argan without his drugs and doctors – dangerously strains the limits of comedy. Hence the arbitrary and artificial dénouements for which Molière is renowned. They result, not from an inability to handle plot, but from a theatrical necessity to escape the logic of character which must otherwise lead to the tragic. 'What!' cries the rank-conscious comtesse d'Escarbagnas, when her marriage to a local lawyer is proposed, 'To mock a person of my quality in that way?' 'No offence is meant to you, Madam, and comedies require these kind of things.'

As an observer of society, Molière is much plainer. From the standpoint of an immensely shrewd middle class, he paints the manners of that class in *Tartuffe*, *L'Avare*, *Le Bourgeois Gentil-homme*, or *Le Malade imaginaire*, or else sizes up the aristocracy in an early comedy-ballet like *Les Fâcheux* (1661) or in *Le Misanthrope*. No social deformation escapes him and his work in this respect completes La Bruyère and the chief memoir-writers and letter-writers. He captures the tone of voice, the fashionable or typical utterance, sometimes in verse, sometimes in prose – in which several of his best comedies were written. The dialect of his peasants and his other provincial characters may not always be realistically accurate. That is a matter of philological debate, but at least it brings to the stage a dimension not contained in the cultivated speech of the salons and Versailles. What words in all their variety can do to enrich drama, and what Scarron had attempted

more self-consciously, Molière achieves with an easy zest. The age
was against a Rabelaisian verbal inventiveness, but Molière takes
or makes as much as anyone needs. The delightful free verse of
Amphitryon, creating a poetic drama outside the conventional
alexandrine is another example of his astonishing range.

Even badly translated or flatly acted, his plays can hold the stage
because they were rooted in experience of the theatre. As literature
they contain more, artistically and psychologically, than any but
the greatest actors could hope to execute. Thus a full discovery of
them is usually a fruit of reading, with an imaginary stage somewhere on the mind's horizon. This was the first European comedy,
except Shakespeare's and to a lesser degree Jonson's, which seems
even now to be fully dramatic yet belongs to the first rank of
literature.

Around Molière, only Racine produced a really memorable
comedy in *Les Plaideurs* (1668). It is, very freely based on Aristo-
phanes, a satire on the French law courts and on the mania of
private persons for going to law. It is uproariously funny in
situation and language and is a perfect example of intelligent burlesque. Unfortunately Racine, probably disappointed by its first
reception and deciding to specialize in tragedy, attempted nothing
more in this vein. Edme Boursault (1638–1701), a busy secondary
figure in letters, joined in the 'Comic War' with a short sketch, *Le
Portrait du peintre*, which Molière brushed briefly aside in *L'Impromptu de Versailles*. Later, he wrote *Ésope à la ville* (1690) and
Ésope à la cour (1701), two moralizing comedies, of indirect social
application, incorporating verse fables in La Fontaine's manner.
But for the most part the comedies of the later seventeenth century
were light occasional pieces often written by actors (Hauteroche,
Montfleury *fils*, Champmeslé, Baron) to fill gaps in their company's
repertoire. Florent Carton Dancourt (1661–1725) was one such
actor, recruited into the profession by his runaway marriage with
an actor's daughter, 'after which outburst he could see no career
open to him except the stage'. He may perhaps be allowed the
description of a lightweight successor of Molière. His are mildly
satirical social comedies in prose, many in one act. Of fifty such
plays, his most notable were *Les Vendanges de Suresnes* (1698), a
comedy in one long act, and the full-length *Le Chevalier à la mode*

(1687), *Les Bourgeoises à la mode* (1692) and *Les Bourgeoises de qualité* (1700). *Les Bourgeoises à la mode* is the source of *The Confederacy* by Vanbrugh, who borrowed freely from Dancourt and other French dramatists, including Boursault and Molière (*Le Dépit amoureux* gave *The Mistake*; *Monsieur de Pourceaugnac* gave, in collaboration with Congreve and Walsh, *The Cornish Squire, or Squire Trelooby*). The imitations by the English Restoration dramatists of Molière and Molière's imitators usually stress the more grossly farcical features, substitute John Bullishness for the lighter touches, or, as in Wycherley's *Plain Dealer*, turn the civilized tabu-ridden Misanthrope into a blunt puritan preaching virtue. This is perfectly normal, since comedy must grow native roots, but it shows that the English borrowings were confined to themes and situations. There could be no close resemblances of tone between the two national comedies.

Beside the actor-dramatist, an occasional gentleman-playwright (like Vanbrugh and Congreve in England) became absorbed in the comic stage and its financial rewards. Jean-François Regnard (1655–1709) was prosperous enough to travel Byronically for pleasure in his youth and to taste the experience of being captured by Algerian pirates, or so he says in his novel *La Provençale*. Settling in Paris, he produced numerous light pieces for the Italians, such as *Arlequin homme à bonnes fortunes* (1690), and then wrote more ambitious comedies for the Comédie-Française, of which the first of importance was *Le Joueur* (1696), suggested by the contemporary rage for gambling. Others were *Le Distrait, Attendez-moi saus l'orme, Les Folies amoureuses,* and *Le Légataire universel* (1708), his best play. It contains a situation – reminiscent of Ben Jonson's *Volpone* – in which an old man who was believed to be dead revives to disconcert his would-be heirs. Regnard, who was ranked immediately below Molière by eighteenth-century opinion, had a talent for comic intrigue but little feeling for character. He reflects with a certain fantasy, which once sparkled but now often seems flat, the social manners of his time. His chief plays are written in verse, supple and capable of rendering several different tones. It is on the stylistic count that he comes nearest to Molière.

His plays, with *Turcaret* (1709) of the novelist Lesage and the light-sketched comedies of situation and character of Charles

Rivière Dufresny (*c.* 1654–1724), amused theatre-goers during the last years of Louis XIV and the Regency. But the first writer with a new conception of comedy, which also belonged typically to the new century, was Pierre Carlet de Chamblain de Marivaux (1688–1763), also a journalist and novelist. He wrote over thirty plays, preferably for the Italians, who could give him freer and more buoyant renderings than the official theatre. But he has long been as firmly installed in the repertory of the Comédie-Française as Molière and Musset. His first success, *Arlequin poli par l'amour* (1720), was followed by *La Double Inconstance* (1723), *L'Île de la raison* (1727), the second *Surprise de l'amour* (1727; the first dates from 1722), *Le Jeu de l'amour et du hasard* (1730), *Les Fausses Confidences* (1737). A score of shorter pieces, such as *Le Legs*, *L'Épreuve*, *La Dispute*, *Le Préjugé vaincu*, complete his production.

There are few loud laughs in Marivaux and no clownings or grotesque characters. The plot ripples easily forward through the delicately conversational prose – stylized just sufficiently not to become amorphous – in which all his plays are written. This style and the delicate but not trivial sentiments which it serves to express have been dubbed *marivaudage*, meaning the language of affected love-making. But the reproach fits his imitators better than Marivaux himself and, given his themes, he could hardly have used a more suitable idiom. The approach of love, its unconscious stirrings and its ultimate revelation to fundamentally innocent and even adolescent characters form the main basis of his plays. Love in Marivaux is never a passionate force, neither is it brutal or licentious. He pictures it as a delicately pleasurable sensation filling his characters with the same delight they would find in a fine summer morning or a properly-ordered party among congenial friends in the right surroundings. All this takes place in a slightly fantastic country, which might be Chekhov's with a clearer skyline. The characters are called La Comtesse, Le Marquis, Araminte, Lucidor. They have their servants called Lubin, Dubois, Lisette, who are almost part of the family and are familiar without being thought insolent. This is not quite the France of Louis XV. It floats just above it, emanating from it more directly than did the comedy of Louis XIII's time. Unlike that, this is native. In its gracefully etched innocence it is rather touching, both for its contrast with the

cynical manners of the time and as a still shy forerunner of the unashamedly loud sensibility which is all too soon to come. Because
Marivaux announces this, without himself developing it, his sentiment is sometimes called bourgeois. No doubt he was, in his general
kindheartedness and his desire that difficulties should have a cheerful outcome. And who but a bourgeois could have created his
delightful aristocrats, or for that matter his delightful bourgeois?

His best-known play, *Le Jeu de l'amour et du hasard*, contains
the twin disguise of Silvia as her own maid and of Dorante, who
thinks of marrying her, as his own valet. This conventional device,
which Scarron among others had partly used in *Jodelet* (in which
the master changes clothes with his valet), acquires fresh possibilities because of the double substitution. Both Silvia and Dorante
think they are falling in love with servants. The sentimental awakening of both man and woman can be traced and so can Silvia's
scruple after she has discovered who the lovable valet really is. In
older comedy, appetite or social directness would have caused her
to reveal herself at once, or else to continue the disguise for a malicious pleasure in the intrigue. Silvia continues because she wants
to be loved for herself alone, which of course she is. These comedies are only not romantic because they are unsubstantial and
avoid the appearance of ever going deep.

The sentimentality latent in Marivaux came fully to the surface
in the 'tearful comedy' of La Chaussée, as later in the *drame bourgeois*, both of which were discussed in the previous chapter. In
the same way his implicit morality becomes open moralization in
such 'philosophical' comedies as those of Philippe Néricault Des-
touches (1680–1745), who tried to construct his plays round
'characters' with laughable eccentricities – a resource from which
Molière and La Bruyère had patently skimmed the cream. *Le
Glorieux* (1732) is his best example. Others, composed between 1712
and 1736, were *L'Ingrat*, *L'Irrésolu*, *Le Médisant*, *Le Philosophe
marié*, *L'Envieux*, *Le Dissipateur*. But the true spirit of Marivaux
passed out of literature proper into the comedy with songs and
music which the Italians and the theatres of the fairs had first
popularized when, under pressure from the Comédie-Française, they had been forbidden to perform completely spoken
plays. So was born the *comédie vaudeville* soon called the *opéra-*

comique, whose chief exponent was Charles-Simon Favart (1710–92), author of *Bastien et Bastienne, Ninette à la cour, Annette et Lubin, Les Moissonneurs*. Others were written by Sedaine (*Rose et Colas, Les Sabots, Le Déserteur, Richard Cœur de Lion*), while Jean-Jacques Rousseau's only musical successs, *Le Devin du village* (1753), also belongs to the genre.

Historically considered, most of this was light pastoral, with all the conventions and illogicalities that go with pastoral, adapted here for popular audiences but with a pedigree that made tragedy look like a new immigrant, since *opéra-comique* could look back to the thirteenth-century *Robin et Marion* of Adam de La Halle. It would have been the only kind of comedy worthy of the name after 1750, but for a lucky stroke by Beaumarchais, who thus succeeded in at least one of his many enterprises.

Pierre-Augustin Caron (1732–99) was a watchmaker's son who began by following his father's trade. He took the name of Beaumarchais at the age of twenty-four when he married the widow of a court official and secured an entrée to the golden opportunities awaiting the adventurer in that period of political and financial confusion. His career was certainly stranger than his work. He became a music-teacher to the royal princesses, engaged, like Voltaire, in ambitious business schemes, ran guns to the Americans during the War of Independence, edited and published the first complete (Kehl) edition of Voltaire's works, visited Spain as a self-appointed economic adviser to Carlos III and England and other countries as an agent of the French Government. He dodged in and out of France during the Revolution and died in Paris with his pockets empty but his head still on his shoulders.

He wrote in the hope of making money and so followed the fashion of the *drame bourgeois* in his undistinguished *Eugénie* (1767), *Les Deux Amis* (1770) and *La Mère coupable* (1792). His opera, *Tarare* (1787), was also a failure. Only two plays, whose popularity has no doubt been increased by the operas composed on them by Rossini and Mozart, ensure his fame. *Le Barbier de Séville* (1775) and *Le Mariage de Figaro* (written 1778, banned until 1784) were throw-backs in the age of the *drame* to the old comedy of intrigue. In the first, Count Almaviva, ably seconded by Figaro, his ex-servant turned barber, surgeon, musician, and dramatist, wins the hand of the innocent and beautiful Rosine, who is kept isolated, like Agnès in Molière's *École des femmes*, by her guardian Bartholo. In terms of the *commedia dell'arte*, Figaro is Harlequin or Scaramouche, Bartholo is Pantaloon, while Don Bazile, the complaisant music-master, is no doubt the Pedant. *Le Mariage de Figaro* uses the same characters less conventionally, while adding others such as the *soubrette* Suzanne and the page Chérubin who might have come from Marivaux, though the atmosphere is less innocent. Chérubin is really Beaumarchais's invention, as certainly is the idea of showing the hero and heroine of the previous comedy (the Count and Rosine) in their not too smooth married life. This was exceptional if not unique. Figaro, since anything is now possible, proves to be the natural son of old Bartholo and at the same time finds a much-wronged long-lost mother, by Rétif de La Bretonne out of La Chaussée. The mainspring of the plot is Suzanne's successful campaign to be securely married to Figaro, notwithstanding the Count who finds her attractive.

These two plays show a rich mixture of influences which combine to produce comedy quite original in its speed and dancing gaiety tinged with acceptable sentiment. In Figaro, the comic valet is renewed by taking on something of the author's own picaresque character. He also turns out to be a democrat, preaching equality in long epigrammatic monologues which can still be swallowed and which once gave the plays their burning topicality. 'Because you are a great lord you think you have a great talent. . . . What have you done to deserve all these things? You took the trouble to get born, nothing more.' Such speeches have become almost proverbial. They explain the original ban on *Le Mariage de Figaro*, finally lifted through the efforts of members of the aristocracy. Five years before the Revolution, the social conscience had made sufficient progress among the privileged classes, in earnest or as a fashion, for them to distinguish between good aristocrats and bad aristocrats. The good aristocrats applauded *Le Mariage*. The bad ones intrigued to have Beaumarchais briefly imprisoned. To console him for this, the less radical *Barbier* was acted at Versailles, with Marie Antoinette in the part of Rosine. Of this mad world Beaumarchais was himself typical. Fundamentally, he was far less revolutionary than Molière. Opportunism, bravado, and a for once candid projection of his own experience led him to express sentiments popular at the time, believing that, like his plays, everything would end in songs.

So the eighteenth century at last produced topical comedy which has not dated. But in spite of a few fine speeches, it cannot be called political comedy.

CHAPTER 11

Poetry from Marot to Chénier

ONE of the two great centuries of French poetry, the sixteenth –
though less rich than the nineteenth – was no less remarkable for
the revolution which it achieved. One sees the poets of the late
Middle Ages performing like endlessly interbred mice in a cage spun
by decades of craftsmanship and then, after a space of about fifty
years, the justified boasts of freedom and renewal made by the poets
of the Pléiade. These also considered themselves as the heirs of a
tradition, but it was an older and certainly a broader one. Exploited
boldly and only half explored in the century of the Renaissance, the
legacy of the Greek and Latin poets seemed then to be inexhaustible. The limits which force writers to rebound towards a central
repetition were not felt or even suspected. This domain was so
roomy that Ronsard's generation felt only the excitement of discovery.

The discovery was not wholly theirs, though the main achievement was. Through Italian scholarship and Italian poets some
awareness of new horizons had begun to reach France in the early
years of the century. It had seeped through in such late *Rhétoriqueurs* as Jean Lemaire de Belges. It appeared intermittently in the
greatest of hybrid poets, Clément Marot (1496–1544), the son of
another *Rhétoriqueur*, the minor court poet Jean Marot. Thanks to
his father's teaching, Clément Marot was expert in the old, ingenious forms and some of his best verse is cast in *rondeaux* and
ballades, though also in the freer *chanson*. His medieval interests
show in the editions which he published of the *Roman de la Rose*
and of Villon's poems. But the taste of the court, and particularly
the court of Marguerite d'Angoulême, who protected him when he
fell under suspicion of heresy, gradually turned him towards Italian
and humanistic models. He read Martial and translated Ovid. He
wrote the earliest sonnets in French, including six translated from
Petrarch. But he was never a learned poet, nor did he leave any one
great poem. *L'Enfer*, which he wrote after his imprisonment in

1526 (he was denounced by a woman for having boasted that he had eaten bacon in Lent – the crime looks comic, but the consequences, after an inquiry with torture, could, with ill-luck, be atrocious), is topically interesting in these days of political persecution. Like Villon, he was several times in prison, but for ideological (i.e. religious) reasons. He began a metrical translation of the Psalms which led to his condemnation by the Sorbonne and his flight to Geneva (1542). He was, however, an independent rather than a convinced Calvinist. Geneva stifled him. He moved on to Savoy and died at Turin.

Much of Marot's verse was occasional, written to praise or petition his patrons or to record episodes in his own turbulent life. He is not a great lyric poet and his treatment of love is superficial – though playful and charming, as in his *rondeaux*. Apart from the nobility of his *Psaumes*, his best vein is in the broad satire of his *Épigrammes* and some of his *Épîtres*. Even when not satirical he shows a humour more often reminiscent of Villon and Rabelais than of the niceties of the *Rhétoriqueurs*. Though on analysis he was transitional, his witty and racy verse has the strong individual quality of a poet who felt quite at home in his age.

While Marot bowed in certain poems to the contemporary Italian influences, he cannot be said to have absorbed them. Two influences, neo-Platonism and Petrarchism, were now reaching France, to affect profoundly the poetry of her full Renaissance. Plato, who had been little read or understood during the Middle Ages – dominated by the philosophy of Aristotle – had been revived in the late fifteenth century by a group of intellectuals in Florence. Foremost among them was a priest, Marsilio Ficino, whose translation and commentaries of Plato were of decisive importance in the contemporary conception of his philosophy. Ficino associated Plato's teaching with Christianity, of which he made him one of the great forerunners. The connection was intimately close in the Platonic theory of love, as Ficino deduced it from *The Symposium* and elsewhere. According to this, the soul on earth still retains vague memories of the world of perfect beauty in which it once existed. Though now imprisoned in the body, the sight of physical beauty stirs longings, at first imprecise but not carnal. The soul gradually recognizes that the body is only the imperfect envelope of another soul, and so through perception and contemplation of ever higher forms of beauty it rises to a unity with the perfection of God, on which divine level beauty, love, and goodness are one and the same. Earthly love, in the neo-Platonic sense, is thus a first step on the ladder to divine love and the first can only find its true fulfilment in the second.

Another face of this theory, of equal importance for philosophy and poetry, is that which shows that the objects which surround us on earth are simply reflections or projections of their own perfect archetypes in heaven. The latter, which Plato calls Ideas (one might loosely say, Ideals), are dimly remembered by us as we move about life and are the cause of our passionate attachment to their imperfect copies. So imagination is memory and aspiration is nostalgia – but a nostalgia which, if cultivated and refined, can lead us up (or back) to the original heights.

Among the many appearances which the theory of Ideal Beauty and Ideal Love make in Renaissance verse, one of the purest is Du Bellay's sonnet beginning

> Si notre vie est moins qu'une journée
> En l'éternel . . .

and ending

> Là, ô mon âme, au plus haut ciel guidée,
> Tu y pourras reconnaître l'Idée
> De la Beauté qu'en ce monde j'adore.

Between 1530 and 1550 the chief centre of the new Platonism in France was the court of Marguerite d'Angoulême. Here Antoine Heroët (c. 1492–1568), in *L'Androgène* and *La Parfaicte Amie*, expressed the new conception of spiritual love with woman as its worthy medium. Marguerite's own poems show a mixture of Platonic conceptions with a Christian mysticism which easily harmonized with them. In most French poets, however, the influence of Plato was crossed and enriched by that of Petrarch. The fourteenth-century *Rime* of the Italian poet had traced in a succession of short related lyrics the development of Petrarch's love for Laura, including at first his own inner conflict between flesh and spirit. The death of Laura marks a division in the book (composed intermittently throughout Petrarch's lifetime), after which the spiritual side of his love becomes progressively stronger and recollection curves to meet adoration of the beloved now in paradise. The final lyric is addressed, not to Laura, but to the Virgin Mary. The accidental points of resemblance between Petrarch's work and neo-Platonic doctrine are obvious, as are Petrarch's debts to the lyric tradition of troubadour poetry. He refined and perfected that tradition, in much the same way as the *Roman de la Rose* of Guillaume de Lorris had epitomized the more worldly (i.e. social) tradition of chivalrous love found in the medieval romances. As a literary model, congenial to the fifteenth-century Italian poets who transmitted him to France, he created the psychological love-story told in a series of short poems, he used the sonnet-form extensively though not exclusively, and he evolved a poetic style full of symbolism and allusion which might sometimes fall into affectation, but whose indirectness, like the indirectness of religious mysticism, was the only possible language for his theme. The sixteenth-century version of Petrarch was the sonnet sequence containing the praise of the beloved and the analysis of the lover's feelings towards her, from Du Bellay's *L'Olive* to Sidney's *Astrophel and Stella*.

The main entry-point of Petrarchism into France was Lyons, a city well placed geographically and culturally to receive the new influence. Through it, from Paris to Lombardy or Rome, passed soldiers, cardinals, diplomats, and scholars. It was an important centre of printing. It had its own lettered society, one of whose leaders was the poet Maurice Scève (*c.* 1501–*c.* 1563). An ardent admirer of Petrarch, Scève incurred much publicity together with some suspicion by discovering at Avignon what he claimed to be the tomb of Laura in a chapel belonging to the de Sade family. It is one of the ironies of literature that the real Laura may have belonged to the family which produced the eighteenth-century marquis de Sade, but it is highly improbable that the scattered bones found by Scève were hers.

In his work, however, Scève was a worthy Petrarchist. He wrote, in *Délie, object de plus haulte vertu* (1544), a long book of poems praising his mistress in verse of a difficult symbolism which well rewards the effort of following it. The form used is the *dizain*, a ten-line stanza on four rhymes modelled on the Italian *canzone*.

Had he used the sonnet, Scève might well have been recognized as a greater pioneer. His other works are *La Saulsaye, églogue de la vie solitaire* (1547), in which a fable of nymphs and shepherds is developed in the pastoral setting of the Saône valley, and *Microcosme* (1562), a philosophical-religious poem tracing the progress of man since the fall of Adam.

Délie, the ideal mistress, has been explained as an anagram of *l'Idée*. There is, however, a strong presumption that these poems were inspired by a real woman, the young poetess Pernette du Guillet (*c.* 1520–45), who was certainly Scève's literary disciple. Her *Rymes* (1545) show his influence on the playfully learned songs of passion which they contain, though something of the Greeks and of Marot has been seen in other poems of hers in the same book. A second poetess completes the Lyons group. Louise Labé (*c.* 1524–65) has been the subject of romantic legends which send her to war in male armour and also make her a lettered courtesan. She belonged in fact to the rich merchant class and no doubt rode a horse as well as most gentlewomen. The innuendoes of a zealous puritan seem to have created the rest. Her single volume of *Euvres* (1555) contains three elegies and twenty-four sonnets of frank and seemingly personal passion which have made her work representative of woman's longing for the unattainable lover – in this case a fully human figure, and perhaps the poet Olivier de Magny.

Lyons was on the periphery, while Paris, then as now, was crushingly central. The high tide of Renaissance poetry could only flow in there. The group which was known later as the Pléiade began to form when Ronsard turned at the age of eighteen from the life of a court page to become a student under the humanist teacher Jean Dorat. An illness which left him partially deaf was the probable cause of his change of direction. His early companions were Jean-Antoine de Baïf and Du Bellay. By 1548 the three had joined with several others to form a group of student-poets called *La Brigade*. These others, except perhaps Denisot, are now very obscure names. They quickly dropped out, to be replaced in the fifteen-fifties by disciples and sympathizers such as Pontus de Tyard and his cousin Des Autels – both from Lyons – Jodelle, remembered for his experiments in drama, La Péruse, a tragic dramatist and lyric poet who died young of plague, Jacques Peletier du Mans, a scholarly poet who wrote an *Art Poétique* (1555), and Rémy Belleau, the first Frenchman to translate Anacreon (1556). The definitive Pléiade consists traditionally of Ronsard, de Baïf, Du Bellay, Jodelle, de Tyard, Belleau, and Dorat, but this does not cover all the writers who belonged to the movement. Even the name Pléiade was used only allusively by Ronsard and not adopted formally in his time. The thing was in fact a movement and cannot be represented by an exact list of names.

The first acts of Ronsard's young group showed that they considered the old poetry as dead and had something much better to put in its place. They condemned the 'confectionery' of the *Rhétoriqueurs*, attacked the half-hearted Italianism of the court poet Mellin de Saint-Gelais, and impatiently brushed aside the school of Marot, which had dominated French verse until their day. (Later, Ronsard did Marot greater justice.) Their first manifesto was Du Bellay's *Deffence et illustration de la langue françoise* (1549), a somewhat confused essay arguing that the way to enrich French literature was through the study and imitation of Greek and Latin writers. As an ardent classical student, Du Bellay took almost for granted the actual (though not the fundamental) inferiority of French, but believed that it could be raised by an assimilation of foreign thought and by a deliberate cultivation of the language as a means of expression. In the same year he published his sonnet-sequence, *L'Olive*. Ronsard followed in 1550 with his first book of *Odes*, whose preface developed in more technical detail the ideas of Du Bellay. Their triumph was rapid, for they filled what was almost a poetic vacuum and nearly every young writer was with them. The main achievements of the Pléiade, as they were consolidated during the next twenty years, were to bring French poetry more fully abreast with contemporary humanistic scholarship, to link it more directly with Greek and Latin poetry than had been done before – though without compromising its independence – to endow it with the nobler tones necessary to express great national and religious themes, and above all to create a true personal lyricism. Until then (apart from the Lyons poets) the French lyric had either resembled a song (assimilating the poet to the professional singer) or it had been mixed with humour, as in Villon and Marot (the poet as jester). Now the poet was a person who first experienced feeling on exactly the same uncalculated plane as other men, before rising above them by his greater insight and artistry.

In the technical field, the Pléiade poets obliterated for the time being such medieval forms as the *rondeau* and the *ballade*. They acclimatized the sonnet, which henceforth appeared indispensable, as well as practising other less stylized forms like the ode. They established the alexandrine, the twelve-syllable line which the Middle Ages had almost ignored, but which after Ronsard came to be recognized as the chief instrument in the French poet's armoury – as natural and native a metre as blank verse has become in English. Some of their experiments proved less lasting, while others, like their attempt to found a native tragedy, needed a long time to mature.

Most of these innovations owed their lasting success to Pierre de Ronsard (1524 or 1525-85), who was quickly recognized as the leading poet of his generation. He was born in Vendôme of a minor noble family and was intended for a career of arms and diplomacy. His early experience at court served him well when, after the break which he made to equip himself as a poet, he returned to satisfy his ambitions through literature. He became the favourite poet of two kings, was richly endowed with abbeys and benefices, and only in the reign of Henri III, when literary fashions began to change, did he feel less welcome at court. His production was immense, and of great technical variety, since he was continually experimenting. While his early odes might perhaps be classed as exercises in the manner of Horace and Pindar rather than of Anacreon, many have the delightfully free-and-easy quality of successful transplantations. With the *Amours de Cassandre* (1552-3), a book of sonnets and other short poems addressed to a mistress adored from a certain distance, he entered his true domain of delicately sensual love-poetry and wrote such memorable poems as *Mignonne, allons voir si la rose . . .*

His second *Amours* (1555-6) were inscribed to Marie, a country girl of his native province. The setting is pastoral (the banks of the Loire), the feeling freer, relieved now from the Petrarchan restraint which sometimes marks the Cassandre collection. Over twenty years later a group of lovely sonnets on the death of Marie were added to the second *Amours*, so pointing with a virtuoso's melancholy the Renaissance moral: 'The rose does not last; love while you may.' But the best of this kind of verse is in the *Sonnets pour Hélène* (1578), written by an ageing Ronsard for a famous court beauty, Hélène de Surgères. His grave passion perfectly suits the human and social circumstances. Whether the by now arthritic poet laureate really intended to offer the young maid-of-honour more than his friendship and his homage is unimportant. The clearest product of their connection was a foreseen literary immortality for both:

> Quand vous serez bien vieille, au soir, à la chandelle,
> Assise auprès du feu, dévidant et filant,
> Direz, chantant mes vers, en vous émerveillant:
> 'Ronsard me célébrait du temps que j'étais belle.'

It would be pointless to pursue Ronsard biographically through his loves for Cassandre, Marie, Hélène, Astrée, Genèvre, Sinope, and others hinted at in occasional verses. Much of this is literature, sharpened however by real feeling, not so much for any one person (to attribute that to Ronsard the poet would be an anachronism) as for the sentimental pains of life and its sensual and cultural pleasures:

> Soit que m'amie ait nom ou Cassandre ou Marie,
> Neuf fois je m'en vais boire aux lettres de son nom.

For the Renaissance poet these pains and pleasures are one and indivisible, as is the man who experiences them. But when he reflects on human destiny, his first reaction is to exclaim that life is too short to enjoy all the possibilities which the new age has suddenly shown him. The effect of the collapse of medieval religion was to offer paradise here and now, but without the immortality necessary to enjoy it. Some of the sixteenth-century melancholy was of course inherited from the Latin poets, but at the same time life was literally short in the general expectation. The contrast between the little that was physically possible and the much that humanism promised was the underlying anguish of the age. Ronsard renders it in his own idiom, writing in terms of drooping flowers and pretty girls who must grow old and die. Such symbols may well conceal the fundamental dilemma from the modern reader, conditioned as he is by science and insurance to expect a long stretch of pensionable years.

For *Hélène* and for most of the poems to Marie, Ronsard had used the alexandrine. At the same time he had been using it, rhymed in couplets in the way that most poets after him would adopt, for a different kind of verse. In the *Hymnes* (1555–6) and the *Discours* (1560–70) he aimed at expressing national themes. He writes as a Prince of Poets to princes (never, like Marot, with the familiarity of the court buffoon), comments on great events, engages in debate with the Protestants, deplores the fratricidal wars of religion. Since, however, he is not a religious poet, his main appeal is to patriotism and national unity. He rises unexpectedly often to the high political note and, like Milton, can forget Corydon and Amaryllis to write verses of impressive dignity.

His ambition – the same that has obsessed French poet after French poet from the Renaissance until today – was to write a modern epic, in his case the epic of the French monarchy founded by an invented Francus of Troy, as an invented Brutus of Troy had founded the English monarchy in the *roman* of the twelfth-century Norman, Robert Wace. But though Vergil could bring off Aeneas for the Roman emperors, no one has succeeded in imitating him. The historical and literary moments have been as much at fault as the poets. To write *La Franciade* (1572), Ronsard misguidedly dropped the alexandrine and used ten-syllable lines. The poem in any case fell flat and was abandoned after the first four books.

Ronsard's other work consists of occasional poems such as court masques and *bergeries*, of familiar poems describing his everyday life, and of much easy verse in praise of nature, fruits, and flowers. He remains a universal poet, sometimes obscure for those who cannot follow his classical allusions but never complicated in his reactions and feelings. In scope and achievement he is among the great European poets. Disowned by Malherbe's generation, he suffered the unusual fate of being virtually forgotten for two hundred and fifty years, until the Romantics rediscovered him. Though he cannot be forgotten a second time, today he is again somewhat neglected. Narrower poets like Scève, whose work contains a richer mine of psychological symbolism, appeal more strongly to the modern sensibility.

The second great poet of the Pléiade was Joachim Du Bellay (1522–60), Ronsard's companion at the Collège de Coqueret. He became an accomplished Latinist and was to publish a book of Latin verses (*Poemata*, 1558). This may provide one clue to the disillusion which characterizes his best work. Four years after writing the manifesto of *La Deffence et illustration* he went to Rome in the suite of his kinsman, Cardinal Jean Du Bellay – the same cardinal whom Rabelais had accompanied on earlier misssions. Du Bellay's Roman years, though they gave him cultural maturity, seem to have been a bitter personal disappointment to him. The great Rome of antiquity, he found, was not only in ruins, it was infested by Italians. He did not get on well with them, nor was he a good enough courtier to please his uncle the Cardinal.He became homesick, and during his four years' exile longed for the quiet life which, with less ambition, he might have led in his native Anjou. Such at least are the conclusions which emerge from his two finest books of sonnets, *Les Regrets* and *Les Antiquités de Rome* (both 1558). In them he was, of course, developing a literary theme, as is shown by the fact that his friend Olivier de Magny (1529–61), who was in Rome at the same time and worked with him, produced a similar book of sonnets, *Les Soupirs*. But, whatever the models, the mood of Du Bellay was no invention. He returned to France in 1557, tried unsuccessfully to pick up the threads in Paris, and died suddenly on New Year's Day, 1560.

Du Bellay was the first great master of the sonnet in France. His early sonnet-sequence, *L'Olive* (1549–50), was the first of its kind in a non-Italian language and followed the Petrarchan plan of singing the praises of his mistress. The verse is more varied and more fluent than the sonnets in Ronsard's *Amours de Cassandre*. In *Les Regrets* and *Les Antiquités* (which Edmund Spenser, acknowledging his debt to Du Bellay, translated in *The Complaints*) the verse is sharper and sometimes harsher, though always obedient to Du Bellay and his sonnet-form. He holds out his hands and iron-beaked phrases, squawking with poetry, fly into them. When he binds them into his verse, the result is not always neat. It is

terrific, like an eagle in a sack. His vision of Ancient Rome linked
to his sense of personal loneliness make some of his lines ring with
a note of defiant desolation:

> Telle que dans son char la Bérécynthienne,
> Couronnée de tours, et joyeuse d'avoir
> Enfanté tant de dieux, telle se faisait voir,
> En ses jours plus heureux, cette ville ancienne.

His nostalgia, though less broadly based than Ronsard's,
appears deeper because more personal. It is the common lot to
grow old, to lose one's looks and one's appetites. But it is a condition of Du Bellay's exile from home and from his fellow-men
that he feels it as a particular case. A further condition is that he
blames himself and seeks the cause of an isolation due to both
circumstance and temperament in some mistake of his own. Inevitably he is a Platonist – the soul exiled from heaven – though
while he is in Rome the Loire province of his youth usually
appears heaven enough.

To express this melancholy, each time reducible to a short re-
curring mood crystallized on a single concept, the sonnet is the
perfect instrument. (The French sonnet is based on the Italian and
rhymes *abba abba* followed by some such combination as *ccdeed*.
It does not end with the snap imparted by the final couplet of the
Shakespearian sonnet.) Du Bellay also used the form to render the
irony and satire which often went with his disillusionment. He
wrote besides other short poems of great metrical lightness, some
on pastoral subjects. They appeared in the *Odes* (1549), the *Divers
Poèmes* (1552), and the *Jeux rustiques* (1558).

The other poets of the Pléiade group and generation have already been listed. While they have their individual excellences and
collectively make up the greatest poetic 'school' in France since
the troubadours, they hardly extend the range of poetry in directions not covered by Ronsard and Du Bellay. The same tradition
was continued more artificially by Philippe Desportes (1547–1606),
who was Ronsard's successor as the official court poet. His earlier
work shows the influence of Ariosto and of the later Italian
Petrarchists, as Bembo. In his forties he began to compose religious
verse and made, after Marot and de Bèze, a new verse rendering of

the Psalms. Desportes was a competent and pleasant poet who followed literary fashion a little too mechanically.

Religious poetry, in an age when religion could satisfy all the idealistic and combative instincts, tended in France to be extra-verted. Songs of praise and vengeance, often linked to the noble commonplace of spiritual life springing from physical death, may obscure the lack of great mystical poets in this period. They will remain lacking until Hugo, a baffling and perhaps not authentic case. What religious mysticism there was in the sixteenth century cannot be easily separated from Platonism. As the two had been mingled in Marguerite d'Angoulême, so they meet in Jean de Sponde (1557–95), in whose verse an English reader may some-times detect a foretaste of Donne. There is a different symbolism, of great and curious beauty, in the five hundred sonnets which make up the *Théorèmes spirituels* of Jean de La Ceppède (*c.* 1550–1622), a southern Frenchman and incidentally a relative of St Teresa of Ávila. One may quote as an example his sonnet in which the stag, plunging into a river to escape the hunters, is compared to Christ swimming the river of death to escape the Jews, then clambering out on the 'immortal shore'.

Another memorable collection of sonnets was *Le Mépris de la vie et consolation contre la mort* (1594) of Jean-Baptiste Chassignet (*c.* 1570–*c.* 1635). They may be called religious in that all 434 of these sonnets harp on the conventional theme of the inevitability of death, with the warning, stated or implied, that this physical world is vanity and the soul's true home is elsewhere, in a heaven which appears both Christian and Platonic. But the strength of Chassignet is less in his theme than in the bold and ingenious imagery which he uses to express it.

Chassignet wrote his *momento mori* poems young and lived on for another forty years. La Ceppède's *Théorèmes spirituels* were published in two books in 1613–21, by which time the two most powerful religious poets of the century seemed, at least temporarily, to be out of date. Guillaume de Salluste Du Bartas (1544–90) was a militant Protestant steeped in the narrative and imagery of the Bible. He read it both as proof of the workings of God's providence and as a historical prelude to his own times. He was a descriptive-didactic poet, recounting and preaching with equal energy and basing his religious convictions on a foundation of scientific knowledge (as, that the earth is the centre of the physical universe) which was soon to appear grotesque. Du Bartas stands as a permanent warning to those well-intentioned persons who seek to make science a handmaid to religion in any literal way. He was wedded to the long poem in which his Gascon garrulity could have free play, as his first works (*Uranie*, *Le Triomphe de la foi*, and *Judith*) show .His masterpiece was the two *Semaines*, of which only the first was finished (1578). This ambitious poem recounts the seven days of the Creation, beginning with the stars and planets and passing on to the animals and man. The second *Semaine* was to continue the story through biblical times with Eden at the outset. Except in name, it was no longer a 'week', for each 'day' was divided into four cantos with different subjects, giving twenty-eight in all. Half that number were actually written. The *Semaines* have an evident affinity with the medieval Mystery play, or rather cycle of plays, which treated the same theme, from the Creation to the Passion, on a lavish scale. Du Bartas's didacticism is medieval too, though the knowledge and philosophy he displays belong to the Renaissance. If Rabelais had set out to write a Mystery, then had been told that it could be printed but not performed, something similar might have resulted. Du Bartas's verbal exuberance, his uncouth linguistic inventions in a serious work have made it difficult for French critics to concede him the high place which he seems to deserve. They cannot help smiling at onomatopoeic words like *sou-soufflant* or *bou-bouillonnant* which inevitably suggest the burlesque poetry of the next century. He coined other words which were not taken up (as did Ronsard, but less outrageously), and nothing can be more damaging to a writer's reputation. 'Where French cannot travel, let Gascon go,' Montaigne once remarked, and there is a good parallel in English and Irish. But the Gascon Du Bartas has not carried the French with him. For them he remains an impressive curiosity. He has done better abroad. Since Baudelaire admired the verse of Poe, it would be only reciprocal (though it is not proved) that Milton should have admired Du Bartas and borrowed some tips from him.

The second great religious poet, Agrippa d'Aubigné (1551–1630), has a first-hand sincerity which dispels any suspicion of quaintness. His father was a Protestant gentleman from Pons, south of La Rochelle. Riding with him through Amboise at the age of nine, the young d'Aubigné was shown the newly-decapitated heads of their friends exposed there as a warning after an abortive Huguenot plot, and was made to swear there and then that he would dedicate his life to avenging them. He became a soldier in merciless campaigns which pitted him against hard-bitten veterans like Monluc, was wounded, he says, twelve times, and for twenty years was the companion and counsellor of Henry of Navarre. Henry's conversion to Catholicism which secured him on the throne and brought peace to France disgusted the rigid-principled d'Aubigné. He forgave his master in time, but in the reign of Louis XIII he emigrated to Geneva, where he was received with honour, helped to fortify the town, and ended his days. His son Constant was an unprincipled scoundrel whose daughter Françoise married, first, the poet Scarron, then Louis XIV, by whom she was created marquise de Maintenon. The collector of ironies will appreciate the probability that she was partly responsible for the revocation of the Edict of Nantes, an act which put an end to ninety years' toleration of the Protestants in France.

D'Aubigné was not exclusively a soldier. He received a classical education at various universities and was familiar with the courts of France and Navarre. His first verses, published long after his death as *Le Printemps du Sieur d'Aubigné*, were love-sonnets begun in 1570 in emulation of Ronsard, and inspired by Diane Salviati, the niece of Ronsard's Cassandre. Seriously wounded in 1577, d'Aubigné turned from such trifles to begin his great ideological poem, *Les Tragiques*. He worked on it for many years, publishing it only in 1616. *Les Tragiques* is the fighting epic of French Protestantism, the long cry of indignation of an unconquerable minority comparable in many passages to the voices of the Hebrew prophets, which d'Aubigné consciously echoed. It is divided into seven books: *Misères*, describing the lamentable condition of France during the civil wars; *Princes*, a bitter satire on the Valois kings and their favourites; *La Chambre dorée*, an allegory of the corrupt judges of the Parlement de Paris; *Les Feux*, describing the sufferings of the Protestant martyrs; *Les Fers*, an account of the wars of religion, with a tremendous evocation of the St Bartholomew's Day massacre; *Les Vengeances*, dealing with God's various punishments of the unjust, beginning with Cain; and *Jugement*, an apocalyptic vision of Judgement Day in heaven.

In this poem, allegory, satire, invective, and rhetoric are mingled. The tone and symbolism are precisely those of Milton's lines from *Lycidas*, which might easily have been translated from d'Aubigné:

> The hungry sheep look up, and are not fed,
> But swoln with wind and the rank mist they draw
> Rot inwardly, and foul contagion spread;
> Besides what the grim wolf with privy paw
> Daily devours apace, and nothing said.

In prose, d'Aubigné wrote a number of political pamphlets, ranging in tone from the solemn to the comic. Geneva was scandalized by some of the Rabelaisian anecdotes in *Les Aventures du baron de Faeneste*. Towards the end of his life he wrote his autobiography in the third person as an example for his children, entitling it *Sa vie à ses enfants*. This book, not always free of self-glorification, is as revealing of personal character as are the *Essais* of his contemporary, Montaigne. His greatest prose work is the *Histoire universelle*, which recounts the Protestant struggle in Europe from 1553, the birth-date of Henri IV, until the reign of Louis XIII. Mainly composed between 1600 and 1612, it combines personal experiences with impersonal accounts of events based on information gathered in an unpartisan spirit. The relationship between d'Aubigné and Henri IV reminds one of Joinville's relationship to Louis IX, while his autobiographical treatment of history strengthens the resemblance.

By the date when d'Aubigné's work was published, a new conception of poetry had begun to grow up. It owed much to François de Malherbe (1555–1628), whose influence, like some of his verse, stood for discipline and dignity at the outset of a century which, from one point of view, led up to the classical doctrine of Boileau. Malherbe was fifty years old before he obtained full recognition at the court of Henri IV and there was something of the spirit of vengeance in his condemnation of his predecessor, Desportes. As for the dead Ronsard, after covering half his printed poems with corrections, Malherbe's patience gave out. He took his pen and deleted all the remainder ... These were the crotchets of a newly-arrived dictator intent on forgetting his origins, for Malherbe's early verses had been as fanciful as anything written by Desportes or Ronsard and when, towards 1600, he struck his characteristic manner in the official ode, he invented nothing that had not been established by Ronsard in his *Hymnes* and *Discours* forty years earlier. This type of noble, impersonal poetry was also being written on the eve of Malherbe's reign by Jean Bertaut (1552–1611) and Jacques Davy Du Perron (1556–1618), both of whom attained high ecclesiastical position, the latter becoming a cardinal. Malherbe's odes, addressed either to friends, like his much-anthologized *Consolation à Du Périer*, or to his royal patrons on national occasions, mark the perfection of formal poetry rather than its beginnings. So do his religious poems based on the Psalms. This verse is stiffly rhetorical, excluding warmth and familiarity, which would be out of place in the atmosphere which it creates. The rhythm moves with a slow and measured pace. The metaphors are lofty and general, never descending into detail. In this monumental way Malherbe, writing of the death of kings, treats the theme of *Golden lads and girls all must, As chimney-sweepers come to dust*:

> Ont-ils rendu l'esprit, ce n'est plus que poussière
> Que cette majesté si pompeuse et si fière
> Dont l'éclat orgueilleux étonna l'univers;
> Et dans ces grands tombeaux où leurs âmes hautaines
> Font encore les vaines,
> Ils sont mangés des vers.

Malherbe is remembered as much for his teaching as for his verse, but he published no comprehensive work on literary theory and depends much on sayings reported by his followers, such as Racan in his *Mémoires pour la vie de Malherbe* (1672). He insisted first on the use of pure French, rejecting importations from Greek and Italian, the kind of learned and compound words invented by the Pléiade or Du Bartas, and 'trivial' terms belonging to the

spoken tongue. These were linguistic recommendations which
showed that literature was beginning to grow conscious of its social
standing. As for the form of poetry, Malherbe advocated an alexandrine scanning regularly with a break in the middle (the caesura)
and a slight sense-pause at the end of the line. There should be no
rejets, or overflowings of the phrase from one line to the next. The
rhyme, on which the voice was thus encouraged to dwell, should
be a full rhyme (*univers* and *vers* would be better than *fers* and *vers*)
and various inadmissible rhymes and combinations of vowel-sounds
which appeared ugly were banned by either Malherbe or his disciples. These 'classical' rules, observed on the whole by minor
rather than major poets, now belong to the museum of French
prosody. They amounted historically to a tightening and tidying-
up of the alexandrine, as part of a general movement towards
uniformity and proportion.

But it was not an exclusive movement. The development of
literature towards what, for convenience, may be called its classical
stage, was opposed or sometimes diverted by tendencies which
most historians of French literature now group as 'baroque'. The
wisdom of applying to poetry a word used to classify other arts is
in any case doubtful; here it is positively confusing. As applied to
specific styles in post-Renaissance painting, sculpture, and architecture, baroque suggests the curved or contorted line coupled with
a certain opulent fantasy in the execution. Theoretically, baroque
is the reverse of the stable and centralized; it has been taken to
consist in the mobile, the extravagant, the intricate, or the ornate.
Philosophically, it renders the anguish of men living among changing and uncertain values. It has been found in d'Aubigné, Sponde,
the early Malherbe, Saint-Amant, Scarron, Corneille, and could no
doubt be detected in many later poets. But long before that point
was reached, its inadequacy to suggest the texture and stuff of verse
would become clear. Even limited to a period of perhaps eighty
years running from about 1580, it blurs essential distinctions
between poets more than it illuminates their resemblances. The
fact is that, just as in architecture and the plastic arts there was no
native French baroque, so baroque poetry hardly has a meaning
outside Germany, Italy, and Spain. The term may perhaps be
applied to work by Marino and Góngora. But no French poet

resembles either of these. What is found in the French poets with non-classical tendencies is the sense of anguish (in religious verse), fantasy – sometimes of a humorous kind – and often a curious (for the classics, a perverse) juxtaposition of incongruous ideas and an exploration of the detail of imagery which for Malherbe and Boileau was the mark of a puerile mind. The baroque tendency appeared in snatches in many French poets, not excluding the most classical, but it nowhere came to full fruition. Instead, it split, giving on the one hand the humorous exaggeration of burlesque, on the other the mannered sentiment of *précieux* poets, executed in minor verse.

Poets who were in conscious disagreement with Malherbe's theories were Régnier and Théophile de Viau. Mathurin Régnier (1573–1613) was a satirist not unlike Marot in temperament; his treatment of the foibles of humanity announces Molière and Boileau. The satire had already been roughed out as a French poetic genre by Jean Vauquelin de La Fresnaye (c. 1535–1606), a writer within the orbit of the Pléiade. Régnier's more talented work may be said to have established it. He had a roving mind and pen, and with Juvenal as one of his distant models, followed his own whims in his choice of subjects. Literature – with humorous reflections on the way poets live – and social types and manners are his chief targets. He has a philosophic bent and prefers the general to the personal. His best known satire is *Macette*, the portrait of an old *fille de joie* turned outwardly pious, but still practising slyly as a go-between. Her advice to one of her protégées recalls Villon's *Belle Heaulmière*, less the sting of mortality:

> Prenez à toutes mains, ma fille, et vous souvienne
> Que le gain a bon goût, de quelque endroit qu'il vienne.
> Estimez vos amants selon le revenu:
> Qui donnera le plus, qu'il soit le mieux venu.

The first thirteen of Régnier's satires were published between 1608 and 1613, others posthumously.

Théophile de Viau (1590–1626) was sentenced to be burnt at the stake for the 'impieties, blasphemies, and abominations' found in a work which he denied having written. Though the sentence was remitted, the two years which he spent in prison while the interrogation and trial were in progress led to his death soon after his release. He was a Bohemian writer dependent on various patrons, wrote an early tragedy, *Pyrame et Thisbé* (1623), was accused of atheism, and was in any case a *libertin* by temperament. His verse which matters consists of short personal poems filled with a sometimes sensuous feeling for nature more directly felt and expressed than in conventional pastoral. His language is simple and almost free of the urban affectations which were beginning to find favour in the salons. Though not an exciting poet, he commands attention for his insistence on 'natural' poetry. Its writing, he observes in his *Élégie à une dame*, should be a pleasure, not a laborious science. Whereas the followers of Malherbe 'go scratching at French until they tear it to pieces', for his part:

> La règle me déplaît, j'écris confusément:
> Jamais un bon esprit ne fait rien qu'aisément.

His friend Antoine-Girard de Saint-Amant (1594–1661) was another free-living poet – a traveller, soldier, musician, and notable drinker. Heartiness and melancholy often appear together in his work. An early poem, *Les Visions*, concerned with ghosts and sorcery, promised a very interesting writer. But Saint-Amant preferred to devote his powers of verbal invention to the humorous extravagance of *Le Passage de Gibraltar* (on a sea voyage), *Albion* (against the sourly puritanical English), and *Rome ridicule* (1643). The last is a kind of Saturnalia in which Ancient Rome becomes merely a site for ludicrously gross episodes. Far from approaching the Eternal City with the reverence of a Du Bellay, or – to draw an American parallel – in the sensitive spirit of a Henry James, Saint-Amant jeers at it with all the exuberance of a coarser Mark Twain. In the years since the Pléiade some French poets at least had acquired new confidence in their native wit, though the results did not always justify it.

Burlesque poetry, born of the same impulse which had inspired earlier prose parodies such as Sorel's *Berger extravagant*, was popular in France between about 1645 and 1660. Its favourite targets were the great Latin poets, as in the most notable of the verse parodies, Scarron's mock *Aeneid* or *Virgile travesti* (1648–59). Others who practised the diversion were d'Assouci (burlesquely called 'The Emperor of Burlesque') in *Le Jugement de Pâris en vers burlesques* (1648), and *Ovide en belle humeur* (1650), Furetière in *Les Amours d'Énée et de Didon* (1649), the Perrault brothers in *Les Murs de Troie* (1653), and Georges de Brébeuf in *Lucain travesti* (1656). Such works sprang from the impatience of essentially literal minds with authors whose qualities they were unable to appreciate, but which had been held up since Renaissance times as models. Their attitude was somewhat schoolboyish, as often was their humour. The technique was to take Achilles and Hector and to show them talking slang, or tripping over their shields. Anachronisms – unintentional in the seriously-meant romances – were here cultivated for the fun of it. It was a process of reducing the over-remote to the over-familiar, not near enough the mark to be good literary parody, but belonging to the dreary history of pedantic humour. Burlesque only touches the history of poetry as a sign of revolt against the solemnity of Malherbe and the ascendancy of the Greeks and Latins – also as a sign that a certain liveliness of style remained current even in this debased form. The loquacity of a Du Bartas was hardly to blossom again in serious poetry until Hugo. Seventeenth-century burlesque was one of the preservative mediums: hence the impression of frozen exuberance which it makes on the modern reader.

The society of the salons encouraged a contrasting type of poetry, written in such forms as the madrigal, the *villanelle*, the sonnet, and the revived *rondeau* and *ballade*, as well as the longer elegy and *épître*. The masters of this elegant society-verse were Vincent Voiture (1598–1648), a favourite of the Hôtel de Rambouillet; Jean-François Sarasin (*c.* 1610–54); Jean Regnault de Segrais (*Athis*, 1653, and *Poésies diverses*, 1658); Isaac de Benserade (1613–91), who wrote verses for Lully's ballets; and Gilles Ménage (1613–92), who was also a philologist and Mme de Sévigné's tutor. Our perspective has changed since Molière wrote *Le Misanthrope*. Unlike Alceste, we would hardly blame these poets for being insufficiently blunt or sincere. We would wish them to have had a stronger faith in their skill and perhaps in their Italian forerunners and to have written verse ingenious to the point of obscurity. As it is, their ingenuity usually stops short at prettiness.

Slightly earlier, pleasant pastoral verse smacking less of the salon was written by Honorat de Beuil de Racan (1589–1670) who, with François Maynard (1582–1646), is considered the chief of Malherbe's disciples. The poetry of Tristan L'Hermite (1601–55), better known as a dramatist, lies half-way between the *préciosité* of the salons and a delicate expression of personal feeling.

Meanwhile the heritage of Malherbe – his feeling for the dignity of language – had passed into the plays of Corneille and his chief contemporaries. This is also true of Corneille's religious poetry (*L'Imitation de Jésus-Christ*, 1651; *L'Office de la Sainte Vierge*, 1670), though here Corneille was clearly the suppler and greater poet. In fact, the dramatists wrote the most consistently good verse of a century which almost lost the art of subjective poetry and in which the individual thought so little of himself that he dare hardly appear without clowning or simpering. The sense of the incongruous, so overworked by the burlesque school, is rendered in Molière's dramatic verse with a feeling for proportion which trebles its effect, while Racine's verse is both as regular as Malherbe would have desired yet full of controlled imagination.

Of the non-dramatic poets, certainly the most interesting was Jean de la Fontaine. Born in 1621 and dying in 1695, he belonged to the libertine tradition. He was, however, a libertine in his love of cultivated pleasures and his passive escape from obligations, not by any active rebellion. He should have followed his father as a forestry official in Champagne, but instead he gradually severed his local connections, including that formed by his marriage, to drift in apparent idleness through Parisian and aristocratic society. The various patrons who maintained him were all people of wit and discrimination, from the Chancellor Fouquet to Mme de La Sablière, the cultured wife of a financier. For the first he composed his two early mythological poems, *Adonis* and *Le Songe de Vaux*, as well as several shorter elegies. Another patron suggested the subject of his didactic poem, *Le Quinquina* (1682), the fashionable remedy which smart people were just then drinking by the bottleful. Between the two he wrote his most considerable prose work, *Les Amours de Psyché et de Cupidon* (1673), re-telling the Greek myth with a grace which the eighteenth-century writers of fairy-tales could not better, and a poem of religious edification, *La Captivité de Saint Malc* (1673). Late in life he tried his hand at opera libretti and produced *Astrée*, with the music of Colasse, in 1691. He also seems to have collaborated with the actor Champmeslé in a number of short comedies, but La Fontaine's share in these is not easy to decide.

Altogether, under an appearance of nonchalance, he was a thoroughly professional writer, whose main self-indulgence was his *Contes et nouvelles en vers*. Produced in four parts between 1665 and 1674, these stories, predominantly scabrous, needed some living down when, later, he was trying to conquer the solidity of an accepted writer. They undoubtedly delayed his election to the Académie française. The anecdotes they enshrine are very various, drawn from the kind of popular sources which once fed the *fabliaux*, from the *Cent Nouvelles nouvelles*, Boccaccio, Rabelais, or Marguerite d'Angoulême. La Fontaine makes some effort to tone down the honest coarseness of his originals to suit the more polished taste of the *Grand Siècle*. His slyness and his narrative gift found a more perfect outlet in the *Fables*, of which the first were published in 1668, the last (completing twelve books) in 1694, the year before his death. The immense success of these has rightly overshadowed the rest of his considerable production.

There is no need to go back to Marie de France's *Isopet* or to the *Roman de Renart* to find ancestors for the ever-popular verse fable, which La Fontaine merely renewed, taking his themes from the several prose collections of Aesopian fables published during his own century and from a book of Indian fables translated in 1644. After him, the verse fable became a common poetic exercise, practised during the next hundred years by Furetière, Aubert, Imbert, Florian, and other scarcely-remembered writers. If only La Fontaine is still read, it is because his manner of telling the fable has had a very wide appeal. He is (at his best) a worthy contemporary of Mme de Sévigné, La Rochefoucauld, La Bruyère, in the lightness and economy with which he can evoke an impression or relate an anecdote. He is concise, sober, and rapid and, within those limits, picturesque. He uses those composite adjectives admired in Homer, pompously, as in *l'oiseau porteur de Ganymède* (the eagle), neatly in *le chat grippe-fromage* or *Dame belette au long corsage* (the weasel). His talkative magpie is called Margot, also Caquet-bon-bec, which derives from French country speech rather than from literature. These animals live in their own world, and are nowhere caricatures of contemporary humans. Their separateness is emphasized by the comparison formally pointed out in the moral. This is not satire but neatly-ticketed philosophy. The ethics of La Fontaine's 'morals' are practical and often cynical – a traditional feature of the fable which has no particular bearing on La Fontaine's own position as a moralist. Far from spoiling the tale, the moral rounds it off. Children like it, because it tells them exactly where they stand. Grown-ups take it as a didactic seasoning to the simple enjoyment of the story. It is a fair comment on French classicism that its maturity produced, not Donne and Jonson, not Góngora and Calderón, but, after Racine, La Fontaine's *Fables* and Perrault's *Fairy Tales*.

The purest statement of classicism has been held to be contained in the writings of Nicolas Boileau (1636–1711), usually known as Despréaux to his contemporaries. His work has suffered in the past from being credited with a greater critical load than it can really bear. He was a plain man with a few clear principles, by stressing which he achieved a reputation which might well be envied by cleverer writers. A lawyer's son, he belonged to that same shrewd middle class which produced Molière, La Fontaine, La Bruyère and Racine. Though he qualified for the bar, his only serious profession, which a small private income enabled him to follow, was literature. The majority and best of his twelve *Satires* were published in 1666–8, having circulated previously in manuscript. They concerned contemporary literature more or less directly, with exceptions such as the *Satire sur l'homme*, of Jansenist inspiration, or *Les Embarras de Paris*, a comic description of the noises and inconveniences of the capital. A parallel series of twelve *Épîtres* ran from 1669 to 1698. These were occasional poems on public events, such as *Le Passage du Rhin* (1672), or more relaxed digressions on Boileau's personal life and opinions. His most sustained flight of humour and literary parody was *Le Lutrin* (1674), a mock-epic story of an ecclesiastical quarrel over the placing of a lectern which prolonged the burlesque tradition. In the same year he published

L'Art poétique, his ambitious attempt to define the principles – and indeed the rules – of poetry. All these works were written in well-aligned alexandrines and nearly all were previous to his appointment as Royal Historian to Louis XIV, jointly with his friend Racine. After 1677 he wrote little, but consolidated his critical doctrines in the prose *Réflexions sur Longin* (1694) and in prefaces to various editions of his works.

The case for Boileau the critic is that he insisted that the function of literature is to express the normal man's view of the normal world. Normality (as apparently in Molière) is equated with nature. Nature can be known through reason, which also teaches the artist how to render it. This doctrine condemns obscurity of style as a darkener of truth, pedantry as incompetence, and complication of fantasy as affectation.

The case against Boileau is longer because its separate heads are more numerous, though collectively not so much more impressive. He identified clarity with truth, symmetry with beauty, and craftsmanship with art. In his admiration for the Latins, he misunderstood the French national heritage, beginning with the Middle Ages (this was understandable at the date) but including the best poets of the sixteenth century. He had no feeling for the lyricism of either a Ronsard or a d'Aubigné. In his own age, he attacked literary fashions (such as *préciosité*) which were already out of date and writers who were already dead or of no contemporary importance. (True though this is in the main, it is almost impossible at this distance of time to see the literary scene as Boileau saw it. In finishing off the dying, he may well have thought that they still had life in them.) He proclaimed his admiration for Corneille, Molière, and Racine, but only after their reputations were established. On the other hand, he had no public praise for La Fontaine and when La Bruyère first showed him *Les Caractères* he did not realize his importance. The gravest charge against Boileau bears, however, on the dogmatism of the *Art poétique*, on his preference for the 'sublime' rather than the sensitive, and on the danger that, pushed to extremes, his doctrine of perfectionism severs literature from whole fields of human experience. It denies it both the means and the right to deal with them.

During the years of his ascendancy, Boileau was engaged, as the champion of antiquity, in 'The Quarrel of the Ancients and the Moderns', which brought to a head a fifty-year-old feeling of resentment against the Greeks and Latins. Charles Perrault opened the main phase of the dispute by reading his poem *Le Siècle de Louis le Grand* (1687) at a meeting of the French Academy. His motives were pride in the achievements of the age, a belief in progress, and a notion that literary qualities are related to the climate of the time – that there are no absolute standards of excellence. The dispute ended in an inconclusive reconciliation. In 1713, after Boileau's death, it was renewed by less illustrious champions on the occasion of a translation of the *Iliad* by Houdar de La Motte which, with its critical preface, offended the stricter Hellenists. This second phase is interesting for the light it throws on the standing of poetry at that date.

It would be fair to say that no poetry had been written in France since Racine's *Athalie* in 1691, if one expects from poetry some effective communication of feeling. This might be found in the epic, the ode, the hymn, and the satire and does not limit us to a narrow reliance on 'lyric' poetry, but it does suppose some trace of direct feeling beyond the writer's pleasure in his work as an aesthetic creation. Good though they are, La Fontaine's *Fables* are something other than poetry; so are Boileau's *Satires* – there is not enough hate in them. With such examples before it, it was natural, if wrong-headed, for the eighteenth century to ask: What can poetry express that prose cannot express better and more easily? Is it not a waste of time to count syllables and match rhymes, especially when the result must in some degree deform the original thought? The extreme case was put by Houdar de La Motte, who wrote: 'The aim of speech being to make oneself understood, it seems unreasonable to submit to constraints which often defeat that end,' and 'The art of poetry, like all other arts, is only an intellectual exercise which is learnt at the cost of neglecting something else.' The defenders of poetry, among whom was Voltaire, could point out the advantages of the poetic 'constraints' and also the charms of 'harmony', but their arguments were not entirely convincing and the example of the verse they wrote hardly supported them. Attention had become too narrowly concentrated on the mechanism of verse, for which the insistence of Boileau (and of

Malherbe before him) on the laborious acquisition of a technique was largely responsible. Both these poets had composed with difficulty and were therefore over-obsessed with the art of writing, by which they meant primarily the workmanship.

With such conceptions of the nature and functions of poetry, it is hardly surprising that the eighteenth century should have expressed its deeper emotions in prose. On the other hand, no poet appeared with a sufficient passion for aesthetic values to build up towards great poetry from that side. The verse of the eighteenth century can therefore be classified briefly without doing much injustice to the individuals who wrote it.

The chief vehicle of 'noble' poetry was the ode, reminiscent of Malherbe and of which Boileau had proposed a new model in his *Ode sur la prise de Namur*. He claimed that this sort of poem,

> Élevant jusqu'au ciel son vol ambitieux,
> Entretient dans ses vers commerce avec les dieux.

Of indeterminate length, but never very short, it could serve for patriotic, religious, or philosophic subjects, or be addressed to a friend on some special occasion. Its most skilful user was certainly Jean-Baptiste Rousseau (1671–1741), a cobbler's son who was driven from France at forty as the result of a literary feud and spent most of the remainder of his life abroad. His *Odes et Cantates* (1723) were first published in London. His most successful disciples were Jean-Jacques Lefranc, marquis de Pompignan (1709–84), the author of the *Odes chrétiennes et philosophiques* (1771), and Ponce-Denis Écouchard Lebrun (1729–1807), a writer also of *Élégies* and *Épîtres*. This sort of verse was written to be bound in tooled calf and placed in gentlemen's libraries, since it was too long to be inscribed on their tombs. Great moral elevation, impeccable sentiments, and a classical apparatus of nymphs and gods are its chief outward marks. It has, of course, its own language, as all poetry of character has, but it is not a language which contains many secrets worth learning. Inflated with abstract words and phantom images, it floats or rolls at roof-top level like a giant carnival balloon. Seeing it, we cannot exclaim, 'Take eloquence and twist its neck', for the eighteenth-century ode had no neck to twist. The

spectacle of its buoyant pomp is harmless and even exhilarating.
Who could take offence at such inspired conceit as J.-B. Rousseau's
in:

> Qu'aux accents de ma voix la terre se réveille.
> Rois, soyez attentifs: Peuples, ouvrez l'oreille.
> Que l'univers se taise, et m'écoute parler.
> Mes chants vont seconder les accords de ma lyre.
> L'esprit saint me pénètre, il m'échauffe et m'inspire
> Les grandes vérités que je vais révéler.

Of longer kinds of poetry, the epic had not ceased to be written
in the seventeenth century. While the burlesque epics had been
classical, the serious epics contemporary with them had been
Christian or national, as Saint-Amant's *Moïse sauvé* (1653),
Chapelain's *Pucelle d'Orléans* (1656), or Desmarets de Saint-
Sorlin's *Clovis* (1657). Voltaire continued this tradition in his first
considerable work, *La Henriade* (1724–8), which is the saga of
Henri IV and plods somewhat mechanically over the ground once
covered by d'Aubigné's muse of fire. After this, the old-style epic
disappeared and the didactic poem returned to favour. It was
philosophic, as in Voltaire's relatively short *Poème sur le désastre de
Lisbonne* (1756), containing his reflections on the great Lisbon
earthquake in which thirty thousand people died and whose effect
on thinkers might be compared to that of the Hiroshima atom
bomb. It was pastoral and chiefly descriptive in Saint-Lambert
(1716–1803), whose poem *Les Saisons* (1769) was suggested by the
Seasons of the English poet Thomson. Similarly, Jean-Antoine
Roucher (1745–94) described country life in the twelve cantos of
Les Mois (1779). Both of these were pleasing and even vigorous
examples of the revival of nature poetry, though still somewhat
artificial. Jacques Delille (1738–1813) published *Les Jardins* in 1782
and survived the Revolution to write *L'Homme des Champs* (1800),
L'Imagination (1806), *Les Trois Règnes de la Nature*, and other
works. He observes, paints, and comments with the felicity of a
mild water-colourist, his mediocrity rather cruelly underlined by
the contrast with his English contemporaries. More learned poems
on Happiness, Man, and the Thermometer were written by two
generations from Helvétius to Fontanes, but the century produced
nothing to equal the sublime absurdities of Du Bartas.

Some poetry was more modest in its subjects and forms. In the hands of Voltaire, Piron, and Écouchard Lebrun the epigram served as the small ammunition of endless literary vendettas. Good light poetry was written by Jean-Baptiste-Louis Gresset (1709–77), the author of *Le Lutrin vivant*, *Le Carême impromptu*, and *Vert-Vert*. The hero of the last is a parrot, brought up by nuns and then transferred to another convent. During the journey he picks up sailors' oaths, with the scandalous sequel that can be imagined. Gresset is also remembered for his comedy, *Le Méchant* (1747). Educated, like Vert-Vert, by ecclesiastics, he returned later to religion and repented sincerely of his literary sins.

As a writer of lightly sensual love-poetry, the Vicomte de Parny (1753–1814) stands out among the 'little poets' who in the previous century would have written madrigals. His verse, a Parisian eighteenth-century version of the Latin elegiac poets, has grace, wit, and occasional foreshadowings of the Romantic melancholy. The young Lamartine considered himself as Parny's disciple. Parny's verse has a colloquial flavour, more fluid than in La Fontaine, and in striking contrast to the over-blown odes of his contemporaries. His variation on the Pléiade theme of 'Gather ye rosebuds while ye may' is revealing in its restraint:

> Mais le Temps, du bout de son aile
> Touchera vos traits en passant;
> Dès demain vous serez moins belle,
> Et moi peut-être moins pressant.

Such verses were typical of the *Poésies érotiques* of 1778. After the Revolution, Parny published anti-religious poems, such as *La Guerre des dieux* (1799). This, like Voltaire's earlier *La Pucelle d'Orléans* (1755), was a vulgar descendant of the old burlesque epic, daring now to be grossly anti-Christian as well as anti-classical.

The most considerable poet of the eighteenth century was André Chénier (1762–94), who has also been regarded as a forerunner of Romanticism. Though brought up in France from early childhood, he was born in Constantinople and his mother was a highly-cultured woman whose family came from the Greek islands. Her influence and his own knowledge of Greek gave him a more direct feeling for the Hellenic world than any poet since Racine. It impregnates his earlier poems, the *Bucoliques* and some of the *Élégies*, in which his adolescent longings are projected into an Arcadian Hellas with its gods and heroes. In the fashion of his century he also wrote odes and planned several long didactic poems, of which *Hermès* and *L'Amérique* were the chief. Though only fragments were written, these were to have been enthusiastic surveys of modern knowledge, particularly scientific knowledge.

When the Revolution broke out, Chénier held an appointment in the French Embassy in London. He returned to France full of enthusiasm for the new régime, but was presently led to protest against its excesses. He was arrested during the Terror and executed after four months' imprisonment. While in the prison of Saint-Lazare, he wrote his most immediately striking poems, *Les Iambes*, which were smuggled out by his friends. They deal with the horror and pity of his own situation and contain indignant invective against the betrayers of the Revolution. Only two of Chénier's poems, of minor importance, were published in his lifetime, and a few others, separately, during the next twenty-five years. Not until 1819 did his work become at all generally known through an edition published by Henri de Latouche. It aroused great interest among the young Romantics, who thought they recognized a kindred spirit. There are close echoes of Chénier in the early verse of Lamartine and of Vigny, though still unresolved questions of dating make it uncertain whether he could actually have influenced the latter. Seventy years later, his influence appeared again in the *Trophées* of J.-M. de Heredia, who, indeed, published a new edition of Chénier's bucolic poems.

Chénier suggests Romanticism by the personal accent in his verse, expanding at times into self-pity. But this can be paralleled by other poets of his generation, while in prose there was, of course, the example of Rousseau. The *moi* of Chénier, audible at normal pitch in his early poems, becomes shriller in the shadow of the guillotine, but it cries in the language of an angry Fénelon, not of a Hugo or even a Musset. In the technical field, Chénier never thought of rejecting classical models. His imagery and allusions belong to the Ancient World, which, however, was for him a living enough thing to be blended into his sensibility. His metre is a

supple alexandrine, less stiff than in Boileau, and above all charged
with feeling. In the *Iambes*, he alternates it with the eight-syllable
line, to create an effect of 'skimming and dipping' which gave
French poetry a new rhythm:

> Comme un dernier rayon, comme un dernier zéphyre
> Animent la fin d'un beau jour,
> Au pied de l'échafaud j'essaye encor ma lyre.
> Peut-être est-ce bientôt mon tour.

While Chénier looks a pale and modest figure if placed beside
the great Romantics, in the eighteenth century on the verge of the
Revolution he retains his full stature. He has the elegiac note of
sadness tinged with sensuality, the enthusiasm inseparable from
foreboding which all the more sensitive young men of his generation must have felt. He had inherited a poetic idiom in which
elegance and rhetoric still counted for much and which, inadequate
though it may now seem to render the confusion and violence of
his own period, apparently satisfied him.

But for the break in French literature during the Revolution
and the First Empire, the problem of 'placing' Chénier on one side
or other of the divide would probably never have arisen. One does
not trouble about transitions between Cowper, Blake, Wordsworth, Coleridge, and Byron. In France, however, when a good
poet at last appears, to be followed by twenty-five years' silence
broken only by the indefatigable purring of Delille, questions begin
to be asked. Chénier, who happened – quite legitimately – to be
there at the time, is scrutinized minutely in the search for an answer.
He serves at least as a reminder of how much had been lost or
forgotten since the time of Ronsard: the fact that it is possible to
think of the Pléiade in reading him is perhaps the highest tribute
that he can be paid.

III

FROM THE ROMANTICS TO THE PRESENT DAY

CHAPTER 12

The Novel in the Nineteenth Century

WITH the nineteenth century a new period opened in French literature, but the break with the past was not so complete as it had been at the Renaissance. In spite of the political and social upheaval of the Revolution, followed by the Napoleonic régime and the short-lived restoration of the Bourbons, some of the chief trends of the eighteenth century continued across the divide. One was the emotionalism typified by Rousseau and especially his conception of the individual as the central figure in the scheme of things. Another, allied to this, was the rekindled interest in spiritual values which had appeared in unorthodox form in such eighteenth-century theosophist sects as the Martinists. These *illuminati*, claiming direct contact with the divine, were forerunners of a type of mysticism which became common among the Romantic writers and competed with orthodox Catholicism when this had acquired new dynamism as a social and literary force. The contrary tendencies – the rationalism of Voltaire, the materialism of the Encyclopaedists – were temporarily in eclipse, but they were to operate again after 1850 in new and strengthened forms.

Yet if the nineteenth century prolonged the eighteenth in certain important respects, it differed profoundly in others. By the end of the First Empire, the three-hundred-year-old tradition of the Renaissance was finally exhausted. That tradition may be called classicism without limiting it too narrowly to the interpretation put on it by the age of Boileau. That was only one – though a very brilliant – moment in the long period during which Frenchmen had looked back to the Greeks and Romans as their cultural ancestors. No doubt they had often misunderstood them, no doubt also they had sometimes rebelled against them, intentionally or not. But if there was one view to which the majority of Frenchmen, from Ronsard and Montaigne to Montesquieu and Chénier, would have subscribed, it was that the Ancient World could provide models for their world, whether in literature, in political institutions, or in human conduct. They believed the experience of the Athenians and the Romans to be still relevant to the human situation as they found it two thousand years later.

This general habit of thought, shaken but not displaced in the eighteenth century by the spread of scientific thinking, was transferred in the nineteenth and twentieth centuries to a minority – the classical scholar and the professional philosopher – who became specialists in one particular field of knowledge rather than interpreters of a central tradition. Highly educated people could now echo the words of Molière's uncultured but sensible character: 'Les anciens sont les anciens, mais nous sommes les gens de maintenant.'

This change was reflected in French literature, which quickly became open to modern European influences – German through such intermediaries as Mme de Staël, English (Ossian, Scott, Byron, a rediscovered Shakespeare, De Quincey), and, later, American (Poe, then Whitman) and Russian. Such new communications were characteristic of the Romantic Movement, which was international, leaving no culture untouched, but which originated principally in Germany and England.

Far-reaching social changes also came into play. The middle class, which had been increasing in power throughout the eighteenth century, so consolidated itself after the Revolution that no return of the aristocracy could seriously shake its position. The social structure had altered fundamentally and had given literature new patrons with new tastes. Besides this, the Industrial Revolution, particularly after 1830, created an urban proletariat whose influence on literature was twofold. As readers, they called into existence a mass of popular and lively fiction including the adventure and the crime novel. As subjects, they offered writers a whole new field for observation and comment. The mere description of their lives and environment was rich material for the realistic writer, while the problems of social reform which they raised preoccupied other kinds of novelists throughout the century.

Most of this would have been foreign to the classical tradition, which in France had developed canons of taste identifying it closely with the aristocratic sensibility. Nineteenth-century writers with classical or aristocratic temperaments – or both at once – are inclined to consider themselves as isolated (Stendhal, Mérimée,

Baudelaire, Leconte de Lisle, Barbey d'Aurevilly, Mallarmé) and in most cases to write consciously for a small élite. This is not merely a difference between the 'popular' and the 'literary' author, though that consideration may also enter in. Primarily, it is the difference between the man who feels in tune with his age and the man who does not.

In spite of the renewed importance of poetry, the novel became the most representative genre of the age, and has continued to be so until today. It was the form best suited to the new reading public, with whom it occupied a place comparable to that held in the Middle Ages by the *chansons de geste* and the verse romances. Enlarged in scope and raised in status, the nineteenth-century novel not only mirrored society but expressed much more comprehensively than before the general philosophy of the times. To a great extent the novelist took over the parts formerly played by the moralist and the essayist. He also came to look on his profession as an art and his interpretation of the age as something approaching a mission. There was now a theory of the novel, whereas earlier there had only been theories of poetry and of drama. As the medium of expression of Stendhal, Balzac, Flaubert, Zola, and a score of somewhat lesser men, it amply justified its new place in the literary hierarchy.

It was not, however, until 1830 that the greater novelists began to appear. Before that, the chief innovation had been the short biographical or 'confessional' novel, which could take as many tones as there were individual writers. In the *Obermann* (1804) of Senancour, in the *Atala* (1801) and *René* (1802) of Chateaubriand, the Romantic hero, doomed to unhappiness by temperament or circumstances, is already taking shape. *Obermann* is essentially its author's sentimental and spiritual diary, told in letters. The two others were illustrative tales attached to Chateaubriand's ambitious defence of religion, *Le Génie du Christianisme. Atala*, the story of an Indian girl who commits suicide rather than break her vows of chastity, exploits to the full the grandeur of American scenery and the charm of half-savage customs. *René* is no more than a short story, providing, after Goethe's *Werther*, the classic illustration of Blake's remark: 'If any could desire what he is incapable of possessing, despair must be his eternal lot.' The contrary condition, with its very different overtones, was the motif of Benjamin Constant's *Adolphe*, a short but major work transparently based on its author's life.

Constant (1767–1830) was a cultured and travelled man of good family, born at Lausanne but later a naturalized Frenchman. After the restoration of the Bourbons he rose to political prominence as a leader of the liberal opposition and published important studies on religion and politics. His more personal writings were *Le Cahier rouge*, a cynical account of his youth, the *Journal intime*, which continues his experiences into middle life, and *Adolphe*, suggested by his long liaison with Mme de Staël, a possessive woman whose domination he came to resent. His hero is a young man who makes love, as a sentimental experiment, with an older woman from whom he wins a passionate response. He grows tired of her while pitying her, and is persuaded by a family friend to break free for practical reasons. She dies and Adolphe finds that he is left with an empty life before him. This story, written with great psychological penetration and in a style approaching dryness when compared with Chateaubriand's lyrical prose, is a curious blend of the eighteenth-century and nineteenth-century sensibilities. The hero appears to behave deliberately and cynically, while being aware of the necessity of a fuller emotional response. But he cannot contrive it. He plots intellectually for possession which, once attained, he is unable to enjoy. Neither does the success of the mere intrigue reward him, as it might reward a character of Choderlos de Laclos. His tragedy is that he realizes his emotional impotence and suffers from it – as do those with whom he comes in contact – but he has no remedy. One is tempted to think that such a book could only have been written at that particular date. As a terribly lucid analysis of the mechanism of passions recognized and understood, but not felt, it stands unrivalled. Probably in 1811, Constant began a second novel, *Cécile*, based on his relationship with Charlotte von Hardenberg, who became his wife. It was an unfinished and unsatisfactory work, which lay undiscovered until 1951, when it was unearthed and published as a curiosity.

Adolphe, written in 1807 and published in 1816, thus remained alone in its period. The main trend then, or soon after, was for stories of Gothic horror and historical stories inspired by such English writers as Anne Radcliffe and Scott. But Henri Beyle, in literature Stendhal (1783–1842), was already working through his curious career and preparing his unsentimental observations on the psychology of love, published as *De l'amour* (1822).

Henri Beyle was born at Grenoble and intended for a career in mathematics or engineering. This, however, he baulked, and he was found a place in the War Office by an influential cousin. He became a second lieutenant and followed Napoleon's armies to Italy; later he was in Germany and Russia as a non-combatant officer in the supply services. As an interlude in his early twenties, he followed a young actress to Marseilles, where he served behind the counter of a grocery-shop. After the fall of Napoleon, he decided to give his whole time to literature and lived for seven years in Milan, a city whose civilization enchanted him. Requested to leave by the police, who suspected him of subversive activities, he spent the next nine years in Paris (1821–30). Here he led a full social life, made his first close acquaintance with the young Romantic Movement, and published his first novel, *Armance* (1827). After the July Revolution, he was appointed French Consul at Civita Vecchia, in the Papal States. He held this post until his death, with frequent visits to Rome and Paris.

Stendhal's two outstanding novels are *Le Rouge et le Noir* (1831) and *La Chartreuse de Parme* (1839). Certainly they are not autobiographical in any direct sense, but in both he employed settings which had been important in his own life, while that constant self-analysis in which he delighted caused him to transfer his own features to his characters with more frequency than is usual in a purely 'objective' novelist. It is that peculiar combination of the revelation of character from the inside (not dissection) with a profound and unillusioned view of society that makes Stendhal's greatness. He is the observer who participates, and his frequent recourse to irony would seem to be due to the observer pulling up the participator when he fears that he is about to compromise him. Stendhal saw himself as an ultra-sensitive man who must hide his hand if he was to achieve the two ends which he prized most: happiness, through love; power, through 'energy'. Both eluded him.

In *Le Rouge et le Noir* Stendhal the liberal wrote what is in one sense a political novel. It was set in contemporary France. The hero,

Julien Sorel, is a passionately ambitious young man who chooses the black robe of the priest rather than the red uniform of the soldier to make his way up the ladder. He becomes secretary to an ultra-royalist aristocrat, whose political salon is brilliantly depicted, and wins over his daughter, Mathilde de La Mole. A marriage is agreed to, in spite of the social difference, but before it can take place Julien is denounced as an adventurer by Mme de Rênal, an older woman whom he had seduced while tutor to her children in his first post – and who still loves him. The end is melodramatic, yet in keeping with the self-consciously romantic characters, who perform by rule acts which their imagination tells them must be heroic. Julien takes vengeance on Mme de Rênal by shooting and wounding her. He is tried and guillotined. Mathilde, carrying his severed head in her arms, has him buried in a cave in the mountains.

Le Chartreuse de Parme is set in the Italy which Stendhal loved and deals in considerable detail with the intrigues of the small court of Parma, where politics are inextricably entangled with personal and sentimental interests. The hero, Fabrice, is again a young man, but of a less calculating nature than Julien. The opening chapters, in which he runs away to join Napoleon and rides about the battlefield of Waterloo with no clear notion of what is happening, are rich in ironical comedy. The later chapters have the complexity and fascination of a chess game, and contain some of Stendhal's finest political and psychological observation.

Of Stendhal's other novels, the best is *Lucien Leuwen*, which depicts the finance-ridden politics of France under Louis-Philippe, and was left unfinished. The early *Armance*, concerned with sexual-emotional problems, and the posthumous *Lamiel* both contain partial projections of the author's character or experiences, but there is far more substance in the *Journal*, in the *Souvenirs d'égotisme*, and, particularly, in *La Vie de Henry Brulard*, which are all frankly auto-biographical. Henri Beyle was a richer character than any he created – hence the many passionate admirers of the man Beyle, as distinct from the admirers of the novelist Stendhal. Both aimed at complete precision in the definition of feeling and motive, and hence in style. With most writers it would be a crippling limitation, or would turn frankly to comedy. Here it does not, and as a result Stendhal is one of the lightest of serious novelists.

It would not be altogether unjust to say the opposite of his contemporary, Honoré de Balzac. With a ponderous comprehensiveness he leads us round the society and the thought of his period, spanning fifty years from the Revolution to about 1840 and covering almost all walks of life. Crammed into this fantastic museum is every physical feature and material object that the novelist could lay hands on, preserved under its descriptive coating. Breathing heavily behind us, the author-guide explains at length the philosophy of his heroes, points out the angelic virtues of his 'good' characters, and exhibits, with a keener interest than the moralist should properly show, the evil machinations of the bad ones. If this were just realistically-furnished melodrama, one could enjoy it with admiration for Balzac's skill and intensely serious verve, but with amusement at the disparity between the means and the end. That is the natural reaction after reading only one or two of his books, particularly the more philosophically ambitious ones, but it cannot be maintained in face of the eighty-odd titles (including short stories) of the *Comédie humaine*. To explore further is to discover the existence of a true Balzacian world, consistent within itself and united by a kind of crazy cousinship with what we are pleased to call the 'real' world.

The creator of this world was born at Tours in 1799 of a middle-class family which had recently emerged from the peasantry. His early attempts at writing (novels of various types, from the Gothic thriller to the historical story) proving unsuccessful, he took a partnership in a printing-firm which went bankrupt. Left at thirty with a load of debt which he could never shake off, he returned to literature with a kind of dedicated fury, wrote *Les Chouans* (1829), the story of a royalist rising during the Revolution, then embarked on the twenty years of labour which ended only in his death from overwork. In his heroic bouts of composition he would write for weeks with lit candles and drawn curtains, never going out. One of his novels was drafted in seventy-two hours and rewritten on the proof-sheets. Between times, he lumbered heavily into society, imagined grandiose financial schemes which never succeeded, and slipped away – sometimes as far as St Petersburg – to meet Eveline Hanska, the Polish countess with whom he kept up a passionate correspondence for eighteen years. Their marriage in March 1850 relieved him for the first time of financial worries, but five months later he was dead.

The title of *La Comédie humaine* was settled by Balzac in 1842 and applied retrospectively to most of the books he had already written as well as to those still to come. It gives an appearance of method to his total production and suggests, as he intended, a 'scientific' attempt to classify the various social species. But in fact the *Comédie humaine* is not systematically planned, as Zola's *Rougon-Macquart* series can be said to be, nor is it an organic whole, like Proust's vast single novel. Although the same characters appear in different novels, each story exists quite separately. There is neither completeness nor balance in the total plan, which is imposed rather arbitrarily on the work. Nevertheless, it provides a convenient classification of Balzac's vast output and an indication of his programme – which, it must be remembered, he did not have time to complete.

He made two main divisions, the *Études de mœurs* and the *Études philosophiques*. The first, which is much the largest, was subdivided into several unequal sections of which the chief, with some of the better-known books they contain, were these: 'Scenes of Private Life': *Le Père Goriot*. 'Scenes of Provincial Life': *Eugénie Grandet*, *Les Illusions perdues*, *Ursule Mirouët*, and the short *Curé de Tours*. 'Scenes of Country Life': *Le Médecin de campagne*, *Le Curé de village*. 'Scenes of Parisian Life': *César Birotteau*, *La Cousine Bette*, *Le Cousin Pons*, *Splendeurs et misères des courtisanes*.

Among the *Études philosophiques* were classed *La Peau de chagrin*, *La Recherche de l'absolu*, and the two 'mystic' novels *Louis Lambert* and *Séraphîta*. There is also a strong element of sentimental mysticism in *Le Lys dans la vallée*, placed by Balzac among the 'Scenes of Country Life'. These philosophical novels, all written between 1831 and 1835, reflect the most obvious side of Balzac's Romanticism. They contain vaguely passionate characters searching in melodramatic circumstances for various ideals of happiness or knowledge which they usually fail to attain. *Louis Lambert* and *Séraphîta* both reflect the doctrines of Swedenborg, the Scandinavian visionary whose influence on French writers, from Senancour to the later Hugo, was considerable. It led Balzac to juxtapose other-worldly happenings and characters with the human and the material. The symbolism of these ambitious but cloudy novels has now lost much of its significance and they cannot be counted among his most successful works.

His Romanticism extends, however, into his more realistic books. Here the settings are as solid as observation and recollection can make them, but the characters and their actions are inflated beyond any rational – or reasonable – view of humanity. The purity of the chaste mother or of the young girl is 'angelic' without further examination. The cynicism of the villain and his sneering ugliness in defeat is absolute, as is the malice of the old maid, the saintliness of certain priests, the corruption of the courtesan, the integrity of the honest businessman, the glitter of Parisian high society. Unlike Stendhal, Balzac rarely enters into his characters, some of which are more or less intended caricatures of types which he could not have known well. He writes of them with an intense excitement. In Paris he is always the gaping provincial whose remarks show ignorance, penetration, and humour all at once. His provincial scenes are the most successful with their evocation of stagnant little towns where everything significant happens behind closed shutters. The contrast between these and the maelstrom of the capital is a recurrent feature of his work. Questions of realism and Romanticism apart, his contribution to the novel was twofold. He established the principle of the series of 'documentary' novels on contemporary society, in which the importance of money was fully recognized. He then elaborated a picture so violently coloured that the reason must reject it, though the imagination may accept it. The imagination may be right. After all, there are in actual life characters as colourful, as extreme, as twisted as any in Balzac. What if they are not, or were not always, the exception? It is at least a fact that humanity has recognized its image in Balzac more readily than in Stendhal.

In Balzac's heyday, the more typically Romantic personal and sentimental novel was written by George Sand (1804–76). This was the pen-name of Aurore Dupin, who, after separating from her husband, set about earning her living by her pen and exploited her own emotional and sexual experiences in such books as *Indiana* (1831), *Valentine* (1832), and *Lélia* (1833). Naturally labelled 'promiscuous' (her distinguished list of lovers included Musset and

Chopin and she was on terms of friendship with the artistic *élite* of her time), she was a feminist of the kind who claims, not equality of professional opportunity with men, but equality of freedom to make emotional experiments. She succeeded at least partially in creating the unsatisfied Romantic heroine as a counterpart to (not a consolation for) the unsatisfied Romantic hero. She was then converted to an idealistic socialism which inspired such novels as *Le Meunier d'Angibault* (1845) and *Le Péché de Monsieur Antoine* (1847). The last phase found her living serenely in her country house at Nohant, surrounded by her grandchildren and her tenants, writing a series of simple pastoral novels beginning with *La Mare au diable* (1846), and befriending and encouraging younger writers such as Flaubert. Traces of realism can be found in her last books, but in general her reputation has suffered cruelly from the facility which caused Musset to say: 'We worked all day. By evening, I had written ten lines of verse and drunk a bottle of brandy. She had drunk two pints of milk and written half a volume.'

The historical novel also flourished in this period. The journey to the distant age or country – in Baudelaire's phrase, 'anywhere out of the world' – was typical of another side of the Romantic temperament. With it went a love of the picturesque, a taste already whetted by Chateaubriand's descriptions of his travels in the New World and the Near East, or of Gaul and Greece in early Christian times in his prose epic, *Les Martyrs*. Other travellers in time or space told their tales, while after 1820 Walter Scott was much read in France and provided immediate models for historical fiction.

The first notable French example was Vigny's *Cinq-Mars* (1826) – the story, set in Louis XIII's reign, of a plot against Richelieu, carrying the moral undertones usual in its author. There was historical fiction among Balzac's early experiments and the historical novelist's preoccupation with his material setting (to lend authenticity to a remote period) persisted visibly in his mature work, although the period was now contemporary. In 1831, Victor Hugo published *Notre-Dame de Paris*, his evocation of medieval Paris with its monstrously simplified characters and its compelling atmosphere. Such a book was not far from popular fiction, but it was left to Alexandre Dumas *père* (1803–70) to develop the Romantic interest in the past into something that could be universally enjoyed.

He had begun as a dramatist, writing historical dramas in prose contemporary with Hugo's in verse. Over ten years later, he struck his vein as a novelist, helped by collaborators who did his research for him. But historical correctness hardly mattered. All that was needed was a decent 'period' appearance for these exciting adventure-tales with their bold and lively characters. His first and greatest success was the trilogy consisting of *Les Trois Mousquetaires*, *Vingt ans après*, and *Le Vicomte de Bragelonne* (1844–7). Others were *Le Comte de Monte-Cristo* (1845), in which the happenings described were supposed to have occurred in Dumas's lifetime, but which appears as 'historical' as the rest; *La Reine Margot* (1845); and *La Dame de Montsoreau* (1846). These novels were among the first works serialized in the popular press, which thus provided the writer with an important new source of income.

The most accomplished exponent of local colour, but with a deliberately anti-popular bias, was Prosper Mérimée (1803–70). Mérimée was a cultured civil servant, like his friend Stendhal, and was deeply interested in archaeology and languages. His post of Inspector of Ancient Monuments led him to travel widely, in France and abroad. His friendship with the family of Eugénie Montijo, who married Louis Napoleon and became Empress of France in 1852, made him an intimate of the Imperial Household, which he served as an unofficial literary adviser. But by that date he had virtually ceased to write.

His earliest works were plays and sketches, some of them pseudo-Spanish and pseudo-Illyrian (he presented them playfully as the genuine article), others medieval. He then produced an historical novel, *La Chronique du règne de Charles IX* (1829), concerned with the tumultuous times of the St Bartholomew's Day massacre and an excellent book of its kind. His main reputation, however, is based on the *nouvelle* – the short and long-short story – colourful in setting but dry in sentiment, with characters who act and react violently under the stress of primitive emotions. The most famous is *Carmen* (1845), the innocent source of the opera, which inevitably sacrifices the ironic humour of the original and somewhat blunts the contrast between the prudent northern hero (Don José) and the untamed gypsy-girl. In *Colomba* (1841), the story of a Corsican vendetta, there is a similar contrast between the attractively primitive sister and the more civilized brother through whom she must act. To these should be added a dozen shorter tales, such as *Les Âmes du Purgatoire* (a version of the Don Juan legend), *La Vénus d'Ille* (an archaeological ghost story), and *Tamango*, an account of the voyage of a slave-ship told with bitter restraint.

Mérimée may fairly be classed as a repressed Romantic, looking for an integrity of feeling which he could not find in the Parisian civilization to which he belonged. Having found it elsewhere, he was perhaps over-impressed by it. He puts on a poker-face to conceal his nervousness and adds irony to divert the impact. This in his best work. Elsewhere, he can tell a traveller's tale with ease and wit (*Notes d'un voyage en Corse; Lettres d'Espagne*). Another of his virtues was to be one of the first Frenchmen to take an interest in Russian literature. He made translations from Gogol and Turgenev.

After 1850, the French novel underwent a change. For the time being the autobiographical novel was dead, notwithstanding isolated examples such as *Dominique* (1862) by the painter and traveller Eugène Fromentin (1820–76). The historical and adventure novel, typical of another facet of Romanticism, was also neglected. New conceptions of realism and later of naturalism began to rule literature, pinning the writer to often sordid contemporary themes and stamping his work with a new pessimism.

The turning-point can be found in Gustave Flaubert (1821–80) and, more precisely, in his first published novel, *Madame Bovary* (1857). This story of a provincial doctor's wife who attempts to escape from the monotony of her environment by illicit love-affairs which she invests with a false glamour is, in one sense, one of the cruellest comments ever written on the Romantic mentality. The drab stupidity of life in the little Normandy town cannot be overcome by such moral or material resources as Emma Bovary possesses and she is hunted from expedient to expedient until she commits suicide in circumstances which are described in repulsive detail.

The disgust with 'life as it is' linked with an urge to depict it minutely runs, in less immediately obvious form, through Flaubert's second great contemporary novel. *L'Éducation sentimentale* (1869). Against the wider background of Paris, a young man of the Romantic generation exhausts his enthusiasms in vain projects.

Aspects of the social and artistic worlds are drawn with intimacy, but also with a flatness which gives an impression of formlessness. This was Flaubert's depressing intention, his way of showing that human hopes end not so much in a sudden tragic disillusionment as in gradual disintegration. Finally, in his unfinished *Bouvard et Pécuchet* (1881), he depicts human inanity in the shape of two retired copying-clerks who are interested in every form of 'modern' knowledge without possessing the mental capacity to understand it. This somewhat laborious book may be taken as a satire on the short-sighted scientific positivism of the *petite bourgeoisie* of the time.

A different aspect of Flaubert's talent appears in two other works. *La Tentation de Saint Antoine*, which occupied him intermittently for twenty-five years before its publication in 1874, is a symbolic review of ancient religions developed in a series of *tableaux*. The point of departure was in fact a picture by Brueghel. *Salammbô* (1862), undertaken as a colourful excursion after the four and a half years' labour of writing *Madame Bovary*, is, broadly, an historical novel. But the term is inadequate to convey the savage splendour of this evocation of ancient Carthage with its astonishing mixture of war, cruelty, sex, and primitive religion. The novel is certainly over-loaded, and the immense and exact research which went into it does not appear sufficiently assimilated, yet the total effect is impressive. Working on a grander scale than his contemporary, Leconte de Lisle, Flaubert plunged into the distant past and returned with a monstrous specimen quite unlike anything that his contemporary civilization contained.

Flaubert, the apostle of 'impersonality', held that 'the artist should so arrange matters that posterity will believe that he has never lived'. Though this should discourage any examination of his work from the biographical point of view, the almost sadistic morbidity which runs through his books certainly had its source in his own nature. What this source was is not entirely clear. As the son of the chief surgeon of the hospital at Rouen, he was brought up in a macabre proximity to the dissecting-room. In his early twenties he was attacked by a mysterious nervous disease which affected him throughout his life and determined his retirement to the country house which his father had bought at Croisset, near Rouen.

Here he remained until his death, apart from frequent trips to Paris and a journey to the Near East and another to Tunis when he was planning *Salammbô*. There were two women in his life. One, Elisa Schlesinger, whom he met when fifteen, always remained the object of a platonic and almost mystical adoration. The other was the cultured Louise Colet, who was his mistress for several years. But in essentials he was always 'the hermit of Croisset', leading an outwardly humdrum bourgeois life, rooted in the detested Norman soil and slaving at his novels with the conscientiousness of a good, if not a supreme, artist. For his first book alone Flaubert would be a very important novelist. The others support that position but do not raise him any higher.

Whatever else Flaubert has to offer, his *Madame Bovary* may be said to have established the realistic novel, which was dominant in France for the next thirty years. The novel was to be an exact record of contemporary society, based on the same kind of research and 'documentation' which the historian or the biographer employs for his work. Such was the principle of the Goncourt brothers, Edmond (1822–96) and Jules (1830–70), who at first wrote books on the society and art of the eighteenth century, then turned, in the eighteen-sixties, to novels of contemporary life. Among these, which have one central and usually neurotic character, were *Renée Mauperin*, *Germinie Lacerteux* (an early proletarian novel), and *Madame Gervaisais*. After his brother's death, Edmond de Goncourt continued to write novels (*Les Frères Zemganno*, 1879) and continued also the famous *Journal* which they had begun together in 1851. This, a mine of observations and anecdotes on the Paris they knew, was also intended as raw material for their novels. Edmond's will instituted the Académie Goncourt whose members (ten eminent writers) meet yearly to award a literary prize which still has considerable prestige.

It was a writer of much coarser fibre than the Goncourts who became the leader of the naturalistic school which emerged in the late eighteen-seventies as an extreme development of Flaubertian realism. As defined by Émile Zola (1840–1902), the new novel was to be based on the laws of scientific determinism which, according to the thought of the time, governed human nature. The relatively new theory of evolution, applied to psychology and thence – by such critics as Taine – to literature, was at the root of this curious idea. Accepting environment and heredity as decisive factors in the formation of the personality, it was the novelist's business to carry out 'experiments' (comparable to those made by the laboratory-worker) which should throw more light on the general laws. Having felt his way in a couple of early novels, Zola proceeded to put his theory into practice in the long Rougon-Macquart series of books published over a period of twenty-two years (1871–93). On the one side, the fact that different members and generations of the allied Rougon and Macquart families appear throughout the series provides a 'scientific' framework, based on a somewhat superficial application of the laws of heredity. On another, the novels were intended to give the panorama of an age – the second Empire – which Zola mapped out as his period in the same way as Balzac had covered the Restoration and the July Monarchy.

The principles which Zola put forward, partly for self-justification or self-advertisement, cannot be altogether discounted in reading his work. If his characters appear as symbols or as automata, the reply is that such was his intention: it would be beside the point to speak of weakness in characterization. If the physical is sometimes stressed to the point of nausea, the novelist who has compared his skill to that of a surgeon conducting a post-mortem has a ready answer to his reader's protests. This is, or was, life. It calls for an objective examination. Suppose, however, that these arguments are rejected and the whole of Zola's mechanistic view of humanity is dismissed as outmoded and irrelevant, there still remains something. With the help of an imagination which can fairly be called poetic, he succeeds admirably in creating an atmosphere of places and of identifying it with the group-life which goes on in them. Thus, his picture of the Parisian working-class in *L'Assommoir* (1877) is inseparable from the drink-shop of the title and its immediate surroundings. The miners, the mine, and the mining-village form an entity in *Germinal* (1885), probably his finest novel. The primitive crudity of the peasant grows out of the farmland in *La Terre* (1887). In *La Débâcle* (1892), his novel of the Franco-Prussian war, there are several settings, but the spirit of the doomed army, first in its confused marches and counter-marches, then in defeat, is excellently rendered.

The Rougon-Macquart cycle was Zola's main work in life. Born in Provence, he had gone to school in Paris and begun work early as an ambitious young journalist and serial-writer. When the last Rougon-Macquart book (*Le Docteur Pascal*) was finished in 1893, the hitherto objective novelist turned his attention to politics. His views, as put forward in *Les Trois Villes* (Lourdes, Rome, Paris, 1894-8), were those of a strongly anticlerical positivist. A second series, *Les Quatre Évangiles* (of which only three were completed), expounded Zola's new-found humanitarian socialism. As literature, these verbose books are second-rate. Between the two series, Zola championed the cause of Dreyfus in articles which led to his trial and his temporary flight to England. He died accidentally, suffocated in his bedroom by the fumes from a stove.

No other serious writer carried naturalism as far as Zola. But a loosely-knit group formed round him, united, at least for a time, by broadly similar aims. Besides the older Flaubert – whose attitude was often critical – and Edmond de Goncourt, the group included Alphonse Daudet, Huysmans, and Maupassant. Guy de Maupassant (1850-93), the acknowledged master of the realistic short story, was a Norman like his master Flaubert, who guided him in his early writings. He published his first story, *Boule de suif*, at the age of thirty, in *Les Soirées de Médan*, a volume written collectively by Zola and his friends. During the next eleven years, giving up his post as a minor civil servant, he produced nearly three hundred stories and six novels, of which *Une Vie* (1883) and *Bel Ami* (1885) were the first and most successful. His health, undermined by venereal disease contracted in youth, gave way under the pressure of his work. He became mad, and ended his days in the clinic of Dr Blanche, who over thirty years before had had Gérard de Nerval as his patient.

Maupassant is at his best when writing of the middle class and of the peasants of his native Normandy. Through some simple and often basically absurd anecdote he reveals their moral blindness and the frightening banality of their lives. The peasants in particular are neither the idealized innocents of George Sand nor the animated vegetables of Zola – who after all idealized the physical by rooting it in a kind of Life Force – but all too patently human beings in their average brutality, their matter-of-fact lechery, and their overriding cupidity. The moral comment which he refrains from making is implicit in his picture of man cut off from both the brute and the angel and so incapable of development in either direction. This explains both the limitations and the force of his work and provides one reason why realism of this kind is inseparable from pessimism. His short stories, first printed in newspapers, were published in such collections as *La Maison Tellier* (1881), *Contes de la Bécasse* (1883), *Contes du jour et de la nuit* (1885). As his health deteriorated and his fear of madness grew, he wrote several uncanny tales reflecting his morbid fears such as *Apparition* and *Le Horla*.

Though Maupassant was the most influential of the nineteenth-century short-story writers, many others practised the art. It is sufficient to recall, besides Mérimée, the symbolic and fantastic tales of Charles Nodier (1780–1844), the author of *Smarra ou les Démons de la nuit*, *Trilby*, and *La Fée aux miettes*; the mystical *Filles du feu* (1853) of Gérard de Nerval, considered in a later chapter; and the occasional productions of other writers more famous as poets or novelists. Such were Vigny's *Servitude et grandeur militaires* (1835); Balzac's varied short tales and his *Contes drolatiques* (1832–7), a curious attempt, in consciously quaint old French, to pastiche the broader storytellers of the sixteenth century; and Flaubert's carefully-worked *Trois Contes* (1877), a fitting pendant to his novels. Barbey d'Aurevilly (1808–89), an ultra-Catholic and ultra-royalist writer and a stimulating and merciless literary critic, produced, after several novels (as *Un prêtre marié*, 1865), a book of short stories entitled *Les Diaboliques* (1874). These stories of 'devilish' wickedness in modern settings appear today as quaint as *Dracula*, and hardly more credible. Their idealized aristocrats, mechanical psychology, and jewelled prose announced the decadents of the nineties. A writer with a somewhat similar outlook, Villiers de l'Isle-Adam (1838–89), attacked his own materialistic age in the *Contes cruels* (1883) and other collections of stories some of which contain macabre and terrifying episodes. In a period dominated by naturalism, his play *Axel* proclaimed the ascendancy of spiritual qualities and looked forward to the Symbolist drama.

Alphonse Daudet (1840–97) was perhaps remembered too exclusively as the author of the *Lettres de mon moulin* (1869), tales evoking with considerable charm the landscapes and legends of his native Provence; also for his caricature of the irrepressibly boastful southerner in *Tartarin de Tarascon* (1872) and its sequels – in which the mainspring of the humour is the contrast between publicity and performance. His second volume of short stories, *Les Contes du lundi* (1873), dealing largely with the Franco-Prussian war and its aftermath, was already more realistic. The remainder of his work attaches him, at least nominally, to the naturalistic group, since it is concerned with the contemporary scene and sometimes with the poorer classes in Paris (*Froment jeune et Risler aîné*, 1874; *Jack*, 1876; *Le Nabab*, 1877; *Numa Roumestan*, 1881; *Sapho*, 1884). However, a certain sentimentality prevents these books from being fully realistic in the manner of Maupassant. Although Daudet's contemporary reputation was built on them, later readers were not so far astray in preferring the picturesque fantasy of his earlier period.

With Joris-Karl Huysmans (1848–1907), the development is in the opposite direction. He was at first a whole-hearted adherent to Zola's group and wrote proletarian novels in which life was petty and sordid (*Les Sœurs Vatard*, 1879; *En ménage*, 1881). But this could not satisfy him. This was the period, not only of naturalism, but of a new orientation of aesthetic values reflected in Impressionist painting, in the conscious emergence of Symbolist poetry, in the discovery of the darker and more immediately striking side of Baudelaire's art. Huysmans's novel *À rebours*, published in 1884, therefore remains in literature as a notable wax model of the protesting aesthete attempting to transform an abhorred materialism into a spiritualism full of strange thrills. Its hero, Des Esseintes, turns in disgust from society to live alone among beautiful things and the sensations generated by decadent literature and art. Finally, this artificial paradise proves to be not the solution. Des Esseintes is ordered back into the world by his doctor and begins to glimpse a curative in religion. The spiritual Odyssey of Huysmans was continued in *Là-bas* (1891), concerned with diabolism and black-magic, then in several novels filled with a form of Christian mysticism to which the chief road was a love of medieval ecclesiastical art (*La Cathédrale*, 1898; *L'Oblat*, 1903). A prose stylist of great richness and originality, Huysmans represented a state of mind very common at the century's end. He provided one of the more tortuous ways by which the author's personality, temporarily banished from literature by realist theory, could come back to haunt his works.

There were other ways. The first trilogy of Maurice Barrès (1862–1923), collectively entitled *Le Culte du Moi* (*Sous l'œil des barbares*, 1888; *Un Homme libre*, 1889; *Le Jardin de Bérénice*, 1891), was the work of a temperament not totally unlike Huysmans, an aesthete in revolt against the impersonal values of naturalism. In his second trilogy, *Le Roman de l'énergie nationale* (1897–1902), concerned with the political ferments of the time, he began to champion Catholic and traditional values and it was this Barrès who adhered for a time to the neo-royalist *Action Française* movement, though he remained essentially an individualist. The first novel in this trilogy, *Les Déracinés*, deals with a group of young Lorrainers (Lorraine was Barrès's native province) attempting to make their mark in the Paris of the eighteen-eighties, but failing spiritually because they had 'uprooted' themselves. This kind of regional sentiment merged passionately into nationalism at a time when Alsace and Lorraine were under German annexation. Lorraine again furnished the inspiration of Barrès's most technically perfect novel, *La Colline inspirée* (1913). His strongly personal sense of atmosphere appears best in his travel-books, whether on Spain (*Du Sang, de la volupté et de la mort*, 1894), on Venice, or on Greece, or again in his story of medieval crusaders in Syria, *Un Jardin sur l'Oronte* (1922). These were still pilgrimages of an aesthete in search of sensations, in close and sometimes violent communion with what appeared to him to be the spirit of the place.

His influence has been considerable in France, since he has expressed with remarkable insight the anti-democratic and anti-materialistic bias of a cultured minority. He was an active journalist and politician, but without political action he would have exerted the same influence through his fastidious sensuality and his rejection of the middle-class values which had come to dominate the nineteenth century. Though his traditionalist leanings opposed him to Gide, he can be compared to him as a disseminator of ideas. He used the novel to express a state of mind, at once personal and topical, and his books marked a break in the novel-writing tradition which had reigned from Balzac to Zola. In his earliest work the divisions between fiction, autobiography, the meditation, and the parable had already begun to grow shadowy, so pointing to the less differentiated literature of the twentieth century. It also marked the ebb of naturalism.

What Barrès's travel-books could do for the romantically-minded intellectual, the books of Pierre Loti (1850–1923) did for a wider and simpler public. By profession a naval officer, whose real name was Julien Viaud, he re-told in an early novel, *Aziyadé* (1879), the story of his own love-affair with a Turkish girl in Constantinople. This tale foreshadowed most of his other work. His novels are personal experiences, more or less written-up; most are love-stories ending unhappily in a parting, and to which in any case the barriers of race and religion give a sense of impermanence; they describe persuasively the beauty of various foreign settings: Tahiti in *Rarahu* (1880), Japan in *Madame Chrysanthème* (1887) and *La Troisième Jeunesse de Madame Prune* (1905), Senegal in *Le Roman d'un Spahi* (1881), and elsewhere India, Persia, the Balkans, Morocco. His Breton novels, particularly *Pêcheur d'Islande* (1886), show him as a true writer of the sea, with an understanding of the simple people whose lives it shapes. In his day, Loti represented a sentimental protest against the mechanical progress of the West, an understandable escape into the calm of Asia and elsewhere which world events have terribly dated. Of several 'colonial' novelists who followed him – some were influenced by Kipling – the most interesting was Claude Farrère (born in 1876), who wrote *Les Civilisés* (1905), *L'Homme qui assassina* (1907), and the short stories of *Fumée d'opium* (1904). However, the brutal psychology of Farrère is quite unlike Loti's.

If Loti is hardly read today, he has at least been spared the spectacular fall of Anatole France (Jacques-Anatole Thibault, 1844–1924), who, after being grossly overrated in his lifetime, has been almost as grossly neglected since. Revivals are constantly predicted, but they do not come. Today he appears as a pleasantly dry but minor writer of philosophical and satirical fiction. His first success, *Le Crime de Sylvestre Bonnard* (1881), was full of a learned and sentimental irony which seemed to promise yet another alternative to the prevailing naturalism of the time. Stories such as *Thaïs*, set in Alexandria in early Christian times, or *La Rôtisserie de la*

Reine Pédauque (1893), which contained the character of the out-spoken eighteenth-century *abbé* Jérôme Coignard, established France as a playful rationalist steeped in classical culture. In his most ambitious undertaking, the series' of four novels entitled *L'Histoire contemporaine* (1896–1901), France attempted to mirror his age in a subtly malicious portrait of provincial society. From that date, his sceptical detachment turned more and more strongly into the kind of socialism associated with extreme anti-clericalism. This appeared in his denigratory *Vie de Jeanne d'Arc* (1908) and, more effectively, in his two best satirical works, *L'Île des pingouins* (1908) and *La Révolte des anges* (1914). Between the two, he published *Les Dieux ont soif* (1912), a novel on the French Revolution, in which he condemned the fanaticism of the Jacobins as strongly as he had attacked religious extremism elsewhere. Anatole France, using the novel to air theories and expose pretensions more than to create character, has inevitably been compared to Voltaire because of his rationalistic approach. But he lacks Voltaire's passion and, besides, the strong eighteenth-century strain in his work appears as too deliberately studied and suggests only an indirect reaction to the realities of his time. The direct reaction came from Zola, Bloy, Barrès, even Huysmans. France has therefore incurred the damning charge of being too 'literary' a writer. The standpoint and style which once caused him to be praised as a reincarnation of traditional French qualities have lost their appeal for readers who no longer appreciate elegant irony, particularly when it is out of period. If there is a future rehabilitation, it might well bear on his *Histoire contemporaine* series.

With Anatole France, the list of novelists who were formed in the nineteenth century comes almost to an end. A few more names must be mentioned, and first two writers who were in violent revolt against society. Jules Vallès (1832–85) was a militant socialist whose trilogy of novels, collectively entitled *Jacques Vingtras* (1879–86), is bitterly autobiographical and ends, in *L'Insurgé*, with an eyewitness account of the Paris Commune. Léon Bloy (1846–1917) was an incontinent writer inspired by an even greater loathing of his time, but for him salvation was in religion – a religion which came to him directly rather than through the Church. On his own initiative he called down fire from heaven, and no doubt believed that it would literally come. His prolific work had great influence on the twentieth-century revival of Catholic literature, exercised as much through his eight-volume *Journal* (1898–1920) as through his two novels: the violent and pessimistic *Le Désespéré* (1886) and *La Femme pauvre* (1897).

With Jules Renard (1864–1910), rebellion is transposed to the minor key of family relationships, at least in his famous story of an unloved boy, *Poil de carotte* (1894). A realist with a wry sense of humour, Renard excelled in other books in depicting village characters, while his *Histoires naturelles* are unique in French literature for their slyly picturesque portraits of animals, which he wisely leaves as portraits where a different writer might have worked them up into fables. He also left an important *Journal*, concerned chiefly with the literary scene of his time.

Such work has proved more lasting and humanly authentic than the so-called 'psychological novel' which began to emerge in the eighteen-nineties. The general theme here is the human heart as it beats on – usually – the higher and richer levels of society, and too many talented writers went astray down this profitable road of fame. Amorous entanglements, divorce, 'moral' problems, and social dilemmas are subjected again and again to tedious examinations in the light of a momentary code which makes such books unreadable a few years after they were the success of the season. In so far as they reflect changing fashions in social morality, they acquire in time an historical interest, and future research students may well have to examine them from that point of view, just as Mlle de Scudéry's novels are examined for patterns of conduct in the seventeenth century. For such purposes they would be more rewarding than the work of an original genius like Proust, who cannot help imposing his personal vision on whatever he describes. Paul Bourget (1852–1935) was no doubt the most gifted of the numerous 'psychological' novelists and can at least be quoted as representative. He remained a popular and prolific writer almost until his death, but there was little progression beyond his early successes (*Cruelle énigme*, 1885; *Le Disciple*, 1889). His critical writings, particularly the *Essais de psychologie contemporaine* (1885), have survived in better shape.

Of novelists belonging to the turn of the century whose work still commands respect, the most noteworthy are Paul Adam (1862–1920), a disciple of Zola in his luxuriant style and his studies in mass-psychology; Charles-Louis Philippe (1874–1909), the author of *Bubu de Montparnasse* and *Marie Donadieu*; and René Boylesve (1867–1926), in whose delicately incisive studies of provincial characters some critics have seen an aborted forerunner of Proust, since the original complexity of his richly analytical style was pruned on the advice of literary 'experts'.

CHAPTER 13

The Novel in the Twentieth Century

IN the twentieth century, the novel takes on still greater importance as a means of expressing very varied approaches to life. It is difficult to think of even a score of writers of the first rank who have not used it, while among those who have done so have been men whose talent appeared equally in other forms of literature, such as the essay and the drama. If these have produced good and sometimes remarkable work alongside that of the more specialized novel-writers, it is because the bounds of the novel have widened corres-pondingly. It has become impossible to give any definition covering the vast range of books that are published as novels and accepted as such by the public; nor is there more than a relative value in classi-fications such as 'ideological', 'documentary', 'autobiographical', since the distinctions between them are often imprecise. They may serve to underline the chief characteristic of one novel or novelist, but they can seldom be used to point to any significant differences or resemblances. The twentieth-century novel is a story of almost any length over fifty thousand words based on its author's lived experience, his imaginative life, his observation of other individuals or of society as a whole or of particular events; to observation, re-search is sometimes added. This embraces most novels, so long as the word 'story' is interpreted liberally, both as to the conception of what a story is and as to the manner of its telling.

This expansion of the novel has of course been paralleled in other literatures, and in some cases was initiated by them. It is not specifically French. Moreover, it was already well advanced in the nineteenth century and on any theoretical count of 'types' of novel the twentieth century might appear to have invented little. It is possible to speak of continuation rather than of transformation, after allowing for inevitable changes in the conception both of society and of the individual psychology which the novel mirrors with more or less directness. Such changes have been vast, especially since 1925, and they have naturally been accompanied by the realization on the part of many novelists – though by no means all – that they cannot be rendered in the old forms. Innovations in technique, stemming for the most part from surrealism, existentialism, or from modern linguistics, provide the most evident contrast between this century and the last. It is here, rather than in thematic differences, that the principal developments have lain.

Is any pattern discernible in all this? Rough maps have been drawn, but when one actually tries to use them one finds them unreliable in whole or in part. We are still too close to the wood – we are in fact in the middle of it – to be able to give it an intelligible outline. We can see various giant trees and others, smaller but curious or striking, which seem to be the real landmarks and to yield in themselves as much pattern as is needed. Whatever the future historian may find, the best way for us through the modern novel is still to move from individual to individual, while noting the principal features of the space they occupy.

Before the First World War, a writer appeared who seemed to possess a new breadth and nobility of vision. Romain Rolland (1868–1944) was by vocation an idealistic biographer, seeking in the lives of his heroes evidence of the greatness of humanity, its fraternity on the highest level and its hopes for the future. The subjects of his biographies are a sufficient illustration: Beethoven (1903), Michelangelo (1905), Tolstoy (1911), Gandhi (1924), Ramakrishna (1929), Vivekananda (1930). His interest in the philosophy of India was contemporary with an enthusiasm for the Soviet Union, which led him to try to reconcile Leninism and Gandhism, and this was only an extreme extension of the disinterested internationalism which he had shown in the First World War, which he spent in Switzerland (*Au-dessus de la mêlée*, 1915). Late in life he returned to an early theme and wrote the six volumes of his massive *Beethoven, les grandes époques créatrices* (1927–43). In the year of his death he published an outstanding study of Péguy, who had been his friend and editor forty years before.

It was in Péguy's *Cahiers de la Quinzaine* that Rolland made his first appearance as a novelist. There he began publication of the long *roman-fleuve* which made his name, *Jean Christophe* (1904–12). This ten-volume work can be seen as a prolongation of the biographies on an imaginative plane. Its fictional hero is a musician of genius, born in the Rhineland and with an instinctive sympathy for both German and French culture (Rolland himself was of pure French stock). In his personal life and in his opinions on the contemporary world, he represents the warm but somewhat vague humanitarianism of his author. More than a novel of ideas, this was a novel of pure feeling, which painted a quite unreal picture of its period (measured by political events) but was moving because of the conceptions of personal freedom and of universal brotherhood which it contained. A second *roman-fleuve*, *L'Âme enchantée* (1922–33), lacked the human interest of at least the early volumes of *Jean Christophe* and appeared in its period as even more out of touch with contemporary possibilities. Half a dozen shorter novels (as *Colas Breugnon*, 1919), autobiographical writings, essays on music, and an unsuccessful attempt to found a 'people's drama', make up the remainder of Rolland's production. As Anatole France throws back, superficially, to Voltaire, Romain Rolland can be more fitly compared to Rousseau. An anti-rationalist, an opponent also of the Catholic and national tradition as Maurras and Barrès conceived it, he had an almost mystic belief in humanity, emotional sympathies not unconnected with his love of music, and a largely subjective vision of the world. But unlike Rousseau, he lived at a time when these qualities were very little in demand, in Western Europe at least.

It is sometimes difficult to think of him as a contemporary of André Gide (1869–1951), who became well known only in the nineteen-twenties, and whose influence remained immense until the Second World War. In contrast to Romain Rolland, Gide's attraction lay in his famous *disponibilité* – his suppleness, it may be, in adopting constantly the most advanced attitude of the time, which he later qualifies – his chronic incapacity to remain long of one mind either as a thinker or as an artist; or (the obverse of the medal), in his rejection of authority, his determination always to keep a way open for new moral explorations. It was naturally on the strength of the second alternatives that he came to be accepted as a pioneer of the French conscience, and the true verdict appears to be that his perpetual revisions were a proof of his sincerity.

Gide was not primarily a novelist. He was a moralist and a critic (of ideas and of literature). In fact, he only consented to call one of

his books – *Les Faux-monnayeurs* – a *roman*. Yet an important part
of his work consists of stories which are certainly novels, or sometimes *nouvelles*, and in spite of their symbolic or philosophical
qualities they still remain in that category. At the same time, they
are so closely related to the rest of Gide's production that it is best
to consider them in the context of the whole.

André Gide's parents were Protestants and he was brought up in
an atmosphere of biblical religion dominated by strict puritanical
values. His work has been seen as a running conflict between this
early influence, reinforced by his marriage to his cousin, and the
sensuality which was paramount in his own nature. This was revealed to him – no longer as a sin but as a necessary response to life
– by the Symbolist circles in which he moved as a young man (the
sensuous factor in art), through his admiration for Oscar Wilde, and
by a journey to Algeria – the first of several – undertaken in 1893.
While Barrès at the same date was discovering in Spain *le sang, la
volupté et la mort*, Gide found in Africa *le soleil, la volupté et la vie*,
together with his own capacity for enjoying them. This gave the
dominant note of *Les Nourritures terrestres* (1897), a book of poetic
meditations and descriptions, followed in 1902 by *L'Immoraliste*, a
semi-autobiographical story – in fact a short novel – based on the
same experiences. It was also an avowal of the homosexuality which
Gide was to proclaim more openly in the Socratic dialogues of
Corydon (1924) and in *Si le grain ne meurt*, the memories of his
childhood and youth, not published until 1926. *L'Immoraliste*,
however, is not primarily a study of the homosexual but a voyage
of discovery beyond all the moral laws which his young hero had
hitherto believed binding. Thus, he connives at a petty theft by an
Arab boy, joins the poachers in snaring his own game, and almost
wantonly causes the death of his wife.

Having liberated himself from his Protestant scruples (at least
experimentally, in literature, but with a dilettantism which a purer
rebel might find profoundly shocking), Gide might have been expected to develop the 'paganism' characteristic of the early nine-
teen-hundreds if one considers chiefly the lesser writers. His interest
is that he did not, or could not. Disregarding his secondary books,
his main work for another twenty years was concerned with questions of conscience in religious contexts. The short *Retour de*

l'enfant prodigue (1907) in which, when the prodigal son of the parable comes home defeated, his younger brother sets out in search of the same freedom, shows that nothing is settled. *La Porte étroite* (1909), perhaps Gide's finest novel, is a drab but moving book turning on the idealism of its heroine, who is temperamentally impelled to sacrifice her human love to her conception of the absolute. *La Symphonie pastorale* (1919) again contrasts profane love with the purity – and the constraints – of religion before reaching its disastrous climax. That this was still a vital personal issue for Gide is shown by the religious crisis he traversed at about the date when he was writing *La Symphonie pastorale* and which he transcribed later in *Numquid et tu* (1926). But before this he had apparently relaxed in *Les Caves du Vatican* (1914), a semi-buffoonish exploitation of contemporary ideas and certain Catholic tendencies which he labelled a *sotie*. It contains the famous example of the motiveless act (*l'acte gratuit*), in which a character kills a complete stranger by pushing him out of a railway-carriage with no other reason than to show his own independence of the laws of cause and effect. This, which like much else might appear as a mere intellectual gambit on Gide's part, has been taken at least as seriously as it deserves as a classic instance of: 'I act wilfully, therefore I am', and points directly to one facet of existentialist philosophy.

Something of the *sotie* still persists in the seriously-intended *Faux-monnayeurs* (1925), brilliant as a study of a group of schoolboys and adolescents in Paris, but in other respects an interesting failure. For his adult characters and his plot, Gide uses the clumsiest devices of the stock 'psychological' novel but leaves, characteristically, a loophole by declaring his disdain of 'classic' fiction whose conventions he is thus free to exploit ironically. One of his characters is himself writing a novel entitled *Les Faux-monnayeurs*, and further commentary was provided by Gide's 'log-book', *Le Journal des Faux-monnayeurs* (1927), in which he noted his problems and intentions while composing the original. This is an irritatingly self-conscious work if read at its face value as a story of personal relationships, but it can also be seen as a notable anticipation of the later technique of presenting the 'story' from several different points of view. A final fictional trilogy (*L'École des femmes*, 1929;

Robert, 1930; *Geneviève*, 1937) abandoned the experimentalism of *Les Faux-monnayeurs*. These three short novels, dealing with the problems of two partners in a failed marriage and then of their daughter, are remarkably un-Gidean in their 'classic' (i.e. completed) presentation and characterization, and in a different writer one would notice with less surprise the influence of the drawing-room.

Towards his sixtieth year, Gide became interested in political-social questions. A journey in Equatorial Africa produced *Voyage au Congo* (1927) and *Retour du Tchad* (1928), fascinating travel books and at the same time effective protests against the exploitation of native peoples by the white man. Soon after, he was attracted, like so many Western intellectuals at that period, by the human promise of communism. He reversed his views after a visit to Russia, where he found social inequalities as grave as in capitalist countries and an insistence on the blind orthodoxy which he had been fighting all his life (*Retour del'U.R.S.S.*, 1936). From then on, Gide remained detached from political problems, living in North Africa during the German occupation of France and seeing his vast *Journal* (covering 1889–1949) through the press. A postscript to his thought, if no final verdict, was contained in the short *Thésée* (1946). Theseus, founder of Athens and conqueror of monsters (including the voluptuous but stupid Minotaur), meets the blinded Oedipus, the heroic victim who has renounced the external world. Theseus says: 'I remain a child of this earth and believe that man, whatever he may be like and however tainted you consider him, should make the best of the cards he holds.'

Gide's great influence was largely personal, whether exercised directly on the numerous writers he launched or encouraged, or through the *Nouvelle Revue Française* which he helped to found in 1909 and which, with the publishing firm which grew out of it, became a focal point of French letters. As a literary critic, he was one of the most penetrating and universal of his time (*Prétextes*, 1903; *Nouveaux Prétextes*, 1911; *Dostoïevsky*, 1923; *Incidences*, 1924; *Interviews imaginaires*, 1942; etc.). As a novelist, he had the faults of his own eternal youthfulness, which he insisted were not faults and perhaps are not when they are related to his work as a whole. As a dramatist, his plays, as *Saül* (1903) and *Oedipe* (1931), were treatises hardly designed for the theatre, though they have been acted. As a moralist conducting a long and frank self-examination in the tradition of Montaigne and Rousseau, he is immensely interesting, and it is conceivable that he should be read for his *Journal* alone, with *Si le grain ne meurt* as a prelude and, possibly, *Thésée* as an enigmatic afterthought. It was only natural that his influence should have declined, temporarily at least, after the Second World War. Political and social questions required *engagement* and open-mindedness could too easily be construed as a state of dithering.

While Gide's thought was dispersed among many different books, the whole of Proust is contained in one vast work – rambling and episodic in appearance but possessing a fundamental unity. *À la recherche du temps perdu* is, moreover, a true novel. Whatever its links with lived experience, it presents a world of the imagination to which ideas, observation, characters, and even the author's own character are all subordinate. The reader who cares to look for external applications is free to do so, but they are only incidental to Proust's main intention. If Gide's function was to act as a gadfly, Proust is the spider who invites you in.

Marcel Proust (1871–1922), the son of a Jewish mother and an eminent Parisian doctor, came of a family rich enough to allow him an apparently idle social life. As a young man, he was welcomed in salons ranging from the aristocratic to the cultured bourgeois, and he himself entertained lavishly. His mother, on whom he was greatly dependent, died in 1905. Not long after, he retired to the flat on the Boulevard Haussmann where, between 1909 and 1919, the bulk of his great novel was written. From boyhood he had suffered from asthma and, though he may subconsciously have cultivated ill-health, the figure of the hypersensitive invalid meditating in the silence of his cork-lined bedroom, taking elaborate precautions when, more and more rarely, he went out, is of central importance when one approaches his work. The first part, *Du côté de chez Swann*, was published in 1913 at his own expense, after being refused by various publishers and by the *Nouvelle Revue Française*. The second part, *À l'ombre des jeunes filles en fleurs* (1918), was awarded the Prix Goncourt, and the completion of the book by its now recognized author became, physically, a race against death. It was concluded, though Proust would probably have rewritten the last volume, or even prolonged the work, if he had had time. He did not live to see it all published. (*Le Côté de Guermantes*, 1920; *Sodome et Gomorrhe*, 1920–2; *La Prisonnière*, 1923; *Albertine disparue*, 1925; *Le Temps retrouvé*, 1927.)

À la recherche du temps perdu is several things in one. It is a study of French society – and most strikingly, though not exclusively, of the aristocracy and its satellites – from the eighteen-eighties to just after the First World War. It does not hesitate to show, by irony and the humour of exaggeration, that that society is in decay. Proust has been called, perhaps rightly, a snob, but his nostalgia was for something other than the old hierarchy. He is the observer rather than the partisan, aiming to reflect his period as Saint-Simon and Balzac had reflected theirs. At the same time he is an analyst of love, as profound and sceptical as anyone since Stendhal. His theory of *absence* is a step beyond Stendhal's theory of *crystallization*, according to which one is already disposed to fall in love, as one might be disposed to catch a disease, without having any particular person in view. An 'object of love' appears, upon whom are deposited, like crystals on a branch left in a salt-mine, all the qualities already prepared in the mind of the lover. For Proust, love is even more a subjective creation of the imagination – so much so that it cannot thrive in the presence of its object. Physical absence or inaccessibility, a refusal to respond, or the suspicion of infidelity creating desire through jealousy, are necessary to maintain it. While this idea, over-simplified, can appear the most banal truism, in Proust's hands it lends itself to elaborate and fascinating developments – if never to the presentation of those thwarted or mutually exclusive passions found in a master like Racine. Compared with these, the Proustian passion is nearer the level of a collector's passion. In the same way, while Proust introduces homosexuality as a major theme both in his analysis of society and of the individual psychology, his treatment of it appears more superficial than in Gide. One reason is that there is a strong element of humour in his greatest homosexual character, the baron de Charlus.

Proust is himself deeply involved through the character of Marcel, who is at once the narrator and an actor in the story. How closely narrator and author should be identified is probably as fruitless a question as the search for exact originals of the other characters, but the fact that there is at least considerable identification gives the book personal and poetic qualities which a mere 'chronicle' would lack. Much has been written of Proust's theories of time and of the 'involuntary memory' by which some accidental sense-association recalls a scene from the past more vividly than when it was actually occurring. What was once part of a fugitive present can be 'recaptured from past time' (this is the significance of the work's title) by the writer. It becomes part of a new, more real, present – part, therefore, of the self. Worked out independently of both Bergson and Freud, Proust's attempt to remount the stream of time by a kind of intuition gives a curiously dreamlike quality to some of his writing, makes it difficult (and unimportant) to establish an exact chronology of his story, and leaves him at the centre of it, since the whole thing is being continuously re-created in his own mind. His style, with its long and complex sentences, is that of a man discovering, qualifying, and enriching in the act of writing and is an essential part of his subjective approach.

Apart from *À la recherche du temps perdu*, Proust's work consists of an early book of stories and sketches, *Les Plaisirs et les Jours* (1896), and other slight volumes of essays published later or posthumously (*Pastiches et Mélanges*; *Chroniques*; *Contre Sainte-Beuve*). In 1951–2, the literary world was surprised by the publication of *Jean Santeuil*, a long, unfinished novel recently discovered among Proust's papers. Of absorbing interest to students of Proust's psychological and artistic development, it is best read as a lengthy sketch in preparation for his great novel. Composed probably between 1895 and 1899, then laid aside, it shows that he carried his chief work within him during the whole of his adult life.

Another genuinely personal world, simpler but rendered with very great art, is that of Sidonie-Gabrielle Colette (1873–1954). After a delightful country childhood in Burgundy with the mother whom she depicted racily and tenderly in *Sido* (1929), she married the popular novelist 'Willy' (Henry Gauthier-Villars), with whom she collaborated in her early Claudine books (1900–03). These tell what was essentially the story of her own girlhood, her first experiences in Paris, her marriage and its breakdown. The occasionally scabrous note was the contribution of Willy, a professional in quest of sales. Colette's own sensuality, in evidence in many later books, is a more open and natural feature. Divorced, earning her living for a time on the music-halls, later remarrying, she continued to write of her own memories and experiences in books which inclined now to the autobiography, now to the novel (*La Retraite sentimentale*, 1907; *La Vagabonde*, 1911; *La Maison de Claudine*, 1923; *Le Fanal bleu*, 1949, etc.). Of her less immediately personal books, distinguished by their more objective characterization, the chief are *Chéri* (1920) and *La Fin de Chéri* (1926), which are concerned with a liaison between a middle-aged courtesan and a nerveless young man and achieve an unsentimental pathos not far removed from tragedy. The deliberately limited universe of Colette is a universe of the senses, whose perceptions she expresses with astonishing skill. It is not surprising that she has written so well about animals: in her early *Dialogues des bêtes*, or better, *La Paix chez les bêtes*, or in *La Chatte* (1933), a short novel in which a cat plays a decisive part in the life of a young married couple. Such a theme could only be made plausible on the plane of physical sensation.

Adolescents totally unlike animals, with their aura of idealism and make-believe still clinging to them, were the characters of *Le Grand Meaulnes* (1913), the only novel of Alain Fournier (Henri-Alban Fournier, 1886–1914). Introducing a fairy-tale atmosphere into a real setting – in other words, evoking a child's world – the book was a crystallization of feeling and fantasies round a girl whom the author had seen only once, at the age of twenty. The parallel with Gérard de Nerval's stories is sometimes drawn. As far as the general atmosphere is concerned, a better comparison would be with some of the verse *romans d'aventure* of the Middle Ages. Though it set a fashion after 1920, *Le Grand Meaulnes* remains a unique book.

The shattering national experience of the First World War left comparatively little mark in the novel. The best-known books inspired by the actual fighting, such as *Le Feu* by Henri Barbusse (1873–1935) or *Les Croix de bois* by Roland Dorgelès (b. 1886), have lasted badly and lack the realistic truth of a classic like Remarque's *All Quiet on the Western Front.* There was more of that quality in Duhamel's quietly bitter *Vie des martyrs* and *Civilisation*, based on his experiences as an army doctor. Another exception was the four volumes of *Ceux de Quatorze* (1916–21) in which Maurice Genevoix (b. 1890) described with sober realism the soldier's immediate experience of the fighting. But twenty years had to pass before the war was shown in some perspective as part of the great national drama in the middle volumes of Jules Romains's *Hommes de bonne volonté*.

As for the aftermath of war, the 'restless twenties' saw the rise or development of half a dozen important novelists, but none of them can be considered as typical of that anarchic period. In a very general way, surrealism might be said to have broadened the conception and technique of the novel – though the influence of Proust was of much greater importance – but no outstanding work came as yet from that particular source. Relatively conservative, the French novel in an experimental decade produced no name comparable to Kafka or James Joyce. In the category of the monstrous there was, indeed, the *Voyage au bout de la nuit* of Louis-Ferdinand Céline (1894–1961), a book nihilistic in its obscenity and its disgust with human nature, written in a strange and violent prose which has suggested comparisons with Rabelais and Lautréamont. But published only in 1932, it was inter-war rather than post-war and reflected a mood of demoralization which was to contribute to the collapse of 1940. Céline's later books, as *Mort à crédit* and *L'École des cadavres*, added nothing to his first success, while his personal reputation was tarnished by his anti-semitism during the German occupation.

Meanwhile the writing which now seems most typical of the twenties is found in the rapid and lively work of Paul Morand (b. 1888). The predominantly cynical short stories of *Ouvert la nuit* (1922), *Fermé la nuit* (1923), *L'Europe galante* (1925), *Magie noire* (1928), together with his travel books (as *Rien que la terre*, *Londres*, *New York*) established him as a brilliant social observer. His full-length *Bouddha vivant* (1927) dealt with a young Asian prince who practises the austerest Buddhism in the modern Western world and whom his admirers would like to set up as a guru, mainly for social and materialistic reasons. Morand went on to write more novels with serious undertones, but even in the latest, a bitter study in stoicism (*Tais-toi*, 1965), his style did not lose its sparkle.

To the more frivolous side of the twenties might be attached the best work of the poet and novelist of the dubious Bohemia of Montmartre and Montparnasse, Francis Carco (1886–1958). Carco's toughness hides a soft centre of the kind so often exploited in the Parisian music-hall, but has a fascination beyond the conventionally typical (*La Bohème et mon coeur*, poems, 1912; *Jésus-la-Caille*, 1914; *L'Homme traqué*, 1921; *Perversité*, 1925; *Rue Pigalle*, 1927, etc. He also wrote biographies or memoirs on Verlaine, Utrillo, Katherine Mansfield, and others). Add to these the unsubstantial and sensitive novels of Giraudoux, as *Simon le pathétique* (1918), *Suzanne et le Pacifique* (1921), *Siegfried et le Limousin* (1922), *Bella* (1926), and of Cocteau (*Le Grand Écart*, 1923; *Thomas l'imposteur*, 1925; *Les Enfants terribles*, 1929), and the decade of the first post-war period would appear to have a character either of light cynicism or of escape into personal fantasies as a reaction against an experience too dreadful to contemplate steadily.

But at the same time novelists of greater stamina were on the march. The inter-war years saw the growth of the *roman-fleuve* to heroic proportions, as exemplified in the work of Jules Romains (1885–1972), Georges Duhamel, and Roger Martin du Gard. The first two had been members of the Unanimist group which came together in the early years of the century inspired by a conception of humanity in the mass partly derived from Zola and Verhaeren. Their concern was to express the collective spirit of social communities, of towns, of streets, rather than to explore the psychology of individuals. The medium they at first preferred was poetry, and Romains continually produced quietly sincere verse in line with his original theory, from *La Vie unanime* (1908) to *L'Homme blanc* (1937). He has also distinguished himself as a playwright, but his chief work is the twenty-seven volumes of *Les Hommes de bonne volonté* (1932–47), which paint the social and political life of France during precisely twenty-five years from October 1908 to October 1933. This huge fresco represents the age by picturing the impact of events on many different characters and social *milieux*. There is no attempt to give it unity by writing of a single hero or family. In this at least it is faithful to the principle of Unanimism. The continual shifting of perspective chequers the work as a whole, though certain volumes are excellent in themselves. It remains as an impressive monument to a perhaps unworkable formula.

When Georges Duhamel (1884–1966) came to write his chronicle novels, he used a different method. His *Vie et aventures de Salavin* (5 volumes, 1920–32) centres upon a sensitive and continually unhappy character who was perhaps for Duhamel what René was for Chateaubriand, though he never became the image of a generation. The more important *Chronique des Pasquier* (10 volumes, 1933–45) is established solidly on the story of a middle-class family which to a considerable extent was Duhamel's own. Running from the eighteen-nineties to the nineteen-twenties, it shows both the strength and weakness of the French bourgeoisie at a time when it was the chief power in France, and it indicates through the personal experiences of its characters the main ideological conflicts which were then declared or developing. Duhamel is a somewhat disillusioned humanist, capable of irony but more often inclined to pity. He is an excellent story-teller, but in the tradition of the great secular moralists he looks beyond the immediate meaning of his material. His war books and his travel books, as well as several lesser novels, illustrate his gift for deductive observation.

Les Thibault of Roger Martin du Gard (1881–1958) covers much the same period as *La Chronique des Pasquier*. Its eleven volumes, written between 1922 and 1940, also show the French bourgeoisie as the background to a single family. But it shows that class in dissolution, torn by internal disputes. The two Thibault brothers, on whom the main interest focuses, seem outside their class because of their wider interests. One is a doctor, the other a revolutionary intellectual. But when the 1914 war comes, considered as the end of an epoch, neither is able to survive it morally. Roger Martin du Gard inherited features of nineteenth-century naturalism; faced with the pessimism of *Les Thibault*, one may see in it the disillusionment of the scientific materialist, who had expressed his earlier faith in intellectual progress in the lengthy *Jean Barois* (1913).

These are only the chief *romans-fleuve*. With them might be compared, for length, the immense *Histoire d'une société* of the Belgian-born René Béhaine (1888–1966). Comparatively short cycles of three or four volumes, as Jacques Chardonne's *Les Destinées sentimentales* or Montherlant's *Les Jeunes Filles*, were common in the thirties. The form survived the Second World War, after which Aragon, in *Les Communistes*, continued his pre-war series entitled *Le Monde réel*, while Sartre embarked on *Les Chemins de la liberté* and Paul Vialar (b. 1898) published the eight volumes of *La Mort est un commencement*, followed this with the ten-volume *La Chasse aux hommes* and began, in 1948, the still vaster *Chronique française du 19e siècle*. The Belgian ex-communist Charles Plisnier (1896–1952) published two realistic cycles, *Meurtres* (1939–41) and *Mères* (1946–9). Obviously such works have little in common except their length, and even that varies widely. Yet, after setting aside those cycles excessively concerned with the author's own personality or devoted to an ideology, it is possible to reach some general conclusions. Most of the *romans-fleuve* deal with the near past, which they attempt to record before it has moved into the more impersonal field of history. The authors do not look on themselves as historians, but as imaginative chroniclers drawing on their own experiences and backgrounds to suggest the spirit of the time more faithfully than a factual record could achieve. But none are as deeply involved, in their own persons, as Proust. The main inspiration comes rather from Balzac and Zola. The prospect of painting a huge canvas, of settling down for the next ten or twenty years to produce a work of both literary and social importance, also attracts certain temperaments. They are assured of continuity, in tone, events, and usually characters, and spared the difficulty (as it is for some writers) of repeatedly casting round for a new theme and re-establishing contact with their readers. These are artistic and material considerations valid for almost any time and place. But there is also, in the French *romans-fleuve* of the thirties, the desire to depict a vanishing society, based on the old bourgeois and family values, before it finally disappears. This aspect may have become clearer since 1945, and in any case a social novelist whose subject extends over several years is necessarily concerned with the past. Yet even in the nineteen-twenties a writer sensitive to change could easily sense that the old order was coming to an end, and conceive the plan of his work accordingly. There is at least a valedictory element in the novel-cycles of Martin du Gard, Romains, and Duhamel which is not only due to later events. They will be read in the future, in part or in whole, as 'testimonies', as well as for their narrative interest and the vitality of a few of their characters. The persistence of the cyclic novel into the nineteen-sixties, but in this case more clearly historical, is seen in the work of Henri Troyat, considered on a later page.

In contrast to these broad canvases are the novels more particularly concerned with the fate of individuals. The moral aspect – the question of how to live and to what purpose – is felt to be of primary importance and few of the greater recent novelists have not wrestled with it. From the Catholic point of view, the most uncompromising writer has been Georges Bernanos (1888–1948), a spiritual descendant of Léon Bloy, some of whose violent convictions he shared. This appears most strikingly in his polemical works, in which he attacked with uncompromising independence the materialism of the orthodox bourgeoisie (*La Grande Peur des bien-pensants*, 1931), Franco and his ecclesiastical supporters outside Spain (*Les Grands Cimetières sous la lune*, 1938), the men of Munich and the Vichy Government. His first novel was *Sous le soleil de Satan* (1926), in which, in an atmosphere of witchcraft and brimstone, he shows a priest at grips with supernatural powers and incidentally goes out of his way to introduce a caricature of Anatole France, for him the incarnation of the godless rationalist. In *Le Journal d'un curé de campagne* (1936), his best-known novel, he develops the same theme in a quieter and more realistic manner. His extraordinary *Nouvelle Histoire de Mouchette* (1937) shows a fourteen-year-old girl suddenly destroyed by a series of spiritual disasters, and would be melodramatic but for the bitter sincerity of the writing. His last novel, *Monsieur Ouine* (1946), had an incoherence which suggests that Bernanos's obsession with damnation had grown beyond the resources of literature. His film scenario, *Dialogue des Carmélites* (1949) was a moving evocation of the guillotining of a community of nuns under the Terror.

Similar problems of conscience underlie the more disciplined work of François Mauriac (1885–1970), whose numerous novels show strangely introverted characters at grips with their passions and vices, but with no open intervention of the supernatural. He has created a portrait-gallery of sinners on a classical model which throws back to Racine. If there is also a suspicion of Paul Bourget in it, it is saved from insipidity by a view of the human personality made genuinely poignant by the issues of damnation and divine

grace. This is especially visible in the unhappy character of Thérèse
Desqueyroux, who appears in three novels (*Thérèse Desqueyroux*,
1927; *Ce qui était perdu*, 1930; *La Fin de la nuit*, 1935). Other outstanding books are *Le Baiser au Lépreux* (1922), *Génitrix* (1923),
Nœud de Vipères (1932) and *Le Mystère Frontenac* (1933). The hot-
house temperature of Mauriac's family conflicts is heightened by the
atmosphere of the Landes, the country round Bordeaux in which
most of them are set. This was also the setting of his most successful
play, *Asmodée* (1938).

Julien Green (b. 1900) might be broadly classed as a Catholic
writer, though with considerable modifications explicable by his
life. Born in France of American Protestant parents, educated partly
in the United States, this bilingual author was attracted by Catholicism, then entered a long Buddhist phase, and was finally converted
at the age of forty. The Christian struggle between God and the
world, spirit and flesh, underlies most of his pessimistic novels, as
in Mauriac. But while Mauriac is relatively realistic, the atmosphere
of Green's novels is one of hallucination. After his early novels set
in the French provinces (*Adrienne Mesurat*, 1927; *Léviathan*, 1929),
the setting becomes more and more dreamlike, whether it is some
vaguely apprehended town as in his masterpiece, *Minuit* (1936), or
some legendary sea-wood. Through these his somnambulant
characters, haunted by fate and death, move in psychological
patterns peculiar to the author (*Le Visionnaire*, 1934; *Varouna*,
1940; *Moira*, 1950; *Chaque homme dans sa nuit*, 1960). Similar
characters, neurotically or erotically obsessed, appear in his plays
(*Sud*, 1953; *L'Ennemi*, 1954; *L'Ombre*, 1956).

It is even more hazardous to class Henry de Montherlant (1896–
1972) as a Catholic, though he would at least have sympathized
with the militant masculine Christianity of the *chansons de geste*.
He has also been described as a 'pagan', but there is no necessary
contradiction if one remembers the example of Barrès. In the same
way Montherlant travelled as a Catholic traditionalist in search of
violent sensation. Spain gave him much inspiration, from his early
novel *Les Bestiaires* (1926), concerned with Mithraism and the bull-
fight, to the four-volume series *Les Jeunes filles* (1936–9), which
is both sensuous and anti-sentimental, in the manner of the original
Don Juan. *La Rose de sable* (1954, revised 1968) has a North

African setting and an anti-colonialist theme. In *Le Chaos et la nuit* (1963) he returns to Spain to draw the portrait of a Spanish Republican in exile . Outstanding among his non-fictional writings are his early *Chant funèbre pour les morts de Verdun* (1924) and the moral reflections contained in *Service inutile* (1935) and *Carnets* (1957). Turning with success to the theatre with *La Reine morte* (1942), he wrote a number of plays, in some of which the Spanish influence is again perceptible. These are arguably the most important part of his work and are considered separately in Chapter 17.

Montherlant's work, varied in form and smacking of several influences, has nevertheless made its chief appeal as the very personal voice of a somewhat brutal aristocrat in love with more absolute values than those of modern democracy. It is often over-inflated and the reality of the values can be questioned. The heroic in a modern writer so easily becomes heroics. Nevertheless his work, with its emphasis on violent and dangerous activities, including war, in which Montherlant participated, and its denigration of the feminine, was symptomatic, at least in the thirties, of a widespread desire for a literature of action. Many Frenchmen were tired of 'psychology' – the eternal fishing in the home-pond that Racine, Proust, and, say, Mauriac had fished so thoroughly – and desired a different revelation of character, robuster if less subtle. A rough American parallel would be a preference for Hemingway over Henry James.

This desire has been best satisfied by André Malraux (b. 1901), undoubtedly one of the great modern French writers. His material is modern and actual, and he has been personally involved in the events he describes – as a witness of the Chinese revolution of 1926, as an organizer and pilot of the Republican Air Force in the Spanish Civil War, and as a fighter in the French Resistance Movement, which led him finally to reject communism and to join de Gaulle. His novels arise from these experiences. The first group – *Les Conquérants*, *La Voie royale*, and the outstanding *La Condition humaine* (1933) – concerns events in China; *Le Temps du mépris* (1935) deals with the fate of a Czech communist in Nazi Germany; *L'Espoir* (1937) is a fine novel of the Spanish War. *Les Noyers de l'Altenburg* (1948) – part of a longer, unfinished work – is more explicitly philosophic. Though it opens with the French defeat of 1940, its characters – some of whom are Alsatians of German culture – discuss a much wider range of political and human themes.

All these are more than political novels. Against backgrounds of violence and confusion, the characters are driven to examine their own situation as individuals, and hence their own nature. There is no formal analysis by the author, but abrupt, fragmentary conversations thrown up by the pressure of circumstances. The communist tortured by the Gestapo who may be saved by the sacrifice of a comrade, the airman or the saboteur undertaking a suicide mission, the prisoner awaiting the firing squad face a particular concentrated form of reality. In Malraux's hands, they reveal, not only character, but reactions to the human situation as a whole which ring true both in the immediate circumstances and well beyond them. It is doubtful if a writer with a set scheme of values, religious or other, could have achieved this spontaneous truth, and in this connection it must be said that Malraux was never an orthodox communist, blindly following the party line. In serving de Gaulle as Minister of Culture he still showed much independence. The great problem explored in his novels is how to reconcile individual liberty with the fraternity of the human race, in both of which he believes passionately. His main work after the war was the four volumes of the *Psychologie de l'art* (1947–57), which established him as a philosophic art historian of great originality, possessed of a deeply humanistic culture in the tradition of Jacob Burckhardt.

A somewhat similar combination of thought and action is found in Antoine de Saint-Exupéry (1900–44), a pioneer civil airline pilot who served during the war in the French Air Force and disappeared on a reconnaissance flight. Only his first book, *Courrier-Sud* (1929), was cast as a novel; the others (*Vol de nuit*, *Terre des hommes*, and *Pilote de guerre*) speak directly of his experiences and contain the beautifully written meditations which these suggested to him. An unfinished and rather disappointing symbolical story was published posthumously (*Citadelle*, 1948). Saint-Exupéry can be read as a classic of the air, as the great sea-writers are read for their descriptions and their accounts of hardships overcome. But there is also the factor of self-realization through the exercise of a dangerous profession – the same that Malraux found in his militant political activities. It is because of Saint-Exupéry's professional acceptance of the risks involved and his complete identification with his material that his books are more than true adventure stories. Through long familiarity combined with high literary skill a unity is established between man, his experiences, and the physical surroundings in which they occur.

There are similarities in the books of two other writers. Joseph Kessel (b. 1898) served as a pilot in the First World War and wrote up his experiences as novels in *L'Équipage* (1923) and *Vent de sable* (1929). He continued to lead an adventurous and sometimes dangerous life, romancing and rather over-dramatizing his material (*Le Coup de grâce*, 1931; *Le Lion*, 1958; *Les Cavaliers*, 1967, etc.). Much of this can be described as imaginative reporting, as in some of Hemingway, in which action is preferred to reflection. With Jules Roy (b. 1907), another pilot and a professional soldier, but in World War II, the search for a moral meaning is more evident. It is open in his essays, *Le Métier d'armes* (1948) and *L'Homme à l'épée* (1957), but continually present also in his novels, of which the first, *La Vallée heureuse* (1946), draws on the allied bombing raids on Germany. The 'happy valley' was the Ruhr. *Le Navigateur* (1954), *La Femme infidèle* (1955) and *Les Flammes de l'été* (1956) have similar themes, written from the point of view of the airman by this admirer of Saint-Exupéry, to whom he devoted a book. Following the wars of his period, Jules Roy wrote as a historian-reporter of Indo-China in such works as *La Bataille dans la rizière* (1953) and of North Africa in *La Guerre d'Algérie* (1960). In 1968 he embarked on a long novel-cycle on Algeria from the beginning of French colonization in 1830 (*Les Chevaux du soleil*).

Virile action, including sport, was a theme of the early essays of Jean Prévost (1901–44), killed while fighting in the Resistance. This brilliant left-wing intellectual, a pupil of Alain's like André Maurois and Simone Weil (see p. 252 below), left two remembered novels on working-class life, *Les Frères Bouquinquant* (1930) and *Le Sel sur la plaie* (1934) among his numerous critical and political writings.

From realization of the self and its universe through action it is only a step to considering action as the *sole* valid definer of personality. To invoke for a moment historical circumstances, this was brought home to Frenchmen during the German occupation, when many of them were faced with a choice between collaboration with the invader and resistance. It was a personal choice, psychologically rather different from the collective choice made by an uninvaded nation. In making it and in performing – sometimes in isolation – the acts which followed inevitably, the individual discovered that old groupings and values no longer meant much. Patterns of class and creed fell away as irrelevant, and the sense of having to remake oneself through one's own acts was strong. This was pure Malraux, the theme which runs throughout his work and which he had put in extreme form as early as 1933 in *La Condition humaine*: 'A man is the sum of his acts, of what he has done and of what he can do – nothing else.'

This approach was adopted by Albert Camus (1913–60) in his novel *La Peste* (1947). Ostensibly the story of a North African town isolated by an outbreak of plague, it refers obliquely to the dilemmas raised by the German occupation of France. The chief character, a doctor, decides after rejecting religion and every sort of idealism that his best choice is still to devote himself to his fellow-men. What emerges is a kind of pessimistic humanism. A comparable theme, dramatized and treated more symbolically, gave *L'État de siège*, produced by Barrault in 1948. Other plays were *Le Malentendu* (1944), *Caligula* (1945) and *Les Justes* (1949). However, in an earlier novel, *L'Étranger* (1942), Camus demonstrated what he calls the *absurdity* of the human situation by creating a character who drifts through life, including crime, with no will either to construct a philosophy or to react in any way. The conviction that reaction is necessary in order to assert, and so preserve, the human personality, underlies *L'Homme révolté* (1951), a study of the psychology of both personal and political revolt in modern Europe, beginning with the marquis de Sade and the Jacobins. A final novel, *La Chute* (1956), philosophizes around these theories of Camus, which are more memorably expressed in his essay *Le Mythe de Sisyphe* (1942) and his posthumous *Carnets* (1962–64), published after his meaningless death in a road accident. His short stories, *L'Exil et le royaume* (1957), are partly concerned with his own Algerian background.

Here, then, are the two main sides of existentialism: the negative conception of the absurd or meaningless state in which the majority of people live and the positive conception of becoming something by freely decided acts. Both Malraux and Camus refused, however, to be classed as existentialists and there was no challenge to the leadership of Jean-Paul Sartre (b. 1905), who popularized the doctrine immediately after the war which had created such a favourable climate for it. He has expounded his system for his fellow-philosophers in several works, of which *L'Être et le néant* (1943) and *Critique de la raison dialectique* (1960) are the most substantial. He has enlarged on his theories and applied them to various fields in such studies as *Situations* (articles reprinted from his review, *Les Temps Modernes*, and which in themselves, together with other topical essays, make him one of the major social and literary critics of his time), in *Baudelaire* (1947), in *L'Idiot de la famille* (1971, on Flaubert) and in *Saint Genet* (1952). This last work proposed as an example of the existentialist hero the remarkable figure of Jean Genet, a lyrically coarse contemporary writer of great originality who had defied a society which rejected him, had been in prison and was proud of it. (See Chapter 17 below for Genet's plays.) For Sartre he represented – in the simplest terms – the integrity of the deliberate evil-doer faced with the hypocritical respectability of the property-owning class. Besides such an example from life, Sartre has presented fictitious cases in plays, films and novels, composed with great skill to reach the widest possible audience. His plays are considered in Chapter 17. His novels and stories have stressed the negative aspect of existentialism by showing characters in states of hopeless indecision like the hero of *La Nausée* (1938), or in various pathological conditions from which they can find no outlet, as in the short stories of *Le Mur* (1939). But Sartre's most ambitious experiment in fiction was his novel-cycle *Les Chemins de la liberté*, begun in 1945 with *L'Age de raison* and continued with *Le Sursis* (1949), *La Mort dans l'âme* (1950) and the unfinished *La Dernière chance*. Here characters were shown floundering in the morass of recent events, presented with brutal rapidity and including the year of Munich and the fall of Paris in 1940.

Such novels contain naturalistic portraits of man at his most abject. Reflecting a widely-felt disgust with society as it is, they were intended to act as a kind of purge before the unpalatable and perhaps illusory existentialist remedy was taken. If this is refused, they become merely nihilistic studies in disintegration, like Céline's

Voyage au bout de la nuit. Purely as literature, they fascinate, then strain credibility. They are not so much observed as constructed, which in the long run would appear fatal to their arguments. Though existentialists deny this, the observation of Flaubert and, in a different order, of Zola, carries conviction if no philosophy. Sartre's hell-on-earth comes nearer to an ideal of evil than to its reality.

Yet his attitude can perhaps be justified. He is no armchair philosopher. He has mingled forcefully and dangerously in all the main political controversies of his period, inclining for a time to communism but rejecting it definitely after the Russian invasion of Hungary in 1956. Completely a-religious, loathing reactionary capitalism, the whole of his mature work could be seen as a quest for some alternative solution which is not idealistic.

Simone de Beauvoir (b. 1908) became known as Sartre's principal disciple, as well as his close companion, but in spite of a common philosophical outlook, her work is very different. In her novels (*L'Invitée*, 1943; *Le Sang des autres*, 1945; *Tous les hommes sont mortels*, 1946; *Les Mandarins*, 1954; *La Femme rompue*, 1967) and her play *Les Bouches inutiles* (1945), her handling of psychology is lighter and subtler. By temperament she seems an analytical writer in the classic tradition. She is at her best in the closely-reasoned analytical essay, as *Pour une morale d'ambiguïté* (1947), *Faut-il brûler de Sade?* (1952) and her long militant defence of woman, *Le Deuxième sexe* (1949). There is a strong personal element in much of her work, confirmed by her four autobiographical volumes, from *Mémoires d'une jeune fille rangée* (1958) to *Une mort très douce* (1964) on her mother's death from cancer. These strengthen her reputation as a different and independent mind.

Novelists having no connection with existentialism and who have so far gone unmentioned must be dealt with more briefly than several of them deserve.

Switzerland had a great novelist in Charles-Ferdinand Ramuz (1878–1947), whose books express the spirit of his native canton of Vaud but whose tragic sense makes him much more than a mere regional writer. There was also a heady local flavour in the Provençal novels of Jean Giono (1895–1970), who wrote in his earlier work of nature and peasant characters with a Rousseauesque lyricism which some critics considered overstrained. After the war this considerable novelist developed a completely new manner, tautening and pruning his style and switching to historical subjects whose heroes have been justly described as Stendhalian (*Le Hussard sur le toit*, 1951; *Angelo*, 1958; *La Bataille de Marignan*, 1963, etc.). The natural poetry and superstitions of Provence fill the books of Henri Bosco (b. 1888), such as *Le Mas Théotime* (1945), who has remained faithful to regionalism. In his earlier novels André Chamson (b. 1900) dealt with peasant life in the Cévennes before turning to subjects of more immediate contemporary significance. He fought in the Resistance and, as with Giono, the war marked a turning-point in his production.

While the southern novels are the work of poets if not visionaries, conscious of a pantheism which the picturesque Daudet never felt, the northerners are realistic, urban, and disillusioned. Of the Belgians, Plisnier (1896–1952), the grim ex-communist chronicler of a corrupt society, has already been mentioned as a writer of *romans-fleuve*. Georges Simenon (b. 1903) hunts human nature into its most squalid corners in his countless short detective novels. A Frenchman, Maxence Van der Meersch (1907–51), set most of his puritanical social studies in the industrial north-east, though not his best-known book, *Corps et âmes* (1943), a resounding attack on the medical profession.

Other novelists have been more concerned with the individual psychology – sometimes their own – explored in a series of restless books. Marcel Jouhandeau (b. 1888) is a self-tormented Christian nearer to Bernanos than to Mauriac. He invented the odd provincial town of Chaminadour (a caricature of his home-town) and the character of Monsieur Godeau to illustrate his savage and sometimes burlesque conceptions of human relations and the married state (*Chaminadour*, 3 vols, 1934–41; *L'Oncle Henri*, 1943). His abundant production includes also *Chroniques maritales* (1938), *L'Imposteur* (1950) and the six-volume autobiographical *Mémorial* (1950–58).

With Jean Schlumberger (1877–1968) and Jacques de Lacretelle (b. 1888), who were both influenced by Gide, we return to the central French humanist tradition. Lacretelle's chief books are *Silbermann* (1922), the story of a young Jewish intellectual in France, and

Les Hauts-Ponts (1932–6), a four-volume cycle on the decline of a family – a theme also used by Schlumberger in *Saint-Saturnin* (1931). Two examples of sentimental analysis in the purest classical manner were written by Raymond Radiguet (1903–23) before his early death: *Le Diable au corps*, on the premature emotional initiation of an adolescent, and *Le Bal du Comte d'Orgel*, a modern version of the theme of *La Princesse de Clèves*.

For contrast, there are the humorous novels and short stories of Marcel Aymé (1902–67), who successfully mingles the real and the ridiculous, the gross and the fantastic in a satirical commentary on various types and levels of society. Among his best books are *La Table-aux-crevés* (1929), *La Jument verte* (1933), *Travelingue* (1941) and *Les Contes du chat perché*, children's short stories (1934). He also became a successful playwright with *Lucienne et le boucher* (1947), *Clérambaud* (1950) and *La Tête des autres* (1952).

A humorous satirist of a younger generation, with at least as sharp a bite, is Jean Dutourd (b. 1920), the author of *Au bon beurre* (1952), *Les Taxis de la Marne* (1956), *Les Horreurs de l'amour* (1963), etc. Finally, Gabriel Chevallier (1895–1969) owed his fame to *Clochemerle* (1934), the preposterous saga of a village urinal. A one-book author, who has never managed to repeat this success.

By about 1950 nearly all the novelists so far considered had either finished their careers or were continuing to write in their already established vein. What has occurred since?

The most notable development was the emergence in the fifties of the *nouveau roman*. This well-publicized term, easier to pick to pieces than to define, represented a trend of potentially vast importance, though whether literature will in fact be transformed by it and, if so, how rapidly, is a very open question. The discovery of perspective in the fifteenth century revolutionized painting, but not immediately; the twentieth-century discovery that perspective is unnecessary revolutionized it again, yet considerable artists still practise earlier techniques. The 'new' techniques in the novel – not all of them new and not all confined to the members of any particular group – are aimed in general at a fresh way of representing human existence in a verbal medium. Two main factors are involved, of which the first, sometimes labelled *chosisme*, is an apparently obsessive preoccupation with material objects. However, this is less a cult of objects for their own sake than a recognition of the high place they occupy in human consciousness and sometimes a rearrangement of them to correspond more faithfully to lived experience. The old well-plotted story, admired by Aristotle 2,300 years ago, put them in the places where generations of writers had led us to expect to find them and subordinated them to traditional rules of design.

To reduce this to a simple analogy, the motor-car of the advertisements is a complete and aesthetically attractive object whose 'truth to life' can be checked by viewing a stationary car at a short distance from the outside. But when one gets into the driving-seat and moves off it is entirely different. The driver sees a steering-wheel, controls, instruments, a windscreen and various external things either stationary or moving. These occupy not only his vision but his awareness or conscious experience of the car while he is driving it. At that time they make up a reality far truer than the sleek model in the saleroom. One can call this a change of view-point and this, applied to literature, is an important consideration, but one cannot stop there. There are times when the whole car becomes and 'is' nothing but a steering-wheel and a couple of vital pedals.

This simplified example may serve to illustrate the basis of *chosisme* and also to indicate that it is not a dehumanizing process but a transposition of conventional representation to a more meaningful plane. Through perception it affects consciousness, with profound consequences for the psychological reactions of the individual. To suppose that these are neglected by focussing the attention on objects is a complete mistake. In fact the psychological reactions are sometimes over-elaborated and the objects are even given symbolical meanings which in this kind of art are totally outside their sphere.

The second factor is that of time. Bergson and, as has been seen above, Proust had already rejected the traditional conception and later writers and theorists have developed their ideas. A 'story' could move freely backward and forward in time and, more important perhaps, could expand, contract or neglect certain periods of it as measured by the clock. What mattered was not their literal sequence or duration, but the impression made on the individual consciousness. Some 'New Novelists' have exploited such well-tested theories rather self-consciously, linking them with Structuralism (returned to in Chapter 14) in what appear to be deliberate exercises. Their open interest in composition is, however, another feature of the New Novel and is evidence of their desire to discard traditional techniques ('the height of art is to conceal art') and to propagate openly and didactically a new manner of rendering life.

Two main influences are perceptible in the New Novel and related literature. On the philosophical level there is the phenomenology of Heidegger and Husserl, either directly or derived through Sartrean existentialism; on the technical level, that of the film, in which the practices of focussing on particular objects, photographing them from 'unusual' angles, manipulating 'natural' time and so on are too familiar to need detailed description here. Incidentally, they have long been accepted as normal by the general public.

Such, in outline, is the main theory. What has it so far produced in practice?

If one could apply the old criteria to Alain Robbe-Grillet (b. 1922) one would say that his novels were melodramatic stories in exotic settings, such as the West Indian banana-plantation of a deceived husband or a luxurious brothel-restaurant in Hongkong Harbour frequented, among others, by spies. His characters investigate or commit crimes and indulge in sexual fantasies which they apparently put into practice with sadistic ingenuity. But this is not Somerset Maugham or James Bond. The different technique, based on the principles outlined (particularly the question of time), presents the whole novel through the mind of the involved narrator and leaves the reader in doubt as to what has happened objectively. Beginning with *Les Gommes* (1953) and continuing with *Le Voyeur* (1955), *Dans le labyrinthe* (1959) and *La Maison de rendez-vous* (1965), Robbe-Grillet has written what can be classed as psychoanalytical novels cast in the new form. His essay, *Pour un nouveau roman* (1963), and films, beginning with *L'Anneé dernière à Marienbad* (1961) throw further light on this author who has no desire to be obscure for the general public.

This is less certain of Michel Butor (b. 1926), whose *Passage de Milan* (1954), *L'Emploi du temps* (1955), *La modification* (1957), his first prominent novel, and *Degrés* (1960), are psychological studies also, but with outwardly ordinary characters and settings. They are as non-melodramatic as Sartre's *La Nausée* and no less drab. Butor is a brilliant intellectual, deeply interested in the purpose and construction of the novel (this tends to show in his), and an original and probing critic. After Sartre, he took up the term *anti-roman*, which defines his own fiction better than the word 'new'. His conceptions of literary meaning and method are expounded in *Répertoire 1–3* (1960–68) and *Essai sur les essais* (1968). With Roland Barthes (see below, pp. 255–6) he is one of the best, if more difficult, theorists of the new order.

'New' novels have also been written by Claude Simon (b. 1913) in half a dozen books from *Le Vent* (1957) to *Histoire* (1967). His long involved sentences, inevitably dubbed Proustian and conveying shifting perspectives and constant qualifications, provide an excellent subject for stylistic study, but their purpose is the tentative expression of a psychology based once again on phenomenology and the time-syndrome. His novels abound in sexual imagery and descriptions of sexual acts and, so far as this is relevant, most have bourgeois settings. An exception is *La Route de Flandres* (1960), which revolves round the rout of a French cavalry regiment in the Second World War.

Nathalie Sarraute (b. 1902) joined the movement, as it then appeared to be, in the fifties. But her much earlier work, *Tropismes* (1938), had prepared the kind of literature that was to be written twenty years later. She went on as both a theorist (*L'Ère du soupçon*, 1956) and a novelist (*Portrait d'un inconnu*, 1957, written in 1949; *Martereau*, 1953; *Le Planétarium*, 1959; *Les Fruits d'or*, 1963) to confirm her position as a leading 'new' writer among much younger novelists. Yet she shows little trace of the same influences. She has rejected tradition independently (except perhaps that of the Russian novelists; she herself was Russian-born) to elaborate new patterns of human relationships which seem more genuine if more complex because of her luxuriant style.

As for Marguerite Duras (b. 1914), she was first claimed as a New Novelist on the strength of *Les Petits chevaux de Tarquinia* (1953) and her play, *Le Square* (1955), followed by *Moderato cantabile* (1958). These applied the new techniques to the same material that her earlier books had treated more conventionally: the attempted but always elusive analysis of feeling in ostensibly simple characters. Making full allowance for method, these again are psychological novels, written in a rigorously spare style. She wrote the film script of *Hiroshima mon amour* (1960), more plays, including *Des journées entières dans les arbres* (1966), and such later novels as *Le Vice-Consul* (1966) and *L'Amante anglaise* (1967).

Other writers associated with the New Novel, for the most part younger and whose work is still far from complete, are Claude Mauriac, François Mauriac's son, Claude Ollier and Robert Pinget.

It is easier to speak of the New Novel than to pinpoint the New Novelists. All those so far mentioned would subscribe to the general principles indicated, but each applies them in his own way. This is hardly surprising if they have any originality at all. A comparison might be drawn with naturalism – though this does not mean that these are naturalistic writers and they have formed no group comparable even to that which centred for a time on Zola* (see above p. 206). But in both cases tendencies already in existence were strengthened by a recognition of common aims, developed in different ways by individual writers (and eventually rejected by some), and either had, or may have, a lasting influence on literature. At the same time they do not monopolize it. They resemble an injection rather than a major operation. It takes with some, fails with others, while others again seem never to have heard of it, yet contrive to remain healthy. Among these last are several novelists, not all of them traditionalists, whose main reputations were established after 1950.

A major figure is Henri Troyat, the pseudonym of Lev Tarassov (b. 1911 in Moscow), whose family emigrated to France, where he was educated, in 1920. After several shorter novels he embarked on his big *romans-fleuve* with *Tant que la terre durera* (1947–50), followed by *Les Semailles et les moissons* (1952–6) and *La Lumière et les justes* (1959–63). These chronicle-cycles, set principally in nineteenth-century Russia and terminating before the Bolshevik Revolution, resuscitate a vanished society with remarkable realism and vigour in a now outmoded form. They are no less impressive for that. They have been called Tolstoyan, with some justice. Troyat's sympathy with his native country's past reappears in his excellent biographies of Dostoievsky (1940), Tolstoy himself (1965) and other nineteenth-century writers. He is a further example of the recurrent influence of Russian literature on France, both through expatriates and on the native French themselves. In 1965 he began the saga of a great French family (*Les Eygletière*).

A more popular vein is exploited in the historical novels of Maurice Druon (b. 1918), who went far back into the national past to write his colourfully exciting *Les Rois maudits* (1955–60). He returned to history after publishing a first cyclic novel on modern French society, *Les Grandes familles* (1948–51). Aided by collaborators and researchers he has inevitably been hailed as a modern Elder Dumas.

Popular again (and why not?) is Françoise Sagan (b. 1935), who published her best-selling *Bonjour tristesse* at the age of eighteen and followed it with *Un Certain sourire* (1956), *Dans un mois, dans un an* (1957) and a number of other novels and plays (as *Château en Suède*, 1960), to *La Garde du coeur* of 1968. A minnow beside the giant chroniclers and a natural writer in the classic style, she finds her material in the rudderless youth of the upper and middle classes, depicted wistfully but unsentimentally, with no sociological undertones. She has captured the spirit of a generation which perhaps should not have existed, but did. If Radiguet has been long remembered and even read, Sagan may be also.

It may seem shocking to close this chapter with a reference, after Sagan, to Jean Cayrol (b. 1911), a Catholic poet of high quality who turned to the novel after surviving the horrors of a Nazi concentration camp. Their common feature is the sense of rootlessness, however differently conceived and expressed. In a series of novels beginning with *Je vivrai l'amour des autres* (1947–50) Cayrol presents broken-down outcasts meditating vaguely on the meaning of life – that of themselves and of others. Unlike Beckett's, they have a Christian conscience and think there may be hope somewhere, but they cannot define or fulfil it and this increases their difficulties. Another example of the Absurd, taken very seriously indeed.

CHAPTER 14

Other Prose since 1800

THIS chapter is chiefly concerned with prose-writers who cannot be attached to the history of the novel but who belong to literature either through their immediate influence upon it or through the particular qualities of their work. Philosophers, whether metaphysical or social, tend in the nineteenth century to recede from the world of letters and to form a special study in themselves. They provide a background of thought which must always be taken into account, but which it is rarely the province of literary history to explore. Its business lies more directly with the critic, the general essayist, and with certain kinds of historian.

The generation exiled by the Revolution contained some of the most original minds in France. Mention has already been made of Mme de Staël (1766–1817), who more than any other individual was responsible for calling attention to German culture and for formulating the idea of a northern alternative to the clear, dry literature of the 'classical' south. Her two principal books, *De la littérature considérée dans ses rapports avec les institutions sociales* (1800) and *De l'Allemagne* (1810), were heavily drawn on by the theorists of Romanticism, including Hugo in the Preface to *Cromwell*, and did much to guide them towards a new aesthetic. One of her contentions was that literary works are products of environment – Montesquieu had said the same of political institutions – and that in approaching them one should take account of the period and country in which they were written, as well as of geographical and climatic conditions. The misty hills of Scotland had produced Ossian (then accepted as an authentic Gaelic bard), the hard sunlight of Greece, Homer. This fruitful idea announced the Romantic interest in the local peculiarity and also refuted the classical conception of absolute standards in art. The critic is no longer asked to judge art by universal criteria, but to understand it in its various local and historical manifestations.

Exile also widened the horizon of François-René de Chateaubriand (1768–1848). This aristocratic writer fought in the *émigré* army, wandered to England and America, was recalled and employed as a diplomat by Napoleon, but broke with him when he found his policy too tyrannical. Under the Bourbon Restoration he filled important ambassadorial and ministerial posts and was responsible as Foreign Minister for giving armed support to the monarchist absolutists in Spain. Though his views afterwards became more liberal, he refused to serve the July Monarchy and retired from politics after 1830. His immense influence on the younger Romantics was exercised partly through *René*, in which the whole of a lost generation recognized its image, partly through the work of which it formed a small part, *Le Génie du Christianisme* (1802). This book was the fruit of Chateaubriand's recovery of his religious faith after a period of spiritual indecision. In reaction against the eighteenth-century agnostics, it argued the truth of Christianity by pointing to its achievements in the fields of art, learning, and social action. Maintaining that European culture was built on Christianity rather than on the 'paganism' of Greece and Rome, it attacked the classical tradition from another angle than Mme de Staël's. Its arguments were expressed in a lyrical style which was itself an illustration of the emotional and aesthetic inspiration which a living religion can give the writer. *Les Martyrs* (1809), with its colourful evocations of early Christian times, was another illustration deliberately planned, and showed how history could be approached imaginatively. Geography also, in such books as *L'Itinéraire de Paris à Jérusalem* (1811), *Les Natchez* (1827), and *Voyage en Amérique* (1827), all based on Chateaubriand's travels or on themes suggested by them. After his retirement in 1830, Chateaubriand's major works were *La Vie de Rancé* (1844), the biography of a seventeenth-century priest in whose life Chateaubriand discovered a reflection of his own, and the openly autobiographical *Mémoires d'Outre-tombe* (1848), written to be published only after his death. Here the man and the writer are both shown at their richest and a portrait is painted of the whole stormy period through which he had lived, beginning with his youth under the Old Régime.

All the chief Romantic qualities were contained in Chateaubriand: his projection of his personality into his works, his religious lyricism, his feeling for the Christian and medieval past, his feeling for nature in its more dramatic and sombre aspects, his love of the exotic. His prose, with its powerful rhythms and images, was, in certain respects, the French counterpart to Byron's poetry and preceded by up to twenty years the verse poetry of Lamartine and Hugo.

Chateaubriand showed the way to the great descriptive historians of the mid-century, particularly Thierry and Michelet. Augustin Thierry (1795–1856) was the master of the picturesque narrative. His *Récits des temps mérovingiens* (1840), written after he had gone blind, used what was essentially a novelist's technique in describing events and personages in Ancient Gaul, to which he had first been attracted as a schoolboy by a passage in Chateaubriand's *Martyrs*. It was near to the period in which d'Urfé had once set his pastoral novel *L'Astrée*, though the result was understandably different.

For Jules Michelet (1798–1874), the greatest of Romantic historians, history was even more a matter of vision – a vision in which the past of his native country came vividly to life. His chief work was the *Histoire de France* (1833–67), running from the origins in Roman Gaul to the Revolution. The fruit of immense research, it yet reads often as an imaginative work because of its impassioned style. Michelet was a man of humble birth who rose to high academic posts. He was in love with France and believed in the nobility of the people, whom he championed – at the expense of accuracy, in his later volumes – against the Monarchy and the Church. Except for his consistent anti-clericalism, he announces Péguy, and his influence has been of the same kind. He is one of the modern creators of an *idea* of France, which looks back to the Middle Ages but perhaps could not be formulated before the nineteenth century, when it was born of a combination of democratic enthusiasm and knowledge based on research. Michelet interrupted his main work for a time to write his *Histoire de la Révolution française* (1847–53), a strongly partisan account of the revolutionaries and an idealization of the Republican outlook. His short *Jeanne d'Arc* (1853) dealt with another subject dear to his heart.

In taking stock of their country's development, the historians of this period looked on the Revolution of 1789 as the great dividing-line, significant either as the end of an epoch or as the key to their own age. In either case, it obsessed them. It was analysed from the socialist point of view by Louis Blanc (1812–82), who published a *Histoire de la Révolution française* between 1847 and 1862, having previously written a history of the July Monarchy and a book on political theory, *De l'organisation du travail* (1840). Adolphe Thiers (1797–1877), a politician who was to become the first President of the Third Republic, was predominantly descriptive in his *Histoire de la Révolution* (1823–7) and *Histoire du Consulat et de l'Empire* (1845–62), but his method was to amass factual detail rather than to suggest atmosphere. His political rival, François Guizot (1787–1874), was more broadly analytical and studied, not the French Revolution itself, but the rise of the middle class to political power, which he read as the most important lesson of European history. He wrote a history of the English Revolution and histories of civilization in Europe and France.

A stronger background influence on literature, though their own writings hardly fall into that field, was exerted by early social philosophers such as Charles Fourier (1772–1837), a Utopian reformer on whose theories short-lived communities (*phalanstères*) were founded; and by Félicité-Robert de Lamennais (1782–1854), a Teilhard de Chardin of his time, who attempted to reconcile, not indeed religion and science but religion and the secular political order, unsuccessfully. A more realistic and revolutionary writer, who played a serious part in the development of early socialism, was Pierre-Joseph Proudhon (1809–65). He coined the famous phrase: 'La propriété c'est le vol'. The place of all these is in the history of social/political ideology, but hardly as historians themselves.

Of the analytical historians proper, the greatest was Count Alexis de Tocqueville (1805–58), an objective observer and lucid political thinker whose *L'Ancien Régime et la Révolution* (1856) examines the political, social, and economic causes which led to the French Revolution and shows it to have been inevitable. The exactness of his research and of his interpretations makes him still an authority to be read. Though no lover of democracy, he realized that it had come to stay and was concerned to make the best of it. He defined his object in writing as: 'To show, if possible, how in a democracy men may avoid submitting to tyranny or sinking into imbecility.' Early in life he had spent a year in America on an official mission. The visit had given him his first book, *La Démocratie en Amérique* (1835–40). Here he not only described the conditions and working of democracy in that country – with one eye on the possible developments in France – but also drew general conclusions which have proved prophetically accurate.

There is still something of the historian in Charles-Augustin Sainte-Beuve (1804–69), the greatest literary critic of his age. For him, criticism included biography, since its aim was to examine the whole personality of a writer as a means to appreciating his work. To this end every clue, psychological or material, may be of value, since: 'I may be able to *enjoy* a work, but it is difficult for me to *judge* it without knowledge of the man who wrote it. I am always inclined to say: "Such a tree gives such fruits." ' This search for the individual essence resulted in various collections of *Portraits* and in the long series of *Causeries du lundi* (1851–62) and *Nouveaux lundis* (1863–70), which appeared first as weekly articles in the press. They are descriptive more than analytical, based on a combination of research and intuitive understanding, and still illuminating, though much of their scholarship is necessarily out-dated. Often subjective or unjust when dealing with his contemporaries (though valuable as an eyewitness), Sainte-Beuve is at his best with the second-rank writers of the seventeenth and eighteenth centuries. His only long study, the monumental *Histoire de Port-Royal* (1840–60), originally given as a lecture-course, had laid him a solid foundation in the *Grand Siècle*. Later in life, he modified his individualistic conception of literature and subscribed to the evolutionary theory according to which writers could be classified in terms of species. But he himself hardly put it into practice and he always maintained that literary criticism, however scientific in its method, must remain an art in its application.

But the prevalent creed of the eighteen-sixties was more rigorous than this. Positivism, launched by the social philosopher Auguste Comte (1798–1857) as an anti-metaphysical movement recognizing only the evidence of facts, was now spreading into literary criticism and history. In those fields its most brilliant exponent was Hippolyte Taine (1828–93), whose mechanistic system reduced the artist to little more than an automaton. According to Taine, a writer's character is entirely determined by three factors: heredity, environment, and the historical moment (*La race, le milieu, le moment*). The combination of these factors creates a 'dominant faculty' (*faculté maîtresse*) which infallibly causes him to produce works of a certain kind. This theory, which was an extreme systematization of the theories of Mme de Staël and others, Taine applied to literature in *La Fontaine et ses Fables* (1853 and 1860) and in the *Histoire de la littérature anglaise* (1863), to art in *La Philosophie de l'art* (1865–99), and to history in *Les Origines de la France contemporaine* (1873–94). It proved an intellectually attractive method of explaining every human activity. Intended to be comprehensive, it gave, in the abstract, some highly interesting results. It provided a philosophy for naturalism (Zola, as has been seen, adopted it). It left its mark for a long time on literary criticism: Brunetière's theory of the evolution of literary genres derived from it, while the exacting historical methods of academic critics such as Lanson owed much to Taine, while rejecting his more rigid limitations. Today, Taine's reputation as a critic stands lower than Sainte-Beuve's, entirely because he attempted to prove too much with too little data. But as a historical landmark, representing the philosophy dominant between 1860 and 1890, he is indispensable.

With Taine must be considered Ernest Renan (1823–92), a less rigorously systematic thinker whose chief interests lay in the history of religion. He had begun as a candidate for the priesthood, but religious doubt followed by a revelation of the possibilities which science appeared to offer humanity caused him to break off his training. Throughout life, however, he retained a belief in some ideal force beyond the physical. In writing his principal work, the *Histoire des origines du christianisme* (1863–81), he approached the subject with strong emotional and aesthetic sympathies, if without faith. His biblical scholarship was thorough and he had travelled in the Palestine he described. The book opens with a short *Vie de Jésus*, hailed by Oscar Wilde as a Fifth Gospel, but which treats its theme with the inadequate charm of a pastoral. Too much of Renan is like this. He is a fluid, insinuating writer – disconcertingly so for a rationalist. His desire was to resurrect the past, like Michelet or Chateaubriand, but to shear it of mystical elements and present

it in a familiarly human light. In reconstructing the historical conditions in which Christianity was born, then its diffusion by the
disciples and St Paul until its establishment in the Roman Empire,
he paints a plausible and interesting picture, though too many of
his conjectures have proved wrong for it to have more than a
literary value today. His later works, principally the *Dialogues
philosophiques* and the *Drames philosophiques*, show great subtlety
in the play of ideas but no settled convictions of any kind. His
autobiographical *Souvenirs d'enfance et de jeunesse* (1883)
goes far to explain the character of this insufficiently tormented
thinker.

Positivism as a literary influence was already declining before
Renan's death, as was shown by the novels of Huysmans and
Barrès and by the Symbolist movement in poetry. The work of
Henri Bergson (1859–1941) marked its rejection by a philosopher
who stands as the most conspicuous dividing-point between the
two centuries. By asserting the superiority of intuition over intellect
as a means of apprehending reality, by his discovery of the distinction between spatial (clock) time and 'duration', or time as it is
actually experienced, and by his insistence on human freedom from
systems of materialistic determinism Bergson challenged the basic
assumptions of 'scientific' philosophy. His theories, expounded in
Les Données immédiates de la conscience (1889), *Matière et mémoire*
(1896), and *L'Évolution créatrice* (1907), had an incalculable effect
on the writers of his generation. At the least, these were no longer
committed to a static conception of psychology, nor to the constraint of intellectual analysis, nor to a step-by-step technique in
handling time. At the most, they recovered a whole spiritual universe which positivism and naturalism had removed from their
reach. Bergsonism seconded the revival of Catholic literature and
in later life the philosopher himself, who was Jewish, moved near
to Catholicism.

Bergsonism was an early influence on the most widely known of
modern Catholic philosophers, Jacques Maritain (1882–1971),
though afterwards he attacked it as incompatible with pure
Christian doctrine. Maritain applied Thomism (the teaching of St
Thomas Aquinas) to the problems of his time and wrote in a
progressive spirit on aspects of morals, politics, and aesthetics

(*Primauté du spirituel*, 1927; *Humanisme intégral*, 1936; *Christianisme et démocratie*, 1943; *Art et scolastique*, 1920; *Frontières de la poésie*, 1935). Maritain, who was of the same generation as Bernanos and Mauriac, was a Protestant who owed his conversion to Catholicism to Léon Bloy.

His contemporary, Pierre Teilhard de Chardin (1881–1955), was a Jesuit priest who trained in palaeontology, researched for many years in China, and became a distinguished anthropologist. His fame, mainly posthumous, rested on his philosophical writings which aimed at reconciling Christianity with modern scientific knowledge and theory. Highly unorthodox by traditional Catholic standards, they have exercised an immense influence in the direction of modernism and are open to interpretation as the removal of the old nineteenth-century barrier between faith and scientific materialism. His whole thought demands study, but outstanding separate works are *Le Phénomène humain* (1955), *Le Groupe sociologique humain* (1956) and *L'Avenir de l'homme* (1959).

Religion in France, whether opposed or related to secular philosophies, has inspired so many modern thinkers that even a mere listing is impracticable. But two individuals should not be passed over. Ernest Psichari (1883–1914) was killed, like Péguy, in the first few weeks of the First World War. A grandson of Renan and a professional soldier, he was converted to Catholicism at the age of thirty after deep meditation on life in relation to his career. The starting-point is similar to that of Vigny's *Servitude et grandeur militaires*. He left two books which have retained a lasting interest, *L'Appel des armes* (1913) and *Le Voyage du centurion* (1916). The Second World War threw up Simone Weil (1909–43), a Jewish yet anti-semitic woman whose life was marked by psychological and physical torment, but who never abandoned the attempt to understand it and never allowed herself bodily relaxation. An ascetic beyond all reason, driving herself to exhaustion in factory and farm in human solidarity with the workers, she belonged to the breed of the medieval saint and martyr but, though more than half converted, she refused to enter the Church. Yet religion, and particularly Christianity, conditioned her uncompromising personal search for truth, no less than her quest for a purer and juster ordering of society. After her death in an English sanatorium, her works were published and widely read in their French and English versions. They include *La Pesanteur et la grâce* (1947), *L'Enracinement* (1949), *Attente de Dieu* (1950), *La Connaissance spirituelle* (1950), and *La Condition ouvrière* (1951).

Simone Weil can be attached to no 'school', though some affinities may be found with Personalism, a movement started in the thirties by Emmanual Mounier (1905–50) and centred on the review *Esprit*. After the war it attracted young Catholics preoccupied with social questions and harmonized with the ideas of the Worker Priests.

This, though another sign of the modernization of French Catholicism, has had relatively insignificant effects on literature. Apart from Bergsonism and Existentialism, the principal modern movements which have affected the intellectual climate and so coloured the writer's world have been Marxism and Freudianism, both of non-French origin. Surrealism owes a considerable debt to Freudian and other psychology, but it hardly contains a coherent doctrine and its main interest, paradoxically enough, lies in its art-forms. A minority political movement, at the opposite pole to the liberal Catholicism described above and based on an ideology local to France, has had a seemingly disproportionate influence on her literature. This was the ultra-nationalistic, militantly Catholic, and anti-semitic *Action Française* movement, founded in the eighteen-nineties at the time of the Dreyfus case. Its declared aim was the restoration of the Bourbon monarchy. For forty years it had a potential attraction for any right-wing Catholics who believed that democratic corruption was undermining their country and that the antidote was in a powerfully centralized hierarchy guided by the clear Latin genius which Romanticism (after the Protestant Reformation) had clouded. Its leader throughout was Charles Maurras (1868–1952), a Provençal who was a disciple of the poet Mistral. His writings embraced a vast output of daily journalism, political pamphlets, stories (*Les Chemins de Paradis*, 1891), and literary criticism (as *Les Amants de Venise*, 1902; *Barbarie et poésie*, 1925; *Un Débat sur le Romantisme*, 1929). His interest was naturally in the moral and social significance of literature, and his bold general conclusions are highly stimulating even when unacceptable.

Of the many less immediately militant critics and essayists, one at least must be singled out. Alain (the pseudonym of Émile Chartier, 1868–1951) has left numerous volumes of short, two-page essays, entitled *Propos*, written with all the insight and precision of the humanist intellectual. His longer books commenting on the same questions – literature, art, politics, war, and peace – include *Système des Beaux-Arts* (1920), *Stendhal* (1935), *Avec Balzac* (1937), *Mars ou la Guerre jugée* (1921), *Le Citoyen contre les pouvoirs* (1928). His approach is that of Descartes rather than of Bergson, and he is at once clear, profound, and eminently readable. As a schoolmaster, first at Rouen, later at the Lycée Henri-Quatre in Paris, he influenced a number of variedly brilliant pupils, one of whom was Simone Weil and another André Maurois.

André Maurois (Émile Herzog, 1885–1967) excelled in biography, often choosing English subjects (*Ariel, ou la Vie de Shelley*, 1923; *Disraeli*, 1927; *Byron*, 1930; *Lyautey*, 1931; *Voltaire*, 1935; *Chateaubriand*, 1938; *Lélia, ou la Vie de George Sand*, 1952). His early biographies were 'romanced' somewhat in the manner of Lytton Strachey – that is, they employed a novelist's technique in imposing an aesthetic pattern on a historical subject. This method, infuriating to the academic type of critic who can rarely stomach an imaginative synthesis and is particularly shocked when the inner life of a writer is rendered in terms of externals, succeeded with the general public to an extent which has perhaps over-shadowed the sober and solid workmanship of the later biographies, from *Lyautey* on. In *À la recherche de Marcel Proust* (1949), Maurois wrote an excellent and penetrating study of the novelist. As a novelist himself (*Bernard Quesnay*, 1926; *Climats*, 1932; *Terre promise*, 1945, etc.) he was less successful. His numerous essays and historical studies were well organized rather than original.

In Maurois's time and since, biography has not thrown up any other considerable writers who have specialized in that genre. Most of the good biographers have also been novelists, or are considered as such, beginning with Romain Rolland. Other 'biographies' have been written from a more openly critical or polemical angle and their classification is dubious. At the other end of the spectrum the bookshops of the first half of the century teemed with undistinguished *vies romancées* which had a ready sale and which, if they had to be classified, could be attached also to the novel in its popular form. The same is true of 'history', written with an eye on a semi-cultured public interested in the national past so long as it was presented readably. There was literary talent in some of these books as well as some lightly-worn erudition. But nothing stands out among them and on a long view they were a debasement of Michelet, emptied of his passionate convictions and retaining only a husk of colourful information. That other heritage of Romanticism, the historical novel, has been much better done and can be respected as literature in its own right. History proper is now of course a specialized study, not intended for the general reader, but potentially a background influence exercised in several fields of thought, of which literature is only one.

As for autobiography, contrary to the view that the ego-centred theme died with nineteenth-century Romanticism, it has never been more prevalent. It takes different forms, from the relative directness of Sartre's *Les Mots* and Malraux's *Antimémoires* to writings whose authors call less ostensibly on personal experience yet use it as a basis for their testimonies, reflections, pleadings or attacks.

Among these might be placed Jean Guéhenno (b. 1890) on the evidence of such books as his *Journal d'un homme de quarante ans* (1934) and his *Changer la vie* (1961), in which he describes the life of the French working-classes before 1914 and his own experiences as a boy sent to work in a factory. By his own efforts he educated himself through the formidable State examinations to reach high University posts and membership of the French Academy. Part of his work is first-hand 'testimony', of both social and personal interest. Part is advocacy of 'humanist' (some would say 'idealistic') socialism, strongly opposed to the impersonal face of Marxism (*Conversion à l'humain*, 1931). Another part is literary criticism and interpretation, such as his homage to Michelet (*L'Évangile éternel*, 1931) and his trilogy on Rousseau (*Jean-Jacques*, etc., 1948–52). His championship of the workers, traceable directly to his origins, has been unaffected by his success in a somewhat different world.

Most literature, including the novel, has some autobiographical content, but how much is a question requiring examination in each separate writer. Most of Gide's work might be called autobiographical, though in this book he has been discussed under the novelists. The works of Proust, Colette, Alain-Fournier, Duhamel, Montherlant, Malraux, Camus and others can all be approached as partly autobiographical, though this means ignoring the literary form in which they are presented. There remain a great number of occasional books produced by novelists, poets and dramatists, in which they recount their lives or phases of them but which are not typical of their work and, as with the biographies, cannot be claimed in a brief survey to be of the first importance in themselves. There is no modern writer (except again, perhaps, the Protean Gide) to place in this chapter in the line of Montaigne, Rousseau or Chateaubriand. As for the political memoir-writers, their best place is with the historical researchers, who have a professional interest in reading them.

We are left with literary criticism and the doctrines and theories on which it is usually based. Criticism wears out quickly, no doubt because, as an excellent modern critic, Georges Poulet, has said, it is ' *littérature au second degré* '. It may acquire a historical interest, either in the history of criticism or as a reflection of the judgements and sensibility of its time. Only the greatest are still read for their own sake, like Sainte-Beuve, right or wrong. But where are the great names of the turn of the century, Lemaître, Brunetière, Faguet, Lanson? Ignored or outdated, in spite of good books they wrote and a few of which must still be consulted because they deal with subjects which no one has treated adequately since.

This is our justification for skipping two generations of gifted critics, some of them still influential, still alive, and for coming near to the present day. In the fifties, along with the Nouveau Roman, was born the term Nouvelle Critique. It was only moderately useful because, although it signalled a radical renewal of approaches and methods, these were too heterogeneous to suggest a definable group. All that its practitioners had in common was a rejection of traditional assessments. In various ways they began fruitfully tearing apart the academic conception of French literature and giving it a new face. This has not been done wantonly or ignorantly, but by men who have made a deep study of literature and some of whom have undergone a rigorous academic training.

In spite of what has been written above, one must go back a little in time to Gaston Bachelard (1884–1962) who ended a brilliant university career as Professor of the Philosophy of Science at the Sorbonne. In his fifties he switched in his writings from a scientific to a psychological approach influenced by Jung and surrealist types of poetry which led him to explore the poetic imagination in new terms. In several remarkable books, beginning with *Psychoanalyse du feu* (1937), he relates it to the natural elements and attaches great importance to dreams and imagery. His ideas may prove questionable and his richly imaged prose style critically suspect, but what cannot be questioned is his standing as the master of a new variety of psychological criticism.

The critical essays of Maurice Blanchot (*Faux-pas*, 1943; *L'Espace littéraire*, 1955; *Le Livre à venir*, 1959), who is primarily a novelist, form a kind of bridge between psychology and the formalist approach of the linguistic critics. By these it is language itself which is re-examined and analysed, either in one particular literary work or as a means of communication in general. At its lowest this can become a pedantic exercise, having little more relevance than the 'parsing' of the old Latin grammarians, but in really gifted hands it can yield results of considerable significance. Linguistic exegesis is allied to Structuralism, the most conspicuous new development in criticism. Structuralism is not confined to literature. In the work of Claude Lévi-Strauss (b. 1908), the social anthropologist, it provides a method and a philosophy for an interpretation of the whole field of human relationships and activities (*Les Structures élémentaires de la parenté*, 1940; *Tristes Tropiques*, 1955; *Anthropologie structurale*, 1958; *La Pensée sauvage*, 1962, etc.). In its most general sense, Structuralism gives first place to the ordering of things, to the way they are put together. Its application to literature is obvious – easy in the traditional five-act play, more difficult in a less rationally organized novel or poem. Some of the results are nevertheless illuminating and only misleading if they are taken to represent the 'true' significance of the work, to the neglect of other elements. Superficially at least the main emphasis must appear to bear on form and technique.

A notable exponent of the Structuralist and linguistic approach (though he is not confined to it) is Roland Barthes (b. 1915), whose inquiries into language and 'writing' – not 'literature' – in such works as *Le Degré zéro de l'écriture* (1953), *Eléments de sémiologie* (1965), *L'Empire des signes* (1970), have revealed a critic with revolutionary brilliant talents.

Structuralism, a system conceived for the social and physical sciences, may prove in time to be neither more nor less relevant to literature than the theory of evolution in the nineteenth century (see p. 248 above for Taine, and Brunetière's *L'Évolution de la poésie lyrique au 19e siècle*, 1894, etc.). Literature is a product of the imagination, an ill-defined term certainly, but explorable in other ways which appear to be more promising.

CHAPTER 15

Poetry from Lamartine to Mallarmé

IF the nineteenth century expressed itself most typically in the novel, it was also an age of great poetry. In fact no other period can show a comparable vitality and variety in its poets within so short a time. Seventy-five years separate the first simple and musical verses of Lamartine from the intricate obscurity of Mallarmé's last work. In the interval Hugo, Baudelaire, and Rimbaud had written, to name only the chief among a number of poets whose influences can still be felt today. But first it is necessary to go back to the revival of lyric poetry in the eighteen-twenties and thirties which was the Romantic Movement's most positive contribution to literature.

The four major Romantic poets – Lamartine, Vigny, Hugo, and Musset – did not form a closely-knit group like Ronsard's Pléiade. Although they were conscious of each other's work and at some points were in sympathy, their individual differences went deep. What they had in common will appear better when some outline has been given of their work and that of their immediate successors.

The earliest in date, Alphonse de Lamartine (1790–1869), was certainly the mildest of revolutionaries. But his first book, the *Méditations poétiques* (1820), struck a note new to French verse. These and the *Nouvelles Méditations* (1823) are a sheaf of monologues expressing the regrets and hopes of a young man as he ruminates among mountains and woods never too sharply described. Biographically, they were the product of a childhood spent in Burgundy – his staunchly Royalist and Catholic family owned a château near Mâcon – of early travels in Savoy and Italy, and of various experiences in love of which the most memorable was with a woman met one summer at Aix-les-Bains who died soon after of tuberculosis. But the *Méditations* are not 'confessions'. They are memories caught just at the point where they are merging into general experience, and Lamartine's achievement was to have used a harmonious and half-blurred language which seems in his best poems to flow partly below the level of consciousness. When he is too explicit he is weak, as in the more philosophical verse of *La Mort de Socrate* (1823) and *Le Dernier Chant du Pélerinage d'Harold* (1825) – on the death of Byron – in both of which his poetic language is reminiscent of Chénier. But in *Les Harmonies poétiques et religieuses* of 1830 he became again a great 'natural' poet. Here religion speaks with the voices of planets and of trees; songs of prayer and praise go up to a God who is universally present in nature; emotion of a particularly pure and eager kind is at last expressed in French verse capable of containing it.

Meanwhile Lamartine had begun to plan a great Christian epic, to be entitled *Les Visions*. Only two unrelated parts were finished: *La Chute d'un Ange* (1838) and *Jocelyn* (1836). The first, intended as the prologue, concerns the love of an angel for a woman which dooms him to remain endlessly on earth. The second was an almost contemporary tale set at the time of the Revolution in the Savoy Alps, which provide a background of beauty and grandeur. The story, naïvely sentimental by modern standards, turns on the blameless love of a young man, awaiting ordination as a priest, for a girl whom he has saved from death in the mountains. His religious obligations compel them to separate and the heroine finally dies, like other female martyrs of Romanticism. *Jocelyn* was an attempt at the familiar epic which could not be successfully written in Lamartine's idiom, or perhaps in any. But it contains many examples of the inimitable Lamartinian quality:

> Le jour s'est écoulé comme fond dans la bouche
> Un fruit délicieux sous la dent qui le touche,
> Ne laissant après lui que parfum et saveur.

After publishing *Les Recueillements* (1839) Lamartine abandoned verse except for a few isolated poems, among which *La Vigne et la Maison* (1858), inspired by a visit to his old home, might stand as his poetic testament. By that date he had acquired, and lost, importance as a politician. He had sat for eighteen years in the *Chambre des députés* in somewhat contemptuous isolation, had figured prominently in the 1848 Revolution as the incarnation of an idealistic left wing, and had been driven into retirement by the advent of Louis Napoleon. Most of his voluminous prose writings either revolve round his political activities, like the *Histoire des Girondins* (1847), or were written hurriedly during his later years of poverty and were mainly autobiographical. Lamartine did not attach much importance to these productions. He claimed that his true voice, the voice of the heart, spoke in poetry.

His contemporary, Alfred de Vigny (1797–1863), wrote with much greater reserve, but his pessimism, amounting at times to despair, finally makes a keener impression. He belonged to an old aristocratic family and was brought up on ideas of military glory. Joining the army just after the fall of Napoleon, he found that a smart and idle life were all that it offered to a young officer. Later, his marriage to an Englishwoman was darkened by the incurable invalidism of his wife, whom he looked after devotedly for some thirty years. His craving for feminine companionship led to a liaison with the actress Marie Dorval, which ended in what he considered as her betrayal of him. His public career was not much happier and the reputation gained by his early work seemed soon to be forgotten, though later he realized that his work would live. Part effect, part cause of temperament, these experiences turned Vigny even further inward and made of him a contemplative poet who knows the worst that can happen to a man but constantly looks, without much optimism, for some lightening of the horizon. His attitude has been described as a stoical endurance of suffering, and that indeed is the moral of such a poem as *La Mort du loup*, which asks: Since the animals can meet their fate without whining, why not man? But this poem is too simple to contain his whole philosophy. In the early *Poèmes antiques et modernes* (1826), he had put forward the idea of a relentless Jehovah laying burdens on great men which isolated them from humanity (*Moïse*), destroying mankind without discrimination in natural catastrophes (*Le Déluge*), or damning the purest of angels when human pity moves her to descend from heaven (*Éloa*). His second main group of poems, which began to be published separately in 1843 and were collected in *Les Destinées* (1864), contains, besides *La Mort du loup*, the black religious despair of *Le Mont des Oliviers*, which inquires whether Jesus was not in fact abandoned by God. Here also is the long *Maison de berger* in which, while writing one of the loveliest poems any Romantic poet produced, Vigny denies the usual

Romantic refuge, Nature, and turns instead to Woman, a being as
threatened and transitory as himself:

> Nous marcherons ainsi, ne laissant que notre ombre
> Sur cette terre ingrate où les morts ont passé;
> Nous nous parlerons d'eux à l'heure où tout est sombre,
> Où tu te plais à suivre un chemin effacé,
> A rêver, appuyée aux branches incertaines,
> Pleurant, comme Diane au bord de ses fontaines,
> Ton amour taciturne et toujours menacé.

Yet elsewhere he had proclaimed woman as the inevitable be-
trayer of man. Whichever way Vigny looked, there seemed no
way out. His most positive message is that our knowledge and
experience should nevertheless be passed on, since they may some-
how be of use to a future generation. He differs from the more usual
Romantic type in two ways: he does not indulge in self-pity, but
quietly endures or steadfastly answers back; he avoids the shrill
blasphemies and sarcasms which are often the obverse of the
Romantic optimism. Vigny did not feel himself as a Satanist, but
as a good man unjustly condemned.

His themes and symbols are sometimes classical or contemporary, but predominantly biblical. The Old Testament was the
ground in which his stiff but powerful imagination moved most
easily. A certain stiffness also characterizes his style, in contrast to
the fluidity of Lamartine and the torrential eloquence of Hugo, and
in his hands it is a virtue. He claimed to have created the poetry of
ideas, and the idea is always clearly and firmly stated. His method,
however, is pictorial, and it is for his pictures with their straight-
robed figures and their tawny or stormy landscapes that he can be
read with most pleasure.

The theme of the poet persecuted by a hostile society runs
through his play *Chatterton* (1835) and his prose work *Stello* (1832).
His finest piece of philosophic fiction is *Servitude et grandeur
militaires* (1835), which is full of a stoic 'virtue' which Vauvenargues would have admired. In three tales of army life, it illustrates
the subordination of self to the idea of service. Vigny wrote an
early historical novel, *Cinq-Mars* (1826), and translated three
Shakespearian plays, of which *Othello* was produced at the

Comédie-Française in 1829. His *Journal d'un poète* develops his conception of the poet as a sacrificed and necessary figure in society.

For Victor Hugo (1802–85) the poet was a prophet and leader, or at least the inspired voice which interprets events past, present, and to come. His triumphant personality and work, full of extravagant colours, mark the influx of French Romanticism at its most confident and maintain themselves long after the tide would appear to have ebbed. The son of one of Napoleon's generals and of a Royalist mother, he found success early and by 1830 was a leading figure among the young Romantic writers. In that year, having already made a mark with his ballad-poems and fired a broadside against classical doctrine in the preface to his unacted play *Cromwell*, he conquered the stage with his drama *Hernani* and wrote an outstanding historical novel, *Notre-Dame de Paris*. In the next ten years he established himself as a great lyric poet, saw the decline of the historical verse-drama which he had created, and became increasingly absorbed in political activity. Like Lamartine he remained above or outside parties, but was no Republican at this date. He was created a Peer of France in 1845, two years after the death by drowning of his daughter Léopoldine appeared to have stunned him emotionally. Public and private reasons combined to silence the writer for ten years: public events ensured him a second literary existence. His active opposition to Louis Napoleon in 1851 caused him to go into exile. He fled to Brussels, then to the Channel Islands, where he remained until the downfall of the Emperor in 1870. He spent his last fifteen years in Paris, revered as a figurehead of Republicanism and a Grand Old Man of letters. One of the first acts of his exile had been to write *Les Châtiments*, satirizing Louis Napoleon (1853). He went on to publish *Les Contemplations* (1856), his last great book of personal lyric poetry, and to conceive the main work of his maturity, *La Légende des siècles*. The first volume of *La Légende* appeared in 1859, other volumes in 1877 and 1883, and related poems posthumously. Three long novels, *Les Misérables* (1862), *Les Travailleurs de la mer* (1866), and *L'Homme qui rit* (1869), were also produced in the Channel Islands.

The earliest phase of Hugo's work belongs to the struggle in which he consciously engaged to recover the freedom and movement which he considered that literature had lost in the previous century. Medieval and oriental themes, suggested by the German romantic ballad, by Walter Scott's Border ballads, by Byron, and by the Spanish *Romancero* – a collection of late medieval ballads – offered one fascinating source of renewal. In the early *Odes et Ballades* Hugo touched somewhat timidly on the Middle Ages. In *Les Orientales* (1829), he freely pasticked the *Romancero* and confirmed at one stroke the importance of 'local colour' as one of the new factors in literature. He is, indeed, excessively exotic and picturesque when compared to Lamartine with his faint haze or Vigny painting in monochrome. He outdazzled them also by his bold experiments in metre and rhythm, which seemed once for all to have shown up the tameness of the regularly-scanned alexandrine. From this time, though he would become less strident and more sure, Hugo would remain a great technical master of verse, an innovator as important in his day as Ronsard had been in his.

In the four lyric books of 1831–40 (*Les Feuilles d'automne, Les Chants du crépuscule, Les Voix intérieures, Les Rayons et les ombres*), Hugo turned from the ballad to write chiefly in the first person. His subjects are his own passions, his religion, his family; he writes of contemporary events in relation to his own reactions; occasionally he generalizes his emotional experiences, since the conception of all humanity speaking through the poet's mouth is now shaping in his mind. So were produced the universally intelligible poems, expressing with a kind of familiar eloquence some of the great commonplaces of feeling, which typify 'normal' – one might almost write, 'classic' – romanticism. Sentiment not divorced from sensuality and presented with a philosophy deep enough anyway to serve as a cohesive ensures the permanence of such poems as *La Prière pour tous, Oceano Nox, Tristesse d'Olympio*, and the numerous love-poems addressed to Juliette Drouet, the actress who was so long his mistress that she could almost be considered as his second wife.

Les Contemplations, published after a long silence, contained poems written many years earlier and so directly continued, but in graver tones, the personal lyricism of the earlier books. Some of these poems were meditations on his daughter's death. Others, developing from that point but associated with a crisis of near-madness in the eighteen-fifties during which he became deeply interested in spiritualism, show Hugo's increasing preoccupation with the Absolute. He will no longer speak only with the voice of humanity, but with that of a force of nature and even, it appears at times, with the voice of God himself. His more extreme pretensions make for bad poetry, but they stamp him as a remarkable visionary, if not as the mystic he has sometimes been claimed to be. The first published result of his enlarged conceptions was *La Légende des siècles*, intended as an epic of the human spirit from early biblical times to a distant, apocalyptic future. It consists of a series of separate narrative poems, in which Hugo's powers of pictorial evocation are magnificently displayed. It is heavily weighted in favour of the Old Testament and the Middle Ages, which Hugo saw as a period of savage tyrants. Unsystematic, unhistorical, unscientific and, strictly speaking, unphilosophical and unreligious, many parts of it nevertheless make a striking impact through the force of the poet's imagination weighted with his unrivalled armoury of words. The subject-matter is too mixed to make it an epic in any formal sense, but it catches the epic spirit in its attempt to present legendary and traditional material from the viewpoint of its own age. Other long poems, also imagined and written during the stay in Guernsey, were conceived as continuations of *La Légende des siècles*. Two of them, *Dieu* and *La Fin de Satan*, were published in unfinished states after Hugo's death. In these he makes his most sustained approach to mysticism. The second would, as it were, complete the cycle begun at the Creation by showing the ultimate merging of evil into good. The 'end of Satan' is his integration into a single principle of life.

Victor Hugo, who begins by providing the example of vigorous and sensual egoism necessary to prove that French Romanticism was more than a product of nostalgia or neurosis, ends with the embarrassing appearance of a superman. To say that the truth behind the appearance does not greatly matter is not to condemn him, since he deliberately writes for the immediate and external response. On this level, a plastic Valhalla is as good as the real thing and at first sight probably more impressive without ceasing to be a work of art. (Is the scene-designer less an artist than the architect?) It is only if one tried to inhabit it that the difference would matter, and there is hardly room for other inhabitants in the world of Hugo's imagination. It is already filled to bursting-point with his own multitudinous presence.

None of the cosmic considerations which increase the interest of Hugo's genius by blurring its boundaries are relevant to Alfred de Musset (1810–57), who is clearly contained in his self-allotted rôle of the Flayed God. He sees himself as the sacrificial victim whose sufferings, displayed in his verse, will enlighten and purify humanity. Unlike Vigny, he looks for no solution or lesson, but relies on the shock alone to produce its effect. He reached this consummation at an early age and, it would almost seem, deliberately.

As a young man about Paris whose father was a cultured civil servant, Musset belonged to the circle of young writers which Charles Nodier gathered at the Salon de l'Arsenal and whose leading spirit was Hugo. His first book of poems, *Les Contes d'Espagne et d'Italie* (1830), reflected the influences of Hugo's *Orientales* in its evocations of Madrid and of 'Venise la rouge', which at that date Musset knew only through literature. But other poems showed a disposition to laugh at the Romantic innovations – the intensity and the 'local colour'; Byron became the preferred model and in such poems as *Mardoche* and *Namouna* Musset echoed some of the ironic melancholy of *Don Juan*. But they were not merely imitations. The ability to mock lightly and regretfully at himself and his generation from the more aristocratic heights of the eighteenth century had of course been natural to Byron, who belonged in part to that century. But it was also native to Musset, or at least he made it so. In reaction, like others of his generation, against the commercial and plebeian, he looked back to pre-Revolution days and even as far as Molière and La Fontaine in search of a lost grace and wit. Apart from literature, the attitude of the young Musset was that of the 'dandy' – the man of impeccable fashion and manners who might also be a gambler and a rake. In Musset's case, this character was complicated by fragile health, a chronic longing for some ill-defined and impossible ideal (the *mal du siècle*), and an emotional *naïveté* which practically doomed him from the start. Only when this mixture of qualities and mannerisms is understood and accepted is it possible to take Musset as seriously as he deserves. In a sense he was always in search of a pose, but the search was a necessity and the pose, when found, was maintained to the limits of his strength.

In the summer of 1833, Musset met the novelist George Sand, already celebrated for her love-affairs. In due course the pair of them travelled to Venice, where first Sand and then Musset fell ill and a third person intruded, in the form of an Italian doctor, Pagello. The relationship guttered out stormily, but not before it had crystallized Musset's genius. As a direct result of his experiences of 1834 he wrote his three greatest plays (*Lorenzaccio, Fantasio,* and *On ne badine pas avec l'amour*), his autobiographical novel, *La Confession d'un enfant du siècle*, and his great group of poems, *Les Nuits*. The persons in this story are of small consequence. Musset had been working towards a supreme emotional crisis. It would have come, with George Sand or with someone else. He was also looking for an experience which would fully develop his art. He got it in full measure, though the exploitation of it almost burnt him out. The four *Nuits* poems (*Nuit de mai, de décembre, d'août, d'octobre*), together with the *Lettre à Lamartine, L'Espoir en Dieu,* and *Souvenir*, were written between 1835 and 1840 and cover all Musset's reactions to the broken relationship – at first passionately painful but finally resigned and serene. Rarely has poetry been used for a more open statement of personal feeling, but this, as has been suggested, suited Musset's conception of the poet's function. The religious simile which he uses of the pelican tearing out its heart to feed its young illustrates his obsession.

Nearly all Musset's work was written between the ages of twenty and thirty, and the best of it between twenty-four and twenty-seven. He forced maturity upon himself and then deteriorated quickly, conserving little but his bitter-light touch in a small number of very readable poems. He was a considerably greater poet than modern criticism, which practically ignores him, allows. So far as it is concerned, his self-immolation was fruitless. His work is kept present chiefly through his plays, most of which had been written by 1837. They are considered in Chapter 17.

Of the numerous lesser Romantic poets, many have sunk into an obscurity in which they seem likely to remain, while one or two have been revived for qualities which escaped their contemporaries. There have always been readers for the sincere personal poetry of Marceline Desbordes-Valmore (1786–1859), reflecting with a delicate frankness her own unhappy life (*Poésies*, 1830; *Les Pleurs*, 1833; *Pauvres fleurs*, 1839; *Bouquets et prières*, etc., 1843). Since her first poems, *Élégies et romances*, were published in 1819, a year before Lamartine's *Méditations*, she was historically the first representative of personal Romanticism in poetry. Sainte-Beuve (1804–69), whose greatness lay in criticism, failed in poetry, which the influence of Hugo's circle round 1830 led him to write (*Joseph Delorme*, 1829; *Les Consolations*, 1830; *Les Pensées d'août*, 1837). His unfortunate passion for Hugo's wife inspired *Le Livre d'amour* (published in 1843). He attempted to introduce into French poetry a familiar, homely note which he found in such English poets as Crabbe and Wordsworth but, although this was acceptable in France (as in Lamartine's *Jocelyn* and later, urbanized, in François Coppée; also – with some inevitable dramatization – in the modern episodes of Hugo's *Légende des siècles*), it never appears native in the unrustic Sainte-Beuve. His greater contribution to Romantic poetry was his early *Tableau historique et critique de la poésie française du 16ᵉ siècle*, a study which virtually revealed the Pléiade poets to his generation. Published in 1828 and concerned chiefly with the metrical virtuosity of Ronsard and his group, it had a particular influence on Hugo, whose *Orientales* had yet to be written. Another poet of the same generation whose neglect is more complete than he deserves is Auguste Barbier (1805–82), the author of *Les Iambes* (1831), political and satirical poems full of violent invective. Some of them borrow the form of Chénier's *Iambes*. Barbier never repeated this success, though his *Lazare* (1837), recording a visit to England, is historically interesting. He was a humanitarian socialist whose indignation at the misery of the people beat vainly against his despair at the squalor of the new industrialism. His observations on London belong to the same decade as *Oliver Twist*. It is interesting to compare his coal-fogged city of gin and suicide with the more romantic London, housed with 'cottages jaunes et noirs', which the faunish Verlaine believed he discovered forty years later.

Maurice de Guérin (1810–39), who died young of tuberculosis, is remembered for *Le Centaure* and *La Bacchante*, pieces expressing a pantheistic feeling for nature in classical settings and written in a rhythmic prose more conventionally 'poetic' than Barbier's verse. They are one of the starting-points of the prose poem cultivated more concisely by Aloysius Bertrand (1807–41). His cameos of picturesque medievalism were published posthumously as *Gaspard de la nuit, fantaisie à la manière de Rembrandt et de Callot*, a title echoing Hoffmann's *Fantasie-Stücke in Callots Manier*, which had appeared nearly thirty years earlier. Like the German writer, Bertrand mingled a certain personal craziness (but relatively little) with his evocations of the past – in his case Burgundy in the fifteenth century. The form of his work, though not the content, first suggested to Baudelaire *Les Petits Poèmes en prose*. After noting the somewhat forced frenzy of the verse and fantastic stories of a writer rediscovered by the surrealists, Petrus Borel (1809–59) – self-called *le Lycanthrope*, the Werewolf – we come to the more fundamental and fertile madness of Gérard de Nerval (1808–55), the pseudonym adopted by Gérard Labrunie.

Gérard de Nerval was another member of the young Romantic group of 1830. He translated Goethe's *Faust*, collaborated in play-writing with the elder Dumas, and travelled abroad with Théophile Gautier. At twenty-eight he fell deeply in love with an actress, Jenny Colon, who did not respond and finally married another man. De Nerval's first mental breakdown followed. On recovering, he learnt that Jenny had died. He travelled again, visiting the Near East, Italy, and Germany, then relapsed into intermittent madness. A few months after his last discharge from a mental home he was found hanged in a narrow street near the Châtelet, having presumably committed suicide.

His best work was all written during the last few years of his life, while he was undergoing mental treatment. Until then he had shown, in verse, only the ordinary Romantic sentimentality with some nostalgia for the historical past; and in his stories, a combination of humour and the supernatural perhaps derived from Hoffmann. But in 1853–4 he wrote the novel *Aurélia*, which recounts his own madness and hallucinations; the short stories grouped as *Les Filles du feu*, of which the most moving, *Silvie*, was based on his happy childhood in the country at Mortefontaine; and his sonnets, *Les Chimères*, which embody his finest poetry. All these works revolve on his central obsession with a woman whom he has lost (through his own fault) but who appears in another earthly identity or in a spiritual form and may still be recovered or irremediably lost. Nerval has been quoted as the supreme example of the fusion of the dream-life with reality, and temperamentally he reminds one of Coleridge. The elements which came together in his madness were his recollections of lived experience, his reading of mystics such as Swedenborg (who taught that there was an exact parallelism between the earthly and heavenly worlds and so fathered a doctrine not unlike the New Platonism of the sixteenth century), German Romanticism (particularly the *Faust* he had translated), and his interest in the occult, which he studied deeply. All these things merge in his poetry, which acquires the attractive hidden quality of the emblem or the symbol into whose deeper sense we inevitably desire to be initiated. He thus seems to form a link between the Romantics and the Symbolists. But there is a distinction. The material of the true Symbolist is transmuted in his mind before issuing in verse – the 'poetic alchemy' of Rimbaud – and could only be fully apprehended by following the same imaginative processes as the poet. That is to say, it cannot be understood with complete precision, but always leaves some margin for subjective interpretations. In Nerval, on the other hand, everything seems to be explicable as a definite allusion to his experience or his reading, once one can find the right key. He is therefore more akin to the 'hermetic' poets of the sixteenth century, whose technical language of magical science is mysterious only to the uninitiated, or again to a later poet like Heredia, whose verse is crystal-clear when one recognizes the particular event or legend which he is treating. The interest which Nerval's verse offered to both Symbolists and sur-realists thus depended on *not* tracing each of his allusions to its source, but on preserving the enigmatic bloom of such well-known sonnets as *El Desdichado*, with its final lines:

> Suis-je Amour ou Phébus?. . . Lusignan ou Biron?
> Mon front est rouge encor du baiser de la reine;
> J'ai rêvé dans la grotte où nage la sirène . . .
>
> Et j'ai deux fois vainqueur traversé l'Achéron:
> Modulant tout à tour sur la lyre d'Orphée
> Les soupirs de la sainte et les cris de la fée.

Every line here can be referred with precision to Nerval's biography, or his studies, or his prose tales. (Thus his two victorious crossings of the Acheron were the two spells of insanity from which he recovered.) The final result of such an analysis would be to show him as a poet essentially of the same family as Musset, only vastly more condensed. So much is the quality of poetry in the eye of the beholder.

In some of the verse of Charles Baudelaire (1821–67) there is a deeper sense which cannot be exactly annotated, but on the whole this great poet was classical in his clarity and his handling of form, Romantic in his apparent morbidity, and entirely himself in every line that he wrote. The outline of his life is simple. Though he mingled in the literary and artistic movements of his time, he remained essentially isolated by his own character and was never identified with any group. When he was seven his widowed mother remarried a professional soldier and diplomat. The subsequent conflict of temperament between stepfather and stepson may well have been at the root of Baudelaire's rebellious individualism. At least he refused to take up a suggested diplomatic career or to adopt any other regular profession. On coming of age, he spent most of his own father's inheritance in two years and henceforth depended on a small income doled out to him by the family lawyer and on subsidies from his mother. His life became a characteristic combination of dissipation on small means in the Paris he knew and loved, attempts to earn more money by journalism and books, struggles with his ill-health and his religious conscience, and an unswerving devotion to his art. For him, the poet's mission was not to moralize or prophesy, nor even to interpret, but simply to show the beauty and truth which – for his misfortune, since it makes him an outcast – he sees more clearly than other men.

Beauty and truth may not be the qualities most noticed at a first reading of *Les Fleurs du mal*, the single book published in 1857 which contains nearly all Baudelaire's verse. What immediately strikes the reader is an obsession with death and decay linked to a joyless and often sadistic attitude towards sex; a kind of despair accepted as inevitable; moods of boredom and disgust – the whole elaborated with irony against a sordid yet compelling Parisian background. But on closer acquaintance, one finds that the apparent pose of Satanism, the pervading atmosphere of seamy glitter – important though they are to give body to Baudelaire – are by no means the whole story. Beneath this unhealthily brilliant crust, a mind of quite exceptional honesty and lucidity grapples with the age-old contradiction between the physical and the spiritual. Baudelaire was profoundly religious, believing with perhaps equal conviction in God and the Devil, yet clinging heroically to his own human nature. From his point of view, to renounce the flesh and become a hermit would be a betrayal; so would be Hugo's escape into spiritualism, or Nerval's into madness. He must remain, however painfully, within the limits of the human condition. That was his essence, and anything else would be unreal.

This philosophy has made of Baudelaire a universal writer, in the sense that it is easy to establish direct contact with him. One may reject his outlook, but one cannot accuse it of artifice or remoteness. On the other hand, he expresses it with an art which has given some of the most lovely, as well as moving, verse in French. Most of his poems are short, many are sonnets. He keeps to the alexandrine and two or three shorter metres, with comparatively little indulgence in metrical experiments. The effect is in the perfectly chosen and placed word, in a firmness of phrasing reminiscent of Du Bellay at his best, and in the appropriateness of his rhythms and sound-patterns, which often enchant by their sheer musical beauty. Beyond that – and for later poets and critics this has seemed to be his principal innovation – there is his sense of the associations between different objects, sensations, or concepts, partly expressed in his sonnet *Correspondances*:

> Comme de longs échos qui de loin se confondent
> Dans une ténébreuse et profonde unité,
> Vaste comme la nuit et comme la clarté,
> Les parfums, les couleurs et les sons se répondent.

The theory implied in this gave a new dimension to literature by allowing the whole sensory universe to flow through the poet who is himself part of it and no longer an outside observer. Technically, it creates a more fluid kind of imagery in which one image can merge into another without the necessity of drawing an explicit comparison. Statement and description are entrusted entirely to the metaphor.

But though this has become supremely important in modern poetry, it was by no means always Baudelaire's own practice. Had he lived thirty years later it is impossible that he would have accepted some of the more misty approximations of Symbolism. He was certainly more interested in expressing the intimations of the unconscious in concrete terms, so bringing them into full consciousness. This is the classic side of his genius. As seventeenth-century writers had aimed at giving perfect definition to ideas by means of the *mot juste* – the uniquely appropriate words which express exactly what is intended – so Baudelaire was evidently preoccupied with the *image juste*, the metaphor which should convey his meaning as precisely as possible. The sonnet *Correspondances* itself provides as good an illustration as any, particularly in the sestet:

> Il est des parfums frais comme des chairs d'enfants,
> Doux comme les hautbois, verts comme les prairies,
> – Et d'autres, corrompus, riches et triomphants,
>
> Ayant l'expansion des choses infinies,
> Comme l'ambre, le musc, le benjoin et l'encens,
> Qui chantent les transports de l'esprit et des sens.

While Baudelaire's verse – in all, about one hundred and sixty poems – represents his main achievement, his extensive prose writings are full of interest. His critical essays, first written for magazines and collected as *L'Art romantique* and *Curiosités esthétiques*, discuss contemporary literature, painting, and music and reveal another side of his deeply-cultured mind. His personal note-books, including *Fusées* and *Mon cœur mis à nu*, contain important keys to his work and character and also have more general applications. His translation of Edgar Allan Poe's *Tales of Mystery and Imagination* (*Histoires extraordinaires*, 1856–65) was the most tangible result of his cult of the American writer, whom he revered as an example of the pure artist misunderstood and persecuted by his contemporaries. He took from Poe's critical writings his conception of an art independent of social morality as well as the idea that beauty is most beautiful when mingled with 'strangeness'. In Poe's verse, so different from his own, he seems to have appreciated the 'chiming music' of the sounds and to have been blind to the banality of the conceptions and phrasing. Another foreign model, De Quincey, suggested *Les Paradis artificiels*, which are in part an adaptation of *The Confessions of an Opium Eater*, in part Baudelaire's own observations on the effect of drugs. Finally, *Les Petits Poèms en prose* introduce to us a private world recognizably related to that of the poems in verse. Without the stylization of metre and rhyme, it is more intimate if less immediately striking. For the most part, these are symbolic anecdotes and imaginative meditations rather than the prose poems which the title promises. They were nevertheless an important experiment on the road which led to Rimbaud's *Illuminations*.

Baudelaire's influence has reached so far beyond his own lifetime that he cannot be adequately classed as a Romantic poet – even an embittered or a distorted one. But his work does mark a point in time from which it is possible to survey the chief Romantic characteristics. In the forty years since the publication of Lamartine's *Méditations*, the right of the poet to speak in the first person had been fully asserted. The individual self, whether exalted or detested, had become the established starting-point from which to approach society, religion, or nature. The old classical conception of standard human reactions disappeared and what was now valued was the differentiating feature, the originality or even abnormality of each writer. Work and personality became inseparable, with particularly fruitful results in lyric poetry – the one field in which the Romantic was entirely at home. Feeling was the chief guide and touchstone, superseding Reason, which the eighteenth century had seen as the controlling principle. 'Absolute Reason died at eleven last night,' announces the director of the asylum in *Peer Gynt*, and in an ecstasy of liberation the lunatics prepare to cut their throats. Such violent alternative roads to truth were taken, on the whole, only by the minor Romantics, and they have the obvious literary disadvantage that the findings are incommunicable. Yet the mere recognition of new approaches, whether through sentiment, sensation, or intuition, had a broadening effect on the whole of poetry, which could now claim to be a universal instrument for exploring and expressing the human situation. The language of poetry had been greatly enriched by the practice of new metres and verse-forms and above all by the development of a vocabulary no longer tied to the neo-classic standards of taste which had ruled in the eighteenth century. As for the classical mythology which has always been of central importance in European art, including poetry, there could be no question of rejecting it completely. Prometheus, Venus, the Furies, and the Muses were still necessary symbols to the Romantic poet. But Christian mythology played a much larger part in literature than it had done since the Middle Ages, and this implied drawing not only on the Bible (the main source) but also on medieval beliefs and legends. Satan walked again, though not strictly according to Catholic theology, while the illuminist sects of the eighteenth and early nineteenth centuries contributed their own spirits and angels. Some poets looked to foreign cultures and discovered, or rediscovered, the significance of Faust, the Wandering Jew, or Don Juan. All these were separate tendencies which, though they amounted to a preoccupation with the spiritual in many forms as opposed to the rational and the material, could hardly be the basis of a new culture. A culture and its mythology grow up together, and it would have been quite impossible in a few decades to displace the ancient traditions of Greece and Rome or of orthodox Christianity, or to have formed some new amalgam of them which could have any living force. All that can be said is that the Romantic poets inclined each to use a private mythology, less conventionally classical than before. Thus, Venus and Helen were for the time being relegated to the background. In their place were Eve, Delilah, Elvire, or more often a modern though idealized *elle*.

A characteristic of the Romantic de-standardization was that it extended beyond individuals to racial and cultural minorities. This occurred throughout Europe, giving a 'soul' to new national movements in the form of a revival of languages and literatures which had long lain dormant. In France there was the regional revival of Provençal brought about by the group of poets known as the Félibres, who came together formally in 1854. They organized themselves on the lines of the medieval associations of troubadours, but the old heritage proved to be exhausted and a modern

Provençal literature has failed to develop. Only their leader, Frédéric Mistral (1830–1914), acquired European standing with his long poems woven from southern French legend and tradition, such as *Mireille*, *Calendal*, and *Le Poème du Rhône*.

In terms of poetic 'schools', the Romantics were succeeded by the Parnassians, a name taken from *Le Parnasse contemporain*, an anthology of contemporary poetry published serially between 1866 and 1876. But the Parnassians, while intending a revolt, merely developed certain Romantic tendencies to the neglect of others. For all their somewhat narrow theory, their work is best seen as a by-product of Romanticism.

The origins of the movement can be traced back to Théophile Gautier (1811–72), one of the young Romantics of 1830 and originally a painter. His early poems showed an evident inability to render personal feeling in verse, and he was temperamentally justified in turning to descriptive poetry in which his taste for the macabre and the exotic could have full play. He visited Spain, an experience which developed his strong sense of local atmosphere. As early as 1835, he launched his theory of Art for Art's sake in the preface to his novel, *Mademoiselle de Maupin*. It was reinforced by his main volume of poems, *Émaux et Camées* (1852). He advocated and practised the carefully-chiselled poem, detachment from subjective emotions as well as from contemporary events, and the cultivation of 'colour' which stressed the appearance of places more than the psychology of people. Gautier himself is only a minor poet, though Baudelaire hailed him as his master in the dedication of *Les Fleurs du mal* and there is an external similarity between some of their poems. In the eighteen-fifties and sixties, however, he represented an overdue protest against the self-pitying attitude of some of Musset's disciples and the careless verse into which they emptied their hearts. To his demand for stricter forms was added the plea of Théodore de Banville (1823–91) for greater metrical virtuosity. In *Les Cariatides* (1842) and *Les Odes funambulesques* (1857), Banville revived old verse-forms like the *ballade* and rhymed and punned with a juggler's skill. Going further than Gautier, he declared that art was his religion, though all that he made of it was a specialized craft.

Parnassianism was in fact a convenient term to cover the tem-

porary desire for impersonality, for carefully-composed and somewhat static verse, and a renewal of interest in Greece and Rome,
which were now credited with the same picturesque qualities as
the Middle Ages and the Renaissance. Poets as varied as Baudelaire
and the young Verlaine and Mallarmé contributed to *Le Parnasse
contemporain* and owed something to the tendencies which it
represented. Even Victor Hugo had his Parnassian moments. Only
two considerable poets, however, remained identified with Parnassianism throughout their careers, and the first does not entirely fit
the theoretical definitions.

Leconte de Lisle (1818–94) was a powerfully pessimistic poet
whose work seems based on a fundamental contradiction. He
accepted the scientific positivism of his time, evolution, and the
purely materialistic destiny of man. On the other hand, he had no
faith or interest in material progress. His imagination was stirred
by the splendid savagery of primitive cultures and past epochs,
ranging from Ancient Greece to the Scandinavia of the Norse gods,
and dwelling with particular sympathy on India. In his three main
books, the *Poèmes antiques* (1852), *Poèmes barbares* (1862), and
Poèmes tragiques (1884), he develops, though not systematically,
his idea of the evolution of religions. Each has grown up and
declined with its particular civilization. The last-comer, Christianity, is now dying in its turn. For the human race, as for the individual, there is no foreseeable future – only a growing lassitude and
finally annihilation.

Leconte de Lisle rarely writes in the first person, but some
personal grounds can be found for his pessimism. He was born
and brought up in Réunion, in the Indian Ocean, where his father
was a sugar-planter. His descriptions of tropical scenes, with the
suggestions they often carry of a violent but finished world, are
certainly connected with the nostalgia of the Parisian man of letters
for the island of his childhood. Politically, he was a disillusioned
socialist of Fourier's school, and the despair into which the loss of
a political faith can plunge the individual is easy enough to understand today when it has become equivalent for many people to the
loss of a religion. In Leconte de Lisle's case, it may explain why a
communal hope turned into a cosmic disappointment, embracing
all life rather than the single personality. As Leconte de Lisle's

scientific philosophy dated, his verse came to be read principally for its descriptions, and among these his descriptions of wild beasts and birds. Some of these appear as heavily-loaded set-pieces, too highly coloured and elaborate, whereas they are in fact marvels of caricaturism. The same may be said of his evocations of exotic countries and societies. To relive, say, the Old Testament through the imagination of this peculiarly frustrated Frenchman of the eighteen-sixties is an experience as impressive as reliving it through Milton or through Claudel, though the theology is less familiar. In spite of this, Leconte de Lisle's stock has slumped heavily. Of the greater nineteenth-century poets he is probably the least read. Since his time, poetry has taken a different road.

The purest Parnassian poet was José-Maria de Heredia (1842–1905), a Cuban by birth who spent most of his life in France. Nearly all his verse is contained in the hundred and eighteen sonnets of *Les Trophées* (1893), which are a scholar's exact, pictorial evocations of scenes typical of past cultures, particularly Greece, Rome, and the century of the Renaissance. Heredia has no philosophy, except a general mild melancholy. He comes nearer to the ideal of Art for Art's sake, as Gautier had understood it, than any other poet of his century. The pleasure to be had from his finely-worked sonnets is comparable to the collector's thrill in coming upon a small but perfect new specimen.

The Parnassian conception of poetry was soon overshadowed by a subtler and more profound conception, that of the Symbolists. Symbolism had been already implicit in Baudelaire and Nerval and there is of course no precise point at which it can be said to have emerged. Poets became conscious of it as a definite movement in the eighteen-eighties, but the tendencies which composed it had come into existence some time before that. Some of them were apparent in the work of Paul Verlaine (1844–96).

Verlaine was one of the last Bohemians, though his Bohemianism was modified by a 'respectable' middle-class background from which he never quite broke free. Sly and unheroic, though quite incapable of caution, he has been compared to Villon. So far as there can be a resemblance over a gap of four centuries, he does show some of the same Parisian irreverence, the self-pity, the piety, and the unashamed attitude towards sex. The two most decisive events in his life were his marriage to Mathilde Mauté, the young wife from whom he separated after long and sordid quarrels of his own making: and his association with the poet Rimbaud, with whom he travelled to England, and whom he shot and wounded in the arm during a quarrel in a Brussels hotel. During his consequent imprisonment in Mons gaol, Verlaine was converted to the Catholic piety expressed later in the poems of *Sagesse*. After his release, he took various teaching-posts in England and France, tried farming without success, and drifted back into a life of debauchery in Paris. Several of his last years were spent in hospital, from which he issued periodically to receive the homage and drinks offered by admirers of his now considerable literary reputation. He died almost destitute.

Most of Verlaine's verse can be related to his biography, though his first collection, the *Poèmes saturniens* (1866), contained a number of impersonal descriptive pieces in the Parnassian manner. His *Fêtes galantes* (1869) very successfully evoked the delicate licentiousness of eighteenth-century painters such as Watteau and Fragonard and was one of those 'transpositions of art' recommended by Gautier (painting into poetry), but executed with a new lightness and irony. The three following books (*La Bonne Chanson*, 1870; *Romances sans paroles*, 1874; *Sagesse*, 1881) show Verlaine's allusive personal manner at its best, and the religious poems contained in *Sagesse* alongside others appear different but not discordant. It would be unkind to describe Verlaine's religion as religiosity, but it inclined to a languorous resignation and there was no real battle of conscience of the sort that tortured Baudelaire. Verlaine was a convert who easily relapsed, as, after the two mixed collections of *Jadis et naguère* (1884) and *Amour* (1888), he did openly in *Parallèlement* (1889). He explained this last as a 'cruelly pagan' expression of the senses running 'parallel' to his more edifying books. His best work was now finished and too much of the rest is an undergraduate mixture of sensuality and sentimentality written in a style of distressing flabbiness. Yet one can feel relatively grateful to Verlaine for living to be over fifty without ever acquiring pomp and dignity.

His poem *Art poétique*, published in 1882 but composed in prison eight years earlier, became one of the sacred texts of the Symbolist school, together with Baudelaire's *Correspondances* and Rimbaud's *Sonnet des Voyelles*. It was, protested Verlaine, only a song, but at least it provides an excellent commentary on his own verse. Written in an anti-Parnassian spirit, it insists on music, imprecision, shading but not colour (he meant bright distinctive colours which delimit and separate, whereas shading 'marries dream with dream and flute with horn'). There must be fluidity and lightness, no rhetoric, no clinking and tyrannical rhymes; above all, no 'literature'.

Many of Verlaine's best poems fulfil these conditions. He achieves the desired fluidity of form often by following his own prescription of *l'impair* – the uneven line of seven, nine, or eleven syllables instead of the more usual eight, ten, or twelve. His lack of respect for conventional scansion, syntax, and educated speech gave French poetry a freedom well on the way to free verse, though Verlaine's verse still rhymes and scans in its manner. This was the right instrument to render those fugitive moods and impressions, those flickers of pure feeling good for a score of lines but not much more, which are his greatest contribution to French poetry and remind us at times of a suppler and more sensitive Ronsard. Verlaine, though he preferred the analogy with music, had much in common with the Impressionist painters, and impressionism is the word that has stuck to his verse. He has the defects of his qualities – vagueness with subtlety, triviality with delicacy, and a general lack of firmness in thought and form. To read his verse for long is to feel like a fly drowning in a medium-sweet Sauternes. There is nothing substantial to take hold of – and the point is that there should be nothing.

While the bad imitator of Verlaine may achieve a meaningless prettiness, it would require a literary perverter of genius to do the same with Arthur Rimbaud (1854–91). This astonishing poet, who turned his back finally on literature at nineteen (or, according to a recent theory, a year or two later), invites judgement not merely as a precocious adolescent but as a writer who must be placed on the highest level by any standard. He was born in the industrial town of Charleville, near the Belgian frontier, and brought up by a mother with the strictest of front-parlour mentalities. His father was a roving professional soldier, seemingly of some originality of character, who left the home finally when Rimbaud was six. Rimbaud became a brilliant pupil at the local school, which he left at sixteen, laden with prizes which he sold soon afterwards for twenty francs. He had already begun to write poetry and during the next year composed much of his 'regular' verse. This was also a year of rebellious and adventurous wanderings to Paris, to Brussels, against the disturbing background of the Franco-Prussian war and the Commune. Psychologically, it was a period of the intense passion and receptivity to sensation which can go with adolescence and which Rimbaud tried to exteriorize in the medium he intuitively understood: literature. To express the *totality* of his sensations, the poetry he already knew seemed inadequate. While still sixteen (May 1871) he tried to formulate in letters to two friends a new conception of the poet as a *voyant* (a *seer* in the literal sense) who will arrive at supreme knowledge by experiencing in himself 'every form of love, of suffering, of madness'. He will achieve this after a deliberate preparation: 'The poet makes himself a *voyant* by a long, immense and planned disordering of all the senses.' This theory, which has had tremendous repercussions in French poetry, is easily explained as the still generalized desire of the passionate adolescent to embrace the whole sensory universe and find reality in that ecstatic way, aided by the use of drugs, rather than by the step-by-step method associated with Descartes. (Though even Rimbaud was Cartesian enough to envisage a planned (*raisonné*) disorder.) With Rimbaud it worked for a limited time – after which spiritual exhaustion silenced him for good, exactly as he had foreseen that it would.

Armed with this doctrine and with his masterly poem *Le Bateau ivre*, Rimbaud spent six months in Paris at the invitation of Verlaine, to whom he had sent some of his work. He loathed young literary Paris and it rejected him as rustic and boorish (as he exaggeratedly was). But with Verlaine a bond of sympathy was established which resulted in a year's wandering together to Belgium and London and finally the shooting affair in Brussels. Rimbaud, greatly shaken, retired to a farm in the Ardennes owned by his mother, where he finished *Une Saison en enfer* and had it privately printed (October 1873). This series of meditations in sometimes enigmatic prose reflects his experiences of the past two years, and in a certain measure his disgust, or at least disintoxication.

He confesses the failure of his attempt to reach truth through variety of sensual experience and the 'verbal alchemy' which went with it. But now he has returned to earth and to 'rugged reality'.

This work appears to be Rimbaud's farewell to literature and to follow logically on the prose poems of *Les Illuminations*, which render, as far as words can, the visionary world which Rimbaud had created or discovered – but in any case inhabited – in obedience to his conception of the poet as *voyant*. *Les Illuminations* – first published by Verlaine in 1886, when Rimbaud was far away and had no further interest in them – were dated traditionally before *Une Saison en enfer*, and this seemed to be their natural place. However, in 1949 the critic Henry de Bouillane de Lacoste concluded that *Les Illuminations* is the later work and was composed, or at least fair-copied by the poet, towards 1874–6. His conclusion was based primarily on an examination of Rimbaud's handwriting, which he found more mature in the manuscript of the *Illuminations*. Although his view has by no means won general acceptance, the possibility that Rimbaud returned to his imaginary world after the farewell of the *Saison en enfer* can no longer be ruled out.

In any case, it would have been a short return. Determined now to equip himself for the 'real' world and driven, in the words of one of his biographers, 'by his demon, but no longer by his genius', Rimbaud travelled widely in Europe and even to Java, working in half a dozen capacities from circus-hand to quarryman. In 1880 he settled as a trader at Harar in Abyssinia, and in a tough life now dominated by the material values of his pitiless mother trekked through hitherto unexplored regions with his caravans of rifles and salt. His only remaining literary ambition was to place a few travel articles with French newspapers – which did not print them. After eleven years he was brought home with an agonizing tumour on the knee and died a few months after amputation in hospital at Marseilles.

While the adolescent may be, emotionally, nearest the source of poetry, his verse is often imitative and so seems to be partly the expression of other men's experience. The miracle of Rimbaud is that, having absorbed Hugo, Baudelaire, and some of Verlaine, he still had time to invent a magnificent language of his own. His style, relatively plain in the earliest poems in verse, though already

wonderfully supple, becomes rich and complex because of its subjective images in *La Bateau ivre*, written while he was still sixteen.
Here, inspired by pictures in magazines, Rimbaud, who had not yet
seen the sea, identified himself with an abandoned ship tossing on
an almost fabulous ocean and mixed colour with perfume, sight
with sound, the physical with the abstract, in an interweaving of
metaphor which went well beyond Baudelaire's idea of 'correspondences'.

A little later he wrote his sonnet on the vowels:

A noir, E blanc, I rouge, U vert, O bleu,

a statement of equivalences between sounds and colours which
appears more dogmatic than was probably meant. Some of his
later poems have the deceptive lightness of folk-songs which use
such simple words that they become mysterious. As for the prose
Illuminations, they are the immediate transcription of an inner
experience and so, at many points, indecipherable. That does not
lessen their power of suggestion or the interest of their rhythms
and their daring juxtapositions of ideas and images. Fifty years
later the surrealists would use the same technique more mechanically. But in reading Rimbaud, one cannot feel that his effects were
trick effects.

He is the kind of poet who appeals particularly to the reader
who prefers the intuitive flash to the rationally constructed work.
In his French context, he gives striking proof of the distance
poetry had travelled since Boileau or even Chénier. So extreme is
the contrast that he appears to belong not merely to a different
century, but to a different literature and a different race. On any
reckoning, he is among the greatest French poets. If one had to
pick a quartet combining the highest quality with the widest possible
range, one would list him with Baudelaire, Racine, and Ronsard.
Should there be a fifth place for Mallarmé?

Stéphane Mallarmé (1842–98) was a teacher of English in various
provincial *lycées* and, after 1871, in Paris. Only towards the end of
his life was he able to give up this uncongenial drudgery and devote
himself entirely to literature. His outwardly uneventful life was
shared with his German wife and their daughter. Their flat in the
rue de Rome became a place of pilgrimage for the younger writers

who began in the eighteen-eighties to hail him as a master. His poems present a façade of impersonality constructed with immense patience and skill which – if he is contrasted with Verlaine and Rimbaud – assimilate him to the Parnassians, to whom he at first adhered. But the technique and the final effect are quite different from anything achieved by Gautier or Heredia.

He had begun writing several years before Rimbaud. The first version of his most famous poem, *L'Après-midi d'un faune*, was written in 1865 and twice recast before being published in its definitive form, with illustrations by his friend Manet, in 1876. This, with shorter poems published collectively in 1887 and 1899, constitutes the best of his work, which is virtually completed by the experimental *Un coup de dés jamais n'abolira le hasard* (1897) and his intricate prose writings on literature and art (*Divagations*, 1897). *Hérodiade*, a poem symbolizing virginity or sterility, obsessed him throughout life, rather as *La Tentation de Saint Antoine* obsessed Flaubert. He began it when he was twenty-two and left it unfinished at his death.

An intellectual inhibited by the white sheet of paper which he was too fastidious to violate (a typewriter would have been fatal to his art), Mallarmé might easily have contented himself with tracing elaborate verbal flowers in the margin. With great persistence, he reached the centre, but his was always an indirect approach. He was at once incapable and contemptuous of the plain statement, whose inadequacy (because of its bluntness) repelled him. The 'subject' of *L'Après-midi d'un faune* is the desire of the faun, dreaming and half-dreaming on a warm southern afternoon, for the nymphs of whose reality he is uncertain. The 'subject' of the sonnet beginning:

> Tel qu'en Lui-même enfin l'éternité le change

is the reputation of Edgar Allan Poe whom, following Baudelaire, he greatly admired. The no less famous sonnet which opens:

> Le vierge, le vivace et le bel aujourd'hui

appears to treat metaphorically the poet's artistic impotence, or fear of impotence. But of course such poems cannot be summarized in a prose restatement. Their interest is in Mallarmé's approach to his themes, his probing and turning, the seemingly organic life given to his verse (and thought) by the grafting of image on image and allusion on suggestion. Of necessity, he almost created a new language for poetry – a language in which words took on new meanings, sentences new shapes, while rhyme and sound played an important part in contributing to the final impression. In *Un coup de dés jamais n'abolira le hasard* – his most difficult work – he went even further away from normal language and tried by special printing devices to express concepts which still remain obscure.

This was not – though it may look like it – only Art for Art's sake. Nor was it a substitution of verbal skill for fertility of ideas or lived experience. Mallarmé's close-packed poetry corresponded to his close-packed thought on themes which he found emotionally important. But because these themes have not, on the whole, bulked large in general human experience, his verse has tended to appeal most to other poets and to intellectuals with a developed aesthetic sense. It goes, these declare, to the root of the matter. Others ask whether the root is really so deep and so hidden. They accuse Mallarmé of being largely responsible for the obscurity for which twentieth-century poetry is sometimes blamed. But it must be remembered that without Mallarmé (and in his different way Rimbaud) the plain-speaking tradition of the great Romantics, magnificent though it was in its time, would have degenerated long ago into the same obviousness as late 'classical' verse; or else it would be hiding its poverty under a smoke-screen of rhetoric. In either case critics would rightly be inquiring what poetry could say that prose could not say better. This situation was averted by renewing the mystery of poetry at the source, by removing it altogether from the category of the travel article, the political speech, the sermon, and even the personal confession to priest or psychologist.

Among the contemporaries of the three major poets just described were others whose quality was not appreciated until later. The comte de Lautréamont – such was the pseudonym of Isidore Ducasse (1846–70) – produced in his short life one strange work in poetic prose, *Les Chants de Maldoror*, particularly prized by the surrealists in the nineteen-thirties as an example of 'unconscious' writing. As the work of an adolescent in revolt, obsessed by the predominance of evil, it has been compared to Rimbaud's *Saison en enfer*. But the imagination is far less rich and the literary originality far less profound. Beside the mechanical frenzy of certain scenes, there are other passages which a drunken Chateaubriand might have written. Tristan Corbière (1845–75), who wrote the staccato and close-packed verse of *Les Amours jaunes* (1873), was also a rebel, principally against Romantic sentimentality. The son of a Breton sea-captain, he spent most of his life at Roscoff, in Finistère, sailing his own boat in a deliberately tough protest against his own sickly constitution. While owing something to Baudelaire, he is essentially a poet of the open air, filled with a sardonic Celtic melancholy and with a contempt for 'literature' at least equal to Verlaine's. Almost forgotten for fifty years, he was rediscovered by twentieth-century critics. An opposite case is that of Jean Richepin (1849–1926), who achieved an immediate popularity of scandal with his poems on down-and-outs and vagabonds, *La Chanson des Gueux* (1876), and worked on through ragged Bohemia and the out-of-doors in such collections as *Les Caresses*, *Les Blasphèmes*, *La Mer* (1884). But for some time now this once-relished poet has been unmasked as only an imitation filibuster, with the literary man's sprinkling of picturesque or archaic shock-words.

A more truly original poet was Charles Cros (1842–88), a Parisian Bohemian with many talents (he invented, on paper, colour photography and the gramophone), and a friend of Verlaine and Rimbaud. His two collections, *Le Coffret de santal* (1873) and *Le Collier de griffes* (1908), contain prose poems already suggestive of surrealism and verse full of lively fantasy and of a sometimes macabre humour. There is also fantasy, of an ironical and lightly bitter sort, in Jules Laforgue (1860–87), whose untraditional vocabulary and metres had an appreciable influence on the early T. S. Eliot. He died young of tuberculosis, and there is a bleak gaiety in his seemingly unsubstantial verse in keeping with his destiny. His work is thin both in sensual content and in human experience, but much too keenly and uncomfortably sensitive to be dismissed – as it has been – as the voice of a dying pierrot. His chief collections were *Les Complaintes* (1885), *L'Imitation de*

Notre-Dame la Lune (1886), *Le Concile féerique* (1886), and *Derniers Vers* (1890). He was one of the first French poets to write free verse, as distinct from the prose poem and from Verlaine's *vers libéré* (traditional metres loosely handled). Partly for his technical interest, partly because there is a tonic quality in his melancholy, he tends with many modern readers to take the place of the more musical Verlaine. But to rank him as high would be perverse.

In terms no longer of men but of movements, the nineteenth century ended with the triumph of Symbolism. This had begun, with Verlaine, as a protest against the too deliberate artistry of the Parnassians. It ended, with Mallarmé, in the elaboration of a style which is the antithesis of the spontaneous song. Yet both these poets, in their different ways, prepared French poetry for the task which would face it in the next age – the expression of the unconscious. The Romantics had brought their egos to the surface and, once there, had exhibited them in a bright and often theatrical light. The Symbolists realized how much was lost by this excessive clarity. The true personality must be left to swim in the depths, even if at times it could be only vaguely seen. The blur, the shadow, the sudden illogical shift from level to level were part, not just of its surroundings, but of its nature. They might be rendered by an aesthetic which, like Baudelaire's and Rimbaud's, recognized the merging of sensations, by freer poetic forms and by a telescoping of metaphors which gave greater mobility to verse. But it was as much a matter of outlook as of technique. The poet who conceives it as his function to clarify, or to philosophize over the examples he has fished up, will not even attempt to manœuvre among the shadows; his duty is to dispel them. Whether he is wrong, or whether there is not always room in literature for both kinds of approach, is a question on which criticism constantly divides.

Meanwhile, Symbolism dominated poetry for some twenty years and extended its influence to other European countries, including Belgium, which had a flourishing school of Symbolist poets. While an account of the French-language literature of Belgium is outside the scope of his book, the name of at least Émile Verhaeren (1855–1916) must be mentioned. With a background of Flemish realism apparent in his first book, *Les Flamandes* (1883), he reflected the influence of Symbolism in the more personal phase which followed

(*Les Soirs, Les Débâcles, Flambeaux noirs*). He then became absorbed in socialism and rendered the atmosphere of rustic Flanders and of the monstrous industrial towns in such books as *Campagnes hallucinées* and *Les Villes tentaculaires* (1896). In his final phase, he became almost a prophet of fraternity, reminiscent of Hugo in the rhetorical alexandrines of *Les Forces tumultueuses* or *La Multiple Splendeur* (1906). It is, however, for the rough and powerful free verse of his earlier books, often compared to Walt Whitman's, that he is best remembered. His compatriot, Maurice Maeterlinck (1862–1949), made his chief mark on the French theatre with his poetic dramas discussed in Chapter 17. He wrote an early volume of personal verse in the Symbolist manner, the *Serres chaudes* of 1889.

Such a work points to the domesticated Symbolists of the eighteen-nineties – Albert Samain, Gustave Kahn, Stuart Merrill, Francis Vielé-Griffin, and others – pleasant, melodious poets in their way, but too delicate to survive in this rough world.

A blending of Symbolism and Parnassianism is found in Henri de Régnier (1864–1936), who wrote like a somewhat tenuous Verlaine in the free-verse poems of the *Jeux rustiques et divins* (1897), then, under the influence of J.-M. de Heredia, began to cultivate historical and local colour and to use the sonnet and other short regular forms. Régnier's verse has the kind of beauty associated with rose-scented twilights in comfortable surroundings. It is nostalgic and politely sensual. It is honestly felt and executed within its obvious limits, and there is no good reason why a sensibility of this order should not express itself in pleasing poetry. It would only be a pity if such verse, typical of much of the poetry of the early nineteen hundreds, were mistaken for the culmination of Symbolism rather than its echo in a minor key.

CHAPTER 16

Poetry in the Twentieth Century

FOR the true climax of Symbolism we must look to Paul Valéry (1871–1945), whose early poems, finally published in *Album de vers anciens*, were written in the eighteen-nineties under the influence of Mallarmé. Soon after writing them, Valéry appeared to give up literature. He became private secretary to the director of the Havas news agency, married, and devoted much of his time to study and meditation. The key to his silence can perhaps be found in a prose dialogue which he wrote at the age of twenty-four, *Une Soirée avec Monsieur Teste*. This shows him intensely interested in the processes of the intellect but indicates his objections against expressing them in words: words limit and to some extent falsify thought, creation means movement but execution is static, and then the idea of a public or an audience must disturb the purity of the writer's inner dialogue. This austere theory may well have been Valéry's reason for publishing nothing for twenty years. In 1917 he produced *La Jeune Parque*, his most intricate poem, followed by *Le Cimetière marin* (1920) and *Charmes* (1922), then virtually ceased to write verse. Recognition was immediate. Academic and other honours transformed the solitary thinker into an almost official representative of French culture. In this more social phase of his life he produced the numerous essays on philosophic, moral, and cultural themes which showed his mastery of dialogue and made the prose-writer hardly inferior to the poet. The chief of them are in the five volumes of *Variété* (1924–44), in *L'Âme et la danse* (1921), *Eupalinos ou l'Architecte* (1923), *Degas, Danse, Dessein* (1938), and *Regards sur le monde actuel* (1931–45). His last important work, *Mon Faust* (1946), takes the form of a stage play and is written partly in verse. His fascinating *Cahiers* were also published posthumously (29 vols., 1957–61).

A recurrent theme of the prose writings is the conflict between the artist and the thinker, incarnating action and contemplation. It is certain that such a conflict had taken place in the poet. Yet without

a knowledge of Valéry's life and theories, who would suspect it?
There is none of that stiff struggle between the thinker and his
medium which distinguishes Vigny, little (except in the early verse)
of that torturing of words and phrases to make them yield surprising secrets which was Mallarmé's method of composition. Valéry's
verse flows in traditional metres and verse-forms, with a delight in
sound-patterns which fully explains why he gave his famous, but
one-sided, definition of Symbolism as 'the common intent of
several families of poets (otherwise mutually hostile) to recover
their own birthright from Music'. His own verse is certainly poetry-
music, but it is also poetry-meditation of a kind in which the intellectual and the sensual are inextricably mingled. It is impossible
to say which is leading the other. Narcissus, on whom Valéry wrote
three different poems, never loses sight of his own body, neither
does the Young Fate, neither does the Pythoness, the oracle physically convulsed before she can deliver the divine message which
might be taken to characterize all 'intuitive' poetry:

> Honneur des Hommes, Saint LANGAGE,
> Discours prophétique et paré,
> Belles chaînes en qui s'engage
> Le dieu dans la chair égaré,
> Illumination, largesse!
> Voici parler une Sagesse
> Et sonner cette auguste Voix
> Qui se connaît quand elle sonne
> N'être plus la voix de personne
> Tant que des ondes et des bois!

While Valéry deals with sensations in terms which the
intellectual must respect as supremely intelligent, he is not a poetic
philosopher, since his thinking 'leads nowhere'. Under the dreamlike surface of the verse, there goes on a conscious and highly skilful
counting-over of the ego. But the purpose of this is not self-knowledge which might in some way be used. Indeed, it has no purpose
outside itself. *Dilettante* is a word which is often misapplied. One
of its French meanings is *connaisseur*. Rightly understood, it contains the highest praise that can be given to a poet. One can either
accept Valéry's verse as one of the most marvellous *objets de luxe*

that the French genius has ever produced, or one can, if it seems necessary, discover a different justification of it in Valéry's own phrase: 'L'Homme pense, donc je suis, dit l'Univers.'

Only one poem seems at least partially to break the circle suggested by the title *Charmes* ('Incantations'). This is the beautiful and verbally vigorous *Cimetière marin*, a meditation in a churchyard overlooking the Mediterranean. The sea, the sun, the dead, the self's consciousness of them all and of its own existence, are linked in verse as sinewy and flawless as anything written in French. Published exactly a hundred years after Lamartine's *Méditations*, *Le Cimetière marin* appears, as much as one poem can, as a worthy culmination of a century of poetry.

Poetry different in every way is found in Paul Claudel (1868– 1955). As Valéry's starting-point was Mallarmé, Claudel claimed to descend from Rimbaud, in whose prose poems, *Les Illuminations*, he found the reply to the materialism of the eighteen-eighties and to whose work he attributed his conversion to the Catholic faith. Claudel's poems, however, sometimes suggest Walt Whitman and, more often and more certainly, the language and imagery of the Bible. His religious lyricism appears at its best in the *Cinq grandes odes* (1910) and *La Cantate à trois voix* (1914), which are written in an unrhymed free metre based on the biblical verse (the *verset*), both more forceful and more intense than the earlier free verse of the Symbolists. Much of his other poetry is uneven or frankly bad, but his strength lies in a religious certainty which embraces the whole of life, including the physical universe and by no means excluding the comic and even the trivial. The aesthetic and intellectual considerations which were all-important to Mallarmé and Valéry appear narrow from this point of view, according to which truth does not so much emerge from language as inspire or dictate it. Readers who do not share all Claudel's dogmatically expressed beliefs will nevertheless admire his runs of what in a different poet would be pantheistic emotion, his fusion of self, nature, and the divine in a manner reminiscent of certain Romantics, and his contemptuous rejection of ordinary literary 'taste'. Claudel's poetry, whose virtue is in its vigorous and concrete images more than in its free yet monotonous form, is particularly effective in his dramas, which are the most impressive and original part of his work (see Chapter 17).

His mastery of the prose-poem is shown in *Connaissance de l'Est* (1900), descriptive of Asian scenes.

Charles Péguy (1873–1914) was another of that remarkably varied generation, including Claudel, Gide, Romain Rolland, Valéry, and Proust, which came to maturity in the decade before the First World War. An idealistic socialist, then an unorthodox Catholic, he has come to stand for the sturdy mystical patriotism associated with the Joan of Arc on whom he wrote two dramatic poems (*Jeanne d'Arc*, 1897, and *Le Mystère de la Charité de Jeanne d'Arc*, 1910). These are in free verse alternating with prose; later poems or poem-sequences, such as *Ève* and *La Tapisserie de Notre-Dame* (both 1913), are in regular alexandrines, but in each case Péguy's insistent repetitions (whether of words, of concepts, or of rhymes) are his unmistakable hallmark. The plod of the inspired peasant is in this verse (Péguy was of humble origin and proud of it) and the underlying sequence is earth – motherland – patron saint – deity. A 'natural' and independent poet, Péguy owed even less to contemporary literary influences than Claudel. He has a medieval fecundity, recalling the *chanson de geste* or the mystery play. This is more evident still in his prose writings, contained for the most part in *Les Cahiers de la Quinzaine* (1900–14), the review which he launched, edited, and largely wrote himself. Here he commented on contemporary events in a spirit of complete independence and tirelessly hammered out his view of the 'Harmonious City' of the future.

Two other poets, with none of Péguy's crusading spirit, have written simply about the same anti-intellectual France. Francis Jammes (1868–1938) showed a rustic piety and an often humorous love of familiar things in the verse inspired by everyday life in his native region of the Pyrenees (*De l'angélus de l'aube à l'angélus du soir*, 1898; *Les Géorgiques chrétiennes*, 1911; *Le Livre des quatrains*, 1923, etc.). Paul Fort (1872–1960) devoted most of his life to evoking French folk-lore and history in the forty volumes of the *Ballades françaises et chroniques de France*. He disguises his facile and approximately regular verse by printing it in the form of prose paragraphs. Such poets represented in their day a trend towards apparent artlessness which has persisted in spite of Mallarmé and Valéry, though it has taken other roads. The main dividing-point was the surrealist movement, which was in some measure prepared by Apollinaire.

Guillaume Apollinaire (the pseudonym of Wilhelm Apollinaris de Kostrowitsky, 1880–1918) was of Italian-Polish parentage, though brought up entirely in France. He was in the forefront of the 'modernist' movement in Paris before the First World War, edited short-lived literary reviews, and became linked with Picasso at the time when he was entering his cubist period. Apollinaire's *Les Peintres cubistes* (1913) helped to define and publicize the movement when it was still young. In 1913 he published a manifesto in favour of futurism and in 1917 his *Les Mamelles de Tirésias*, called by the author a 'surrealist play', was performed once in Paris. Meanwhile, he had served in the army and had received a head-wound whose effects contributed to his early death. These activities and publications, added to numerous other occasional prose writings on art and literature and his two principal volumes of verse, *Alcools* (1913) and *Calligrammes* (1918), represent a man of eclectic interests, always avid for novelty and hostile to tradition. His importance as the propagandist of a wide circle of young painters and writers is undeniable. He was cosmopolitan in outlook and conscious of living in a new age of machines and chaotic movement which made nonsense of the barriers of 'literature'. He hoped that his verse would be liked equally, as he wrote in a letter from the front, by 'an American Negro boxer, an Empress of China, a *boche* journalist, a Spanish painter, a young Frenchwoman of good stock, a young Italian peasant-girl, and an Anglo-Indian officer'.

It was too much to hope, though in keeping with his unsettled and half-playful character to wish it. After a period of relative neglect, his reputation as an early 'modern' revived strongly in the nineteen-fifties, though it is possible to attribute each one of his novelties to other poets. His abolition of all punctuation in verse was only a short step beyond Mallarmé's usual practice. His invention of the *calligramme*, or poem printed in some such shape as a heart, a flower, or a fan, also reminds one of Mallarmé's typographical experiments, unless it is taken as a harmless parlour game. It was meant as a half-serious attempt at 'visual' poetry. As for his 'free associations' of words and images, this had not been new since

Rimbaud, though in Apollinaire they take a more arbitrary and irresponsible form:

> Un chapeau haut de forme est sur
> Une table chargée de fruits
> Les gants sont morts près d'une pomme
> Une dame se tord le cou
> Auprès d'un monsieur qui s'avale.

This, however, was also surrealism before the nominal birth of the movement, as was the prose poem *Onirocritique* (written 1908) and, in essentials, the prose fantasy *L'Enchanteur pourrissant* (1909). Apollinaire was thus a pioneer, though it is from that angle that his work is most suspect, since too many of his associations seem mechanical and shallow. He is best appreciated for his less markedly 'modern' poems – particularly the short songs which catch echoes of Verlaine – and for a few longer pieces such as *La Chanson du mal-aimé*, *Les Collines*, or his pathetic poetic testament, *La Jolie Rousse*. In most of these is found the simplicity which was Apollinaire's strongest single quality.

His contemporary Blaise Cendrars (1887–1961), underestimated at the time, can now be seen to have been as originally modernistic as Apollinaire himself, on whom he undoubtedly exerted a certain influence. An apparently genuine world-wanderer in the pre-1914 years when the experience was more novel and stimulating than now, he returned constantly to the same Paris of young writers and painters (Chagall, Modigliani, Braque, Léger, Picasso). He brought with him his three major poems, *Pâques à New York* (1912), *La Prose du Transsibérien et de la petite Jehanne de France* (1913), and *Les Aventures de mes sept oncles* (written 1913, published 1918). The first rhymed roughly in alexandrine couplets, but the later two were rhymeless and completely irregular by all traditional standards. The free associations of Apollinaire's *poèmes-conversations* are very frequent in Cendrars's *télégrammes-poèmes* and elsewhere, showing a more fertile imagination based ultimately and however distortedly on personal experience. This seemingly inconsequential 'poetry', highly colloquial and occasionally trivial, ended in 1924 with *Kodak* after several collections of shorter pieces, but the same imaginative qualities, influenced by film techniques (he wrote scripts for several films) persisted in the lyrical 'prose' of the novels which Cendrars went on to write and whose rich and violent imagery was admired by Henry Miller. Among them were *Moravagine* (1926), *Dan Yack* (1929), *Rhum* (1930), *La Vie dangereuse* (1938), and *Bourlinguer* (1948). These also had a strong autobiographical basis, most obvious in *L'Homme foudroyé* (1945), or they were romanced *reportages*, non-realistic rather than surrealistic.

Surrealism had, or claimed, other forerunners nearer in time than the nineteenth-century ancestor, Lautréamont. One, earlier than Apollinaire and Cendrars, was Alfred Jarry (1873–1907), the author of *Ubu-Roi*, a farce in which grotesque and savage humour combined to launch a destructive attack on the detested bourgeoisie. Jarry's other work, in prose and verse, showed the same social and literary nihilism. In Apollinaire's own circle, the work of André Salmon (b. 1881), the author of surrealist poems on the Russian Revolution (*Prikaz*, 1919) was influential. Max Jacob (1876–1944), though independent of surrealism, pointed in that direction in his prose poems, *Le Cornet à dés* (1917). His verse, particularly after his conversion to Catholicism and his withdrawal from social life, shows a curious mixture of religious mysticism and of humour sometimes expressed in verbal clowning (*Le Laboratoire central*, 1921, *Les Pénitents en maillot rose*, 1925, etc.). His fantasy has great charm and some depth. As for his contemporary, Léon-Paul Fargue (1876–1947), who is usually considered as a link between Symbolism and surrealism, he remains apart in his nostalgic humour and in his individual choice of images, both in verse and prose. He wrote imaginative poems on modern Paris (as *Le Piéton de Paris*, 1927) and was in sympathy with André Breton's group in its early days.

The same group admired the work of Pierre Reverdy (1889–1960), with whom they were in touch through a review which he edited in combination with Apollinaire and Max Jacob. But Reverdy also was essentially an independent, not attracted by movements. Like Jacob, he withdrew from the ordinary world (in 1926) to live as a recluse with strong Catholic leanings. His poetry, in prose and free verse, is apparently very simple, constructed – so far as the comparison can be drawn between different art-forms – on the lines of the great Cubist painters, his contemporaries. His influence and reputation have continued to grow (*Poèmes en prose*, 1915; *Les Épaves du ciel*, 1924; *Flaques de verre*, 1929; *Sources du vent*, 1929, etc.).

The surrealist movement proper came into existence in Paris in 1921–2, when André Breton and other French writers broke away from the Dada movement which had been formed at Zürich by a group of young exiles of various nationalities during the First World War. Dada was 'against everything' (including Dada) and had been composed in unequal proportions of an understandable disgust with world conditions, boredom, and the desire of individuals for self-advertisement. Brought to Paris by Tristan Tzara, a Romanian writing in French, Dadaism found sympathizers among the anarchically-minded post-war generation and added a certain explosive force to the charge already laid by Apollinaire's contemporaries. When Tzara had been shaken off, French surrealism was defined in a well-known formula as:

'Pure psychic automatism by means of which it is proposed to express, either verbally, in writing, or in any other way, the real process of thought – in the absence of all control exercised by reason and outside all aesthetic or moral considerations.'

At the root of this was the conviction that the highest kind of reality exists in the unconscious and that the attempt must be made to capture it before it is distorted by being arranged in some (artificial) category by the conscious mind. To class an impulse as moral or immoral is to have second thoughts about it which falsify its nature; to force a feeling into an existing art-form – whether that is a sonnet or a statue – is necessarily to deform it. This emphasis on the unconscious, and its arbitrary separation from the conscious, stemmed from the theories of Freud, which were still in their novelty for non-specialists and were applied with enthusiasm well outside their original sphere. Applying them to literature and art, the surrealists were led to attach great importance to dreams and to 'automatic writing' – writing performed as nearly as possible in a state of trance.

Surrealism contained a principle of revolt, which is always attractive and remains necessary as a corrective to smug traditionalism. Unlike Dadaism, it was not purely destructive. It proposed to express human nature more truly and more completely than had been done before and its recognition of the unconscious was a vital contribution to literature, going a certain way beyond the discoveries of the Symbolists. The problem it has never solved is the problem of form. Here it could not innovate, since it expressly disclaimed 'aesthetic considerations'. Neither could it reject entirely, since to write at all is to use a form, however unplanned it may appear. So it has simply taken over existing forms and has used them loosely and broadly, free verse drifting into the prose poem and the prose poem sometimes expanding into the long personal, symbolic, or doctrinaire work which may look like a novel but for which no satisfactory name has been found. The distinction between poetry and prose is largely abolished as being of small importance, but because of the stress laid on symbols and images most surrealist writing appears 'poetic' to readers accustomed to associate prose with the realistic and the rational.

After a partial eclipse during the Second World War, surrealism could be seen to be still present in French literature and drama in various forms which still have to be analysed but can be claimed as developments of the original movement. The direct influence of this in its own day extended well beyond the surrealist group and affected writers who at various times broke away from it (often for personal or political reasons) as well as others who (sometimes for the same kind of reasons) have firmly denied that they ever had any connection with it. The only constant surrealist has been André Breton (1896–1966), the leader and theorist of the movement in his several manifestos and his important novel, *Nadja* (1928). Here it should be said that Tristan Tzara (1896–1963), abandoning Dada in the late nineteen-twenties, rejoined Breton's group at the time when he was writing his chief work, *L'Homme approximatif* (1931). He left them again soon after and continued to produce in a more rational and tamer style. Other surrealists of the twenties who also left the movement, to evolve for the most part in a simpler direction, were Robert Desnos (1900–45) and René Char (b. 1907). After his early works, such as *Artine* (1930) and *Le Marteau sans maître* (1934), Char played an active and courageous part in the Resistance movement, reflected in *Seuls demeurent* (1945). This experience seemed to confirm his transformation into a contemplative poet whose work is now firmly rooted in plain human experience and nature, like that of Éluard, whom he resembles in certain ways. He retired to his native Provence and has produced a body of 'private' poetry, difficult at times but not basically obscure, which ranks him among the major poets of his period (*Fureur et mystère*, 1948; *Les Matinaux*, 1950; *La Parole en archipel*, 1962; *Commune présence*, 1964).

A totally different writer, Jean Cocteau (1889–1963), may be said to have looked in on surrealism and to have adapted features of it for a wider public in poems, plays, and films. Jacques Prévert (b. 1900), successful as a writer of film-scripts in the thirties, when he worked with Marcel Carné, made a second reputation with the free verse collected in *Paroles* (1946). He combines social satire with the humour of the incongruous. As for Henri Michaux (b. 1899), he has always protested that he is not a surrealist, but in any general classification he can hardly be placed elsewhere. He expresses a frightening world in which the individual is always at the centre and always threatened. Like, of course, Kafka, he introduces order and logic in places where they have no right to be; the monstrous is presented as customary, while the normal is strange or disquieting. This reversal of the usual kind of dream – the lucid nightmare instead of the chaotic nightmare – is just as impressive. While it might simply result from a superficial spirit of perversity, in the case of Michaux it seems to be the genuine anguish of a strayed Cartesian afflicted by a chronic inability to see things as others see them. His prolific writings – many of them in stylistically lucid prose – include *Qui je fus* (1927), *Un Certain Plume* (1931), *Un Barbare en Asie* (1932), *Voyage en Grande Garabagne* (1936), *Épreuves, Exorcismes,* (1945), *Passages* (1950), and volumes of selections such as *L'Espace du dedans* (1944) and *La Vie dans les plis* (1949). His later works include *Face aux verrous* (1954) and *Connaissance par les gouffres* (1961) based on his experience of mescalin, which he abandoned as a false paradise.

If Michaux has no legitimate literary ancestry, that cannot be said of the two most prominent poets of recent years, Aragon and Éluard. They were among the founders of the surrealist movement, whose characteristics are writ large upon their earlier work at least. For Louis Aragon (b. 1897), this phase ended in the early nineteen-thirties when he parted company with Breton and pinned his faith to communism. His conversion was marked by his poem *Hourra l'Oural* (1934) and by *Les Cloches de Bâle* (1933), the first of a series of politically-slanted novels collectively entitled *Le Monde réel* which make up a loosely constructed and deliberately shapeless *roman-fleuve* on French life since 1900. The series also includes *Les Beaux Quartiers* (1936), *Les Voyageurs de l'Impériale* (1942), and the multi-volume *Les Communistes* (1949, etc.), which deals with the period of the Second World War. This war was Aragon's greatest moment as a poet. Having served in the Medical Corps in 1940 and then engaged in the Resistance, he became the voice of a France defeated, occupied, but still alive and defiant. The poems of *Le Crève-Cœur* (1941) expressed a simple patriotism outside parties which moved many beyond the sealed frontiers of France itself, as did the more personal verses of *Les Yeux d'Elsa* (1942), Aragon's tribute to his wife, Elsa Triolet. The national theme was continued in *Le Musée Grévin* (1943), against Vichy, and *La Diane française* (1944). His later books of poems include *Le Nouveau Crève-Cœur* (1948), *Le Roman inachevé* (1956) and *Le Fou d'Elsa* (1963).

Aragon's war-poetry has worn, as poetry, very badly. Its strongly marked rhythms, too reminiscent of the street-organ or the accordion, its repetitions and other verbal tricks, its echoes of Apollinaire, Péguy, Verlaine and others – all the features which once gave it prestige as the collective voice of a people – seem weaknesses now that the emotion of the moment has passed. Yet to have captured that emotion was something of which a poet less sensitive to the spirit of the time would have been incapable. Aragon's achievement was to write popular poetry, the most successful of the century so far and possibly the last for a long time. He enjoyed a nation-wide readership, only approached by Prévert's in his entirely different way.

Paul Éluard (1895–1952) followed, externally, a development not unlike Aragon's: from surrealism to Resistance and thence to communism. But the order, like the emphasis, was different. His was an idealistic communism, as unpolitical as possible, which developed late (*Une Leçon de morale*, 1949). He simplified surrealism, but never wholly abandoned it. All his poetry is on a quiet, intimate note, including his war poems in *Poésie et Vérité* (1942) and *Au Rendez-vous allemand* (1945). He is essentially a 'private' poet, singing of his own human love and of nature for the most part in uninsistent free verse rhythms. Much of his imagery is sensual, but carried out with such purity of taste that the final impression is one of innocence. Beneath his apparent simplicity lies a sense of the mystery of ordinary life, untouched by any reference to religion, and he is in fact a more difficult poet than he seems or probably wished to be. His influence and his interest as one of the best lyric poets of his time continues to grow. Future readers may be led to study him as the classic of surrealism just as Valéry was the classic of Symbolism. His numerous volumes of verse form a whole, among which are few separately outstanding titles. A *Choix de Poèmes* was published in 1951.

Of the same family of poets was Jules Supervielle (1884–1961), who was born in Montevideo of Basque parents and divided his life between South America and France. The free verse of *Débarcadères* (1922) showed the influence of the South American pampas which was to recur often in his work. A certain incoherence in other books such as *Le Forçat innocent* (1930) suggested surrealism, though Supervielle affirmed his independence and insisted that his aim was to be understood by any normally sensitive reader – in which he nearly always succeeds. He is a sometimes whimsical poet who writes with great charm when his subjects are childhood and animals. His novels and short stories have the same unsubstantial serenity. Most of his best verse is in *Gravitations* (1925), *La Fable du monde* (1938), *Poèmes de la France malheureuse* (1942), *Oublieuse mémoire* (1949) and *Le Corps tragique* (1959).

While Supervielle, Aragon and Éluard have been the most widely read poets of their age, two others have produced work requiring considerable initiation before its qualities can be fully appreciated. Saint-John Perse is the pseudonym of Alexis Saint-Léger Léger (b. 1887), a former high official in the French Foreign Service. His poetry, written partly in *versets* like Claudel's, also reflects a deep culture and the influence of travel from Peking to Washington. But there the resemblance ends. Where Claudel is exuberant in the manner of Hugo, Saint-John Perse pursues a path of more formal reserve in which aesthetic considerations predominate. This mandarin of French poetry has been writing for over fifty years with long intervals of apparent silence. *Éloges* (1911) and *Anabase*

(1924, translated by T. S. Eliot in 1930) were followed by *Exil* (1942), then by the related *Pluies, Neiges* and *Vents* (1946–7). In 1957 he published *Amers* and in 1963 *Oiseaux*, having been awarded the Nobel Prize in 1960. His later work shows a growing use of the short paragraph of 'poetic' prose as an alternative to the *verset* and a more open admission of personal emotionalism. In Pierre-Jean Jouve (b. 1887) the unconcealed dominant emotion is a curious product of religious mysticism. At first in sympathy with the Unanimist group, Jouve passed through a spiritual crisis in his late thirties which led him to disown all that he had written until then. A blend of Catholic doctrine and Freudian psychology is the basis of his mature work, which is rich in sexual imagery and essentially pessimistic in its view of humanity (*Tragiques*, 1923; *Les Noces*, 1928; *Matière céleste*, 1937; *Kyrie*, 1938; *La Vierge de Paris*, 1945; *Diadème*, 1949; *Ténèbre*, 1965). Jouve might be described as a modern baroque writer whose innate eroticism is combined with a strong sense of sin but not, at least consciously, opposed to it. The richness of his difficult poetry is being increasingly recognized.

The influence of Jouve and of Claudel could be felt in a younger generation of Catholic poets who began publishing in the nineteen-thirties. Jean Cayrol, Luc Estang and Patrice de la Tour du Pin were all born in 1911 and the last-named achieved early recognition with *La Quête de joie* (1933). He afterwards incorporated this in a vast spiritual epic in verse and prose entitled *Une Somme de poésie*, of which the first volume appeared in 1946 and which is still unfinished. Pierre Emmanuel (b. 1916) was a declared disciple of Jouve in his early work, as *Tombeau d Orphée* (1941), in which the symbolism is at once sexual and religious. Stimulated by the disasters of the war, he continued to write powerful rhetorical poetry in verse in which the great Christian and pagan myths were linked, more topically than by La Tour du Pin, to questions of contemporary history. His work includes *Combats avec tes défenseurs* (1943), *La Colombe* (1943), *Sodome* (1944), *Babel* (1951), *Évangéliaire* (1961) and, in prose, the autobiographical *Qui est cet homme?* (1948) and *Le Goût de l'un* (1963).

Such, as they appear today, were the most outstanding poets of the first half of the century, with prolongations in several cases into the nineteen-sixties. To their names several others might have been added, among them Victor Segalen (1878–1919), a widely-travelled Frenchman deeply influenced by Polynesian and Chinese culture; Oscar Vladislas de Lubicz-Milosz (1877–1939), a Russian aristocrat educated in France whose work combines symbolism and mysticism in a way not comparable to any native French poet except perhaps, distantly, Jouve and La Tour du Pin; Jacques Audiberti (1899–1965) and Raymond Queneau (b. 1903), both audaciously brilliant manipulators of words owing much to surrealism, both successful as novelists and, in Audiberti's case, as a playwright also; and two more sober poets, André Frénaud (b. 1907) and Eugène Guillevic (b. 1907).

On the whole these are relatively minor poets, with the possible exception of Milosz, and it seems improbable though never impossible that either here or in the previous pages any truly major poet, discoverable by a future generation, has been passed over. What may strike the reader as excessive caution on the critic's part can be justified by the reminder of how nearly Rimbaud was forgotten or, to quote a less striking example in English poetry, Gerard Manley Hopkins.

Since Valéry, however, and to a lesser degree Éluard, the era of the 'great poet' has passed away, temporarily at least, and this becomes more obvious as the century moves through its second half. To begin with, greatness is a title less prized by prominent men in almost any of the fields where it was once conferred automatically. There are great liars, great frauds and great fools, but not so many great heroes. This is particularly true of poets, partly because of a change in the status and function of poetry itself. Victor Hugo could confidently be called a great poet because of his national standing. So could Baudelaire for entirely different reasons, though he would no doubt have refused the title contemptuously. Today would any poet wish to be 'great' any more than he did? It sounds too like an embalmment in a coffin unlikely to be given a funeral in the Pantheon or the Abbey.

Poetry is undoubtedly alive, in France as elsewhere. Scores of poets are writing it and are being published and read by a public which, though admittedly small, is not composed exclusively of critics and academics on the prowl for something new to proclaim.

It looks and often is impersonal, the *moi* of the poet being sub-ordinated to an observation or contemplation of the external world which may indeed reflect back on to human experience, but not directly to that of the poet in any autobiographical sense. Some of this stems from Saint-John Perse, but also from another elder poet, Francis Ponge (b. 1899). Ponge was 'discovered' in the nineteen-forties, when he published *Le Parti pris des choses* (1942) and *Proèmes* (1948) before going on to write other books collected in *Le Grand Recueil* (1961), *Tome Premier* (1965) and *Le Nouveau Recueil* (1967). His theory is to abolish the distinction between man and the natural universe around him – they are all part of the same thing. He thus avoids the anthropomorphism of the Romantics, the symbolism of the Symbolists (his trees and rocks exist in themselves and are not symbolical of human experience) and the self-centred unconscious of the surrealists. There is no kind of spiritual transcendance (as there was in Claudel, a Catholic pantheist) and, although Ponge has not bothered to say so, the conception of a universe created on separate days with Adam and Eve emerging last in the specially favoured shape of God's image is pointedly ignored. Ponge's work has been attached to existentialist phenomenology and, later, to the cult of the *object* in the New Novel, but these associations are accidental and he cannot be grouped. His poetry takes the form of prose paragraphs, descriptive and discreetly contemplative, very carefully composed as to the choice of words, with a deliberate exclusion of lyricism and resonances of any other kind.

Signs of Ponge's influence can be found in some of the poets of a later generation, already mature now. Foremost among them are Yves Bonnefoy (b. 1923), André du Bouchet (b. 1924), Philippe Jaccottet (b.1925) and Michel Deguy (b. 1930). Du Bouchet has written poetry as impersonal and in places as impenetrable as it is possible to go while still using coherent language (*Air*, 1950; *Le Moteur blanc*, 1956; *Dans la chaleur vacante*, 1961), but beneath the sibylline verse of Bonnefoy, approximately regular with occa-sional rhymes, it is easy to detect human feelings, tightly restrained but not emasculated (*Du mouvement et de l'immobilité de Douve*, 1953; *Hier régnant désert*, 1956; *Pierre écrite*, 1965). Jaccottet, while prescribing 'the absolute effacement of the poet', certainly does not exclude humanity and indeed an underlying metaphysical sense from his verse, much of which, like Bonnefoy's, approximates to the traditional forms (*L'Effraie et autres poésies*, 1953; *L'Ignorant*, 1958; *Airs*, 1967; *Leçons*, 1969). He has, however, evolved towards impersonality in his later theories and prose poems (*Paysages avec figures absentes*, 1970). As for Deguy, descriptions of nature not devoid of anthropomorphic significance are an obvious feature of his poems in free verse and prose (*Meurtrières*, 1959; *Fragments du cadastre*, 1960; *Poèmes de la presqu'île*, 1961; *Ouï-dire*, 1966), but he is also engaged, as in *Actes* (1966), on a critical re-examination of the basis and rôle of poetry, and indeed of language, in the world to-day.

There is still a contrary current of more openly personal poetry, no less difficult to decipher but, when that has been done, visibly based on the reactions of the particular individual who is writing it. Like the earlier work of Antonin Artaud (*L'Ombilic des limbes* and *Le Pèse-nerfs*, both 1925), whose more important influence on the theatre is described in Chapter 17, it derives from the still living tradition of surrealism. Three poets can be given as examples: Jean-Pierre Duprey (1930–59), whose *Derrière son double* (1964) was written some years before his suicide; Bernard Noël (b. 1930), the author of *Extraits du corps* (1958) and *La Face de silence* (1967); and Joyce Mansour, an Egyptian living in France whose work contains an eroticism and a destructive social challenge in strong contrast to the poets mentioned in the previous paragraph (*Cris*, 1954; *Les Gisants satisfaits*, 1958; *Carré blanc*, 1965; *Phallus et momies*, 1969). It seems trivial to mention Women's Lib in this connection, but if one needs it, here it is in an aggressive and genuine form, with much else besides.

Besides poetry there is anti-poetry, subscribed to in varying degrees by some of the poets already listed. It is a reaction against tradition, seen at its narrowest as the use of regular versification and its associated prosodic practices and, more fundamentally, as the conventional use of language as a valid means of communication. It could be explicable at this date as a protest against the millions of apparently coherent but ultimately meaningless words poured out by the media and their imbecile commentators and discussionists. In that case it would have a similar motivation to that of the partisans of the anti-popular Art for Art's Sake movement of the nineteenth century, but with very different results. In itself it has many forerunners: Mallarmé, working to create a new poetic language within the traditional verse-forms but also, in *Un coup de dés . . .*, rendering conceptual and linguistic associations by the typographical arrangement of the page; Apollinaire, trying the same thing rather arbitrarily in *Calligrammes*; early surrealism rejecting rational speech, though less stridently than Dada which had proclaimed this as its main object; Henry Michaux, among others, who invented words either as a necessity or a pastime; and, more consistently, the *lettriste* movement of the forties and fifties, founded by Isidore Isou, a Romanian like Tzara and Ionesco, who aimed at re-founding poetry and other writing on letters rather than on words.

To these various experiments and innovations must be added a powerful movement in modern criticism which can be classed broadly as linguistic, though it takes several forms, of which the most prominent is Structuralism. This challenges all previous conceptions of language, going far beyond the verse or the sentence to the basic construction and articulation of the literary work as a whole. (see above, pp. 255–6).

These influences have not suddenly transformed French poetry, nor are they likely to, but they have partially affected many poets writing to-day, with the result that their work is removed ever further from the public domain. The reader can either dismiss it as 'obscure', an understandable but rather defeatist attitude, or be prepared to learn a language within a language. This is not so difficult, neither is it unrewarding, neither is it a frivolous exercise inspired by up-to-dateness for its own sake. One has sobering memories of the dismissal of Cubist painting – and even of Impressionism – in the early decades of this century by the general public. The general public were wrong in every sense, including even their commercial judgement. Without claiming that much modern French poetry has a comparable significance, it has a value and interest which are more than innovatory. Meanwhile there is an enormous body of earlier poetry which has interest and value too, and if one enjoys reading it, it is no disgrace to be caught doing so.

It might seem desirable to end this chapter with a list of modern schools and movements, but any attempt to do this would be misleading. Since surrealism at latest there have been no definable 'schools'. Movements have centred on groups, or rather groupings, for the most part short-lived and quickly dispersed, or leading to dead-ends. Some future manual may succeed in classifying them, if that seems necessary, but for the moment the general indications sketched out in the last few pages are as much as it seems critically legitimate to provide.

CHAPTER 17

The Theatre since 1800

Over the past hundred and fifty years France has had the most continually active theatre in Europe, though other countries may have had greater individual dramatists, at least from the time of Ibsen on. Ibsen, Strindberg, Chekhov, Shaw, Pirandello, O'Neill, Brecht, would be difficult names to match, but they belong to half a dozen literatures. France has produced, in the nineteenth century, Hugo, Musset, the elder and younger Dumas, Becque, Rostand; and in the twentieth, Claudel, Giraudoux, Cocteau, Salacrou, Anouilh, Sartre and Ionesco. Besides these, she has had numerous highly accomplished dramatic craftsmen, from Scribe to Bernstein, while in light comedy she has often excelled. These names reflect enough vitality for Paris to have maintained its position as the main centre of world drama throughout this period as a whole, though other capitals have sometimes taken the initiative temporarily. From the nineteen-twenties to the fifties, indeed, Paris even came near to recovering the supremacy it enjoyed in the time of Molière and Racine.

No lasting alternative to the verse play as they wrote it has appeared, however. The whole history of the French drama since 1830 might be seen as a series of experiments in dramatic idiom which have produced the Romantic verse drama, the imaginative prose of Musset and Giraudoux, naturalistic dialogue, the poetic prose and free verse of the Symbolists and Claudel, and then the collapse or deformation of language itself in recent years. No lasting tradition has been established and the need for one would certainly not be felt today. But in the early nineteenth century the situation was different. Comedy, already familiar in prose, was not immediately in question. What the Romantics were seeking was a rejuvenated kind of noble drama.

The eighteenth century had already seen attempts to introduce more movement and colour into the old classical tragedy while preserving the same literary form. It had also seen the birth of historical and domestic drama, with its popular counterpart in melodrama. These types of play, particularly melodrama, continued to flourish without essential change during the Empire and the Restoration and offered the possibility of renewal from native sources. But at the same time there were foreign examples: perennially Shakespeare, acted in Paris and hissed, for political reasons, in 1822, acted again and applauded in 1827; more immediately, the example of the German historical and idealistic drama (Schiller and Goethe) and the theories of such critics as Schlegel, popularized by Mme de Staël. There were thus two strands ready to be woven together: the actual practice of the French theatre and the doctrines, derived from abroad, which enabled the whole question of renewal to be set and discussed on a higher critical level.

This was done by Stendhal (*Racine et Shakespeare*, 1823) and, with greater force and eloquence, by Victor Hugo in the preface to his play *Cromwell* (1827). Concerned above all with challenging classical doctrine, Hugo rejected the unities of time and place, attacked the separation of the tragic and the comic as an artificial convention, and called for more natural language on the stage. Here he was protesting against the stilted diction which the academic writers of the time still used in imitation of the great classic dramatists and was by no means advocating what would now be called realistic dialogue. On the contrary, he still wanted verse drama, but in the poetic convention of his own age. Beyond that, he demanded a much bolder use of local colour, both in the staging of a play and in the spirit in which it was written. This meant that the playwright's task was to take his audience to the time and place which the play represented, not, as it was argued that the French classics had done – and as such dramatists as Cocteau and Anouilh were certainly to do later – to adapt the remote or the ancient to contemporary taste.

Cromwell was unacted and unactable. Although Hugo had written a resounding manifesto in its preface, another dramatist was a little before him in producing a play which stands historically as the first successful example of the Romantic drama. This was *Henri III et sa cour* by the elder Dumas, a crude story of love and revenge set in sixteenth-century France. Produced in February 1829, it was the first of a series of similar works which during the next ten years made Dumas *père* the most popular dramatist in

France. His plays, written in prose, have few literary qualities and, whether 'historical' like *Henri III* or *La Tour de Nesle*, or 'modern' like *Antony*, are hardly distinguishable from melodrama and remarkable only for their vigour.

Meanwhile Hugo had made a triumphal appearance with *Hernani* (1830), which was the occasion for a violent battle of opinion in which the supporters of the 'classics' were temporarily routed. This, with *Ruy Blas* (1838), represents the height of the Romantic historical drama, as well as Hugo's best writing for the stage. Both plays are set in Spain. Both contain characters of exceptional nobility pitted against circumstances rather obviously manipulated by the author. But they rely on the audacity of plots and settings to induce a suspension of disbelief in the audience. The illusion, once submitted to, is upheld by the theatrical magnificence of the verse at moments of strong feeling and by its ingenuity elsewhere. Between these two plays, Hugo produced *Marion de Lorme* (written before *Hernani*, but banned by the censors and not acted until 1831), *Le Roi s'amuse* (1832), and three mediocre dramas in prose. In 1843, *Les Burgraves*, a complicated experiment in epic melodrama in which Hugo aimed at showing a whole aspect of German medieval history, was hissed off the stage. No doubt Hugo had attempted too much, but it was also a sign that by that date the theatrical fashion had changed.

It was not surprising. In spite of his ambitious theories, Hugo had not succeeded in creating a serious alternative to the old classical tragedy. The new conception towards which he was feeling his way was best realized later in Wagnerian opera which was, in fact, the ultimate development of German Romantic theory. But there, legend on a grand scale takes the place of the rather trivial, semi-historical themes used by Hugo. *Hernani*, he claimed, showed the rise in Spain of the dynasty of Austria, while *Ruy Blas* showed its decline two centuries later. *Les Burgraves* was intended to suggest the greatness and decadence of German feudal society. But no such broad historical sweep emerges from the plays, however much it might seem to be promised by their subjects. Elsewhere, it is not even glimpsed. The spirit of the France of the Renaissance, which might have appeared in *Le Roi s'amuse*, is ignored in order to present a caricature of François I engaged in numerous love-affairs

– much as Henri VIII is represented in English popular plays – and a fictitious court jester, Triboulet, who under his laughable exterior is naturally the nobler character of the two. *Marion de Lorme* was at first entitled *Un Duel sous Richelieu* and is little more than the cloak-and-sword story which that title implies. *Lucrèce Borgia* (1833) is only too expectedly full of poisonings, but hardly at all of the peculiar atmosphere of intrigue and sadism which might be held to characterize the Italian courts of the Renaissance. Although Hugo was conscious of the 'picturesque', he did not possess that deeper historical imagination which might have given his dramas coherence and life. He is content with flatly obvious characters, without psychological interest or truth. On the other hand, they fail to attain meaning as symbols, which is another function of the characters in poetic drama. Hernani, the foredoomed Byronic hero, Charles V, the representative of kingship in the same play, Marion de Lorme, the courtesan purified by love, Ruy Blas, the valet who becomes Prime Minister and stands for the innate nobility of the people, the corrupt aristocrat Don Salluste – none of these, with the glaring contrasts deliberately shown between them, or between their worldly conditions and their inner natures, belong anywhere except in the property-chest. The essential carry-over, the spark for the imagination, the mythical life which would replace realistic plausibility and make it unnecessary, is never present. One does not complain, or even notice, that Tristan and Isolde, or Romeo and Juliet, are not literally of this world. One continually notices and protests, when faced with Hernani and Doña Sol. It is the poet who is at fault as much as the dramatist.

For such reasons, the Romantic historical drama hardly rises above the cloak-and-sword level, for what Hugo could not accomplish no one else could. In another direction, however, the Romantic Movement was to find a dramatist in Musset. Musset's plays are altogether less pompous productions, unburdened by theory and almost free of the stage conventions of spectacular melodrama which date his contemporaries. Depressed by the failure of an early one-act comedy, *La Nuit vénitienne* (1830), he had decided to write henceforth only for publication. Seventeen years later, when nearly all his plays were in print, their dramatic qualities were discovered by an actress of the Comédie-Française. They succeeded admirably on a stage for which they had not been intended, with one or two exceptions, like the almost unmanageable *Lorenzaccio* (1834).

This was Musset's main experiment in historical drama (the other was *André del Sarto*, 1833). It is interesting for its presentation of a character, at times suggestive of Hamlet, who in the setting of sixteenth-century Italy decides to assassinate the tyrant, Alessandro di Medici. He knows that his act will be politically useless, since another tyrant will succeed the first, but is driven to it by the desire to justify his own existence. This subjective and typically Romantic attitude bears some resemblance to Gide's *acte gratuit* and even to the teaching of existentialism. In Musset, however, no coherent philosophy is suggested and his play is an untidy mixture of penetration and platitude. It does, however, throw light on some of his other plays (*Les Caprices de Marianne, Fantasio, On ne badine pas avec l'amour*). These are also concerned with characters in search of an identity, to find which they are placed, or place themselves, in various artificial-seeming situations. It appears a mere game of the emotions with the characters as puppets (as many of them are, though amusing ones), but in fact these are psychological experiments, some of which end in tragedy. No doubt the chief subject of the experiments was Musset himself – who is mirrored partially in several of his characters – and no doubt they are inconclusive. But they have a bearing on human nature such as is not found in Hugo's dramas. Irresolute beings like Fantasio or like Perdican in *On ne badine pas avec l'amour* have more life than Hernani or Ruy Blas just because they are less absolute.

Musset's plays are written lightly, with a blend of playfulness and sentiment. Nearly all are in prose, giving an impression of off-handedness in keeping with the unsubstantial characters and settings. There is no insistence on historical or geographical colour. For the most part they can be classed as slightly fantastic comedies, and this is particularly true of the short pieces, several in one act, which have remained the most popular on the stage. Such are *Le Chandelier, Un Caprice*, and the 'proverbs': *Il ne faut jurer de rien, Il faut qu'une porte soit ouverte ou fermée*, and *On ne saurait penser à tout*. These last revive an eighteenth-century custom of writing a play to illustrate a proverb, but apart from the name they do not differ essentially from the 'comedies'. A further eighteenth-century link is with Marivaux, whom Musset resembles in his delicacy of atmosphere and his treatment of love. He differs from him in his looser technique and in his more lyrical use of language.

As a dramatist, Musset remained a special case, without immediate influence on the trend of the theatre. By the time his work reached the stage, the reaction against Hugo's type of heroic drama was already resulting in a neater and more realistic conception of playwriting which was to rule until near the end of the century. The form, slick and theatrically effective, had been established by Eugène Scribe (1791–1861), who, in the course of writing nearly four hundred plays, developed an almost mechanical expertness in plot-construction. Some of his plays have historical subjects (*Un verre d'eau*, 1842; *Bertrand et Raton*, 1849). Others, such as *Le Mariage d'argent* (1827), *La Camaraderie* (1837), *Une Chaîne* (1842), are comedies of contemporary manners. In both types the medium was prose and the language used was modern. Scribe's success may be said to have ushered in both the social drama and the social comedy which occupied a whole generation of not very distinguished playwrights.

Two of them, Émile Augier (1820–89) and Alexandre Dumas *fils* (1824–95), believed that the theatre could be used as a moral influence. For Augier, typical of the eighteen-fifties and sixties, the basis of virtue was in the middle-class family, unpretentious, hard-working, honest in its acquisition of wealth. It must be protected against adventurers, loose women, the frivolous and the decadent of whatever milieu. (By the merest twist of emphasis, these were the heroes and heroines of Romanticism.) Such are the lessons of *Gabrielle* (1849), *Les Lionnes pauvres* (1858), *Les Effrontés* (1861) and other plays. Sometimes the moral is less stressed, as in his best-known play, *Le Gendre de M. Poirier* (1854), a social comedy written in collaboration with Jules Sandeau. As for Dumas *fils*, his earliest and, ironically, most lasting play was a sentimental portrait of a courtesan, *La Dame aux camélias* (1852). Adapted from his novel of the same name, its sympathetic treatment of the social outcast is in the Romantic tradition of rebel morality against which he soon reacted. Later he was to attack such women as the curse of society. His plays, accompanied by forceful prefaces and pamphlets, put forward with considerable boldness for the period views on illegitimacy, divorce, prostitution, which were new to the stage (*Le Fils naturel*, 1858; *L'Ami des femmes*, 1864; *Les Idées de Madame Aubray*, 1867; *L'Étrangère*, 1876; *Denise*, 1885, etc.). Some of this material was similar to that on which Ibsen was working at the same date. In Dumas *fils*, however, there is little of Ibsen's realism and restraint. Though contemporary, Dumas's situations are extraordinary and, in imitation of Scribe's technique of the well contrived play, end in some neat but unconvincing solution. His characters preach rhetorically, with more verbosity but less logic than Shaw's. It is chiefly this that has dated him, added to the fact that his problems are no longer actual, at least in the form in which he presents them. The stand he took as a moral reformer owes much to his youthful experiences as the illegitimate son of the elder Dumas. He was reacting against the *demi-monde* in which he had been brought up.

No doubt a dramatist's most effective weapon against social abuses is satire, but there is little of this in either Dumas or Augier. It is found, but without much sting and with no reformist purpose, in the lighter dramatists of the time. Of these, Ernest Labiche (1815–88) wrote *Le Voyage de M. Perrichon* (1860), a not unfunny caricature of a worthy merchant seeking self-improvement in travel (the last and lowest manifestation of the Romantic *wanderlust*), and short farces such as *La Poudre aux yeux* and *Un chapeau de paille d'Italie*. Meilhac (1831–97) and Halévy (1834–1908) collaborated in numerous light comedies (as *Frou-Frou*, 1869) and in operettas written for Offenbach's music. For Bizet they wrote the libretto of *Carmen*, based on Mérimée's story. Édouard Pailleron (1843–99) is remembered for *Le Monde où l'on s'ennuie* (1881), a satire – this time both amusing and penetrating – on salon society.

It is obvious that the more serious of the post-Romantic authors were practising a version of the *drame bourgeois* which Diderot had mooted a century before. Their middle-class settings, their pathos and their moralizing approach, their frequent concern with family problems, would all have fitted Diderot's theory. On the other hand, they were more conscious than he had been of questions of class and of money, which interested the new-rich society which gave them both their material and their audiences. Within the limitations of the commercial theatre, they attacked such abuses as they saw, if they never went very deep. They were realistic only in comparison with their predecessors. There is always a gloss, of rhetoric, of sentimentality, or of wit, to protect the audience against shocks in the *pièce à thèse*. The height of artificiality in characterization and plot-construction was reached, however, not by the moral reformers but by Victorien Sardou (1831–1908), Scribe's chief successor in the mastery of stagecraft.

A movement towards greater realism gathered force in the eighteen-eighties, as might be expected in the peak decade of the naturalistic movement. Novels by Zola, Daudet, and the Goncourts were adapted for the stage, though with small success. One original dramatist produced plays which, though they also failed at the time, are now recognized as the chief models of naturalistic drama. *Les Corbeaux* (1882) and *La Parisienne* (1885) by Henri Becque (1837–99) are pieces of dry and powerful writing which concede nothing to sentiment and record without comment, though inevitably with an underlying irony, the unscrupulousness and hypocrisy of contemporary characters. They appear flat but convincing, since the more mechanical tricks of the theatre are not used. The resulting impression of reality is impossible to escape, however depressing it may appear. As a creator of the *comédie rosse*, or bitter social play, Becque occupies a small but important place in the history of the theatre. To his was added the wider influence of André Antoine, an *avant-garde* director and producer who founded the Théâtre Libre in 1887 and kept it open for nine years against the competition of the commercial theatres. Here a naturalistic technique was insisted upon, in dialogue, acting, and décor. Ibsen was acted for the first time in France and a number of French dramatists were launched who could not have been produced elsewhere. Though integral naturalism failed in the drama (as, after much greater triumphs, it failed in the novel), it nevertheless left a mark even on some of its opponents. Henceforth the moralists became less verbose and play-construction in the commercial theatre less obviously artificial.

But this theatre was nevertheless moving towards a dead end. The pseudo-serious play dominant in the early part of the twentieth century (roughly from 1895 to 1915) affected to offer either penetrating studies of human nature or discussions of contemporary problems. It was still Dumas *fils*, under a new technique; or else it was the kind of psychology presented by Bourget in the novel, further simplified for the needs of the stage. The masters of the 'psychological' drama were: Georges de Porto-Riche (1849–1930), Henry Bataille (1872–1922) ,both analysts of love who were rashly hailed as renewers of Racine, Maurice Donnay (1859–1945), also concerned with love, and Henry Bernstein (1876–1953), whose name as an exploiter of powerful emotional conflicts remained before the Parisian public for fifty years. A much smaller following admired the 'drama of ideas' of François de Curel (1854–1928), who confronted his heroically-conceived characters with questions of conscience which no longer seem important. In the direct line of Augier and Dumas *fils* were Paul Hervieu (1857–1915) and Eugène Brieux (1858–1932), both exponents of the *pièce à thèse* and inclined (particularly Brieux) to preach their views on the family and society through characters who are no more than mouthpieces.

In all this dramatic output there are few plays which survive on their own merits. They have an interest – at this date, a morbid interest – for the student of the theatre. They should also prove a mine for the social historian seeking to analyse the tastes and opinions of what might be called without too much distortion the average French Edwardian mentality. In this respect, they provide a much fuller documentation than do their English contemporaries for this country. The parallel is with Pinero, Somerset Maugham, Granville Barker, Galsworthy, and some of the early Shaw, like *Mrs Warren's Profession*.

The light comedy of the period survives in better shape. Robert de Flers (1872–1927) and Armand de Caillavet (1869–1915) collaborated in gay satirical fantasies and in musical plays, much as Meilhac and Halévy had done forty years earlier. Georges Feydeau (1862–1921) wrote farcical comedies of situation from *La Dame de chez Maxim's* (1899) to *On purge bébé* (1910). His slickly constructed plays enjoyed renewed popularity after their inclusion by J. L. Barrault in the repertory of the Comédie-Française in 1948. Tristan Bernard (1866–1947), besides short farces such as *L'Anglais tel qu'on le parle* (1899), has written excellent comedies of character disguised beneath an appearance of ironical frivolity (*Triplepatte*, 1905; *Monsieur Codomat*, 1907; *Jules, Juliette et Julien*, 1929). As a humorist, however, no playwright approaches Georges Courteline (1858–1929), the author of a number of one-act sketches, some of which were dramatizations of his own short stories. He shows the 'little man' at grips with bureaucracy or the law (*Un Client sérieux* 1897; *L'article 330*, 1900; *Le Commissaire est bon enfant*), or in the character of an idiotic soldier struggling with equally idiotic military regulations (*Les Gaîtés de l'escadron*, 1905; *Le Train de 8 heures 47*, 1909). Sometimes the difficulties are domestic, as in *Boubouroche* (1893), his only two-act play, or in *La Paix chez soi* (1903). Often he is content with the slightest of knock-about farces. But his absurd characters, like the situations which develop logically round them, are rooted in exact observation and are instantly recognized as true caricatures by Frenchmen even today. Except in *Boubouroche*, there is no sign of bitterness or of revolt. Courteline's down-to-earth acceptance of the ridiculous prevents him from being a satirist. He has been tentatively compared to Molière, with an eye on Molière's shorter farces; but the better parallel is with the medieval farce, as represented by *Maître Pathelin*. Shrewd and popular in the same way, Courteline was the most genuinely realistic playwright of his period.

Realism and the problem play did not entirely monopolize the serious theatre before the First World War. As early as the eighteen-nineties two other kinds of drama achieved some success, already suggesting that a different development was possible. One was based on a brief revival of Romanticism, the other was a product of the Symbolist movement.

The verse play, broadly in the Romantic tradition, attracted several poets, from François Coppée to Jean Richepin, but was seen at its best in the *Cyrano de Bergerac* (1897) of Edmond Rostand. Rostand (1868–1918) took the character of the seventeenth-century *libertin* writer, rearranged him as a lover, poet, and swordsman with a grotesque nose, invented a handsome but dumb sub-hero and a lovely *précieuse* heroine to heighten the contrast, and surrounded the whole with a *Three Musketeers* atmosphere, a verbal wit owing something to Hugo (whose Don César de Bazan in *Ruy Blas* was the prototype of the stage Cyrano), and a light sentimentality nearer to Musset. This concoction, for such it must be called, takes on a distinct dramatic and poetic life and is a masterpiece in its own

artificial convention. Rostand's other plays hardly approach it. His
earlier *Les Romanesques* and *La Princesse lointaine* are, in comparison, thin and moonshiny pieces. *L'Aiglon* (1900), basing its
highly theatrical appeal on the Napoleonic legend and handicapped
by an impossible hero, has dated sadly, while *Chantecler*, a satire on
humanity with animal characters, demanded a more imaginative
treatment than Rostand gave it.

While he was modernizing and to some extent prettifying the old
Romantic drama in *Cyrano* and *L'Aiglon*, the Symbolists were feeling their way towards a radically new dramatic technique. One or
two short-lived theatre groups attempted to provide it, but only
Lugné-Poe's Théâtre de l'Œuvre – the Symbolist reply to the
naturalism of Antoine's Théâtre Libre – had any measure of success. And even Lugné-Poe was forced to admit that he could not
survive on Symbolist plays alone and to open his doors after 1897
to naturalistic – though still experimental – productions. Before
that, however, he had produced Maeterlinck, who, in *La Princesse
Maleine* (1889), *Pelléas et Mélisande* (1892, with Debussy's music),
and half a dozen lesser plays, had shown shadowy characters
haunted by Death and Fate (also sometimes introduced as characters) in poetic settings such as vaguely medieval castles and forests.
What was intended was an allegory of life, nowhere stated explicitly,
but hinted through ambiguous dialogue and symbolical stage
effects – the storm beating at the window, or the gardener (death,
perhaps?) sharpening his scythe. Mysterious rather than mystical,
Maeterlinck's plays are fuller of suggestions than of conclusions
and he has affinities on that score with Pirandello. But the atmosphere is that of the early Yeats, who owed a good deal to his
influence. The English reader who can imagine a Celtic twilight
de-Celticized will know approximately where he stands with *Pelléas
et Mélisande*. In his later work, Maeterlinck became both less
elusive and more optimistic. *Monna Vanna* (1902) is a straightforward historical melodrama. *L'Oiseau bleu* (1909), a moving
fairy-play, shows the successful search of two children for the Bird
of Happiness.

But for Maeterlinck, the Symbolist theatre would be remembered
mainly as a promising experiment and as the starting-point for
Claudel's drama. Though Claudel (1868–1955) was not yet acted

and wrote the more freely for hardly expecting to be, his earliest work, *Tête d'or* (1889), was in dramatic form and influenced by the metaphysical trends of the period. So were other of his plays written in the nineties, including *La jeune fille Violaine* (1892), which, after two revisions, became the masterly *L'Annonce faite à Marie*, first acted in 1912 by Lugné-Poe. This, called by the author a Mystery play, was set in the Middle Ages, conceived as a period of simple and integral faith. It marked off Claudel from his Symbolist contemporaries, for whereas their approach was indefinitely 'spiritual' and the results evanescent, his was based on religious convictions, and therefore on a powerful moral and psychological tradition. The conflict between a religious vocation and human love, with their final difficult reconciliation, was the motif of *Partage de midi* (1906), which is set, with modern European characters, on an east-bound liner and in the China which Claudel had come to know through his travels as a diplomat. The play lay virtually forgotten until an outstanding production by Barrault's company in 1948. In three other dramas, *L'Otage* (1911), *Le Pain dur* (1918), and *Le Père humilié* (1920), political and social themes – presented sometimes with broad satire – are mingled with the personal conflicts. The background here is the nineteenth century, interpreted imaginatively from the historical point of view. *L'Otage*, for example, invents a kidnapping of the Pope during his enforced visit to France for the coronation of Napoleon. History is treated with an even more imperial freedom in *Le Soulier de satin*, published in 1929. Of this enormous play, 'the scene is the world, and more especially Spain at the close of the sixteenth, unless it be the opening of the seventeenth century'. This enables Claudel to show the working-out of individual destinies against the background of the Spanish conquest of America, the Armada, the defeat of Islam in Africa, all rendered in expressionistic and often cinematographic scenes ranging from the grotesque to the deeply poetic. This early example of 'total theatre' demanded too much of the theatrical resources available and had to be heavily cut when first produced, by Jean-Louis Barrault, in 1943. A similar spirit, though less scenic exuberance, runs through *Le Livre de Christophe Colomb* (1933) and *Jeanne d'Arc au bûcher* (1939), which may be classed as dramatic recitatives. In another vein are his two 'lyrical farces', *L'Ours et la lune* (1917) and *Protée* (1927), in which Claudel's broad humorous fantasy has full play.

Whether an author who has rarely been adequately produced on the stage, and who hardly cared if he was, can be called the greatest French dramatist of his time is open to question. But at least he is the most original. He has shown how it is possible to present great religious and historical themes through fully human characters, has invented a new kind of dramatic speech, in which prose blossoms into free-verse rhythms, has widened the French tradition by borrowings from the medieval drama and the Spanish theatre of the seventeenth century, and has successfully mingled the comic with the sublime in a way that might have delighted Hugo if he could have lived to see it. In years he was a contemporary of Rostand and Bernstein. As an influence, he belonged to the nineteen-thirties and forties.

After 1918 a new epoch opened in the French theatre. It was primarily the work of a great generation of producers and actors who looked back, at least in spirit, to the Symbolist experiments of the nineties. There was, in fact, a living link with that period in the person of Lugné-Poe, who now refloated his Théâtre de l'Œuvre. But the immediate leader of the new movement was Jacques Copeau, who founded the small theatre of the Vieux-Colombier and before his retirement in 1924 had trained or inspired such disciples as Charles Dullin, Louis Jouvet, the Pitoëffs, and Jacques Hébertot. These, with the independent Gaston Baty, were mainly responsible for the inter-war transformation of dramatic art in which Paris certainly led the world. Scenic design was simplified and stylized, the star-actor system was abandoned in favour of the team-performance by the whole company, precise and closely-argued dialogue gave place at times to the poetic monologue and also to mime and 'silent acting', while the well-made plot with its frequent small surprises was jettisoned along with the other more mechanical heirlooms of the nineteenth century. This producer's revolt widened the horizon of the dramatists. If it did not enable them to go as far as Claudel, it encouraged them to stop concentrating on minor ingenuities and to give the imagination fuller play.

Lugné-Poe, Copeau, and Copeau's disciples acted – and in most cases launched – nearly all the more original dramatists of the twenties and thirties, including Romains, Sarment, Achard, Lenormand, Giraudoux, Cocteau, Salacrou, and, later, Anouilh. Not all these are of equal interest, nor can they easily be grouped, but all profited in some measure by the greater freedom which the *avant-garde* theatre had won for them.

To take first the writers of comedy. Jules Romains (1885–1972), besides experimenting with serious drama in *Cromedyre-le-Vieil* (1920), struck a vein of broad social satire in his two plays on *Monsieur Le Trouhadec* and in *Knock, ou le Triomphe de la médicine*, his most perfect comedy (1923). In *Donogoo* (1931), originally conceived as a film-scenario, he described the creation through faith in high-power publicity of a gold-mining centre which at first had existed only on paper. These and a few other comedies, inspired for the most part by his initial concept of Unanimism and at times satirizing it, were clear-sighted but genial comments on the modern world, just fantastic enough to lift them above it but certainly not out of it. Unfortunately for the theatre, Romains became absorbed after 1930 in his vast cyclic novel, *Les Hommes de bonne volonté*. Partly for fortuitous reasons, two late plays, *Grâce encore pour la terre* (1941) and *L'An mil* (1947) made no impact on the theatre.

In Jean Sarment (b. 1897) and Marcel Achard (1899–1974) the themes are treated with a more sentimental kind of humour. The first renewed the whimsical tradition of Musset (*Le Pêcheur d'ombres*, 1921; *Les plus beaux yeux du monde*, 1925). The second introduced a note of irony into his not dissimilar plays (*Jean de la lune*, 1929). Neither author has much increased the reputation he gained in the twenties. Their contemporary Marcel Pagnol (b. 1895) used a more conventional technique in *Topaze* (1928), an excellent satire on crooked business and municipal corruption. He then produced a trilogy of plays with Marseilles characters (*Marius*, *Fanny*, *César*, 1929–31), before leaving the theatre for the cinema.

Whimsical humour and a relatively subtle irony have dated plays of these kinds, in spite of rare revivals. This applies, unfairly enough, even to Romains, whose drama has a sharp cutting edge and in places a robust vulgarity hardly suitable for the old-style drawing-room. It is necessary to say this here because what is broadly labelled 'the theatre of shock' was already germinating in the twenties and thirties in the theories of Artaud, the influence of

Jarry and the plays of Vitrac and others. Dullin, Jouvet and the Pitoëffs were all aware of it. But it was certainly not typical of the time. At most a fringe tendency then, it emerged as a powerful force in the fifties and sixties and will be described more fully on a later page.

Of the serious dramatists of the twenties, Henri-René Lenormand (1882–1951) impressed for a few years with his studies in morbid psychology (*Le Simoun*, 1920; *Le Mangeur de rêves*, 1922; *L'Homme et ses fantômes*, 1924). Their atmosphere is oppressive rather than tragic, their technique cinematographic, calling for rapid successions of short scenes. Though attracted thus early by the same material which began to interest Hollywood in the late nineteen-forties, Lenormand himself remains a might-have-been. His later plays have more than a suspicion of the old *pièce à thèse*. So have those of Gabriel Marcel (b. 1889), prominent as the exponent of Christian existentialism. Since 1921, the date of *La Grâce* and *Le Cœur des autres*, he has been exploring the mystery of the human personality in difficult and somewhat arid plays. Both more detached and more openly philosophic than Mauriac in his novels, he shows characters who have reached a psychological impasse to which the only solution is in a very demanding kind of religious morality (*Un Homme de Dieu*, 1925; *Le Monde cassé*, 1932; *Le Dard*, 1938; *La Soif*, 1938; *Rome n'est plus dans Rome*, 1951). This type of play, more important for the questions it raises than for its theatrical qualities, owed little to the aesthetic revolution which Copeau touched off and so lay outside the main development of the inter-war years.

In the centre of it was Jean Giraudoux (1882–1944), certainly the leading dramatist of his period. His most characteristic contribution was to have taken Greek and biblical themes and to have presented them in a modern, though not a realistic, idiom. Considered theoretically, it was the same process that the dramatists of the seventeenth and eighteenth centuries had followed, but the difference in treatment is so great that all other resemblances disappear. Giraudoux's tone – he writes of course in prose – is nearer to Musset or even to Marivaux than to Racine. He is amusing and obliquely ironical in such a play as *Amphitryon 38* (1929) which treats – for the thirty-eighth time, the title implies – of the love of Jupiter for a mortal woman. In the original legend Alcmena was a faithful wife whom Jupiter could only approach by assuming the shape of her husband. Giraudoux goes further and causes her to convert the master of the gods to her own point of view. In *La Guerre de Troie n'aura pas lieu* (1935) the Trojans are ready to return Helen to her husband and so avoid hostilities. Only a last-minute trick of destiny unleashes the disaster. Produced in the shadow of the coming world war, this play had a grim enough topical interest, but the theme was presented in personal and partly humorous terms. In his first play, *Siegfried* (1928), Giraudoux had also adopted a purely personal treatment in dealing with what might seem the political question of Franco-German relations. His interest is always in individual human qualities, some of them trivial enough for it to be possible to accuse him of frivolity, in face of subjects on which one does not joke. But at his best he maintains an amazing balance between the apparently inconsequential, the decorative notion and metaphor, and a sense of human destiny not greatly inferior to that of the Greeks. It is a remarkable feat, in which neither Cocteau nor Anouilh could succeed so well, but which demanded a prose poet of Giraudoux's particular order, with a producer like Jouvet, to bring it to its difficult perfection, as perhaps in *La Folle de Chaillot* (1945). It is most enjoyable in fantasies like *Intermezzo* and *Ondine*, most moving in the tragic *Électre* (1937). His two biblical plays, *Judith* (1932) and *Sodome et Gomorrhe* (1943), are also openly tragic, but somewhat turgid in their pessimism. Giraudoux was a great enough writer never to be content with charm, but when he dispensed with it his touch became less sure. He should perhaps have accepted it as a natural limitation. Others in his place would have been only too glad to exploit it as the easiest key to success.

This reproach was incurred by Jean Cocteau (1889–1963), a man of brilliant and varied talents, who was actively interested in painting, ballet, music – from early jazz to Honegger and Poulenc – the theatre, and the cinema. He was, like Giraudoux, a novelist, and also a pleasant poet. He seemed to be less a single personality than the spirit, since 1920, of every modern trend that appeared in Paris. Less the spirit than the echo, his critics objected, and that at a level too nicely adjusted to the wealthier middle class. But there is always room for such missionary work and the *avant-garde* could hardly have found a more highly intelligent interpreter of its sometimes incoherent ideas.

He introduced mime and ballet into such early plays as *Les Mariés de la Tour Eiffel* (1924), then turned to modernizations of ancient legends (*Orphée*, 1927; *La Machine infernale*, 1934; *Les Chevaliers de la Table Ronde*, 1937, etc.). His versions contain numerous trick-effects, either scenic or psychological, which too often debase the original material without adding anything of lasting value. Mechanical surprises and strokes of novelettish sentiment abound. If Racine could be criticized in his day for recasting Achilles as a courtly lover, Cocteau does far worse with the tragic figures of Oedipus and Jocasta. What is left when the novelty has worn off is a display of virtuosity comparable to the virtuosity of Rostand's *L'Aiglon*. Yet Cocteau has been too consistently inventive to be dismissed lightly. He has also experimented in modern psychological drama (*Les Parents terribles*, 1938), in tragedy on the French classical model (*Renaud et Armide*, 1943), in historical romance (*L'Aigle à deux têtes*, 1946), and in philosophical allegory (*Bacchus*, 1950). Most of his films have been brilliant adaptations of his plays.

More than ten years after his death, it is still too early to attempt a definitive judgement on Cocteau. An outstanding product of his time, too fashionable then to be fashionable now, he may come to be seen as the last great representative of a truly Parisian culture which can never be reconstituted. Digesting foreign influences, from the Diaghilev ballet to the American film, he gave them back with complete confidence in his own taste and that of his French public. Less superficial than artificial, as so much great art is and especially drama, he was sure of his standing at the main centre of the civilized world. His France has had greater writers, but few, at least since Voltaire, who by the acuity of their minds, their exceptional artistic gifts and the sheer glitter of their wit, have incarnated more completely those qualities that the outside world once looked on as typically and admirably French.

There is something of Cocteau in Jean Anouilh (b. 1910), but much more of Giraudoux. Like Giraudoux's *Siegfried*, Anouilh's first success, *Le Voyageur sans bagage* (1937), hinged on a question of lost memory, though the development was otherwise quite different. He adapted Greek themes in *Eurydice* (1942), *Antigone* (1942), and *Médée* (1946), all tragic plays with intentional anachronisms in dialogue and staging. In *Eurydice* this modernization is somewhat self-conscious, but *Antigone* is a more perfect recasting of the original. It dramatizes movingly, in spite of a few Cocteau-esque touches, the conflict between political expediency and the individual conscience, personified by the daughter of Oedipus. First produced during the German occupation, it had an obvious topical message, but the basic conception was not new to Anouilh and did not require the classical source to suggest it to him. The character (usually a young girl) who refuses to compromise with life and prefers death or certain unhappiness is in most of his plays, beginning with his early *La Sauvage*, and is the most evident sign of an apparently deep-rooted pessimism. He depicts existence as ignoble or absurd and revolt, even when hopeless or apparently perverse, as a necessity for certain natures. Something of this attitude carries over into his comedies, of which the most successful was *L'Invitation au Château* (1947, adapted by Christopher Fry as *Ring round the Moon*). Here, as in *La Répétition* (1950) and *Colombe* (1951), most of the characters are deliberately stylized and suggest, if not puppets, types from the *commedia dell'arte* or from the old French comedy of intrigue which partly derived from it. It is another variety of modernization and another rejection of stage realism – but not, in intention, an escape from reality. To quote from a programme note on *L'Invitation au Château*: 'Harlequin with his mask, his wooden sword and his motley, knew more about life than Zola with his frock-coat and his myopic pince-nez.' In 1953, Anouilh returned to his obsession with revolt. In *L'Alouette* he presented the character of Joan of Arc in the same light as Antigone or as the 'wild girl' of *La Sauvage*.

His most notable play since then, *Becket ou l'Honneur de Dieu* (1959), continued the same theme, with the interesting variation that the 'pure' rebel was the martyred Archbishop and the corruption he rejected personified by Henry II, once Becket's bosom companion in carnal pleasures. The theme was threadbare and 'history' almost as distorted as in the more lightweight *Pauvre Bitos* (1956) and *La Foire d'Empoigne* (1962). But this has never really mattered. What other dramatists have felt obliged to do more furtively, showing some respect for the historians' version before adapting it to their dramatic purposes, Anouilh has done openly, even allowing his characters to change the known course of events in front of the audience. It was as though the Trojan War had really been called off in Giraudoux's play, instead of being nearly averted. This puppet-handling of history brought it straight into the contemporary theatre and allowed of all the topical parallels, social and political, which were so strong a feature of the plays. It also generated satire of a reasonably savage kind, an element often underestimated in Anouilh's drama.

Long recognized as a 'man of the theatre', Anouilh has worked exclusively in and through it, with a virtuosity and a technical inventiveness which every professional must admire. As to his obsessive theme, that the world is ignobly 'absurd', this now appears to be less a significant message than the reflection of a current mood which gave him an immediate rapport with his audiences. Camus and, above all, Beckett have shown that the Absurd is a deeper and more complicated concept. All credit to Anouilh, however, for his early foreshadowing of it, even on a comparatively simple level.

Anouilh's prominence in the nineteen-forties and fifties may have temporarily obscured the achievement of Armand Salacrou (b. 1899), who has over a dozen considerable plays to his credit, beginning with *Tour à terre* (1925). Salacrou is predominantly a writer of psychological drama renewed by methods which were once surrealist or expressionist but have now become an accepted part of dramatic technique. He is expert at juggling with time and with the personalities of his characters, as in *L'Inconnue d'Arras* (1935), in which a suicide at the point of death sees his whole life passing before him. This, Salacrou's first major success, was followed by a more realistic social drama, *Un Homme comme les autres* (1936), a historical play on Savonarola, *La Terre est ronde* (1938), and a smart comedy on marital relations, *Histoire de rire* (1939). At the end of the war came *Les Fiancés du Havre* (1944), a play on personal relationships in some ways comparable to Anouilh's work; *Les Nuits de la colère* (1946), a moving play on the Resistance; *Dieu le savait* (1950), a disillusioned post-mortem on this same Resistance; and *L'Archipel Lenoir* (1947), a bitingly funny satire on family solidarity and pride. A very varied playwright, with a range running from tragedy to farce, Salacrou has obviously moved with – or reflected – his times, but he has a core of despair which seems to be personal. His later work shows an increasing use of naturalism and a reinforcement of his political left-wing convictions, as in *Boulevard Durand* (1961).

Well before 1950 the innovations of Copeau and the *Cartel des Quatre* had spent their revolutionary force. The Symbolism on which this was based had become absorbed into the main practice of the drama, so that even the commercial theatre was familiar with devices like the flash-back, the dream scene, the symbolic and the fractionized character. The influence of Pirandello, the arch-Symbolist, swelled the native French stream. In addition, surrealism, though not at first easily distinguishable from these other trends, had begun to affect dramatic psychology and techniques. Conventional drama seemed dead, but a strong argument that it was not entirely so can be drawn from the work of two undoubtedly important writers whose work (like some of Salacrou's) belonged to that tradition.

Henry de Montherlant (1896–1972) came comparatively late from the novel to the theatre with *La Reine morte* (1942). Like his other principal plays – *Le Maître de Santiago* (1948), *Malatesta* (1950), *Port-Royal* (1954) and *Le Cardinal d'Espagne* (1960) – it has a historical setting, long 'literary' discussions on motive and characters of heroic stature. Some of these dramas recall Corneille, particularly in their pastiche or revival of the Cornelian *moi*, but Montherlant's are actionless in comparison. They hinge on the self-analysis of characters whose psychology is sometimes austere to the point of aridity, such as that of the puritanical Spanish nobleman in *Le Maître de Santiago*, or the community of nuns in *Port-Royal*. They express themselves in carefully written uncolloquial dialogue, and it was a remarkable feat to have made them acceptable to the Parisian stage in the mid-twentieth century. Besides these statu-esque plays Montherlant wrote several having modern bourgeois characters and themes, such as *Fils de personne* (1943), *Demain il fera jour* (1949), *Celles qu'on prend dans ses bras* (1950) and *Brocéliande* (1956). The last two belong to comedy verging on farce. His serious *La Ville dont le prince est un enfant*, published in

1954 but not performed until 1967, is a sympathetic and convincing study of homosexual relationships in a modern Catholic school. Nevertheless if Montherlant's drama survives for long it is likely to be for his 'heroic' plays set in remoter periods.

In contrast, there is no doubt of the total modernity of theme in the plays of J.-P. Sartre, even when he is dramatizing myth or history. His first play, *Les Mouches* (1943), used the legend of Orestes the matricide to expound the existentialist view of human freedom. It was almost the last of such modernizations on the French stage. *Huis clos* (1944), with its three contemporary characters shut up together in a room which soon proves to be hell and condemned to torment each other morally for all eternity, has some of the claustrophobic atmosphere of a Racinian tragedy but none of its emotional logic. If, as one of the characters observes, it is not chance that has brought them together, it is rather too obviously the author intent on proving a point of metaphysics. After this play, Sartre turned to almost contemporary events in *Morts sans sépulture* (1946), which deals naturalistically with the torture of members of the Resistance Movement, wrote a crude little anti-American pamphlet in *La Putain respectueuse* (1946), then attacked communist subservience to the changeable party-line in *Les Mains sales* (1948). Given its timing, *Les Mains sales* appeared above all a political play but it is more important for the self-examination conducted by its hero, who finally decides to die rather than disown responsibility for an act which he has committed. Or rather, his responsibility for the act – the assassination of a party leader – is not in doubt. Only the motive is in question, and it is here that he refuses to adopt the version which the party demands of him. Later, in *Le Diable et le Bon Dieu* (1951), Sartre immensely widened the scope of his arguments in a play constructed on a scale worthy of Claudel and written with a dialectical skill equal to Shaw's. The setting is Germany in the time of Luther. The problems of good and evil, of human responsibility and the existence of God are discussed in dramatic terms against a violent background of war and social unrest. The central character, if somewhat monstrous, is plausibly so in the historical context of the play. Sartre followed this with *Nekrassov* (1955), a satire on professional anti-communism in journalists and politicians, then with *Les Séquestrés d'Altona* (1959), an ambitious play with contemporary characters which returned to the serious probing of human conduct and motive.

This appeared to be Sartre's farewell to the theatre. He had used it, as he used the novel in *Les Chemins de la liberté*, to illustrate a philosophy in action no less than Claudel had done in his major dramas. In the one, existentialism, predominantly in a political context; in the other, a Catholic belief in a providential universe. But while Sartre's plays are much more obviously topical and – unlike Anouilh's – can be seen to carry an immediate social 'message', they cannot be adequately described as *pièces à thèse*. This is only one of their features, but it was made to appear more conspicuous by a complete turning away from any such conception of drama which began in the nineteen-fifties, together with a new upheaval in theatrical techniques.

The drama of the Absurd, as it has been conveniently classified, surfaced most memorably in Beckett's *En attendant Godot*, produced at the small Théâtre de Babylone in January 1953. There had been earlier examples of the Absurd in the sense of a moral nihilism which renders philosophical and religious explanations of the human condition pointless (including the brave affirmations of existentialism that man is potentially free) and implies a negation of all established values which leads either to despair or to a passive acceptance of the void, according to the position from which one starts. Camus and Anouilh had prefigured it in their different ways. Ionesco's first play was produced in May 1950. But *Godot* was, and still is, a landmark, at least where the theatre is concerned. Performed in London over a year and a half later than in Paris (August 1955) it made a deep impression on a small but intellectually influential section of the English-speaking public.

It is an open question whether Samuel Beckett should figure prominently in a survey of French literature. Born in Dublin in 1906 of an Irish Protestant family, he was educated in Ireland, then worked and lived in Paris, meeting James Joyce, and became bilingual in the process. His early work was written in English, but his principal novels (*Molloy*, *Malone meurt* and *l'Innommable*) appeared in French several years before their English versions were published. After *Godot* nearly all Beckett's plays (he has published no more 'novels') have had their first productions in English, with the exception of *Fin de partie* (*Endgame*, 1957–8). Two small but not insignificant works, *Play* (1963) and *Come and Go* (1965), were first performed in German translations on the German stage. When, in 1969, Beckett to his consternation was awarded the Nobel Prize, it was for his international reputation. Basically he has always been an Irish writer, overtly up to and including *Godot*, but still perceptibly in his diminishing production since. His work might be symbolized by some mixed-up old man, full of obscure and unorganized memories, mumbling on about life as he thinks he has experienced it while some faded woman in the background prepares an unappetizing supper. 'The pathetic old fool,' is one's first reaction; but one's second: 'There may be something in what he says, and anyway he says it rather well.' There Beckett appears to stop and quite possibly means to, but at that point the exegetists take over. They have thousands of well-drilled words at their command and a dozen different lines of approach to the significance of a missing fly-button, but as critics or intellectuals they are operating on a different level.

It is impossible to assess with any precision the influence of Beckett (always or mainly through *Godot*) on the theatre in France. In itself it seems to have been quite small. But it helped to show French producers, and also French writers, that it was just possible to hold an audience with a play having no plot, elementary characterization, and apparently elementary and inconsequential dialogue, though in fact this was very carefully written. It offered an alternative, not merely to Scribe, but also to Giraudoux, Sartre and Anouilh.

With Eugène Ionesco (b. 1912), whose Romanian origins have much less significance than Beckett's Irishness, there is no question of the articulateness of the characters in their attempts to reach some understanding of the elusive universe around them. The dialogue ranges from the moronically flat to the sparkling, but the characters' reasoning is always frustrated by the illogicality of their supposed logic, its misdirection, its perceptive and intellectual limitations and the frequent habit of reaching two opposite conclusions at the same time with equal conviction or lack of it. They are uncomfortably true caricatures of the average muddled man, who would hardly know how muddled he is if the external environment were not constantly behaving in unaccountable ways which seem to require comment. Ionesco is an ex-actor, fully aware of the resources of the stage and drawing from them surprising or outrageous effects such as the increasing accumulation of dozens of unoccupied chairs onstage (*Les Chaises*), the gradual lengthening of a huge leg which grows out from the wings (*Amédée*), or the transformation of a table into a toadstool. This was a classic example of surrealist theatre. Unlike Beckett, Ionesco derived his work from surrealism, compounded it quite legitimately with his own dreams and fantasies and presented it to audiences in concrete form. No discreetly symbolic effects, as in Maeterlinck, but actual objects and people which appear, behave, or change in unnaturalistic ways. This concrete presentation of an undefined or experimental psychology may, as in certain painters, appear superficial or phoney. The frontier between the nightmare distortion and the trick effect is difficult to draw. A probable future verdict on Ionesco is that his dialogue saves him from the reproach of fashionable illusionism.

La Cantatrice chauve (1950) first brought him to public notice. A dozen plays followed, nearly all short and performed at little theatres, and including *Les Chaises* (1952), *Amédée ou Comment s'en débarrasser* (1954) and *Tueur sans gages* (1959). Then in 1960 Barrault produced *Le Rhinocéros* at the Odéon-Théâtre de France. This was a full-length play set in a provincial town whose inhabitants are turning into rhinoceroses in increasing numbers. They accept this change and indeed welcome it as the right thing, until the day is near when only one human being will remain, as a freak and an outcast. This parable, which can be variously interpreted, was soberly and realistically staged. Part of it is set in an ordinary office, whose staff absent themselves one by one as they experience the symptoms of rhinocerodom. This marked the climax of Ionesco's originality. In half a dozen more plays he tended to repeat himself, in spite or perhaps because of his consecration by another production at the Théâtre de France and the thorny crown of a production at the Comédie-Française of the full-length and ponderous *La Soif et la faim* in 1966.

Ionesco's drama as a whole has been described as tragic farce. 'Tragic' seems too ambitious a word. But as a practitioner of the Absurd in its most immediately evident form he can hardly be faulted. Not only does he deprive life of any philosophical significance, but he also refuses it sense in relation to any norm, however pragmatic, consequently abolishing the abnormal also. If all his audiences accepted this there could be no farce either, since no incongruities would remain on which to build it. But he does not totally persuade us, as Beckett often comes near to doing, and this margin of disbelief leaves in his plays a strong element of entertainment.

With Ionesco's the name of Arthur Adamov (1908–72) was originally coupled as a dramatist of the Absurd. Nurtured, like him, on surrealism, and also of non-French origin (he retained his native knowledge of Russian literature and his interest in it throughout life) Adamov wrote a handful of plays in the early nineteen-fifties (as *l'Invasion*, 1950; *La Grande et la petite manoeuvre*, 1950; *Le Professeur Taranne*, 1953) filled with a comparable sense of futility, but much more conventional in their staging. All, like Ionesco's in this, concerned the psychology of individuals, fantastically interpreted, though the comic touches were more subtle. In *Le Ping-Pong* (1955) this vein appeared to continue, but there was also a social message for the first time – a condemnation of capitalism. From that date Adamov consciously became a politically committed writer, looking to Brecht as his ideal model, criticizing his own earlier work and condemning Ionesco and his themes as trivial. In *Paoli Paoli* (1957), *Le Printemps 71* (1963) and one or two later plays he began his deliberate progress towards socialist realism. But his political outlook was naïve, his satire lost its subtlety in a laudable but deadening effort to be more accessible to the masses as he conceived them, and a brilliant idiosyncratic talent foundered in these unsuccessful exercises in 'epic theatre'.

Several playwrights have attempted this, without necessarily abandoning the Absurd but using it as a background of accepted ideology for their plays. These, in all their varied and complex forms, might be broadly classed as parody-documentaries with a strong left-wing slant ranging from general anti-bourgeoism, sometimes combined with anti-Americanism, to reactions to specific topical events or situations. To the first category belong *Le Comportement des époux Bredburry* (1960) of François Billetdoux (b. 1927) and the same author's *Comment va le monde, Môssieu? Il* *tourne, Môssieu!* (1964), though in this the topical allusions are much more evident. Armand Gatti (b. 1924) has written powerful plays whose central themes are never in doubt, however richly diffuse their stage presentation may be: the concentration camps in *La Deuxième existence du camp de Tatenberg* (1962), the Sacco and Vanzetti case in *Chant public devant deux chaises électriques* (1966), *La Passion du général Franco* and *V comme Viêt-nam*, whose titles are self-explanatory. These themes are presented through the minds of the characters, often witnesses or survivors, with constantly shifting perspectives and spectacular scenic effects including songs, dances and plays-within-plays. They provide an extreme example of 'total theatre', at the opposite pole to Beckett's Spartan stage technique.*

Gatti's technique has resemblances with that of Jean Genet (b. 1910), though it takes a more exaggerated form. Internationally at least, Genet's five plays to date have earned him greater importance, which he owed initially no doubt to J.-P. Sartre, who first brought him to public notice (see p. 234 above). His themes also are social or political, but conceived so simplistically that beside Sartre's they appear puerile. Only in *La Putain respectueuse* did Sartre ever approach this level of naïve if well-meant protest. Genet's themes, to isolate them, are the oppression of servants by their employer in *Les Bonnes* (1947), the distorted lives of convicts (he had been one himself) in *Haute Surveillance* (1949), colonialism and racism in *Les Nègres* (1958), the brothel patronized by local notabilities in *Le Balcon* (1960) and colonialism again, with a transparent reference to Algeria, in *Les Paravents* (1966). All abuses worth attacking, it might be said, and all still thoroughly alive. But not in the form in which Genet conceives them. The same evils today have shifted their ground and developed new features. Genet never seems to hit them where it hurts and his plays have given comparatively little offence ideologically. He is no satirist, as was Jules Romains or, on a more intimate level, Jean Anouilh. But it must be added at once that he never intends to be. His themes are conventionally Marxian

---

*The fact that *Godot* requires only four actors and that its staging costs virtually nothing was a main reason for the year-long run of the first Paris production. A more expensive production could not have survived on the same box-office receipts.

or near-Marxian, but they serve as hardly more than a pretext for the characteristic features of his work: spectacle, illusionism (the characters play at being other characters), lyrically rich language, and a somewhat contemptuous involvement of the audience in this further example of total theatre.

It can nevertheless be asked whether, after the exploration of individual psychology in the Absurd, there has been a period of political drama to succeed it. While it was inevitable that the events of the fifties and sixties should be reflected in any live theatre, and while in some cases they even occupied the foreground, the general answer is, no. No considerable dramatist has succeeded Sartre in his relatively direct handling of these public problems. What has occurred has been a development of theatricalism in the widest sense, no longer by creating an illusion behind the proscenium arch but by extending it to the whole theatre and including the audience in it by every possible means, both physical and psychological. Making every reservation as to method, it is a return in spirit to the medieval conception of drama, in which actors and spectators were of the same community. A more modern analogy is with pop, which is part of the same movement.

As to influences, the old Symbolist theories have continued to play their part. The notion of the Absurd has lingered on perceptibly, even in dilution. Surrealism, with assumptions and techniques developed from it, has been a pervading force taken almost for granted. The influence of Brecht on the socially-orientated drama has been considerable, while in the nineteen-forties the avant-garde began to recognize a native French influence which grew steadily through the fifties and sixties to reach impressive proportions.

Antonin Artaud (1896–1948) had only one play performed – an adaptation of Shelley's *The Cenci* – but he was in close practical touch with the theatre as an actor in productions by Dullin and Jouvet, as a friend of Barrault and as the founder with Roger Vitrac of a short-lived little theatre of his own. His expression of life was through the theatre, just as Van Gogh's (on whom he wrote an understanding book) was through painting. For him it was much more than an art-form. It was a way of existence, capable of containing all human and extra-human experience, as for a short time poetry had seemed to be to the adolescent Rimbaud before he abandoned it in favour of the rat-race. Artaud could never do this. A confirmed drug-addict, he spent the last ten years of his life in and out of a mental hospital, suffering from visions or hallucinations of a most terrible kind, in which an implacable God seemed to be pursuing him. A mystic convinced of the reality of his religion-conditioned universe, he wrote prolifically of this in the nineteen-thirties, applying his ideas to the theatre in such works as *Le Théâtre et son double* (1938) and launching the concept of 'le théâtre de la cruauté', which can be best translated as 'the theatre of shock'. Theatre should never be a simple entertainment, he protested. It should not depend primarily on words. It should be a ritual involving the audience intimately and forcibly, and this included the arousal of their passions by the sight of violence. This was only one of Artaud's many-sided theories, but it has proved the most popular and readily applicable among a younger generation of dramatists and critics.

As to his predecessors and contemporaries, Artaud looked back with admiration to Alfred Jarry, whose grotesquely savage farce *Ubu-Roi* had first been performed by Lugné-Poe in 1896. Roger Vitrac (1901–52), Artaud's friend and companion in theatrical experiments, wrote a number of equally savage social satires, going well beyond 'bitter comedy' to ruthless comedy in the twenties and thirties (*Victor ou les Enfants au pouvoir*, 1928; *Le Coup de Trafalgar*, 1934; *Loup-Garou*, 1939). The Belgian Michel de Ghelderode (1898–1962) expressed a deep-rooted sense of horror in terms of farce in plays going back to 1925, though he was hardly known in France before the late nineteen-forties (*Fastes d'enfer*, 1949). His compatriot Fernand Crommelynck (b. 1885) made his first Parisian impact with *Le Cocu magnifique* (1921) and went on to produce other plays of a robustly poetic vulgarity, as *Chaud et froid* (1934). The 'shock' in these authors was mainly psychological and verbal, based on an outrageous upturning of accepted ideas of morality and behaviour.

Some of the dramatists of the sixties mentioned above went very much further, encouraged to do so by freer social attitudes and richer theatrical resources, but it is arguable that the intention and the spirit were the same, and certain that the writings of Artaud have provided a source of inspiration on which an entirely new drama could be built. Perhaps it never will be and perhaps Artaud's work is not strictly a 'source' but an explanation and justification of the drama of Genet, Gatti, Billetdoux, Arrabal* and others, whose work might have been much the same without him. But at least the theory is there, as, to go to the opposite extreme, the theory of classical tragedy was in the abbé d'Aubignac, though not invented by him.

The last few pages have dealt with the avant-garde because new trends must be recorded when they show vitality and promise, even if this is not ultimately fulfilled. The commercial theatre goes on much as usual, drawing, with the State theatres, at least 90 per cent of the money and the audiences. But it lacks fresh ideas and outstanding playwrights. There may still be a future for the well-made play which the audience sits back comfortably to watch, as it does with television. It needs, however, some injection of the shock and the participatory compulsion practised by the new dramatists and there are signs that it is already receiving this in mild doses. The result would be a compromise, but unless there are radical social changes, requiring a revolution which went far beyond dramaturgy, it is hardly realistic to expect more.

* Fernando Arrabal (b. in Spain, 1932), author of *Le Cimetière des voitures* (1967) and numerous other plays, inventor of 'panic theatre'.

Chief Dates in French Literature

GENERAL HISTORY	LITERATURE

1ST–11TH CENTURIES

Roman domination of Gaul
(1st–5th centuries)

Frankish kingdom formed
under Clovis (510)

6th–9th centuries: Latin chronicles of Gregory
of Tours, Fredegar, Einhard, etc.

Charlemagne (771–814)

Norse invasions (9th century)

First Romance texts: Strasbourg Oaths (842),
Cantilène de Ste Eulalie (c. 880)

Dukedom of Normandy
founded (911)

Lives of Saints (10th and 11th centuries)

First Crusade (1096)

Guillaume d'Aquitaine, troubadour (1071–
1126)

12TH CENTURY

Troubadours throughout century
Chanson de Roland (c. 1100)
Other *chansons de geste* to 13th century
Roman d'Alexandre, Alberic fragment (c. 1120)
Romans d'antiquité (c. 1140–60)
Mystère d'Adam (c. 1150)

English Court of Henry II
(1154–89) and Eleanor
of Aquitaine, centre of
French culture.

Wace: *Roman de Brut* (1155)
Chrétien de Troyes: Romances (c. 1165–90)
Marie de France: *Lais* (c. 1165)
Tristan et Iseut: Béroul (c. 1175)
        Thomas (c. 1175)

Philippe-Auguste (1180–
1223)

First Northern *trouvères* (c. 1180)

Third Crusade (1189)

Original *Roman de Renart* (c. 1175–1205)

13TH CENTURY

Fourth Crusade (1202)

Fabliaux and *romans d'aventure* throughout
century
Robert de Borron: *Joseph d'Arimathie* (c. 1200)

Albigensian Crusade
(1208)

Villehardouin: *Conquête de Constantinople*
(c. 1210)

Louis IX (St Louis)
(1226–70)

Prose Romances of Arthur and Tristan
(c. 1225–35)

GENERAL HISTORY	LITERATURE
Seventh Crusade (1248)	*Roman de la Rose*: G. de Lorris (*c.* 1235) J. de Meung (*c.* 1280)
Last (Eighth) Crusade (1270)	Rutebeuf active (*c.* 1250–85) Adam de la Halle active (*c.* 1275–85)

14TH CENTURY

Popes at Avignon (1309–78)	Joinville: *Histoire de Saint-Louis* (1309) G. de Machaut active (*c.* 1330–77)
Hundred Years War (1337–1453)	
Crécy (1346), Poitiers (1356)	*Miracles de Notre-Dame* (*c.* 1360–1400) E. Deschamps active (*c.* 1370–1400)
French victories under Duguesclin (1369–78)	Froissart: *Chroniques* (*c.* 1370–1400) *Confréries de la Passion* formed (from 1370)

15TH CENTURY

Civil wars: Burgundians and Armagnacs (1400–35)	Mystery plays throughout century Christine de Pisan: *Chemin de long estude* (1402)
Agincourt (1415)	A. Chartier: *Livre des Quatre Dames* (1415), *Quadrilogue invectif* (1422)
Joan of Arc burnt (1431)	Charles d'Orléans: *Ballades* (*c.* 1430–65)
Burgundian Court, centre of letters (*c.* 1440–1500).	Rhétoriqueurs active (*c.* 1440–1500) *Farces, sotties, moralités* (*c.* 1450–1550)
Turks take Constantinople (1453)	A. de La Sale: *Le Petit Jehan de Saintré* (1456)
	Les Cent Nouvelles nouvelles (*c.* 1460)
Louis XI (1461–83)	Villon: *Le Testament* (1461)
Printing introduced into France (1470)	
Discovery of America (1492)	Commynes: *Mémoires* (*c.* 1490–8)

16TH CENTURY

François I (1515–47)	C. Marot active (*c.* 1525–44)
Germany: Luther excommunicated (1520)	Rabelais: *Gargantua and Pantagruel* (1532–64)
	Calvin: *Christiánae Religionis Institutio* (1536) Scève: *Délie* (1544)

GENERAL HISTORY	LITERATURE
Henri II (1547–59)	Du Bellay: *Deffence et Illustration* (1545), *L'Olive* (1549), *Les Regrets* (1558).
	Ronsard active (1550–85)
	Marguerite d'Angoulême: *L'Heptaméron* (1558)
Charles IX (1560–74)	Amyot: *Vies des hommes illustres* (1559)
Wars of Religion intermittently (1562–94)	Garnier: *Porcie* (1568), *Les Juives* (1583)
Henri III (1574–89)	Du Bartas: *La Semaine* (1578)
Henri IV (1589–1610)	Montaigne: *Essais* (1580–8)
Edict of Nantes (1598)	A. d'Aubigné active (1577–1620)

17TH CENTURY

	Malherbe active (*c.* 1600–28)
	Hardy: Plays (*c.* 1600–30)
Louis XIII (1610–43)	H. d'Urfé: *L'Astrée* (1607–27)
Richelieu's Ministry (1624–42)	Corneille: Plays (1630–52 and 1659–74), *Le Cid* (1636)
	Académie française founded (1635)
Thirty Years War (1618–48)	Descartes: *Discours de la méthode* (1637)
Louis XIV (1643–1715)	Scarron active (1643–60)
Fronde (1648–53)	Mlle de Scudéry: *Le Grand Cyrus* (1649–53)
England: Commonwealth (1649–60)	Pascal: *Provinciales* (1656), *Pensées* (*c.* 1660)
	Molière active (1658–73). *Le Misanthrope* (1666)
Colbert's Ministry (1661–83): Versailles rebuilt, Netherlands campaigns.	Bossuet active (1660–1704)
	Mme de Sévigné: *Lettres* (1664–96)
	La Fontaine: *Contes* (1665–74), *Fables* (1668–94)
	La Rochefoucauld: *Maximes* (1665–78)
	Boileau: *Satires* (1666–1711), *Art poétique* (1674)
	Racine: *Andromaque* (1667), *Phèdre* (1677), *Athalie* (1691)
	Mme de la Fayette: *Princesse de Cléves* (1678)
Edict of Nantes revoked (1685)	La Bruyère: *Caractères* (1688–94)
War against League of Augsburg (1688–97)	Perrault: *Parallèle des anciens et des modernes* (1688–97)
	Bayle: *Dictionnaire critique* (1696)
	Fénelon: *Télémaque* (1699)

GENERAL HISTORY	LITERATURE

18TH CENTURY

War of Spanish Succession (1701–13)	Regnard: Comedies (1690–1709)
Louis XV (1715–74) Regency (1715–23)	Crébillon *père*: Tragedies (1707–17)
	Lesage: *Turcaret* (1709), *Gil Blas* (1715–35)
	Voltaire active (1718–78). *Candide* (1759)
	Marivaux: Comedies and novels (1720–46)
	Montesquieu: *Lettres persanes* (1721), *L'Esprit des lois* (1748)
	Prévost: *Manon Lescaut* (1731)
War of Austrian Succession (1741–8)	Saint-Simon writes *Mémoires* (1740–50)
	Diderot active (1745–84). *L'Encyclopédie* (1751–80)
	Vauvenargues: *Réflexions et maximes* (1747)
Seven Years War (1756–63)	Rousseau: *Discours sur l'inégalité* (1754), *Les Confessions* (1764–70)
	Rétif de la Bretonne active (1768–97)
Louis XVI (1774–92)	C. de Laclos: *Liaisons dangereuses* (1782)
America independent (1776)	Beaumarchais: *Mariage de Figaro* (1778–84)
Revolution (1789)	
First Republic (1792–1804)	A. Chénier: *Iambes* (written 1794)

19TH CENTURY

First Empire: Napoleon (1804–14)	Chateaubriand: *Génie du Christianisme* (1802), *Mémoires d'Outre-tombe* (1848)
	Mme de Staël: *De l'Allemagne* (1810)
Restoration: Louis XVIII (1815–24)	Lamartine: *Méditations* (1820), *Jocelyn* (1836)
Charles X (1824–30)	Vigny: *Poèmes antiques et modernes* (1826), *Les Destinées* (1864)
July Revolution (1830)	V. Hugo: Earlier Poems (1822–40), *Hernani* (1830)
Louis Philippe (1830–48)	Balzac: *Comédie humaine* (1829–48)
	Stendhal: *Le Rouge et le Noir* (1831), *La Chartreuse de Parme* (1839)
	G. Sand: *Indiana* (1831), *La Mare au diable* (1846)
	Musset: *Fantasio* (1834), *Les Nuits* (1835–7)
	Mérimée: *Colomba* (1840), *Carmen* (1845)
	A. Dumas *père*: *Les Trois Mousquetaires* (1844)

GENERAL HISTORY	LITERATURE
Second Republic (1848–52)	A. Dumas *fils*: Plays (1852–85)
Second Empire: Louis Napoleon (1852–70)	Gautier: *Émaux et Camées* (1852)
	Leconte de Lisle active (1852–84)
	G. de Nerval: *Les Chimères* (1853)
	Flaubert: *Madame Bovary* (1857)
	Baudelaire: *Les Fleurs du mal* (1857)
	V. Hugo: *Légende des siècles* (1859–83), *Les Misérables* (1862)
	Goncourt Brothers: Chief novels (1860–70)
	Verlaine active (1866–90)
Franco-Prussian War and Commune (1870–1)	Rimbaud active (1870–3)
Third Republic (1870–1944)	Zola: *Les Rougon-Macquart* (1871–93)
	Mallarmé: *L'Après-midi d'un faune* (1876), *Poésies* (1887–99)
	Maupassant: *Contes* (1880–90)
	Becque: *Les Corbeaux* (1882)
	Huysmans: *À rebours* (1884)
	Barrès: *Le Culte du Moi* (1888–91)
Dreyfus Affair (1898–9)	Maeterlinck: *Pelléas et Mélisande* (1892)

20TH CENTURY

	Péguy: *Cahiers de la Quinzaine* (1900–14)
	Gide: *L'Immoraliste* (1902), *Les Faux-monnayeurs* (1926)
	R. Rolland: *Jean Christophe* (1904–12)
	Claudel: *Cinq grandes odes* (1911), *Le Soulier de satin* (1929)
	Apollinaire: *Alcools* (1913)
First World War (1914–18)	Proust: *À la recherche du temps perdu* (1913–28)
	Valéry: *La Jeune Parque* (1917), *Charmes* (1922)
Russian Revolution (1917)	Colette: *Chéri* (1920)
	Cocteau: Poems, novels, plays (1919–50)
	R. Martin du Gard: *Les Thibault* (1922–40)
	F. Mauriac: *Génétrix* (1923), *Le Sagouin* (1951)
	A. Breton: *Manifeste du surréalisme* (1924)
	Éluard: Poems (1926–46)
	Saint-John Perse: *Anabase* (1924), *Amers* (1957)
	Montherlant: *Les Jeunes filles* (1936–9), *Port-Royal* (1954)
	Bernanos active (1926–48)

GENERAL HISTORY	LITERATURE
	Giraudoux: Plays (1928–45)
	J. Romains: *Les Hommes de bonne volonté* (1932–47)
	Duhamel: *Chronique des Pasquier* (1933–45)
Spanish Civil War (1936–9)	Malraux: *La Condition humaine* (1933)
Second World War (1939–45)	Aragon: *Le Crève-cœur* (1941)
	Anouilh: Plays from 1937. *Becket* (1959)
Fourth Republic (1945–58)	Sartre: *Les Chemins de la liberté* (1945 ff.), *Les Séquestrés d'Altona* (1959)
French War in Indo-China (1947–54)	Camus: *La Peste* (1947)
Algerian War (1954–62)	Beckett: *En attendant Godot* (1953)
	Ionesco: Main plays, 1950–60. *La Cantatrice chauve* (1950)
	'New Novel' from c. 1950. Robbe-Grillet: *Les Gommes* (1953), Butor: *La Modification* (1957)
Fifth Republic (1958) (Under de Gaulle, 1958–69)	J. Genet: *Les Nègres* (1958)

Bibliography

TEXTS

Most of the greater French writers are published in the *Bibliothèque de la Pléiade* (Gallimard) and the *Classiques Garnier*. In recent years the latter have adopted a more substantial and scholarly presentation. Both series constantly add to their lists. A cheaper but well-edited series is the *Collection GF* (Garnier-Flammarion), while the *Livre de Poche*, including many titles, particularly modern, is generally adequate for the ordinary reader. Selections from modern poets (nineteenth and twentieth centuries), with introductions and bibliographies, are given in *Poètes d'Aujourd'hui* (Seghers).

Rarer texts, edited by academic specialists, are published individually by the main British and American university presses and also in Italy and Germany. Specialized French series, not aiming at completeness, are those of the *Classiques Français du Moyen Age* (Champion), the *Textes Littéraires Français* (Droz) and the *Société des Textes Français Modernes* (various publishers: particularly plays of the sixteenth and seventeenth centuries).

GENERAL WORKS

C. Pichois (ed.), *Nouvelle Histoire de la littérature française* (1968 ff.). Will cover the whole field when complete in 16 vols.

G. Grente (ed.), *Dictionnaire des lettres françaises* (7 vols, 1951–73). *Moyen Age* to *Dix-neuvième siècle*.

A. Adam, G. Lerminier and E. Morot-Sir (ed.), *Littérature française* (2 vols, illus., 1968). Ex-Bedier et Hazard.

P. E. Charvet (ed.), *A Literary History of France* (6 vols, 1967–74)

R. Jasinski, *Histoire de la littérature française* (2 vols, 1947). Substantial manual.

M. Braunschvig, *Notre littérature étudiée dans les textes* (2 vols, 1953) and *La Littérature française contemporaine, 1850–1925* (1950). An old work, kept reasonably up-to-date. Useful for extracts and bibliographies.

P. Harvey and J. E. Heseltine, *The Oxford Companion to French Literature* (1959)

D. G. Charlton (ed.), *France, A Companion to French Studies* (1972). Covers briefly history, thought, art, literature, music from 16th to 20th centuries.

In the chapter-bibliographies which follow, studies on authors and certain topics connected with them are listed in the order of their appearance in the chapter. When a book has been republished in a new edition, the date of this alone is given.

PART I. THE MIDDLE AGES

GENERAL

See relevant volumes or parts of the general works listed above (p. 340). Also:

E. Jaloux, *Introduction à l'histoire de la littérature française*, Vol. I (1946)
G. Cohen, *La Vie littéraire au Moyen Âge* (1953)
P. Zumthor, *Histoire littéraire de la France médiévale* (1954). Sixth to thirteenth centuries.
J. Crossland, *Medieval French Literature* (1956)

CHAPTER I

J. Bédier, *Les Légendes épiques* (4 vols, 1926–9)
        Les Fabliaux (1964)
J. Crossland, *The Old French Epic* (1950)
I. Siciliano, *Les Origines des chansons de geste* (1951)
        Les Chansons de geste et l'épopée (1968)
J. D. Bruce, *The Evolution of Arthurian Romance to 1300* (2 vols, 1929)
R. S. Loomis, *The Arthurian Tradition and Chrétien de Troyes* (1948)
R. S. Loomis (ed.), *Arthurian Literature in the Middle Ages* (1959)
J. Marx, *La Légende arthurienne et le Graal* (1951)
        Nouvelles recherches sur le roman arthurien (1965)
F. Bogdanow, *The Romance of the Grail* (1969)
E. Hoepffner, *Les Lais de Marie de France* (1935)
C. S. Lewis, *The Allegory of Love* (1936)
G. Paré, *Le Roman de la Rose et la scolastique courtoise* (1941)
J. V. Fleming, *The Roman de la Rose* (1969)
L. Foulet, *Le Roman de Renart* (1914)

CHAPTER 2

A. Jeanroy, *La Poésie lyrique des troubadours* (2 vols, 1934)
        Histoire sommaire de la poésie occitane (1945)
        Les Origines de la poésie lyrique en France (1925). On *trouvères*.
P. Dronke, *The Medieval Lyric* (1968)
G. Cohen, *La Poésie française au Moyen Âge* (1952)
P. Champion, *Histoire poétique de 15e siècle* (2 vols, 1966)
F. Desonay, *François Villon* (1947)
I. Siciliano, *F. Villon et les thèmes poétiques du Moyen Âge* (1934)

CHAPTER 3

For individual chroniclers consult the serious editions and translations of their works, which usually have informative introductions. Also:

F. C. Shears, *Froissart, Chronicler and Poet* (1930)
M. Wilmotte, *Jean Froissart* (1942)
G. Charlier, *Commynes* (1945)

J. M. Ferrier, *Forerunners of the French Novel* (1954). On medieval story-
     writers.
R. Dubuis, *Les Cent Nouvelles nouvelles et la tradition de la nouvelle en
     France au Moyen Age* (1973)

CHAPTER 4

E. K. Chambers, *The Medieval Stage* (2 vols, 1903). General study.
K. Young, *The Drama of the Medieval Church* (1933)
G. Cohen, *Le Théâtre en France au Moyen Age* (2 vols, 1928–31)
G. Frank, *The Medieval French Drama* (1954)

PART II. RENAISSANCE TO REVOLUTION

GENERAL

See relevant volumes or parts of the general works listed above (p. 340). Also:

A. Tilley, *The Literature of the French Renaissance* (2 vols, 1959)
F. Simone, *The French Renaissance* (trans. 1969)
D. R. Haggis, *The French Renaissance and its Heritage* (1968)
A. Renaudet, *Préréforme et humanisme* (1953)
A. Adam, *Histoire de la littérature française au 17e siècle* (5 vols, 1948–55)
W. D. Howarth, *The Seventeenth Century* (*Life and Letters in France, I*,
     1965)
R. Fargher, *The Eighteenth Century* (*Life and Letters in France, II*, 1970)
P. Bénichou, *Morales du Grand Siècle* (1948)
A. Adam, *Les Libertins au 17e siècle* (1964)
D. Mornet, *Histoire de la littérature française classique, 1660–1700* (1947)
H. Peyre, *Qu'est-ce que le Classicisme?* (1965)
E. B. O. Borgerhoff, *The Freedom of French Classicism* (1950)
R. Lathuillière, *La Préciosité*, Vol. I (1966)
R. Bray, *La Préciosité et les précieux* (1948)
J. S. Spink, *French Free-Thought from Gassendi to Voltaire* (1959)
P. Hazard, *La Crise de la conscience européenne* (3 vols, 1935). Trans. as
     The European Mind (1953).
A. Adam, *Le Mouvement philosophique dans la première moitié du 18e siècle*
     (1967)
E. Cassirer, *The Philosophy of the Enlightenment* (1951)
R. Mortier, *Clartés et ombres du siècle de lumières* (1969)
P. Van Tieghem, *Le Préromantisme* (3 vols, 1924–48)

CHAPTER 5

J. Plattard, *La Vie et l'œuvre de Rabelais* (1939)
J. Charpentier, *Rabelais et le génie de la Renaissance* (1941)
K. Kasprzyk, *Rabelais and His World* (1968)
F. Jeanson, *Montaigne par lui-même* (1951)

D. M. Frame, *Montaigne, A Biography* (1965) and *Montaigne's Essays* (1965)

A. Cioranescu, *Vie de Jacques Amyot* (1941)

P. Michel, *Blaise de Moulue* (1971)

A. Grimaldi, *Brantôme et le sens de l'histoire* (1971)

J. D. Charrou, *The 'Wisdom' of Pierre Charron* (1961)

N. Kemp Smith, *New Studies in the Philosophy of Descartes* (1953)

F. Alquié, *Descartes, l'homme et l'œuvre* (1956)

S. V. Keeling, *Descartes* (1969)

R. P. Lajeune, *Saint François de Sales* (2 vols, 1966)

J. Orcibal, *Les Origines du Jansénisme* (4 vols, 1947–8)

C.-A. de Saint-Beuve, *Histoire de Port-Royal* (1840–60). Repr. Pléiade (3 vols, 1953–6)

H. F. Stewart, *Pascal's Apology for Religion* (1942)

J. Mesnard, *Pascal, l'homme et l'œuvre* (1951)

A. J. Krailsheimer, *Studies in Self-Interest from Descartes to La Bruyère* (1962). Pascal: pp. 98–151.

J. Calvet, *Bossuet, l'homme et l'œuvre* (rev. J. Truchet, 1968)

J. Truchet, *La prédication de Bossuet* (1960)

CHAPTER 6

E. Magne, *Voiture et l'Hôtel de Rambouillet* (2 vols, 1929–30)
       Le vrai visage de La Rochefoucauld (1923)

W. G. Moore, *La Rochefoucauld* (1969)

J. Lemoine, *Mme de Sévigné, sa famille et ses amis* (1927)

L. Battifol, *Le Cardinal de Retz* (1929)

G. Michaut, *La Bruyère et Théophraste* (1936)

P. Richard, *La Bruyère et ses 'Caractères'* (1966)

A. Le Breton, *La Comédie humaine de Saint-Simon* (1914)

CHAPTER 7

M. Raymond, *Fénelon* (1967)

G. Lanson, *Le Marquis de Vauvenargues* (1930)

J. Dedieu, *Montesquieu, l'homme et l'œuvre* (1966)

R. Shackleton, *Montesquieu, A Critical Biography* (1961)

M. H. Waddicor, *Montesquieu and The Philosophy of Natural Law* (1970)

H. N. Brailsford, *Voltaire* (1935)

R. Naves, *Voltaire, l'homme et l'œuvre* (1942)

T. Besterman, *Voltaire* (1969)

R. Pomeau, *La Réligion de Voltaire* (1969)

V. W. Topazio, *Voltaire, A Critical Study of his Major Works* (1967)

J. Lough, *The 'Encyclopédie'* (1971)

R. Grimsley, *Jean d'Alembert* (1963)

D. Mornet, *Diderot* (1941)

J. Proust, *Diderot et l'Encyclopédie* (1962)

R. Pomeau, *Diderot, sa vie, son œuvre* (1967)

D. Mornet, *Rousseau, l'homme et l'œuvre* (1950)

J. Guéhenno, *Jean-Jacques* (3 vols, 1948–52)

J. H. Broome, *Rousseau, A Study of His Thought* (1963)

R. Grimsley, *J.-J. Rousseau, A Study in Self-Awareness* (1961)

J. C. Hall, *Rousseau: an Introduction to his Political Philosophy* (1973)

CHAPTER 8

GENERAL

G. Reynier, *Les Origines du roman réaliste* (1912)
  Le Roman réaliste au 17e siècle (1914)

M. Magendie, *Le Roman français au 17e siècle, de 'l'Astrée' au 'Grand Cyrus'* (1932)

A. Le Breton, *Le Roman au 17e siècle* (1890)
  Le Roman au 18e siècle (1898)

R. Barchilon, *Le conte merveilleux Français de 1690 à 1790* (1973). On fairy tales, etc.

V. Mylne, *The 18th-Century French Novel* (1965)

H. Coulet, *Le Roman jusqu'à la Révolution* (2 vols, 1967)

INDIVIDUAL WRITERS

P. Jourda, *Marguerite d'Angoulême* (2 vols, 1930–32)

L. Febvre, *Autour de 'l'Heptaméron'* (1944)

L. Sozzi, *Les Contes de B. des Périers* (1965)

J. L. Palister, *The World View of B. de Verville* (1971)

M. Magendie, *L'Astrée* (1929)

L. Lafuma, *Les Histoires dévotes de J.-P. Camus* (1940)

E. Seillière, *Le Romancier du Grand Condé, La Calprenède* (1921)

C. Aragonnès, *M. de Scudéry, reine de Tendre* (1934)

C. Dédéyan, *Mme de Lafayette* (1956)

J. Raitt, *Mme de Lafayette et 'La Princesse de Clèves'* (1971)

A. Hallays, *Les Perrault* (1926)

M. Soriano, *Les Contes de Perrault* (1968)

F. E. Sutcliffe, *Le Réalisme de Charles Sorel* (1965)

F. Bar, *Le Genre burlesque en France au 17e siècle* (1960)

C. Dédéyan, *A.-R. Lesage: 'Gil Blas'* (1956)

E. J. H. Greene, *Marivaux* (1965)

H. Roddier, *L'Abbé Prévost, l'homme et l'œuvre* (1955)

J. Sgard, *Prévost romancier* (1968)

J. Simon, *Bernardin de Saint-Pierre* (1967)

C. R. Dawes, *Restif de la Bretonne* (1946)

C. A. Porter, *Restif's Novels* (1967)

J. Lély, *Vie du Marquis de Sade* (1952–7)

G. Gorer, *The Marquis de Sade* (1963)

R. Vailland, *Laclos par lui-même* (1958)

A.-A. and Y. Delmas, *À la recherche des 'Liaisons dangereuses'* (1964)

CHAPTER 9

GENERAL

G. Lanson, *Esquisse d'une histoire de la tragédie française* (1926)

G. Brereton, *French Tragic Drama in the 16th and 17th Centuries* (1973)

E. Faguet, *La Tragédie française au 16e siècle* (1912)

R. Lebègue, *La Tragédie française de la Renaissance* (1954)
  La Tragédie religieuse en France, 1514–73 (1929)

J. Marsan, *La Pastorale dramatique en France à la fin du 16e et au commencement du 17e siècle* (1905)

H. C. Lancaster, *French Tragicomedy, 1552–1628* (1907)
  A History of French Dramatic Literature in the 17th Century (9 vols, 1929–42) and *Sunset, 1701–15* (1945). These authoritative surveys cover both tragedy and comedy.
  French Tragedy, 1715–74 (2 vols, 1951)
  French Tragedy, 1774–92 (1953)

F. Gaiffe, *Le Drame en France au 18e siècle* (1910)

M. Lioure, *Le Drame* (1963)

J. Scherer, *La Dramaturgie classique en France* (1959). Concerns both tragedy and comedy.

INDIVIDUAL WRITERS

M. M. Mouflard, *R. Garnier* (3 vols, 1961–4)

M. Gras, *R. Garnier, son art et sa méthode* (1965)

R. Griffiths, *The Dramatic Technique of A. de Montchrestien* (1970)

E. Rigal, *Alexandre Hardy . . .* (1889)

S. W. Deierkauf-Holsboer, *Vie d'A. Hardy* (1972)

G. May, *Tragédie cornélienne, tragédie racinienne* (1948)

B. Dort, *P. Corneille dramaturge* (1957)

G. Couton, *Corneille* (1958)

P. J. Yarrow, *Corneille* (1963)

A. Stegmann, *L'Héroïsme cornélien* (2 vols, 1968)

F. Orlando, *Rotrou dalla tragicommedia alla tragedia* (1963)

J. Morel, *J. Rotrou, dramaturge de l'ambiguïté* (1968)

D. Dalla Valle, *Il Teatro di Tristan L'Hermite* (1964)

D. A. Collins, *T. Corneille, Protean Dramatist* (1966)

T. Maulnier, *Racine* (1936)

P. Moreau, *Racine, l'homme et l'œuvre* (1952)

R. Picard, *La Carrière de Jean Racine* (1956)

R. C. Knight (ed.), *Racine, Modern Judgements* (1969)

M. Turnell, *Jean Racine, Dramatist* (1972)

G. Brereton, *Jean Racine, A Critical Biography* (1973)

E. Gros, *P. Quinault, sa vie et son œuvre* (1926)

G. Lanson, *Nivelle de La Chaussée et la comédie larmoyante* (1903)

For Voltaire's tragedies (also Crébillon and other 18th-century dramatists) see particularly H. C. Lancaster's *French Tragedy, 1715–74* and *French Tragedy, 1774–92* listed above under 'General'.

CHAPTER 10

GENERAL

H. C. Lancaster, *A History of French Dramatic Literature in the 17th Century* (1929–42) and *Sunset, 1701–15* (1945). Cover both tragedy and comedy.

P. Voltz, *La Comédie* (1964). Covers whole of French comedy.

B. Jeffery, *French Renaissance Comedy, 1552–1630* (1969)

E. Rigal, *De Jodelle à Molière* (1911)

G. Attinger, *L'esprit de la commedia dell'arte dans le théâtre français* (1950)

G. Oreglia, *La Commedia dell'arte* (1961), trans. L. F. Edwards (1968)

R. Garapon, *La Fantaisie verbale et le comique dans le théâtre français* (1957)

INDIVIDUAL WRITERS

L. Morin, *Les Trois P. de Larivey* (1937)

L. Rivaille, *Les Débuts de Corneille* (1936)

G. Couton, *Corneille* (1958)

E. Magne, *Scarron et son milieu* (1924)

F. A. de Armas, *Paul Scarron* (1972)

D. Mornet, *Molière* (1943)

R. Jasinski, *Molière* (1943)

W. G. Moore, *Molière* (1949)

J. Lemaître, *La Comédie après Molière et le théâtre de Dancourt* (1903)

A. Calame, *Regnard, sa vie, son œuvre* (1960)

M. Arland, *Marivaux* (1950)

P. Gazagne, *Marivaux par lui-même* (1954)

K. N. McKee, *The Theatre of Marivaux* (1958)

J. Scherer, *La Dramaturgie de Beaumarchais* (1954)

R. Pomeau, *Beaumarchais, l'homme et l'œuvre* (1956)

CHAPTER 11

ANTHOLOGIES

A. J. Steele, *Three Centuries of French Verse* (1956)

A. M. Boase, *The Poetry of France, Vols 1 and 2* (1964 and 1973)

A.-M. Schmidt, *Poètes du seizième siècle* (1953)

V. E. Graham, *Sixteenth-century French Poetry* (1965)

J. Rousset, *Anthologie de la poésie baroque française* (2 vols, 1961)

GENERAL

G. Brereton, *Introduction to the French Poets* (1973)

H. Chamard, *Histoire de la Pléiade* (4 vols, 1939–40)

R. Lebègue, *La Poésie française de 1560 à 1630* (2 vols, 1951)
O. de Mourgues, *Metaphysical, Baroque and Précieux Poetry* (1953)
R. Winegarten, *French Lyric Poetry in the Age of Malherbe* (1954)
J. Rousset, *La Littérature de l'âge baroque en France* (1961)

INDIVIDUAL POETS

P. Jourda, *Marot, l'homme et l'œuvre* (1967)
V.-L. Saulnier, *Maurice Scève* (2 vols, 1948)
    Étude sur P. du Guillet (1944)
F. Zamaron, *Louise Labé, sa vie, son œuvre* (1968)
G. Gadoffre, *Ronsard par lui-même* (1960)
R. Lebègue, *Ronsard, l'homme et l'œuvre* (1966)
T. Cave (ed.), *Ronsard the Poet* (1973)
V.-L. Saulnier, *Du Bellay, l'homme et l'œuvre* (1951)
J. Lavaud, *Un poète de cour, P. Desportes* (1936)
F. Ruchon, *Essai sur la vie et l'œuvre de J. de La Ceppède* (1953)
G. Ortali, *Un poète de la mort, J. B. Chassignet* (1968)
M. Braspart, *Du Bartas, poète chrétien* (1947)
J. Rousselot, *A. d'Aubigné* (1966)
J. Bailbé, *A. d'Aubigné, poète des 'Tragiques'* (1968)
R. Fromilhague, *Malherbe* (2 vols, 1954)
J. Vianey, *M. Régnier* (1896)
A. Adam, *T. de Viau et la libre-pensée française* (1936)
J. Lagny, *Le Poète Saint-Amant* (1964)
P. Clarac, *La Fontaine, l'homme et l'œuvre* (1947)
G. Couton, *La Poétique de La Fontaine* (1957)
R. Bray, *Boileau, l'homme et l'œuvre* (1942)
F. Scarfe, *A. Chénier, his life and work* (1965)

PART III. FROM THE ROMANTICS TO THE PRESENT DAY

GENERAL

See relevant volumes or parts of the general works listed on p. 340. Also:

A. Thibaudet, *Histoire de la littérature française de 1789 à nos jours* (1936)
P. Moreau, *Le Romantisme* (1957)
L. Emery, *L'Âge romantique* (1959)
H. Peyre, *Qu'est-ce que le Romantisme?* (1971)
C. Beuchat, *Histoire du naturalisme français* (2 vols, 1949)
H. Clouard, *Histoire de la littérature française du symbolisme à nos jours* (2 vols, 1947–9)
P. de Boisdeffre, *Une Histoire vivante de la littérature d'aujourd'hui* (1958)
    Dictionnaire de la littérature contemporaine (1962)
A. Bourin and J. Rousselot, *Dictionnaire de la littérature française contemporaine* (1968)

M. Girard, *Guide illustré de la littérature française moderne* (1968)

R.-M. Albérès, *L'Aventure intellectuelle du vingtième siècle, 1900–50* (1950)

CHAPTER 12

GENERAL

A. Le Breton, *Le Roman français au 19e siècle avant Balzac* (1901)

F. C. Green, *French Novelists from the Revolution to Proust* (1931)

M. Turnell, *The Novel in France* (1950). Chapters on Constant, Stendhal, Balzac, Flaubert, Proust.

J.-P. Richard, *Littérature et sensation* (1954). On Stendhal, Flaubert, Fromentin, the Goncourts.

INDIVIDUAL WRITERS

C. Du Bos, *Grandeur et misère de Benjamin Constant* (1946)

H. Martineau, *L'Œuvre de Stendhal* (1945)
    Le Cœur de Stendhal (2 vols, 1952–3)

F. Hemmings, *Stendhal, A Study of His Novels* (1964)

Stefan Zweig, *Balzac* (1947)

H. J. Hunt, *Balzac, A Biography* (1957)
    Balzac's 'Comédie humaine' (1959)

A. Béguin, *Balzac lu et relu* (1965)

M. L'Hôpital, *La Notion d'artiste chez G. Sand* (1945)

A. Maurois, *Lélia, ou la vie de G. Sand* (1953)

H. d'Alméras, *A. Dumas et 'Les trois mousquetaires'* (1929)

H. Cluard, *A. Dumas* (1955)

P. Trahard, *La Jeunesse de Mérimée, etc.* (3 vols, 1925–30)

P. Léon, *Mérimée et son temps* (1962)

A. Thibaudet, *Flaubert* (1935)

V. Brombert, *The Novels of Flaubert* (1966)

E. Starkie, *Flaubert* (2 vols, 1967–71)

J.-P. Sartre, *L'Idiot de la famille* (1971 ff.). On Flaubert.

A. Fairlie, *Flaubert: 'Madame Bovary'* (1962)

F. Fosca, *Edmond et Jules de Goncourt* (1941)

P. Martino, *Le Naturalisme français, 1870–95* (1923)

A. Wilson, *Émile Zola, An Introductory Study* (1952)

F. W. J. Hemmings, *Émile Zola* (1953)

C. Delhorbe, *L'Affaire Dreyfus et les écrivains français* (1932)

F. Steegmuller, *Maupassant, a lion in the path* (1972)

P. G. Castex, *Le Conte fantastique en France de Nodier à Maupassant* (1949)

A. Le Corbeiller, *'Les Diaboliques' de Barbey d'Aurévilly* (1940)

G. V. Dobie, *Alphonse Daudet* (1949)

R. Baldick, *The Life of J.-K. Huysmans* (1955)

F. Livi, *J.-K. Huysmans: 'A Rebours' et l'esprit décadent* (1972)

P. Moreau, *Maurice Barrès* (1946)

P. de Boisdeffre, *Barrès* (1962)

R. de Traz, *Pierre Loti* (1948)

C. Braibant, *Le Secret d'Anatole France* (1935)

J. Levaillant, *Essai sur l'évolution intellectuelle d'A. France* (1965)

U. Rouchon, *La Vie bruyante de J. Vallès* (2 vols, 1932–8)

L. Bollery, *Léon Bloy* (3 vols, 1947–54)

A. Béguin, *Bloy, mystique de la douleur* (1949)

J.-P. Sartre, *L'Homme ligoté* (*Situations, I*, 1946). On J. Renard.

P. Schneider, *Jules Renard* (1956)

M. Mansuy, *Un Moderne, P. Bourget* (1960)

CHAPTER 13

GENERAL

C.-E. Magny, *Histoire du roman français depuis 1918* (1951)

H. Peyre, *The Contemporary French Novel* (1955)

G. Brée and M. Guiton, *An Age of Fiction* (1957)

P. de Boisdeffre, *Métamorphose de la littérature* (2 vols, 1963). Studies of twelve novelists from Barrès to Sartre.

M. Nadeau, *Le Roman Français depuis la guerre* (1964)

R.-M. Albérès, *Histoire du roman moderne* (1962), *Métamorphoses du roman* (1966), and *Le Roman d'Aujourd'hui, 1960–70* (1970). Accounts kept up-to-date by a critic and reviewer.

INDIVIDUAL WRITERS

R. Arcos, *Romain Rolland* (1950)

J. Robichez, *Romain Rolland* (1961)

J. O'Brien, *Portrait of André Gide* (1953)

P. Lafitte, *A. Gide romancier* (1954)

J.-J. Thierry, *André Gide* (1962)

A. J. Guérard, *André Gide* (1969)

A. Maurois, *À la recherche de Marcel Proust* (1949)

G. D. Painter, *Marcel Proust, A Biography* (2 vols, 1961)

G. Picon, *Lecture de Proust* (1963)

J. Mouton, *Proust* (1968)

M. Le Hardouin, *Colette* (1956)

M. Crosland, *Madame Colette* (1973)

R. Gibson, *The Quest of Alain-Fournier* (1953)

M. Hanrez, *Céline* (1962)

B. Delvaille, *Paul Morand* (1966)

M. Berry, *Jules Romains* (1960)

A. Bourin and Jules Romains, *Connaissance de Jules Romains* (1961)

C. Santelli, *Georges Duhamel* (1947)

B. L. Knapp, *Georges Duhamel* (1972)

J. Brenner, *Martin du Gard* (1961)

A. Béguin, *Bernanos* (1959)

M. Estève, *Bernanos* (1965)

C. du Bos, *F. Mauriac ou le problème du romancier catholique* (1933)

M. Jarret-Kerr, *François Mauriac* (1954)

M. Alyn, *François Mauriac* (1960)

J. Sémolué, *Julien Green ou l'obsession du mal* (1964)

R. de Saint-Jean, *Julien Green par lui-même* (1967)

P. Sipriot, *Montherlant par lui-même* (1953)

H. Perruchot, *Montherlant* (1959)

C. Mauriac, *Malraux ou le mal du héros* (1947)

P. de Boisdeffre, *André Malraux* (1952)

M. Migeo, *Saint-Exupéry* (1959)

B. Vercier (ed.), *Les Critiques de notre temps et Saint-Exupéry* (1971)

P. Thody, *Albert Camus, 1913–60, A Biographical Study* (1961)

J. Onimus, *Camus devant Dieu* (1965)

N. A. Scott, *Albert Camus* (1969)

P. Thody, *J.-P. Sartre, A Literary and Political Study* (1960)

M. Cranston, *Sartre* (1962)

R. Lafarge, *La Philosophie de J.-P. Sartre* (1967)

S. Julienne-Caffié, *Simone de Beauvoir* (1966)

G. Guisan, *C.-F. Ramuz* (1966)

C. Michelfelder, *Jean Giono et les religions de la terre* (1938)

P. de Boisdeffre, *Giono* (1963)

J. Cabanis, *Jouhandeau* (1959)

P. Vandromme, *Marcel Aymé* (1960)

J. Sturrock, *The French New Novel* (1969). On Simon, Butor, Robbe-Grillet.

J. Ricardou, *Problèmes du nouveau roman* (1967)

B. Morrissette, *Les Romans de Robbe-Grillet* (1971)

J. Roudaut, *Michel Butor ou le livre futur* (1964)

L. Roudiez, *Michel Butor* (1965)

R. Micha, *Nathalie Sarraute* (1966)

H. Hell, *L'Univers romanesque de Marguerite Duras* (1965)

A. Cismaru, *Marguerite Duras* (1971)

G. Mourgue, *Françoise Sagan* (1958)

D. Oster, *Jean Cayrol et son œuvre* (1967)

CHAPTER 14

Comtesse J. de Pange, *Auguste Schlegel et Mme de Staël* (1938)

V. Tapié, *Chateaubriand* (1965)

P. Moreau, *L'Histoire en France au 19e siècle* (1935)

G. Monod, *La Vie et la pensée de Michelet* (2 vols, 1924)

R. Barthes, *Michelet par lui-même* (1954)

C. Carcopino, *Les doctrines sociales de Lamennais* (1942)

J. Roussel, *Lamennais* (1957)

C. C. A. Bouglé, *Socialismes français* (1933)

A. Pinloche, *Fourier et le socialisme* (1933)

G. Woodcock, *P.-J. Proudhon* (1956)

J. Lively, *The Social and Political Thought of A. de Tocqueville* (1962)

M. Leroy, *La Pensée de Sainte-Beuve* (1940)

D. G. Charlton, *Positivist Thought in France* (1959)

A. Cresson, *H. Taine, Sa vie, son oeuvre, sa philosophie* (1951)

P. Van Tieghem, *Renan* (1948)

I. W. Alexander, *Bergson* (1957)

A. Thibaudet, *Le Bergsonisme* (2 vols, 1924)

H. Bars, *Maritain en notre temps* (1959)

C. Cuénot, *P. Teilhard de Chardin* (1966)

E. Rideau, *La Pensée de Teilhard de Chardin* (1965)

E. W. F. Tomlin, *Simone Weil* (1954)

H. Massis, *Maurras et notre temps* (2 vols, 1951)

A. Maurois, *Alain* (1949)

H. Mondor, *Alain* (1953)

J. Suffel, *André Maurois* (1963)

J. K. Simon (ed.), *Modern French Criticism, from Proust and Valéry to Structuralism* (1972)

P. Quillet, *Bachelard* (1965)

CHAPTERS 15 AND 16

ANTHOLOGIES

A. M. Boase, *The Poetry of France*, Vols 3 and 4 (1967 and 1969)

C. A. Hackett, *Anthology of Modern French Poetry* (1970)
New French Poetry (1973)

G.-E. Clancier, *Panorama critique de Rimbaud au surréalisme* (1953)

J. Rousselot, *Panorama critique des nouveaux poètes français* (1953)

J.-L. Bédouin, *La Poésie surréaliste* (1964)

J. H. Matthews, *French Surrealist Poetry* (1966)

GENERAL

G. Brereton, *Introduction to the French Poets* (1973)

M. Raymond, *De Baudelaire au surréalisme* (1969)

J.-P. Richard, *Poésie et profondeur* (1955). On Nerval, Baudelaire, Verlaine, Rimbaud.
Onze études sur la poésie moderne (1964). On Char, Ponge, Bonnefoy, Jaccottet, etc.

G. Michaud, *Le Message poétique du symbolisme* (4 vols, 1947)

A.-M. Schmidt, *La Littérature symboliste* (1947)

C. M. Bowra, *The Heritage of Symbolism* (1943)

S. Bernard, *Le Poème en prose de Baudelaire jusqu'à nos jours* (1959)

M. Nadeau, *Histoire du surréalisme* (1959)

W. Fowlie, *Age of Surrealism* (1960)

R. Bréchon, *Le Surréalisme* (1972)

J. Rousselot, *Dictionnaire de la poésie française contemporaine* (1968)

R. Gibson, *Modern French Poets on Poetry* (1961)

INDIVIDUAL POETS

Critical introductions to many of these poets, together with selections from
their work, appear in the *Poètes d'Aujourd'hui* series (Seghers).

H. Guillemin, *Lamartine, l'homme et l'œuvre* (1940)
M.-F. Guyard, *A. de Lamartine* (1956)
P.-G. Castex, *A. de Vigny, l'homme et l'œuvre* (1956)
F. Germain, *L'Imagination d'A. de Vigny* (1962)
H. Guillemin, *V. Hugo par lui-même* (1951)
J.-B. Barrère, *V. Hugo, l'homme et l'œuvre* (1952)
    La Fantaisie de V. Hugo (3 vols, 1949–60)
A. Maurois, *Olympio, ou la vie de V. Hugo* (1954)
P. Van Tieghem, *Musset, l'homme et l'œuvre* (1945)
L. Cellier, *G. de Nerval, l'homme et l'œuvre* (1952)
M. Ruff, *Baudelaire, l'homme et l'œuvre* (1955)
J. L. Austin, *L'Univers poétique de Baudelaire* (1956)
E. Starkie, *Baudelaire* (1957)
S. Fauchereau, *Th. Gautier* (1972)
P. Flottes, *Leconte de Lisle* (1954)
M. Ibrovac, *J.-M. de Heredia* (2 vols, 1923)
A. Adam, *Verlaine, l'homme et l'œuvre* (1953)
J. Richardson, *Verlaine* (1971)
C. A. Hackett, *Rimbaud* (1957)
E. Starkie, *Arthur Rimbaud* (1961)
G. Michaud, *Mallarmé, l'homme et l'œuvre* (1953)
J.-P. Richard, *L'Univers imaginaire de Mallarmé* (1961)
C. Chadwick, *Mallarmé, sa pensée dans sa poésie* (1962)
G. Bachelard, *Lautréamont* (1939)
A. Sonnenfeld, *L'Œuvre poétique de T. Corbière* (1960)
W. Ramsay, *J. Laforgue and the Ironic Inheritance* (1953)
P. Reboul, *Laforgue* (1960)
M. Girdlestone, *The Poetry of F. Mistral* (1937)
A. Gourdin, *Langue et littérature d'oc* (1949)
P. Mansell Jones, *E. Verhaeren* (1957)
J. Hytier, *La Poétique de Valéry* (1953)
F. Scarfe, *The Art of P. Valéry* (1954)
A. Mavrocordato, *L'Ode de P. Claudel* (1955)
S. Fumet, *Claudel* (1959)
R. Rolland, *Péguy* (1945)
B. Guyon, *Péguy, l'homme et l'œuvre* (1973)
M. Adéma, *Apollinaire le mal-aimé* (1952)
M. Davies, *Apollinaire* (1964)
J. Rousselot, *Blaise Cendrars* (1955)
G. Rau, *René Char* (1957)
R. Bréchon, *Michaux* (1959)
R. Garaudy, *L'Itinéraire d'Aragon* (1961)

T. W. Greene, *Supervielle* (1958)
J. A. Hiddleston, *L'Univers de Supervielle* (1965)
A. Lorinquin, *Saint-John Perse* (1963)
A. Knodel, *Saint-John Perse, A Study of His Poetry* (1966)
J. Rousselot, *P. J. Jouve* (1956)
M. Callander, *The Poetry of P. J. Jouve* (1965)
J. Thibaudeau, *Ponge par lui-même* (1967)

CHAPTER 17

GENERAL

A. Le Breton, *Le Théâtre romantique* (1923)
F. Brunetière, *Les Époques du théâtre français* (1892)
R. Lalou, *Le Théâtre en France depuis 1900* (1951). Covers 1900–50 briefly.
J. Hort, *Les Théâtres du Cartel* (1947). On Copeau and his successors.
D. Knowles, *French Drama in the Inter-War Years, 1918–39* (1967)
H. Béhar, *Étude sur le théâtre dada et surréaliste* (1967)
J. and J. Guicharnaud, *Modern French Theatre, from Giraudoux to Genet* (1967)
M. Esslin, *The Theatre of the Absurd* (1961)
P. Surer, *Le Théâtre français contemporain* (1964)
G. Serreau, *Histoire du nouveau théâtre* (1966)
W. D. Howarth, *Sublime and Grotesque, a Study of French Romantic Drama* (1975)

INDIVIDUAL WRITERS

S. Chahine, *La Dramaturgie de V. Hugo, 1816–43* (1971)
J. Pommier, *Variétés sur A. de Musset et son théâtre* (1944)
E. A. Taylor, *The Theatre of A. Dumas fils* (1937)
H. Gaillard, *E. Augier et la comédie sociale* (1910)
E. Sée, *H. Becque* (1925)
P. Blanchart, *H. Becque* (1931)
R. Gérard, *E. Rostand* (1935)
J. Portail, *J. Courteline* (1928)
A. Guardino, *Le Théâtre de Maeterlinck* (1934)
J. Madaule, *Le Drame de P. Claudel* (1958)
M. Berry, *Jules Romains* (1960)
P. Blanchart, *Le Théâtre de Lenormand* (1947)
J. Houlet, *Le Théâtre de Giraudoux* (1945)
R.-M. Albérès, *Esthétique et morale chez J. Giraudoux* (1957)
P. Dubourg, *Dramaturgie de J. Cocteau* (1954)
J.-J. Kihm, *Cocteau* (1961)
W. Fowlie, *J. Cocteau, the history of a poet's age* (1966)
P. L. Mignon, *Salacrou* (1962)
S. Radine, *Anouilh, Lenormand, Salacrou* (1951)
P. Jolivet, *Le Théâtre de J. Anouilh* (1963)

P. Vandromme, *Anouilh, un auteur et ses personnages* (1965)

F. Banchini, *Le Théâtre de Montherlant* (1971)

D. McCall, *The Theatre of J.-P.Sartre* (1969)

E. Freeman, *The Theatre of A. Camus* (1971)

J. Fletcher and J. Spurling, *Beckett, A Study of His Plays* (1972)

P. Mélèse, *Beckett* (1966)

R. Cohn (ed.), *Casebook on 'Waiting for Godot'* (1967)

R. Hayman, *Eugène Ionesco* (1972)

J.-H. Donnard, *Ionesco dramaturge* (1966)

J.-P. Sartre, *Saint Genet, comédien et martyr* (1952)

T. Driver, *Jean Genet* (1966)

O. Aslan, *Jean Genet* (1973)

J.-L. Barrault and M. Renaud, *A. Artaud et le théâtre de notre temps* (1958)

J.-L. Brau, *Antonin Artaud* (1971)

H. Béhar, *Roger Vitrac* (1966)

J. Decocq, *Le Théâtre de M. de Ghelderode* (1969)

Index

Principal reference pages are shown in italic figures